THE WORLD'S

A DARK NIGH

AND OTHER STORIES

MRS GASKELL was born Elizabeth Cleghorn Stevenson in 1810. The daughter of a Unitarian, who was a civil servant and journalist, she was brought up after her mother's death by her aunt in Knutsford, Cheshire, which became the model not only for Cranford but also for Hollingford (in *Wives and Daughters*). In 1832 she married William Gaskell, a Unitarian minister in Manchester, with whom she lived very happily. Her first novel, *Mary Barton*, published in 1848, was immensely popular and brought her to the attention of Charles Dickens, who was looking for contributors to his new periodical, *Household Words*, for which she wrote the famous series of papers subsequently reprinted as *Cranford*. Her later novels include *Ruth* (1853), *North and South* (1854–5), *Sylvia's Lovers* (1863), and *Wives and Daughters* (1864–6). She also wrote many stories and her remarkable *Life of Charlotte Brontë*. She died in 1865.

SUZANNE LEWIS is a graduate of the University of Sydney. She is currently working on a critical study of Elizabeth Gaskell.

THE WORLD'S CLASSICS

ELIZABETH GASKELL

A Dark Night's Work

and Other Stories

Edited with an Introduction by
SUZANNE LEWIS

Oxford New York
OXFORD UNIVERSITY PRESS

1992

Oxford University Press, Walton Street, Oxford OX2 6DP

Oxford New York Toronto
Delhi Bombay Calcutta Madras Karachi
Petaling Jaya Singapore Hong Kong Tokyo
Nairobi Dar es Salaam Cape Town
Melbourne Auckland

and associated companies in
Berlin Ibadan

First published as a World's Classics paperback 1992

British Library Cataloguing in Publication Data
Data available

Library of Congress Cataloging-in-Publication Data
Gaskell, Elizabeth Cleghorn, 1810–1865.
A dark night's work and other stories / Elizabeth Gaskell; edited with an introduction by Suzanne Lewis.
p. cm. — (The World's classics)
Includes bibliographical references.
I. Lewis, Suzanne. II. Title. III. Series.
PR4710.A4 1992 823'.8—dc20 91–24416
ISBN 0–19–282807–X

Typeset by Pure Tech Corporation, Pondicherry, India
Printed in Great Britain by
BPCC Hazells Ltd.
Aylesbury, Bucks

CONTENTS

INTRODUCTION

'"I do think I've a talent for fiction, it is so pleasant to invent, and make the incidents dovetail together." '[1] The words are spoken by Faith Benson, a character in Elizabeth Gaskell's second novel *Ruth* (1853); but they could well apply to the author herself, for Elizabeth Gaskell was a natural and gifted storyteller. Although best known as a novelist, and as the first biographer of Charlotte Brontë, Gaskell also wrote over forty tales, poems, essays, and sketches. During her lifetime, her literary reputation was based nearly as much on the popularity of her short fiction as on the success of her novels. This selection of five stories testifies to the quality and diversity of Elizabeth Gaskell's short fiction, showing the way in which she used this medium to experiment with narrative modes and techniques, and, often, to deal in a more radical way with issues considered in the novels.

One significant issue is the place of women in a patriarchal society, and four of the five stories in this collection centre on a woman. Ellinor Wilkins in 'A Dark Night's Work' is a daughter oppressed and blighted by duty to her father; Libbie Marsh, single, poor, and plain, would not even have a place in the fiction of most of Gaskell's contemporaries; Thekla the servant girl, in 'Six Weeks at Heppenheim', is almost drawn into the self-sacrifice of a loveless marriage; while the story of Anna Scherer, the Grey Woman, uses the Gothic mode to challenge conventional ideas about women and marriage. The range of characters Gaskell employs in these stories is matched by the diversity of setting—urban and provincial, English and European—and context: a specific historical age, the recent past, or Gaskell's contemporary Manchester.

These dramatic contrasts refute a traditional critical view of Gaskell as a limited writer, confined to what she could see from the windows of her Victorian drawing-room. On the contrary,

[1] Elizabeth Gaskell, *Ruth* (1853), ed. Alan Shelston (World's Classics edn.; Oxford, 1985), 150.

'Libbie Marsh's Three Eras', 'Six Weeks at Heppenheim', and 'Cumberland Sheep-Shearers' show that Gaskell could step out of her middle-class milieu and enter working-class lives on their terms, not hers. Libbie Marsh, and Thekla in 'Six Weeks at Heppenheim', are underpaid, overworked, and barely literate. Yet, while the veracity of Gaskell's working-class characterization has often been noted, her equally uncompromising approach to her middle-class heroines is largely overlooked.

The stories in this collection stress the economic and personal importance of work for women. In 'Cumberland Sheep-Shearers' the men and women of a community work together and in harmony with the land so that labour is not merely an economic necessity but a satisfying and fulfilling activity. The working-class women in these stories are independent because their social status allows them to work. In contrast, the middle-class heroines, Ellinor Wilkins and Anna Scherer, are unsuited for work. When these women find themselves destitute and without the protection of husband or father, they can only rely on the common sense and capacity for work of their former servants, Miss Monro, Ellinor's governess, and Amante, Anna's maid.

Gaskell herself—wife, mother, hostess, and pivot of a busy household—was a working woman, a female writer in a literary world dominated by men. She experienced the conflicting claims of duty to self and others—'Home duties and the development of the Individual',[2] as she put it—which beset so many women in the nineteenth century. Elizabeth Gaskell never agreed with the advice offered to Charlotte Brontë by Robert Southey that 'Literature cannot be the business of a woman's life, and it ought not to be. The more she is engaged in her proper duties, the less leisure will she have for it.'[3] Yet, writing in a dining-room with three doors, constantly interrupted by servants, children, and visitors, Gaskell must have had in mind her own predicament when, in *The Life of Charlotte Brontë* (1857), she described the effects of the success of *Jane Eyre*:

[2] *The Letters of Mrs. Gaskell*, ed. J. A. V. Chapple and Arthur Pollard (Manchester, 1966), 106. All subsequent references are to this edition.

[3] Elizabeth Gaskell, *The Life of Charlotte Brontë* (1857), ed. Alan Shelston (Penguin edn.; Harmondsworth, 1975), 173.

> Henceforward Charlotte Brontë's existence becomes divided into two parallel currents—her life as Currer Bell, the author; her life as Charlotte Brontë, the woman. There were separate duties belonging to each character—not opposing each other; not impossible, but difficult to be reconciled.[4]

Like Charlotte Brontë, Gaskell felt the need to use a male pseudonym when she began her literary career. In June 1847 'Libbie Marsh's Three Eras' was published in *Howitt's Journal* under the name Cotton Mather Mills, Esq. However, the immediate success of *Mary Barton*, published anonymously in 1848, ensured that its authorship did not remain secret for long. In 1850 Charles Dickens wrote to Gaskell asking her to contribute to his new journal, *Household Words*. His request was presented in the most flattering terms—'I *do* honestly know that there is no living English writer whose aid I would desire to enlist, in preference to the authoress of Mary Barton.'[5] The publication of the short story 'Lizzie Leigh' in the first number of the new periodical marked the beginning of a fruitful but stormy professional relationship between author and editor.

Elizabeth Gaskell valued the financial rewards of her work. She planned to buy a house in the country, independently of her husband, using the proceeds from her last, and longest, novel, *Wives and Daughters* (1864–6). One of the reasons she persisted in publishing with Dickens, despite their increasing personal and editorial differences, was that work which appeared in *Household Words* or *All the Year Round* could be sold first in magazine form and then in volume form. For example, in 1859 Gaskell collected stories previously published in *Household Words* into the two-volume *Round the Sofa* in order to finance a trip to Germany to take her daughter Meta away from the gossip surrounding a broken engagement. When she ran short of money on this holiday, she sent off two hurriedly written stories to Dickens with a request for immediate payment.

In March 1859 Gaskell wrote to Charles Eliot Norton of her story 'Lois the Witch', 'I *know* it is fated to go to this new

[4] Ibid. 334.
[5] 'To Mrs. Gaskell, 31 January 1850', in *The Letters of Charles Dickens*, vi, ed. Graham Story, Kathleen Tillotson, and Nina Burgis (Pilgrim edn.; Oxford, 1988), 22.

Dickensy periodical, & I did so hope to escape it' (*Letters*, 538). The new periodical was *All the Year Round*, and what Gaskell hoped to escape was Dickens's interventionist editorial practice. From 1860 some of her work, including the short story 'Six Weeks at Heppenheim' (1862), appeared in Smith, Elder's *Cornhill Magazine*. The monthly production of this new, high-quality periodical meant that Gaskell was allowed a larger copy space than that available to her in Dickens's weeklies, thus giving her greater scope for the leisurely development of character and situation which is a strength of her writing. But the man who addressed her as 'My Dear Scheherazade' and claimed 'I am sure your powers of narrative can never be exhausted in a single night, but must be good for at least a thousand nights and one',[6] made himself hard to resist. Most of her short fiction, including three of the stories in this volume, appeared in Dickens's *Household Words* or *All the Year Round*.

'Cumberland Sheep-Shearers' and 'The Grey Woman' were, in their different ways, exactly suited to Dickens's requirements. The former is typical of the sketch, part-fiction and part-journalism, that had become so popular with readers of *Household Words*; and it had the advantage of being short enough to be printed in a single number (22 January 1853). 'The Grey Woman', printed in three parts in *All the Year Round* (5, 12, 19 January 1861), contains the melodramatic elements of suspense and horror which so appealed to Dickens. However, Gaskell's next contribution to *All the Year Round*, 'A Dark Night's Work' (1863), illustrates the issues of personality and literary style over which Charles Dickens and Elizabeth Gaskell came into conflict during their professional association.

'A Dark Night's Work' repeated the frustrations of serialization which had arisen over *North and South* (1854–5), frustrations which caused Dickens to exclaim to Wills, his editor, 'Mrs. Gaskell, fearful—fearful. If I were Mr. G. O. Heaven how I would beat her!'[7] Author and editor could not agree on chapter divisions, and the story was far too long for the space allocated by Dickens. But the real problem, as with *North and*

[6] 'To Mrs. Gaskell, 25 November 1851', ibid. 545.

[7] Quoted in A. B. Hopkins, *Elizabeth Gaskell: Her Life and Work* (London, 1952), 152.

South, was that the story was unsuited to publication in weekly parts. The most sensational action takes place over a third of the way into the tale, the preceding pages having carefully established the historical, social, and psychological factors which determine the crime and its aftermath. 'A Dark Night's Work' is one of Elizabeth Gaskell's most perceptive studies of character, but because most of the action is emotional it fails to provide the amount of incident and suspense Dickens wanted to carry reader interest from one instalment to the next.

If Gaskell could be obstinate when it came to preserving the integrity of her story, Dickens could be a high-handed and peremptory editor. On 21 November 1862 he wrote to Wills, 'I see that Mrs. Gaskell *has* put a name to her story—at the end, instead of the beginning—which is characteristic. The addition of one word will make it a striking name. Call the story "A Dark Night's Work".'[8] Not only was the title of the story changed against Gaskell's wishes, but the addition of the word 'Dark' signals a melodramatic element which is suppressed in the grim, terse original, 'A Night's Work'. Although the story centres on a murder, and is concerned with the operation of conscience and remorse, it is deliberately low-key. Edward Wilkins, his servant Dixon, and his daughter Ellinor are haunted, not by any ghost, but by each other. Their shared guilt and misery are more awful than any supernatural apparition.

At almost every point in the narrative Gaskell turns from melodramatic possibilities to the realistic examination of character and motive. For example, local opinion holds that Mr Wilkins's clerk, Dunster, has ruined his employer and absconded to America with a fortune. The truth is that Edward Wilkins hates Dunster because this subservient, hard-working man, devoid of social aspiration, represents everything that the gentry require in their man of business. Edward's father had conformed to this image, dining with his employers but never accompanied by his wife, hunting with them occasionally but only 'after a little coquetting about "professional engagements," and "being wanted at the office"'. However, he makes the

[8] R. C. Lehmann (ed.), *Charles Dickens as Editor: Being Letters Written by him to William Henry Wills his Sub-Editor* (London, 1912), 318.

mistake of sending his son to Eton, then recalling him to Hamley to take over the practice so that Edward had 'to assume the hereditary subservient position to lads whom he had licked in the playground, and beaten at learning'.

Gaskell's descriptions of the Hamley assemblies at which Mr Wilkins, and later Ellinor, are snubbed, show the acuteness of her observations of county society. She was to use the same social milieu to great effect in *Wives and Daughters*, in which she captures the exact relations between the Whig Lord and Lady Cumnor, the Tory Squire Hamley, and the local doctor Mr Gibson. In 'A Dark Night's Work' she recognizes the injustice of the rigid system which has no place for the accomplished and cultivated young Edward, but condemns his slavish imitation of the squirearchy which leads him into extravagance and heavy drinking. He neglects his business in order to cultivate the society of 'dull boors of untravelled, uncultivated squires—whose company, however . . . he never refused'.

Also trapped by worldliness, although in a different way, is Ellinor's fiancé, Ralph Corbet. The one imprudent action of his life is to form an engagement with a girl considered by his family to be his social inferior. However, his persistence in the face of their opposition is motivated by pragmatism as well as by love, for he expects that Ellinor will inherit her father's fortune. Love gives way to loyalty and then descends to mere duty, as Ralph finds that Ellinor's simple charm cannot compete with the challenge of his career and his widening circle of interests in London. Ellinor's hint that the threat of disgrace hangs over her father, and the drunken insults of Mr Wilkins himself, provide the opportunity for Ralph to break off the engagement. Hesitating for a moment, the young man, as he put it, 'gave Ellinor another chance'; and Gaskell's opinion of the kind of morality which needs to justify itself is encapsulated in that almost incidental, but damning observation.

Ellinor's youth and beauty are blighted by the actions of her father and her fiancé. The tranquillity of East Chester Cathedral Close seems to transform her into a kind of Sleeping Beauty, physically and emotionally passive, while the joyous festivity and picturesque beauty of Rome in spring stimulates her spiritual and physical renaissance. The Roman scene in 'A Dark

Night's Work' is informed by a sense of perfect but fleeting happiness which is echoed in Gaskell's recollection of her own trip to Rome in 1857. She wrote to her hosts, 'It was in those charming Roman days that my life, at any rate, culminated. I shall never be so happy again. I don't think I was ever so happy before' (*Letters*, 476–7).

Ellinor is betrayed by her family and her fiancé but sustained by her servants. Miss Monro supports her financially and emotionally while Dixon is prepared to sacrifice his life to keep her secret. In much of Elizabeth Gaskell's fiction, the traditional family structure of authoritarian father and submissive wife and children breeds misery. In three of the stories in this collection, peace and happiness are found in unorthodox households. Ellinor Wilkins shares a home with her former governess on equal terms. In 'The Grey Woman' the servant Amante disguises herself as a man, and she and her mistress, Anna Scherer, live together as man and wife caring for Anna's child. In 'Libbie Marsh's Three Eras' Libbie proposes to Margaret Hall a relationship of friendship, nurture, and mutual support: 'we should be together in the evenings; and her as was home first would watch for the other.'

Libbie's simple words suggest the kind of Wordsworthian lyricism which informs much of Gaskell's fiction. In a letter to Mary Howitt, Gaskell quotes from Wordsworth's 'Cumberland Beggar' to illustrate her belief that 'the beauty and poetry of many of the common things and daily events of life in its humblest aspect does not seem to me sufficiently appreciated' (*Letters*, 33); and in her Preface to *Mary Barton* she refers to 'the romance in the lives of some of those who elbowed me daily in the busy streets'.[9] Libbie Marsh resembles Alice Wilson in *Mary Barton* in that both women are poor, unmarried, and always, in Libbie's words, 'looking round for the odd jobs God leaves in the world for such as old maids to do'. Gaskell's characterization of such simple goodness is never cloying but, rather, reflects her appreciation of the Wordsworthian blessedness attached to acts of charity among the poor.

[9] Elizabeth Gaskell, *Mary Barton* (1848), ed. Edgar Wright (World's Classics edn.; Oxford, 1987), p. xxxv.

Gaskell's vision of the poetry in common things and simple pleasures is also expressed in her description of the working people's Whitsuntide holiday in Dunham woods. The ancient trees and shaded walks; the view of smoky Manchester in the distance 'where God had cast their lives, and told them to work out their destiny'; the Sunday-school children singing hymns; the expressions 'called up by some noble or loving thought': all are a lyrical celebration of the romance in humble life. At the same time, 'Libbie Marsh's Three Eras' is a realistic depiction of Manchester working-class life. The day at Dunham park, like the scene in Green Heys Fields which opens *Mary Barton*, shows the recreations of the common people. Elizabeth Gaskell's detailed knowledge of life in the crowded courts and factory neighbourhoods is revealed in her description of the Dixons, the family with whom Libbie lodges, preparing their tea, adding eggs to thicken the cream, and buying ham to eat with the bread and butter. A good observer would note that the family could afford these things because 'they were fine spinners, in the receipt of good wages', but only the most perceptive would add that they desired them because, 'confined all day in an atmosphere ranging from seventy-five to eighty degrees', they 'had lost all natural, healthy appetite for simple food'.

In 'Libbie Marsh's Three Eras' and in *Mary Barton*, Gaskell comments on those Manchester workmen who, despite long hours of labour, develop an interest and expertise in botany or science or mathematics. In *Mary Barton*, Job Legh's passion is entomology, and in 'Libbie Marsh's Three Eras' Gaskell introduces a barber who is an 'oracle' on the subject of canaries. Not all her readers were charmed by the description of Libbie's purchase of Jupiter the canary as a Valentine for the crippled boy Franky Hall. The poet and critic Leigh Hunt, who had been imprisoned for libel, wrote to Gaskell, 'I cannot see with comfort a gift made to your poor little invalid of another *prisoner*.'[10] Gaskell's gracious reply acknowledged Hunt's criticism, but reminded him of her aim to present an accurate picture of

[10] 'Leigh Hunt to Mrs. Gaskell, date uncertain', in Ross D. Waller (ed.), 'Letters Addressed to Mrs. Gaskell by Celebrated Contemporaries', *Bulletin of the John Rylands Library*, 19 (1935), 127.

Manchester working-class life (*Letters*, 131).

Like 'Libbie Marsh's Three Eras', 'Six Weeks at Heppenheim' and 'Cumberland Sheep-Shearers' display Gaskell's interest in how ordinary people live and work, and how local customs and conventions shape their lives. From 'Six Weeks at Heppenheim' the reader learns many details of German rural life: the rules of the vintage, the household goods a bride is expected to include in her dowry, and the warning to local police required before moving from one town or village to another. Moreover, such detail is never introduced unnecessarily. Rather, it is part of the psychological veracity of Gaskell's narrator, the practical, orderly young tourist who finds himself stranded by illness in a small German town. Thus it is in response to his invalid's wish for grapes that his hostess explains that, in order to prevent pilfering from the unenclosed fields in the weeks before the harvest, access to the vineyards is restricted to certain days; and it is with an invalid's petulance that he grumbles about the restrictive paternalism of German government.

'Six Weeks at Heppenheim' is as much the story of the narrator as it is of Thekla and her lovers. The young Oxford graduate and prospective barrister is precise, methodical, and a little complacent. Because he can, as he thinks, arrange his own life so well, he tries to arrange the lives of others in the same way. He makes assumptions—that Thekla's stepmother is unkind to her, that Thekla will marry her childhood sweetheart and live happily ever after—that are based on literary stereotypes. Illness disrupts his careful plans and he is forced to surrender control of his life into the hands of strangers. His imposed passivity makes him sensitive to the rhythm of daily life around him, and his deeply felt response to the beauty of the setting and the rituals of the vintage reveal to him a moral order which transcends the individual. The working of such a moral order is suggested when the narrator's recovery, the harvest, and the love story of Thekla and Fritz Müller come to completion at the same time.

Gaskell used an immature, male narrator commenting on and imperfectly understanding a young woman's heart again in 'Cousin Phillis' (1863–4), which also appeared in *The Cornhill Magazine*. The similarities between Paul Manning of 'Cousin

Phillis' and the narrator of 'Six Weeks at Heppenheim' show the way in which Gaskell experiments with, and reworks, narrative devices in her fiction. The two stories use the same pastoral image of prayer conducted in the open fields at the close of the day's work. The narrator of 'Six Weeks at Heppenheim' describes the scene after the vintage, in which men, women, and children draw around the pastor to say 'some words of holy thanksgiving' and sing the famous German harvest-hymn 'Wir Pflügen'. Both incident and feeling are echoed in 'Cousin Phillis' when Mr Holman gathers his labourers around him in the fields at the end of the day's work to sing a psalm. In these two stories, and in 'Cumberland Sheep-Shearers' which follows, Gaskell uses the pastoral setting to portray the poetry and beauty of humble lives and traditional customs.

In 'Cumberland Sheep-Shearers', Elizabeth Gaskell's powers of observation and description can be seen at their best. She presents an account, in autobiographical form, of a visit to a Lake District farm during the busy shearing period. Gaskell demonstrates her awareness of both the prosaic and the poetic aspects of the scene before her. She gives a realistic description of the countryside and farm activity, including a calendar of the sheep-farmer's yearly work cycle. She further enlivens the scene by introducing named characters, and even the tantalizingly brief outline of a love affair. Moreover, she places the grandeur of the natural world and the vital, worthwhile work of the farm within the bucolic convention. Her classical allusions—the 'yellow asphodel' said to cover the meadows of Elysium as well as nineteenth-century Cumbrian fields, the scene in the farmyard 'as full of motion as an antique frieze'—give this scene mythical dimensions, a sense of timelessness informing an otherwise highly specific context. A similar effect is achieved in 'Six Weeks at Heppenheim', in which the description of the child Max as 'a little Bacchus' hints at the tradition of the vintage which stretches back beyond Christian history to pagan civilizations; and also in 'Cousin Phillis', in which a Christian minister quotes Virgil in response to the beauty of the agricultural landscape.

Gaskell's allusion in 'Cumberland Sheep-Shearers' to lines from Wordsworth's *Excursion* not only reinforces her vision of a rich, sustained pastoral tradition, but also suggests the poetry of humble life celebrated in 'Libbie Marsh's Three Eras'. The Prestons, with whom the Gaskells lodged when they visited the Lake District in 1849 and 1851, were, Gaskell reports, described by Wordsworth as 'a "Homeric family" ' (*Letters*, 570). Gaskell herself wrote of them, 'They have no ambition but much dignity,—and look at that family of stately sons & daughters!' (*Letters*, 571); and her account of the sheep-shearing conveys that sense of dignity, the simple pride of the Cumberland statesmen who have farmed their family's land for generations.

Elizabeth Gaskell holidayed not only in the Lake District but in many other parts of Britain and Europe. Her letters reveal that the pleasure she derived from travel arose from both her passionate response to new scenes and a sense of release from the work and duty which lay at home in Manchester. As can be seen from 'Cumberland Sheep-Shearers' and the Roman scenes of 'A Dark Night's Work', Gaskell's travel experiences were often incorporated in her fiction. 'Six Weeks at Heppenheim' is, of course, narrated by an English tourist in Germany. In 1841 William and Elizabeth Gaskell toured the Rhine in the region of Heidelberg, where they were introduced to Mary Howitt and her daughter. The English tourists met frequently when, Gaskell records, 'we all told the most frightening & wild stories we had ever heard,—some *such* fearful ones—all true' (*Letters*, 44). 'The Grey Woman', set in the Rhineland in the late eighteenth century, may have been one of these tales of horror. It contains many of the elements of Gothic fiction: a cruel aristocrat, a ruthless robber gang, an imprisoned wife, a faithful servant, murder, flight, and deadly pursuit. Yet the plot turns on the strength of the relationship between two women, the wife, Anna, whose terrible experiences turn her hair and skin grey, and her maid, Amante.

'Clopton Hall', an early piece written for William Howitt, shows an interest in the macabre which Gaskell confined almost exclusively to her short fiction. One incident at Clopton Hall is curiously reminiscent of details in 'The Grey Woman'. Gaskell writes of exploring the Hall on a schoolgirls' excursion:

In one of the bed-rooms (said to be haunted) . . . hung a portrait so singularly beautiful! a sweet-looking girl . . . Charlotte Clopton, about whom there was so fearful a legend told at Stratford church. In the time of some epidemic, the sweating-sickness, or the plague, this young girl had sickened, and to all appearance died. She was buried with fearful haste in the vaults of Clopton chapel, attached to Stratford church, but the sickness was not stayed. In a few days another of the Cloptons died, and him they bore to the ancestral vault; but as they descended the gloomy stairs, they saw by the torchlight, Charlotte Clopton in her grave-clothes leaning against the wall; and when they looked nearer, she was indeed dead, but not before, in the agonies of despair and hunger, she had bitten a piece from her white round shoulder! Of course, she had *walked* ever since.[11]

Both portraits, Charlotte Clopton's and Anna Scherer's, are of beautiful young girls; and both are associated with a dreadful history. There is also a disturbing parallel in the self-mutilation carried out by these women. In the agony of terror and despair Charlotte Clopton tears a piece of flesh out of her shoulder; and Anna Scherer does the same to her hand when she overhears her husband, Monsieur de la Tourelle, and his accomplices discuss their murderous exploits.

Gaskell returned to the themes of violence and female helplessness in 'French Life', a series of sketches written several years after 'The Grey Woman'.[12] In this account of travels in France and Italy, Gaskell relates the story of Madame la Marquise de Gange. This lovely and pious heiress, married, like Anna Scherer, to a man who is her match for beauty but vicious in nature, is tortured and murdered for her fortune by her husband's brothers. There is an extraordinarily explicit account of her suffering. Made to swallow corrosive poison, Madame de Gange forces her hair down her throat to make herself sick and jumps twenty feet from her window to escape. However, she is pursued, and stabbed by her brother-in-law until his sword

[11] William Howitt, *Visits to Remarkable Places* (1840; Philadelphia, 1842), 118–19. Elizabeth Gaskell sent Howitt a four-page account of a visit to Clopton House which he used verbatim, acknowledging his source only as 'a fair lady' (p. 117).

[12] Elizabeth Gaskell, 'French Life', *Fraser's Magazine*, 69 (1864), 435–49, 575–85, 739–52.

breaks in her shoulder. She survives for nineteen days, long enough to testify against her attackers.

Anna Scherer, in 'The Grey Woman', avoids the fate of the Marquise de Gange but the price of escape is high. In tearing a piece of flesh out of her hand and later breaking a front tooth to effect a disguise, Anna inflicts on herself the violence threatened against her by her husband. For a brief time Amante, Anna, and her child establish a loving female community which attempts to exclude masculine violence. However, such a social vision cannot be sustained and, inevitably, the dominant order of society is reasserted, an order in which it is quite possible for husbands to be gaolers and murderers. It is indicative of such a society that Monsieur de la Tourelle is finally brought to justice, not by the testimony of his wife but in revenge for the crime he has committed against another man, a 'wronged' husband, the Baron de Roeder.

Monsieur de la Tourelle pursues Amante for the same reason that he himself is pursued by the Baron de Roeder. Amante has taken away La Tourelle's wife and usurped his place, even to the extent of assuming a masculine identity and acting a father's role towards his child; and so his story that he is pursuing Anna because she has committed adultery is symbolically true. The interchange of gender roles between La Tourelle and Amante may owe something to the Gothic, but Gaskell uses the mode in an original way by reworking the conventional figures of the dark, dangerous lover and the fair mistress/victim. From the start Anna is repulsed by male sexuality, as represented by her father's apprentice Karl. She is attracted to La Tourelle as a lover by his effeminacy, and only recoils from him when he proposes marriage. In contrast, Amante, described as tall and handsome and thus conforming to the stereotype of the Gothic hero far more than the slight, fair La Tourelle, offers faithful protection which, unlike a conventional marriage, does not have to be paid for by sexual favours.

Anna's letter to her daughter, which comprises most of the story, is a warning against marriage. It conveys a more exaggerated and terrifying version of the feeling which prompted Charlotte Brontë to write to her friend Ellen Nussey, 'Indeed—indeed Nell—it is a solemn and strange and perilous thing for a woman to become a wife.'[13] Two important details suggest that Anna's daughter Ursula may be about to repeat her mother's mistakes: her close resemblance to the portrait of the young Anna; and the fact that she knows as little about her fiancé as Anna did about Monsieur de la Tourelle. Nevertheless, Anna's argument that Ursula is prevented by her father's crimes from marrying Maurice de Poissy is not convincing. Indeed, it is possible to envisage a different version of the story in which such a marriage is a means of reparation, a symbol of healing and renewal. As it stands, however, 'The Grey Woman', like 'A Dark Night's Work', emphasizes the heavy price to be paid for 'the sins of the fathers'.

Gaskell's use in 'The Grey Woman' of a first-person narrative allows her to heighten the Gothic terrors of the tale: 'I stole my groping palm upon the clenched and chilly hand of a corpse!' The device also indicates that Gaskell's fiction has a strong basis in storytelling as an oral, rather than written, form. Anne Thackeray Ritchie, daughter of the novelist William Thackeray, wrote of Elizabeth Gaskell, 'the remembrance of her voice comes back to me, harmoniously flowing on and on, with spirit and intention, and delightful emphasis, as we all sat indoors one gusty morning listening to her ghost stories . . . mystery was there, romantic feeling, some holy terror and emotion, all combined to keep us gratefully silent and delighted.'[14] However, the range of stories in this collection shows that Elizabeth Gaskell did not need to rely on Gothic thrills and supernatural terrors to hold her audience. As her close friend Susanna Winkworth declared, 'No one ever came near her in the gift of telling a story. In her hands the simplest incident,—a meeting in the street, a talk with a factory-girl, a country walk, an old family history,—became picturesque and vivid and interesting.'[15]

[13] T. J. Wise and J. A. Symington (eds.), *The Brontës: Their Lives, Friendships, and Correspondence*, ii (Oxford, 1980), 146.

[14] Anne Thackeray Ritchie, Preface to Mrs. Gaskell, *Cranford* (London, 1895), p. ix.

[15] Susanna and Catherine Winkworth, *Memorials of Two Sisters*, ed. Margaret J. Shaen (London, 1908), 24.

NOTE ON THE TEXT

The text of each story is that of the last publication during Elizabeth Gaskell's lifetime, over which it may be assumed she had some editorial control. In general, however, it was not Gaskell's practice to revise her work to any great extent.

'A Dark Night's Work' appeared first in *All the Year Round*, vols. 8 and 9, 24 January to 21 March 1863. It was published in one volume by Smith, Elder in the same year (present text) with only minor changes to the original text.

'Life in Manchester: Libbie Marsh's Three Eras' appeared in *Howitt's Journal of Literature and Popular Progress*, vol. 1, in June 1847. In 1850 the story was published in one volume as *Libbie Marsh's Three Eras: A Lancashire Tale* by Hamilton, Adams in London and David Marples in Liverpool. Chapman and Hall included 'Libbie Marsh's Three Eras' in the collection *Lizzie Leigh; and Other Tales* (Cheap Edition, London, 1855). The text used by Chapman and Hall differs in many details of syntax and punctuation from the original version of the story. Smith, Elder published the story in the collection *The Grey Woman and Other Tales* (London, 1865; present text). The Chapman and Hall (1855) and Smith, Elder (1865) texts are nearly identical.

'Six Weeks at Heppenheim' was published in the *Cornhill Magazine*, vol. 5, May 1862, and reprinted by Smith, Elder in *The Grey Woman and Other Tales* (London, 1865; present text) with only a few minor changes to the original text.

'Cumberland Sheep-Shearers' was published in *Household Words*, vol. 6, 22 January 1853 (present text). It was not reprinted in Elizabeth Gaskell's lifetime.

'The Grey Woman' first appeared in *All the Year Round*, vol. 4, 5–19 January 1861. It was reprinted in the Tauchnitz copyright edition of *Lois the Witch and Other Tales* (Leipzig, 1861), and by Smith, Elder in *The Grey Woman and Other Tales* (London, 1865; present text), which varies in only a few minor details from the original publication. Collation with the manuscript version of 'The Grey Woman' (held by the John Rylands University Library, Manchester) reveals changes in punctuation, and the creation of chapter divisions, but very little revision of the story itself. Any significant variations are given in the explanatory notes.

A few obvious errors have been corrected and in some instances Gaskell's spelling and punctuation have been modernized or otherwise emended: in particular, spelling of European place names has been standardized and Gaskell's use of hyphenated forms such as 'to-morrow' and 'out-door' has been modernized. All except the most minor changes are referred to in the explanatory notes.

SELECT BIBLIOGRAPHY

Elizabeth Gaskell's short fiction has received far less critical attention than her longer works. There are a number of studies of Gaskell's writing which devote a chapter, or give substantial consideration to, the short fiction. These include Aina Rubenius, *The Woman Question in Mrs. Gaskell's Life and Works* (Uppsala and Cambridge, Mass., 1950); Arthur Pollard, *Mrs. Gaskell: Novelist and Biographer* (Manchester, 1965); Edgar Wright, *Mrs. Gaskell: The Basis for Reassessment* (London, 1965); Margaret Ganz, *Elizabeth Gaskell: The Artist in Conflict* (New York, 1969); Angus Easson, *Elizabeth Gaskell* (London, 1979); Enid Duthie, *The Themes of Elizabeth Gaskell* (London, 1980); Coral Lansbury, *Elizabeth Gaskell* (Boston, 1984); and Patsy Stoneman, *Elizabeth Gaskell* (Brighton, 1987).

The two most comprehensive collected editions of Elizabeth Gaskell's works are the eight-volume Knutsford edition, *The Works of Mrs. Gaskell* (London, 1906) edited by A. W. Ward, and the eleven-volume World's Classics edition, *The Novels and Tales of Mrs. Gaskell* (London, 1906–19) edited by Clement Shorter. Both Ward and Shorter provide useful introductions which include consideration of the short stories. Angus Easson's introduction to *Cousin Phillis and Other Tales* (World's Classics edition, Oxford, 1981) and Edgar Wright's introduction to *My Lady Ludlow and Other Stories* (World's Classics edition, Oxford, 1989) contain both biographical material and critical comment on Gaskell as a writer of short fiction. Michael Ashley has chosen to focus on Gaskell's use of horror and the supernatural in his collection, *Mrs. Gaskell's Tales of Mystery and Horror* (London, 1978).

Of the stories in this collection, 'Libbie Marsh's Three Eras' has received the most critical attention. The original text, which appeared in *Howitt's Journal*, was reproduced in a monograph by the Lancashire and Cheshire Antiquarian Society in 1968, with a brief introduction by J. A. V. Chapple. Anna Walters's introduction to *Elizabeth Gaskell: Four Short Stories* (London, 1983) provides detailed critical comment on 'Libbie

Marsh's Three Eras' together with 'Lizzie Leigh', 'The Well of Pen-Morfa', and 'The Manchester Marriage'. The story is also discussed briefly in Alan Shelston's article 'Elizabeth Gaskell's Manchester' in the *Gaskell Society Journal*, 3 (1989), 46–67; and by Joseph Kestner in *Protest and Reform: The British Social Narrative by Women 1827–1867* (London, 1985), 116–19.

Maureen Reddy offers a detailed reading of 'The Grey Woman' in 'Gaskell's "The Grey Woman": A Feminist Palimpsest', *Journal of Narrative Technique*, 15: 2 (1985), 183–93; and Pauline Nestor discusses this story, as well as other short works by Gaskell, in chapters 2 and 3 of *Female Friendships and Communities* (Oxford, 1985).

Mary Thwaite has explored the Italian sources for 'A Dark Night's Work' and several other fictional and non-fictional short works by Gaskell in 'Elizabeth Gaskell and Italy', *Gaskell Society Journal*, 4 (1990), 57–63. J. G. Sharps makes use of detailed background material and biographical information in his study of the novels and the short fiction, *Mrs. Gaskell's Observation and Invention* (Fontwell, Sussex, 1970).

There are two good biographies of Elizabeth Gaskell. A. B. Hopkins's study, *Elizabeth Gaskell: Her Life and Work* (London, 1952) is still relevant, although Winifred Gérin's more recent work *Elizabeth Gaskell* (Oxford, 1980) has the advantage of access to *The Letters of Mrs. Gaskell*, edited by J. A. V. Chapple and A. Pollard (Manchester, 1966).

A CHRONOLOGY OF ELIZABETH GASKELL

1810 Elizabeth Cleghorn Stevenson, second surviving child of William Stevenson and Elizabeth Holland, born in Chelsea 29 September.

1811 (November) After her mother's death, Elizabeth is taken to Knutsford to live with her Aunt Hannah Lumb.

1822–7 Attends school at Misses Byerley's in Warwick and Stratford-upon-Avon.

1828–9 Her elder brother, John Stevenson (b. 1799), disappears while on a voyage to India. Elizabeth goes to Chelsea to live with her father and stepmother.

1829 (22 March) Elizabeth's father dies; she goes to Newcastle upon Tyne, to the home of the Revd William Turner.

1831 Spends much of this year in Edinburgh with Mr Turner's daughter. Visits Manchester.

1832 (30 August) Marries the Revd William Gaskell, assistant Minister at Cross Street Chapel, Manchester, at St John's Parish Church, Knutsford. They live at 14 Dover Street, Manchester.

1833 Her first child, a daughter, born dead.

1834 Her second daughter, Marianne, born.

1837 A poem, 'Sketches among the Poor', by Mr and Mrs Gaskell, appears in *Blackwood's Magazine* (January). Her third daughter, Margaret Emily (Meta), born. Mrs Hannah Lumb dies.

1840 Her description of Clopton Hall included by William Howitt in *Visits to Remarkable Places*.

1841 Mr and Mrs Gaskell visit the Continent, touring the Rhine country.

1842 Her fourth daughter, Florence Elizabeth, born. The family move to 121 Upper Rumford Street, Manchester.

1844 Her only son, William, born; dies of scarlet fever at Festiniog, 1845.

1846 Her fifth daughter, Julia Bradford, born.

1847 'Libbie Marsh's Three Eras' published in *Howitt's Journal*.

1848 'Christmas Storms and Sunshine' in *Howitt's Journal*. Her first novel, *Mary Barton*, published.

1849 Visits London, where she meets Dickens and other literary figures. Meets Wordsworth while on holiday in Ambleside. 'Hand and Heart' published in the *Sunday School Penny Magazine*, 'The Last Generation in England' in *Sartain's Union Magazine*, America.

1850 The family move to 84 Plymouth Grove, Manchester. Dickens invites Mrs Gaskell to contribute to *Household Words*: 'Lizzie Leigh' begins in first number, followed by 'The Well of Pen Morfa' and 'The Heart of John Middleton'. *The Moorland Cottage* published. First meets Charlotte Brontë in August.

1851 'Mr Harrison's Confessions' appears in the *Ladies' Companion*. Continues to write for *Household Words*, the first episode of *Cranford* appearing in December. Visited by Charlotte Brontë in June. Her portrait, now in the National Portrait Gallery, painted by Richmond.

1852 'The Schah's English Gardener' and 'The Old Nurse's Story' in *Household Words*. 'Bessy's Troubles at Home' in the *Sunday School Penny Magazine*. Gives Charlotte Brontë the outline of *Ruth* (April). Visited by Dickens (September).

1853 *Ruth* (January) and *Cranford* (June) published. 'Cumberland Sheep-Shearers', 'Traits and Stories of the Huguenots', 'Morton Hall', 'My French Master', 'The Squire's Story' all in *Household Words*. Begins *North and South*. Visits exchanged with Charlotte Brontë.

1854 'Modern Greek Songs', 'Company Manners' in *Household Words; North and South* begins to appear in September. Her husband succeeds as Minister of Cross Street Chapel, Manchester. Visits France with Marianne: meets Mme Mohl and William W. Story. Meets Florence Nightingale in London. Last meeting with Charlotte Brontë.

1855 'An Accursed Race', 'Half a Lifetime Ago' in *Household Words*. *North and South* and *Lizzie Leigh and Other Stories* published. In June, Charlotte Brontë's father asks her to write his daughter's *Life*. She and Meta spend a month in Paris with Mme Mohl.

1856 'The Poor Clare' in *Household Words*.

1857 *Life of Charlotte Brontë* published. Visits Paris and Rome with her two eldest daughters and Catherine Winkworth.

1858 'My Lady Ludlow', 'Right at Last', and 'The Manchester Marriage' in *Household Words*. 'The Doom of the Griffiths' in *Harper's Magazine*.

1859 *Round the Sofa and Other Tales* published. 'Lois the Witch' and 'The Crooked Branch' in *All the Year Round*. Visits Whitby where she collects material for *Sylvia's Lovers*. Takes her daughters Meta and Florence to Germany, returning via Paris.

1860 *Right at Last and Other Tales* published. 'Curious, if True' in *The Cornhill*. Visits to France.

1861 'The Grey Woman' in *All the Year Round*.

1862 Visits Paris, Normandy, and Brittany with Meta and a friend, returning to London for the Exhibition. Back in Manchester she over-exerts herself in relief work among the workmen, and has to recuperate. Writes a Preface to Vecchi's *Garibaldi*.

1863 'A Dark Night's Work', 'An Italian Institution', 'The Cage at Cranford', and 'Crowley Castle' in *All the Year Round*. 'Cousin Phillis' in *The Cornhill*. *Sylvia's Lovers* published by Smith, Elder. Visits Mme Mohl in Paris, going on to Rome with three of her daughters. Her daughter Florence marries.

1864 'French Life' in *Fraser's Magazine*. *Wives and Daughters* begins to appear in *The Cornhill*.

1865 *Cousin Phillis and Other Tales* and *The Grey Woman and Other Tales* published. Visits Dieppe, and Mme Mohl in Paris. Buys a house, The Lawns, nr. Holybourne in Hampshire, and dies there suddenly on 12 November.

1866 *Wives and Daughters* published posthumously.

A DARK NIGHT'S WORK

CHAPTER I

In the county town of a certain shire there lived (about forty years ago*) one Mr Wilkins, a conveyancing attorney* of considerable standing.

The certain shire was but a small county, and the principal town in it contained only about four thousand inhabitants; so in saying that Mr Wilkins was the principal lawyer in Hamley, I say very little, unless I add that he transacted all the legal business of the gentry for twenty miles round. His grandfather had established the connection; his father had consolidated and strengthened it, and, indeed, by his wise and upright conduct, as well as by his professional skill, had obtained for himself the position of confidential friend to many of the surrounding families of distinction. He visited among them in a way which no mere lawyer had ever done before; dined at their tables—he alone, not accompanied by his wife, be it observed; rode to the meet* occasionally as if by accident, although he was as well mounted as any squire among them, and was often persuaded (after a little coquetting about 'professional engagements,' and 'being wanted at the office') to have a run with his clients; nay, once or twice he forgot his usual caution, was first in at the death, and rode home with the brush. But in general he knew his place; as his place was held to be in that aristocratic county, and in those days. Nor let it be supposed that he was in any way a toad-eater. He respected himself too much for that. He would give the most unpalatable advice, if need were; would counsel an unsparing reduction of expenditure to an extravagant man; would recommend such an abatement of family pride as paved the way for one or two happy marriages in some instances; nay, what was the most likely piece of conduct of all to give offence forty years ago, he would speak up for an unjustly-used tenant; and that with so much temperate and well-timed wisdom and good feeling, that he more than once gained his point. He had one son, Edward. This boy was the secret joy and pride of his father's heart. For himself he was not in the least ambitious, but it did cost him a hard struggle to acknowledge that his own business was too lucrative and brought in too large an income, to pass away into the hands of a stranger, as it would do if he indulged his ambition for his son by giving him a college education, and making him into a barrister. This determination on the more prudent side of the argument took place while Edward was at Eton. The lad had, perhaps, the largest allowance of pocket-money of any boy at school; and he had always looked forward to going to Christ Church* along with his fellows, the sons of the squires, his father's employers. It was a severe mortification to him to find that his destiny was changed, and that he had to return to Hamley to be articled to his father, and to assume the hereditary subservient position to lads whom he had licked in the playground, and beaten at learning.

His father tried to compensate him for the disappointment by every indulgence which money could purchase. Edward's horses were even finer than those of his father; his literary tastes were kept up and fostered, by his father's permission to form an extensive library, for which purpose a noble room was added to Mr Wilkins's already extensive house in the suburbs of Hamley. And after his year of legal study in London his father sent him to make the grand tour, with something very like *carte blanche* as to expenditure, to judge from the packages which were sent home from various parts of the Continent.

At last he came home—came back to settle as his father's partner at Hamley. He was a son to be proud of, and right down proud was old Mr Wilkins of his handsome, accomplished, gentlemanly lad. For Edward was not one to be spoilt by the course of indulgence he had passed through; at least, if it had done him an injury, the effects were at present hidden from view. He had no vulgar vices; he was, indeed, rather too refined for the society he was likely to be thrown into, even supposing that society to consist of the highest of his father's employers. He was well read, and an artist of no mean pretensions. Above all, 'his heart was in the right place,' as his father used to observe. Nothing could exceed the deference he always showed to him. His mother had long been dead.

I do not know whether it was Edward's own ambition or his proud father's wishes that had led him to attend the Hamley assemblies. I should conjecture the latter, for Edward had of himself too much good taste to wish to intrude into any society. In the opinion of all the shire, no society had more reason to consider itself select than that which met at every full moon in the Hamley assembly-room, an excrescence built on to the principal inn in the town by the joint subscription of all the county families. Into those choice and mysterious precincts no townsperson was ever allowed to enter; no professional man might set his foot therein; no infantry officer saw the interior of that ball, or that card room. The old original subscribers would fain have had a man prove his sixteen quarterings* before he might make his bow to the queen of the night; but the old original founders of the Hamley assemblies were dropping off; minuets* had vanished with them, country dances had died away; quadrilles were in high vogue—nay, one or two of the high magnates of ——shire were trying to introduce waltzing, as they had seen it in London, where it had come in with the visit of the allied sovereigns,* when Edward Wilkins made his *début* on these boards. He had been at many splendid assemblies abroad, but still the little old ballroom attached to the George Inn in his native town was to him a place grander and more awful than the most magnificent saloons he had seen in Paris or Rome. He laughed at himself for this unreasonable feeling of awe; but there it was notwithstanding. He had been dining at the house of one of the lesser gentry, who was under considerable obligations to his father, and who was the parent of eight 'muckle-mou'ed'* daughters, so hardly likely to oppose much aristocratic resistance to the elder Mr Wilkins's clearly implied wish that Edward should be presented at the Hamley assembly-rooms. But many a squire glowered and looked black at the introduction of Wilkins the attorney's son into the sacred precincts; and perhaps there would have been much more mortification than pleasure in this assembly to the young man, had it not been for an incident that occurred pretty late in the evening.

The lord-lieutenant of the county usually came with a large party to the Hamley assemblies once in a season; and this night he was expected, and with him a fashionable duchess and her daughters. But time wore on, and they did not make their appearance. At last, there was a rustling and a bustling, and in sailed the superb party. For a few minutes dancing was stopped; the earl led the duchess to a sofa; some of their acquaintances came up to speak to them; and then the quadrilles were finished in rather a flat manner. A country dance followed, in which none of the lord-lieutenant's party joined; then there was a consultation, a request, an inspection of the dancers, a message to the orchestra, and the band struck up a waltz; the duchess's daughters flew off to the music, and some more young ladies seemed ready to follow, but, alas! there was a lack of gentlemen acquainted with the new-fashioned dance. One of the stewards bethought him of young Wilkins, only just returned from the Continent. Edward was a beautiful dancer, and waltzed to admiration. For his next partner he had one of the Lady ——s; for the duchess, to whom the ——shire squires and their little county politics and contempts were alike unknown, saw no reason why her lovely Lady Sophy should not have a good partner, whatever his pedigree might be, and begged the stewards to introduce Mr Wilkins to her. After this night, his fortune was made with the young ladies of the Hamley assemblies. He was not unpopular with the mammas; but the heavy squires still looked at him askance, and the heirs (whom he had licked at Eton) called him an upstart behind his back.

CHAPTER II

It was not a satisfactory situation. Mr Wilkins had given his son an education and tastes beyond his position. He could not associate with either profit or pleasure with the doctor or the brewer of Hamley; the vicar was old and deaf, the curate a raw young man, half frightened at the sound of his own voice. Then, as to matrimony; for the idea of his marriage was hardly more present in Edward's mind than in that of his father—he could scarcely fancy bringing home any one of the young ladies of

Hamley to the elegant mansion, so full of suggestion and association to an educated person, so inappropriate a dwelling for an ignorant, uncouth, ill-brought-up girl. Yet Edward was fully aware, if his fond father was not, that of all the young ladies who were glad enough of him as a partner at the Hamley assemblies, there was not one of them but would have considered herself affronted by an offer of marriage from an attorney, the son and grandson of attorneys. The young man had perhaps received many a slight and mortification pretty quietly during these years, which yet told upon his character in after life. Even at this very time they were having their effect. He was of too sweet a disposition to show resentment, as many men would have done. But nevertheless he took a secret pleasure in the power which his father's money gave him. He would buy an expensive horse after five minutes' conversation as to the price, about which a needy heir of one of the proud county families had been haggling for three weeks. His dogs were from the best kennels in England, no matter at what cost; his guns were the newest and most improved make; and all these were expenses on objects which were among those of daily envy to the squires and squires' sons around. They did not much care for the treasures of art, which report said were being accumulated in Mr Wilkins's house. But they did covet the horses and hounds he possessed,* and the young man knew that they coveted, and rejoiced in it.

By-and-by he formed a marriage, which went as near as marriages ever do towards pleasing everybody. He was desperately in love with Miss Lamotte, so he was delighted when she consented to be his wife. His father was delighted in his delight, and, besides, was charmed to remember that Miss Lamotte's mother had been Sir Frank Holster's youngest sister, and that, although her marriage had been disowned by her family, as beneath her in rank, yet no one could efface her name out of the Baronetage, where Lettice, youngest daughter of Sir Mark Holster, born 1772, married H. Lamotte, 1799, died 1810, was duly chronicled. She had left two children, a boy and a girl, of whom their uncle, Sir Frank, took charge, as their father was worse than dead—an outlaw, whose name was never mentioned. Mark Lamotte was in the army; Lettice had a dependent position in her uncle's family; not intentionally made more dependent than was rendered necessary by circumstances, but still dependent enough to grate on the feelings of a sensitive girl, whose natural susceptibility to slights was redoubled by the constant recollection of her father's disgrace. As Mr Wilkins well knew, Sir Frank was considerably involved; but it was with very mixed feelings that he listened to the suit which would provide his penniless niece with a comfortable, not to say luxurious, home, and with a handsome, accomplished young man of unblemished character for a husband. He said one or two bitter and insolent things to Mr Wilkins, even while he was giving his consent to the match; that was his temper, his proud, evil temper; but he really and permanently was satisfied with the connection, though he would occasionally turn round on his nephew-in-law, and sting him with a covert insult as to his want of birth, and the inferior position which he held, forgetting, apparently, that his own brother-in-law and Lettice's father might be at any moment brought to the bar of justice if he attempted to re-enter his native country.

Edward was annoyed at all this; Lettice resented it. She loved her husband dearly, and was proud of him, for she had discernment enough to see how superior he was in every way to her cousins, the young Holsters, who borrowed his horses, drank his wines, and yet had caught their father's habit of sneering at his profession. Lettice wished that Edward would content himself with a purely domestic life, would let himself drop out of the company of the ——shire squirearchy, and find his relaxation with her, in their luxurious library, or lovely drawing-room, so full of white-gleaming statues, and gems of pictures. But, perhaps, this was too much to expect of any man, especially of one who felt himself fitted in many ways to shine in society, and who was social by nature. Sociality in that county at that time meant conviviality. Edward did not care for wine, and yet he was obliged to drink—and by-and-by he grew to pique himself on his character as a judge of wine. His father by this time was dead; dead, happy old man, with a contented heart—his affairs flourishing, his poorer neighbours loving him, his richer respecting him, his son and daughter-in-law the most affectionate and devoted that ever man had, and his healthy conscience at peace with his God.

Lettice could have lived to herself and her husband and children. Edward daily required more and more the stimulus of society. His wife wondered how he could care to accept dinner invitations from people who treated him as 'Wilkins the attorney, a very good sort of fellow,' as they introduced him to strangers who might be staying in the country, but who had no power to appreciate the taste, the talents, the impulsive artistic nature which she held so dear. She forgot that by accepting such invitations Edward was occasionally brought into contact with people not merely of high conventional, but of high intellectual rank; that when a certain amount of wine had dissipated his sense of inferiority of rank and position, he was a brilliant talker, a man to be listened to and admired even by wandering London statesmen, professional diners-out, or any great authors who might find themselves visitors in a ——shire country-house. What she would have had him share from the pride of her heart, she should have warned him to avoid from the temptations to sinful extravagance which it led him into. He had begun to spend more than he ought, not in intellectual—though that would have been wrong—but in purely sensual things. His wines, his table, should be such as no squire's purse or palate could command. His dinner-parties—small in number, the viands rare and delicate in quality, and sent up to table by an Italian cook—should be such as even the London stars should notice with admiration. He would have Lettice dressed in the richest materials, the most delicate lace; jewellery, he said, was beyond their means: glancing with proud humility at the diamonds of the elder ladies, and the alloyed gold of the younger. But he managed to spend as much on his wife's lace as would have bought many a set of inferior jewellery. Lettice well became it all. If, as people said, her father had been nothing but a French adventurer, she bore traces of her nature in her grace, her delicacy, her fascinating and elegant ways of doing all things. She was made for society; and yet she hated it. And one day she went out of it altogether, and for evermore. She had been well in the morning when Edward went down to his office in Hamley. At noon he was sent for by hurried trembling messengers. When he got home, breathless and uncomprehending, she was past speech. One glance from her lovely loving black eyes showed that she recognized him with the passionate yearning that had been one of the characteristics of her love through life. There was no word passed between them. He could not speak, any more than could she. He knelt down by her. She was dying; she was dead; and he knelt on, immovable. They brought him his eldest child, Ellinor, in utter despair what to do in order to rouse him. They had no thought as to the effect on her, hitherto shut up in the nursery during this busy day of confusion and alarm. The child had no idea of death, and her father, kneeling and tearless, was far less an object of surprise or interest to her than her mother, lying still and white, and not turning her head to smile at her darling.

'Mamma! mamma!' cried the child, in shapeless terror. But the mother never stirred; and the father hid his face yet deeper in the bed-clothes, to stifle a cry as if a sharp knife had pierced his heart. The child forced her impetuous way from her attendants, and rushed to the bed. Undeterred by deadly cold or stony immobility, she kissed the lips, and stroked the glossy raven hair, murmuring sweet words of wild love, such as had passed between the mother and child often and often when no witnesses were by; and altogether seemed so nearly beside herself in an agony of love and terror, that Edward arose, and softly taking her in his arms, bore her away, lying back like one dead (so exhausted was she by the terrible emotion they had forced on her childish heart), into his study, a little room opening out of the grand library, where on happy evenings, never to come again, he and his wife were wont to retire to have coffee together, and then perhaps stroll out of the glass-door into the open air, the shrubbery, the fields—never more to be trodden by those dear feet. What passed between father and child in this seclusion none could tell. Late in the evening Ellinor's supper was sent for, and the servant who brought it in, saw the child lying as one dead in her father's arms, and before he left the room, watched his master feeding her, the girl of six years of age, with as tender care as if she had been a baby of six months.

CHAPTER III

FROM that time the tie between father and daughter grew very strong and tender indeed. Ellinor, it is true, divided her affection between her baby sister and her papa; but he, caring little for babies, had only a theoretic regard for his younger child, while the elder absorbed all his love. Every day that he dined at home Ellinor was placed opposite to him while he ate his late dinner; she sat where her mother had done during the meal, although she had dined and even supped some time before on the more primitive nursery fare. It was half pitiful, half amusing to see the little girl's grave, thoughtful ways and modes of speech, as if trying to act up to the dignity of her place as her father's companion, till sometimes the little head nodded off to slumber in the middle of lisping some wise little speech. 'Old-fashioned,' the nurses called her, and prophesied that she would not live long in consequence of her old-fashionedness. But instead of the fulfilment of this prophecy, the fat bright baby was seized with fits, and was well, ill, and dead in a day! Ellinor's grief was something alarming, from its quietness and concealment. She waited till she was left—as she thought—alone at nights, and then sobbed and cried her passionate cry for 'Baby, baby, come back to me—come back!' till everyone feared for the health of the frail little girl whose childish affections had had to stand two such shocks. Her father put aside all business, all pleasure of every kind, to win his darling from her grief. No mother could have done more, no tenderest nurse done half so much as Mr Wilkins then did for Ellinor.

If it had not been for him she would have just died of her grief. As it was, she overcame it—but slowly, wearily—hardly letting herself love anyone for some time, as if she instinctively feared lest all her strong attachments should find a sudden end in death. Her love—thus dammed up into a small space—at last burst its banks, and overflowed on her father. It was a rich reward to him for all his care of her, and he took delight—perhaps a selfish delight—in all the many pretty ways she perpetually found of convincing him, if he had needed conviction, that he was ever the first object with her. The nurse told him that half an hour or so before the earliest time at which he could be expected home in the evenings, Miss Ellinor began to fold up her doll's things and lull the inanimate treasure to sleep. Then she would sit and listen with an intensity of attention for his footstep. Once the nurse had expressed some wonder at the distance at which Ellinor could hear her father's approach, saying that she had listened and could not hear a sound, to which Ellinor had replied:

'Of course you cannot; he is not your papa!'

Then, when he went away in the morning, after he had kissed her, Ellinor would run to a certain window from which she could watch him up the lane, now hidden behind a hedge, now reappearing through an open space, again out of sight, till he reached a great old beech-tree, where for an instant more she saw him. And then she would turn away with a sigh, sometimes reassuring her unspoken fears by saying softly to herself,

'He will come again tonight.'

Mr Wilkins liked to feel his child dependent on him for all her pleasures. He was even a little jealous of anyone who devised a treat or conferred a present, the first news of which did not come from or through him.

At last it was necessary that Ellinor should have some more instruction than her good old nurse could give. Her father did not care to take upon himself the office of teacher, which he thought he foresaw would necessitate occasional blame, an occasional exercise of authority, which might possibly render him less idolized by his little girl; so he commissioned Lady Holster to choose out one among her many *protégées* for a governess to his daughter. Now, Lady Holster, who kept a sort of amateur county register-office, was only too glad to be made of use in this way; but when she inquired a little further as to the sort of person required, all she could extract from Mr Wilkins was:

'You know the kind of education a lady should have, and will, I am sure, choose a governess for Ellinor better than I could direct you. Only, please, choose someone who will not marry me, and who will let Ellinor go on making my tea, and doing pretty much what she likes, for she is so good they need not try to make her better, only to teach her what a lady should know.'

Miss Monro was selected—a plain, intelligent, quiet woman of forty—and it was difficult to decide whether she or Mr Wilkins took the most pains to avoid each other, acting, with regard to Ellinor, pretty much like the famous Adam and Eve in the weather-glass:* when the one came out, the other went in. Miss Monro had been tossed about and overworked quite enough in her life to value the privilege and indulgence of her evenings to herself, her comfortable schoolroom, her quiet cosy teas, her book, or her letter-writing afterwards. By mutual agreement, she did not interfere with Ellinor and her ways and occupations on the evenings when the girl had not her father for companion; and these occasions became more and more frequent as years passed on, and the deep shadow was lightened which the sudden death that had visited his household had cast over him. As I have said before, he was always a popular man at dinner-parties. His amount of intelligence and accomplishment was rare in ——shire, and if it required more wine than formerly to bring his conversation up to the desired point of range and brilliancy, wine was not an article spared or grudged at the county dinner-tables. Occasionally his business took him up to London. Hurried as these journeys might be, he never returned without a new game, a new toy of some kind, to 'make home pleasant to his little maid,' as he expressed himself.

He liked, too, to see what was doing in art, or in literature; and as he gave pretty extensive orders for anything he admired, he was almost sure to be followed down to Hamley by one or two packages or parcels, the arrival and opening of which began soon to form the pleasant epochs in Ellinor's grave though happy life.

The only person of his own standing with whom Mr Wilkins kept up any intercourse in Hamley was the new clergyman, a bachelor, about his own age, a learned man, a fellow of his college, whose first claim on Mr Wilkins's attention was the fact that he had been travelling-bachelor for his university, and had consequently been on the Continent about the very same two years that Mr Wilkins had been there; and although they had never met, yet they had many common acquaintances and common recollections to talk over of this period, which, after all, had been about the most bright and hopeful of Mr Wilkins's life.

Mr Ness had an occasional pupil; that is to say, he never put himself out of the way to obtain pupils, but did not refuse the entreaties sometimes made to him that he would prepare a young man for college, by allowing the said young man to reside and read with him. 'Ness's men' took rather high honours, for the tutor, too indolent to find out work for himself, had a certain pride in doing well the work that was found for him.

When Ellinor was somewhere about fourteen, a young Mr Corbet came to be pupil to Mr Ness. Her father always called on the young men reading with the clergyman, and asked them to his house. His hospitality had in course of time lost its *recherché** and elegant character, but was always generous, and often profuse. Besides, it was in his character to like the joyous, thoughtless company of the young better than that of the old,—given the same amount of refinement and education in both.

Mr Corbet was a young man of very good family, from a distant county. If his character had not been so grave and deliberate, his years would only have entitled him to be called a boy, for he was but eighteen at the time when he came to read with Mr Ness. But many men of five-and-twenty have not reflected so deeply as this young Mr Corbet already had. He had considered and almost matured his plan for life; had ascertained what objects he desired most to accomplish in the dim future, which is to many at his age only a shapeless mist; and had resolved on certain steady courses of action by which such objects were most likely to be secured. A younger son, his family connections and family interest pre-arranged a legal career for him; and it was in accordance with his own tastes and talents. All, however, which his father hoped for him was, that he might be able to make an income sufficient for a gentleman to live on. Old Mr Corbet was hardly to be called ambitious, or, if he were, his ambition was limited to views for the eldest son. But Ralph intended to be a distinguished lawyer, not so much for the vision of the woolsack,* which I suppose dances before the imagination of every young lawyer, as for the grand intellectual exercise, and consequent power over mankind, that distinguished lawyers may always possess if they choose. A seat in Parliament, statesmanship, and all the great scope for a powerful and active mind that lay on each side of such a career—these were the objects which Ralph Corbet set before himself. To take high honours at college was the first step to be accomplished; and in order to achieve this Ralph had, not persuaded—persuasion was a weak instrument which he despised—but gravely reasoned his father into consenting to pay the large sum which Mr Ness expected with a pupil. The good-natured old squire was rather pressed for ready money, but sooner than listen to an argument instead of taking his nap after dinner he would have yielded anything. But this did not satisfy Ralph: his father's reason must be convinced of the desirability of the step, as well as his weak will give way. The squire listened, looked wise, sighed; spoke of Edward's extravagance and the girls' expenses, grew sleepy, and said, 'Very true,' 'That is but reasonable, certainly,' glanced at the door, and wondered when his son would have ended his talking and go into the drawing-room; and at length found himself writing the desired letter to Mr Ness, consenting to everything, terms and all. Mr Ness never had a more satisfactory pupil; one whom he could treat more as an intellectual equal.

Mr Corbet, as Ralph was always called in Hamley, was resolute in his cultivation of himself, even exceeding what his tutor demanded of him. He was greedy of information in the hours not devoted to absolute study. Mr Ness enjoyed giving information, but most of all he liked the hard tough arguments on all metaphysical and ethical questions in which Mr Corbet delighted to engage him. They lived together on terms of happy equality, having thus much in common. They were essentially different, however, although there were so many points of resemblance. Mr Ness was unworldly as far as the idea of real unworldliness is compatible with a turn for self-indulgence and indolence; while Mr Corbet was deeply, radically worldly, yet for the accomplishment of his object could deny himself all the careless pleasures natural to his age. The tutor and pupil allowed themselves one frequent relaxation,—that of Mr Wilkins's company. Mr Ness would stroll to the office after the six hours' hard reading were over—leaving Mr Corbet still bent over the table, book bestrewn—and see what Mr Wilkins's engagements were. If he had nothing better to do that evening, he was either asked to dine at the parsonage, or he, in his careless hospitable way, invited the other two to dine with him, Ellinor forming the fourth at table, as far as seats went, although her dinner had been eaten early with Miss Monro. She was little and slight of her age, and her father never seemed to understand how she was passing out of childhood. Yet while in stature she was like a child, in intellect, in force of character, in strength of clinging affection, she was a woman. There might be much of the simplicity of a child about her, there was little of the undeveloped girl, varying from day to day like an April sky, careless as to which way her own character is tending. So the two young people sat with their elders, and both relished the company they were thus prematurely thrown into. Mr Corbet talked as much as either of the other two gentlemen; opposing and disputing on any side, as if to find out how much he could urge against received opinions. Ellinor sat silent; her dark eyes flashing from time to time in vehement interest—sometimes in vehement indignation if Mr Corbet, riding a-tilt* at everyone, ventured to attack her father. He saw how this course excited her, and rather liked pursuing it in consequence; he thought it only amused him.

Another way in which Ellinor and Mr Corbet were thrown together occasionally was this. Mr Ness and Mr Wilkins shared the same *Times* between them; and it was Ellinor's duty to see that the paper was regularly taken from her father's house to the parsonage. Her father liked to dawdle over it. Until Mr Corbet had come to live with him, Mr Ness had not much cared at what time it was passed on to him; but the young man took a strong interest in all public events, and especially in all that was said about them. He grew impatient if the paper was not forthcoming, and would set off himself to go for it, sometimes meeting the penitent breathless Ellinor in the long lane which led from Hamley to Mr Wilkins's house. At first he used to receive her eager 'Oh! I am so sorry, Mr Corbet, but papa has only just done with it,' rather gruffly. After a time he had the grace to tell her it did not signify; and by-and-by he would turn back with her to give her some advice about her garden, or her plants—for his mother and sisters were first-rate practical gardeners, and he himself was, as he expressed it, 'a capital consulting physician for a sickly plant.'

All this time his voice, his step, never raised the child's colour one shade the higher, never made her heart beat the least quicker, as the slightest sign of her father's approach was wont to do. She learnt to rely on Mr Corbet for advice, for a little occasional sympathy, and for much condescending attention. He also gave her more fault-finding than all the rest of the world put together; and, curiously enough, she was grateful to him for it, for she really was humble, and wished to improve. He liked the attitude of superiority which this implied and exercised right gave him. They were very good friends at present. Nothing more.

All this time I have spoken only of Mr Wilkins's life as he stood in relation to his daughter. But there is far more to be said about it. After his wife's death, he withdrew himself from society for a year or two in a more positive and decided manner than is common with widowers. It was during this retirement of his that he riveted his little daughter's heart in such a way as to influence all her future life.

When he began to go out again, it might have been perceived—had anyone cared to notice—how much the different characters of his father and wife had influenced him and kept him steady. Not that he broke out into any immoral conduct, but he gave up time to pleasure, which both old Mr Wilkins and Lettice would have quietly induced him to spend in the office, superintending his business. His indulgence in hunting, and all field-sports, had hitherto been only occasional; they now became habitual, as far as the seasons permitted. He shared a moor in Scotland with one of the Holsters one year, persuading himself that the bracing air was good for Ellinor's health. But the year afterwards he took another, this time joining with a comparative stranger; and on this moor there was no house to which it was fit to bring a child and her attendants. He persuaded himself that by frequent journeys he could make up for his absences from Hamley. But journeys cost money; and he was often away from his office when important business required attending to. There was some talk of a new attorney setting up in Hamley, to be supported by one or two of the more influential county families, who had found Wilkins not so attentive as his father. Sir Frank Holster sent for his relation, and told him of this project, speaking to him, at the same time, in pretty round terms on the folly of the life he was leading. Foolish it certainly was, and as such Mr Wilkins was secretly acknowledging it; but when Sir Frank, lashing himself, began to talk of his hearer's presumption in joining the hunt, in aping the mode of life and amusements of the landed gentry, Edward fired up. He knew how much Sir Frank was dipped,* and comparing it with the round sum his own father had left him, he said some plain truths to Sir Frank which the latter never forgave, and henceforth there was no intercourse between Holster Court and Ford Bank, as Mr Edward Wilkins had christened his father's house on his first return from the Continent.

The conversation had two consequences besides the immediate one of the quarrel. Mr Wilkins advertised for a responsible and confidential clerk to conduct the business under his own superintendence; and he also wrote to the Heralds' College* to ask if he did not belong to the family bearing the same name in South Wales—those who have since reassumed their ancient name of De Winton.

Both applications were favourably answered. A skilful, experienced, middle-aged clerk was recommended to him by one of the principal legal firms in London, and immediately engaged to come to Hamley at his own terms; which were pretty high. But, as Mr Wilkins said it was worth any money to pay for the relief from constant responsibility which such a business as his involved, some people remarked that he had never appeared to feel the responsibility very much hitherto, as witness his absences in Scotland, and his various social engagements when at home; it had been very different (they said) in his father's day. The Heralds' College held out hopes of affiliating him to the South Wales family, but it would require time and money to make the requisite inquiries and substantiate the claim. Now, in many a place there would be none to contest the right a man might have to assert that he belonged to such and such a family, or even to assume their arms. But it was otherwise in ——shire. Everyone was up in genealogy and heraldry, and considered filching a name and a pedigree a far worse sin than any of those mentioned in the Commandments. There were those among them who would doubt and dispute even the decision of the Heralds' College; but with it, if in his favour, Mr Wilkins intended to be satisfied, and accordingly he wrote in reply to their letter to say, that of course he was aware such inquiries would take a considerable sum of money, but still he wished them to be made, and that speedily.

Before the end of the year he went up to London to order a brougham* to be built (for Ellinor to drive out in in wet weather, he said; but as going in a closed carriage always made her ill, he used it principally himself in driving to dinner-parties), with the De Winton Wilkinses' arms neatly emblazoned on panel and harness. Hitherto he had always gone about in a dog-cart—the immediate descendant of his father's old-fashioned gig.

For all this, the squires, his employers, only laughed at him, and did not treat him with one whit more respect.

Mr Dunster, the new clerk, was a quiet, respectable-looking man; you could not call him a gentleman in manner, and yet no one could say he was vulgar. He had not much varying expression on his face, but a permanent one of thoughtful consideration of the subject in hand, whatever it might be, that would have fitted as well with the profession of medicine as with that of law, and was quite the right look for either. Occasionally a bright flash of sudden intelligence lightened up his deep-sunk eyes, but even this was quickly extinguished as by some inward repression, and the habitually reflective, subdued expression returned to the face. As soon as he came into his situation, he first began quietly to arrange the papers, and next the business of which they were the outward sign, into more methodical order than they had been in since old Mr Wilkins's death. Punctual to a moment himself, he looked his displeased surprise when the inferior clerks came tumbling in half an hour after the time in the morning; and his look was more effective than many men's words; henceforward the subordinates were within five minutes of the appointed hour for opening the office; but still he was always there before them. Mr Wilkins himself winced under his new clerk's order and punctuality; Mr Dunster's raised eyebrow and contraction of the lips at some woeful confusion in the business of the office chafed Mr Wilkins more, far more, than any open expression of opinion would have done; for that he could have met, and explained away, as he fancied. A secret respectful dislike grew up in his bosom against Mr Dunster. He esteemed him, he valued him, and he could not bear him. Year after year, Mr Wilkins had become more under the influence of his feelings, and less under the command of his reason. He rather cherished than repressed his nervous repugnance to the harsh measured tones of Mr Dunster's voice; the latter spoke with a provincial twang which grated on his employer's sensitive ear. He was annoyed at a certain green coat which his new clerk brought with him, and he watched its increasing shabbiness with a sort of childish pleasure. But by-and-by Mr Wilkins found out that, from some perversity of taste, Mr Dunster always had his coats, Sunday and working-day, made of this obnoxious colour; and this knowledge did not diminish his secret irritation. The worst of all, perhaps, was, that Mr Dunster was really invaluable in many ways; 'a perfect treasure,' as Mr Wilkins used to term him in speaking of him after dinner; but, for all that, he came to hate his 'perfect treasure,' as he gradually felt that Dunster had become so indispensable to the business that his chief could not do without him.

The clients re-echoed Mr Wilkins's words, and spoke of Mr Dunster as invaluable to his master; a thorough treasure, the very saving of the business. They had not been better attended to, not even in old Mr Wilkins's days; such a clear head, such a knowledge of law, such a steady, upright fellow, always at his post. The grating voice, the drawling accent, the bottle-green coat, were nothing to them; far less noticed, in fact, than Wilkins's expensive habits, the money he paid for his wine and horses, and the nonsense of claiming kin with the Welsh Wilkinses, and setting up his brougham to drive about ——shire lanes, and be knocked to pieces over the rough round paving-stones thereof.

All these remarks did not come near Ellinor to trouble her life. To her, her dear father was the first of human beings; so sweet, so good, so kind, so charming in conversation, so full of accomplishment and information! To her healthy, happy mind everyone turned their bright side. She loved Miss Monro—all the servants—especially Dixon, the coachman. He had been her father's playfellow as a boy, and, with all his respect and admiration for his master, the freedom of intercourse that had been established between them then had never been quite lost. Dixon was a fine, stalwart old fellow, and was as harmonious in his ways with his master as Mr Dunster was discordant; accordingly, he was a great favourite, and could say many a thing which might have been taken as impertinent from another servant.

He was Ellinor's great confidant about many of her little plans and projects; things that she dared not speak of to Mr Corbet, who, after her father and Dixon, was her next best friend. This intimacy with Dixon displeased Mr Corbet. He once or twice insinuated that he did not think it was well to talk so familiarly as Ellinor did with a servant—one out of a completely different class—such as Dixon. Ellinor did not easily take hints; everyone had spoken plain out to her hitherto; so Mr Corbet had to say his meaning plain out at last. Then, for the first time, he saw her angry; but she was too young, too childish, to have words at will to express her feelings; she only could say broken beginnings of sentences, such as 'What a shame! Good, dear Dixon, who is as loyal and true and kind as any nobleman. I like him far better than you, Mr Corbet, and I shall talk to him.' And then she burst into tears and ran away, and would not come to wish Mr Corbet goodbye, though she knew she should not see him again for a long time, as he was returning the next day to his father's house, from whence he would go to Cambridge.

He was annoyed at this result of the good advice he had thought himself bound to give to a motherless girl, who had no one to instruct her in the proprieties in which his own sisters were brought up; he left Hamley both sorry and displeased. As for Ellinor, when she found out the next day that he really was gone—gone without even coming to Ford Bank again to see if she were not penitent for her angry words—gone without saying or hearing a word of goodbye—she shut herself up in her room, and cried more bitterly than ever, because anger against herself was mixed with her regret for his loss. Luckily, her father was dining out, or he would have inquired what was the matter with his darling; and she would have had to try to explain what could not be explained. As it was, she sat with her back to the light during the schoolroom tea, and afterwards, when Miss Monro had settled down to her study of the Spanish language, Ellinor stole out into the garden, meaning to have a fresh cry over her own naughtiness and Mr Corbet's departure; but the August evening was still and calm, and put her passionate grief to shame, hushing her up, as it were, with the other young creatures, who were being soothed to rest by the serene time of day, and the subdued light of the twilight sky.

There was a piece of ground surrounding the flower-garden, which was not shrubbery, nor wood, nor kitchen-garden—only a grassy bit, out of which a group of old forest-trees sprang. Their roots were heaved above ground; their leaves fell in autumn so profusely that the turf was ragged and bare in spring; but, to make up for this, there never was such a place for snowdrops.

The roots of these old trees were Ellinor's favourite play-place; this space between these two was her doll's kitchen, that its drawing-room, and so on. Mr Corbet rather despised her contrivances for doll's furniture, so she had not often brought him here; but Dixon delighted in them, and contrived and planned with the eagerness of six years old rather than forty. Tonight Ellinor went to this place, and there were all a new collection of ornaments for Miss Dolly's sitting-room made out of fir-bobs, in the prettiest and most ingenious way. She knew it was Dixon's doing, and rushed off in search of him to thank him.

'What's the matter with my pretty?' asked Dixon, as soon as the pleasant excitement of thanking and being thanked was over, and he had leisure to look at her tear-stained face.

'Oh, I don't know! Never mind,' said she, reddening.

Dixon was silent for a minute or two, while she tried to turn off his attention by her hurried prattle.

'There's no trouble afoot that I can mend?' asked he, in a minute or two.

'Oh no! It's really nothing—nothing at all,' said she. 'It's only that Mr Corbet went away without saying goodbye to me, that's all.' And she looked as if she should have liked to cry again.

'That was not manners,' said Dixon, decisively.

'But it was my fault,' replied Ellinor, pleading against the condemnation.

Dixon looked at her pretty sharply from under his ragged bushy eyebrows.

'He had been giving me a lecture, and saying I didn't do what his sisters did—just as if I were to be always trying to be like somebody else—and I was cross, and ran away.'

'Then it was Missy who wouldn't say goodbye. That was not manners in Missy.'

'But, Dixon, I don't like being lectured!'

'I reckon you don't get much of it. But, indeed, my pretty, I daresay Mr Corbet was in the right; for, you see, master is busy, and Miss Monro is so dreadful learned, and your poor mother is dead and gone, and you have no one to teach you how young ladies go on; and by all accounts Mr Corbet comes of a good family. I've heard say his father had the best stud-farm in all Shropshire, and spared no money upon it; and the young ladies his sisters will have been taught the best of manners; it might be well for my pretty to hear how they go on.'

'You dear old Dixon, you don't know anything about my lecture, and I'm not going to tell you. Only I daresay Mr Corbet might be a little bit right, though I'm sure he was a great deal wrong.'

'But you'll not go on a-fretting—you won't now, there's a good young lady—for master won't like it, and it'll make him uneasy, and he's enough of trouble without your red eyes, bless them.'

'Trouble—papa, trouble! Oh, Dixon! what do you mean?' exclaimed Ellinor, her face taking all a woman's intensity of expression in a minute.

'Nay, I know nought,' said Dixon, evasively. 'Only that Dunster fellow is not to my mind, and I think he potters* the master sadly with his fid-fad* ways.'

'I hate Mr Dunster!' said Ellinor, vehemently. 'I won't speak a word to him the next time he comes to dine with papa.'

'Missy will do what papa likes best,' said Dixon, admonishingly; and with this the pair of 'friends' parted.

CHAPTER IV

The summer afterwards Mr Corbet came again to read with Mr Ness. He did not perceive any alteration in himself, and indeed his early-matured character had hardly made progress during the last twelve months, whatever intellectual acquirements he might have made. Therefore it was astonishing to him to see the alteration in Ellinor Wilkins. She had shot up from a rather puny girl to a tall slight young lady, with promise of great beauty in the face, which a year ago had only been remarkable for the fineness of the eyes. Her complexion was clear now, although colourless—twelve months ago he would have called it sallow—her delicate cheek was smooth as marble, her teeth were even and white, and her rare smiles called out a lovely dimple.

She met her former friend and lecturer with a grave shyness, for she remembered well how they had parted, and thought he could hardly have forgiven, much less forgotten, her passionate flinging away from him. But the truth was, after the first few hours of offended displeasure, he had ceased to think of it at all. She, poor child, by way of proving her repentance, had tried hard to reform her boisterous tom-boy manners, in order to show him that although she would not give up her dear old friend Dixon at his or anyone's bidding, she would strive to profit by his lectures in all things reasonable. The consequence was, that she suddenly appeared to him as an elegant dignified young lady, instead of the rough little girl he remembered. Still, below her somewhat formal manners there lurked the old wild spirit, as he could plainly see, after a little more watching; and he began to wish to call this out, and to strive, by reminding her of old days, and all her childish frolics, to flavour her subdued manners and speech with a little of the former originality.

In this he succeeded. No one, neither Mr Wilkins, nor Miss Monro, nor Mr Ness, saw what this young couple were about—they did not know it themselves; but before the summer was over they were desperately in love with each other, or perhaps I should rather say, Ellinor was desperately in love with him—he, as passionately as he could be with anyone; but in him the intellect was superior in strength to either affections or passions.

The causes of the blindness of those around them were these. Mr Wilkins still considered Ellinor as a little girl, as his own pet, his darling, but nothing more. Miss Monro was anxious about her own improvement. Mr Ness was deep in a new edition of Horace,* which he was going to bring out with notes. I believe Dixon would have been keener-sighted, but Ellinor kept Mr Corbet and Dixon apart for obvious reasons—they were each her dear friends, but she knew that Mr Corbet did not like Dixon, and suspected that the feeling was mutual.

The only change of circumstances between this year and the previous one consisted in this development of attachment between the young people. Otherwise, everything went on apparently as usual. With Ellinor the course of the day was something like this. Up early and into the garden until breakfast time, when she made tea for her father and Miss Monro in the dining-room, always taking care to lay a little nosegay of freshly-gathered flowers by her father's plate. After breakfast, when the conversation had been on general and indifferent subjects, Mr Wilkins withdrew into the little study, so often mentioned. It opened out of a passage that ran between the dining-room and the kitchen, on the left-hand of the hall. Corresponding to the dining-room on the other side of the hall was the drawing-room, with its side-window serving as a door into a conservatory, and this again opened into the library. Old Mr Wilkins had added a semicircular projection to the library, which was lighted by a dome above, and showed off his son's Italian purchases of sculpture. The library was by far the most striking and agreeable room in the house; and the consequence was that the drawing-room was seldom used, and had the aspect of cold discomfort common to apartments rarely occupied. Mr Wilkins's study, on the other side of the house, was also an afterthought, built only a few years ago, and projecting from the regularity of the outside wall: a little stone passage led to it from the hall, small, narrow, and dark, and out of which no other door opened.

The study itself was a hexagon, one side-window, one fire-place, and the remaining four sides occupied with doors, two of which have been already mentioned, another at the foot of the narrow winding stairs which led straight into Mr Wilkins's bedroom over the dining-room, and the fourth opening into a path through the shrubbery to the right of the flower-garden as you looked from the house. This path led through the stable-yard, and then by a short cut right into Hamley, and brought you out close to Mr Wilkins's office; it was by this way he always went and returned to his business. He used the study for a smoking and lounging-room principally, although he always spoke of it as a convenient place for holding confidential communications with such of his clients as did not like discussing their business within the possible hearing of all the clerks in his office. By the outer door he could also pass to the stables, and see that proper care was taken at all times of his favourite and valuable horses. Into this study Ellinor would follow him of a morning, helping him on with his great-coat, mending his gloves, talking an infinite deal of merry fond nothing, and then, clinging to his arm, she would accompany him in his visits to the stables, going up to the shyest horses, and petting them, and patting them, and feeding them with bread all the time that her father held converse with Dixon. When he was finally gone—and sometimes it was a long time first—she returned to the schoolroom to Miss Monro, and tried to set herself hard at work on her lessons. But she had not much time for steady application; if her father had cared for her progress in anything, she would and could have worked hard at that study or accomplishment; but Mr Wilkins, the ease and pleasure loving man, did not wish to make himself into the pedagogue, as he would have considered it, if he had ever questioned Ellinor with a real steady purpose of ascertaining her intellectual progress. It was quite enough for him that her general intelligence and variety of desultory and miscellaneous reading made her a pleasant and agreeable companion for his hours of relaxation.

At twelve o'clock, Ellinor put away her books with joyful eagerness, kissed Miss Monro, asked her if they should go a regular walk, and was always rather thankful when it was decided that it would be better to stroll in the garden—a decision very often come to, for Miss Monro hated fatigue, hated dirt, hated scrambling, and dreaded rain; all of which are evils, the chances of which are never far distant from country walks. So Ellinor danced out into the garden, worked away among her flowers, played at the old games among the roots of the trees, and, when she could, seduced Dixon into the flower-garden to have a little consultation as to the horses and dogs. For it was one of her father's few strict rules that Ellinor was never to go into the stable-yard unless he were with her; so these *tête-à-têtes* with Dixon were always held in the flower-garden, or bit of forest ground surrounding it. Miss Monro sat and basked in the sun, close to the dial, which made the centre of the gay flower-beds, upon which the dining-room and study windows looked.

At one o'clock, Ellinor and Miss Monro dined. An hour was allowed for Miss Monro's digestion, which Ellinor again spent out of doors, and at three lessons began again and lasted till five. At that time they went to dress preparatory for the school-room tea at half-past five. After tea Ellinor tried to prepare her lessons for the next day; but all the time she was listening for her father's footstep—the moment she heard that, she dashed down her book, and flew out of the room to welcome and kiss him. Seven was his dinner-hour; he hardly ever dined alone; indeed, he often dined from home four days out of seven, and when he had no engagement to take him out he liked to have someone to keep him company: Mr Ness very often, Mr Corbet along with him if he was in Hamley, a stranger friend, or one of his clients. Sometimes, reluctantly, and when he fancied he could not avoid the attention without giving offence, Mr Wilkins would ask Mr Dunster, and then the two would always follow Ellinor into the library at a very early hour, as if their subjects for *tête-à-tête* conversation were quite exhausted. With all his other visitors, Mr Wilkins sat long—yes, and yearly longer; with Mr Ness, because they became interested in each other's conversation; with some of the others, because the wine was good, and the host hated to spare it.

Mr Corbet used to leave his tutor and Mr Wilkins and saunter into the library. There sat Ellinor and Miss Monro, each busy with their embroidery. He would bring a stool to Ellinor's side, question and tease her, interest her, and they would become entirely absorbed in each other, Miss Monro's sense of propriety being entirely set at rest by the consideration that Mr Wilkins must know what he was about in allowing a young man to become thus intimate with his daughter, who, after all, was but a child.

Mr Corbet had lately fallen into the habit of walking up to Ford Bank for *The Times* every day, near twelve o'clock, and lounging about in the garden until one; not exactly with either Ellinor or Miss Monro, but certainly far more at the beck and call of the one than of the other.

Miss Monro used to think he would have been glad to stay and lunch at their early dinner, but she never gave the invitation, and he could not well stay without her expressed sanction. He told Ellinor all about his mother and sisters, and their ways of going on, and spoke of them and of his father as of people she was one day certain to know, and to know intimately; and she did not question or doubt this view of things; she simply acquiesced.

He had some discussion with himself as to whether he should speak to her, and so secure her promise to be his before returning to Cambridge or not. He did not like the formality of an application to Mr Wilkins, which would, after all, have been the proper and straightforward course to pursue with a girl of her age—she was barely sixteen. Not that he anticipated any difficulty on Mr Wilkins's part; his approval of the intimacy which at their respective ages was pretty sure to lead to an attachment, was made as evident as could be by actions without words. But there would have to be reference to his own father, who had no notion of the whole affair, and would be sure to treat it as a boyish fancy; as if at twenty-one Ralph was not a man, as clear and deliberative in knowing his own mind, as resolute as he ever would be in deciding upon the course of exertion that should lead him to independence and fame, if such were to be attained by clear intellect and a strong will.

No; to Mr Wilkins he would not speak for another year or two.

But should he tell Ellinor in direct terms of his love—his intention to marry her?

Again he inclined to the more prudent course of silence. He was not afraid of any change in his own inclinations: of them he was sure. But he looked upon it in this way: If he made a regular declaration to her she would be bound to tell it to her father. He should not respect her or like her so much if she did not. And yet this course would lead to all the conversations, and discussions, and references to his own father, which made his own direct appeal to Mr Wilkins appear a premature step to him.

Whereas he was as sure of Ellinor's love for him as if she had uttered all the vows that women ever spoke; he knew even better than she did how fully and entirely that innocent girlish heart was his own. He was too proud to dread her inconstancy for an instant; 'besides,' as he went on to himself, as if to make assurance doubly sure, 'whom does she see? Those stupid Holsters, who ought to be only too proud of having such a girl for their cousin, ignore her existence, and spoke slightingly of her father only the very last time I dined there. The country people in this precisely Boeotian* ——shire clutch at me because my father goes up to the Plantagenets* for his pedigree—not one whit for myself—and neglect Ellinor; and only condescend to her father because old Wilkins was nobody-knows-who's son. So much the worse for them, but so much the better for me in this case. I'm above their silly antiquated prejudices, and shall be only too glad when the fitting time comes to make Ellinor my wife. After all, a prosperous attorney's daughter may not be considered an unsuitable match for me—younger son as I am. Ellinor will make a glorious woman three or four years hence; just the style my father admires—such a figure, such limbs. I'll be patient and bide my time, and watch my opportunities, and all will come right.'

So he bade Ellinor farewell in a most reluctant and affectionate manner, although his words might have been spoken out in Hamley market-place, and were little different from what he said to Miss Monro. Mr Wilkins half expected a disclosure to himself of the love which he suspected in the young man; and when that did not come, he prepared himself for a confidence from Ellinor. But she had nothing to tell him, as he very well perceived from the child's open unembarrassed manner when they were left alone together after dinner. He had refused an invitation, and shaken off Mr Ness, in order to have this confidential *tête-à-tête* with his motherless girl; and there was nothing to make confidence of. He was half inclined to be angry; but then he saw that, although sad, she was so much at peace with herself and with the world, that he, always an optimist, began to think the young man had done wisely in not tearing open the rosebud of her feelings too prematurely.

The next two years passed over in much the same way—or a careless spectator might have thought so. I have heard people say, that if you look at a regiment advancing with steady step over a plain on a review-day, you can hardly tell that they are not merely marking time on one spot of ground unless you compare their position with some other object by which to mark their progress, so even is the repetition of the movement. And thus the sad events of the future life of this father and daughter were hardly perceived in their steady advance, and yet over the monotony and flat uniformity of their days sorrow came marching down upon them like an armed man. Long before Mr Wilkins had recognized its shape it was approaching him in the distance—as, in fact, it is approaching all of us at this very time; you, reader, I, writer, have each our great sorrow bearing down upon us. It may be yet beyond the dimmest point of our horizon, but in the stillness of the night our hearts shrink at the sound of its coming footstep. Well is it for those who fall into the hands of the Lord rather than into the hands of men; but worst of all is it for him who has hereafter to mingle the gall of remorse with the cup held out to him by his doom.

Mr Wilkins took his ease and his pleasure yet more and more every year of his life; nor did the quality of his ease and his pleasure improve; it seldom does with self-indulgent people. He cared less for any books that strained his faculties a little,—less for engravings and sculptures—perhaps more for pictures. He spent extravagantly on his horses; 'thought of eating and drinking.'* There was no open vice in all this, so that any awful temptation to crime should come down upon him, and startle him out of his mode of thinking and living; half the people about him did much the same, as far as their lives were patent to his unreflecting observation. But most of his associates had their duties to do, and did them with a heart and a will, in the hours when he was not in their company. Yes! I call them duties, though some of them might be self-imposed and purely social; they were engagements they had entered into, either tacitly or with words, and that they fulfilled. From Mr Hetherington, the Master of the Hounds, who was up at—no one knows what hour, to go down to the kennel and see that the men did their work well and thoroughly, to stern old Sir Lionel Playfair, the upright magistrate, the thoughtful conscientious landlord—they did their work according to their lights; there were few laggards among those with whom Mr Wilkins associated in the field or at the dinner-table. Mr Ness—though as a clergyman he was not so active as he might have been—yet even Mr Ness fagged away with his pupils and his new edition of one of the classics. Only Mr Wilkins, dissatisfied with his position, neglected to fulfil the duties thereof. He imitated the pleasures, and longed for the fancied leisure of those about him; leisure that he imagined would be so much more valuable in the hands of a man like himself, full of intellectual tastes and accomplishments, than frittered away by dull boors of untravelled, uncultivated squires—whose company, however, be it said by the way, he never refused.

And yet daily Mr Wilkins was sinking from the intellectually to the sensually self-indulgent man. He lay late in bed, and hated Mr Dunster for his significant glance at the office-clock when he announced to his master that such and such a client had been waiting more than an hour to keep an appointment. 'Why didn't you see him yourself, Dunster? I'm sure you would have done quite as well as me,' Mr. Wilkins sometimes replied, partly with a view of saying something pleasant to the man whom he disliked and feared. Mr Dunster always replied in a meek matter-of-fact tone, 'Oh, sir, they wouldn't like to talk over their affairs with a subordinate.'

And every time he said this, or some speech of the same kind, the idea came more and more clearly into Mr Wilkins's head of how pleasant it would be to himself to take Dunster into partnership, and thus throw all the responsibility of the real work and drudgery upon his clerk's shoulders. Importunate clients, who would make appointments at unseasonable hours and would keep to them, might confide in the partner though they would not in the clerk. The great objections to this course were, first and foremost, Mr Wilkins's strong dislike to Mr Dunster,—his repugnance to his company, his dress, his voice, his ways,—all of which irritated his employer, till his state of feeling towards Dunster might be called antipathy; next, Mr Wilkins was fully aware of the fact that all Mr Dunster's actions and words were carefully and thoughtfully pre-arranged to further the great unspoken desire of his life—that of being made a partner where he now was only a servant. Mr Wilkins took a malicious pleasure in tantalizing Mr Dunster by such speeches as the one I have just mentioned, which always seemed like an opening to the desired end, but still for a long time never led any further. Yet all the while that end was becoming more and more certain, and at last it was reached.

Mr Dunster always suspected that the final push was given by some circumstance from without; some reprimand for neglect—some threat of withdrawal of business which his employer had received; but of this he could not be certain; all he knew was, that Mr Wilkins proposed the partnership to him in about as ungracious a way as such an offer could be made; an ungraciousness which, after all, had so little effect on the real matter in hand, that Mr Dunster could pass it over with a private sneer, while taking all possible advantage of the tangible benefit it was now in his power to accept.

Mr Corbet's attachment to Ellinor had been formally disclosed to her just before this time. He had left college, entered at the Middle Temple,* and was fagging away at law, and feeling success in his own power; Ellinor was to 'come out'* at the next Hamley assemblies; and her lover began to be jealous of the possible admirers her striking appearance and piquant conversation might attract, and thought it a good time to make the success of his suit certain by spoken words and promises.

He needed not have alarmed himself even enough to make him take this step, if he had been capable of understanding Ellinor's heart as fully as he did her appearance and conversation. She never missed the absence of formal words and promises. She considered herself as fully engaged to him, as much pledged to marry him and no one else, before he had asked the final question, as afterwards. She was rather surprised at the necessity for those decisive words.

'Ellinor, dearest, will you—can you marry me?' and her reply was—given with a deep blush I must record, and in a soft murmuring tone—

'Yes—oh, yes—I never thought of anything else.'

'Then I may speak to your father, may not I, darling?'

'He knows; I am sure he knows; and he likes you so much. Oh, how happy I am!'

'But still I must speak to him before I go. When can I see him, my Ellinor? I must go back to town at four o'clock.'

'I heard his voice in the stable-yard only just before you came. Let me go and find out if he is gone to the office yet.'

No! to be sure he was not gone. He was quietly smoking a cigar in his study, sitting in an easy-chair near the open window, and leisurely glancing at all the advertisements in *The Times*. He hated going to the office more and more since Dunster had become a partner; that fellow gave himself such airs of investigation and reprehension.

He got up, took the cigar out of his mouth, and placed a chair for Mr Corbet, knowing well why he had thus formally prefaced his entrance into the room with a—

'Can I have a few minutes' conversation with you, Mr Wilkins?'

'Certainly, my dear fellow. Sit down. Will you have a cigar?'

'No! I never smoke.' Mr Corbet despised all these kinds of indulgences, and put a little severity into his refusal, but quite unintentionally; for though he was thankful he was not as other men,* he was not at all the person to trouble himself unnecessarily with their reformation.

'I want to speak to you about Ellinor. She says she thinks you must be aware of our mutual attachment.'

'Well!' said Mr Wilkins. He had resumed his cigar, partly to conceal his agitation at what he knew was coming. 'I believe I have had my suspicions. It is not so very long since I was young myself.' And he sighed over the recollection of Lettice, and his fresh, hopeful youth.

'And I hope, sir, as you have been aware of it, and have never manifested any disapprobation of it, that you will not refuse your consent—a consent I now ask you for—to our marriage.'

Mr Wilkins did not speak for a little while—a touch, a thought, a word more would have brought him to tears; for at the last he found it hard to give the consent which would part him from his only child. Suddenly he got up, and putting his hand into that of the anxious lover (for his silence had rendered Mr Corbet anxious up to a certain point of perplexity—he could not understand the implied he would and he would not*), Mr Wilkins said,

'Yes! God bless you both. I will give her to you, some day—only it must be a long time first. And now go away—go back to her—for I can't stand this much longer.'

Mr Corbet returned to Ellinor. Mr Wilkins sat down and buried his head in his hands, then went to his stable, and had Wildfire saddled for a good gallop over the country. Mr Dunster waited for him in vain at the office, where an obstinate old country gentleman from a distant part of the shire would ignore Dunster's existence as a partner, and pertinaciously demanded to see Mr Wilkins on important business.

CHAPTER V

A FEW days afterwards, Ellinor's father bethought himself that some further communication ought to take place between him and his daughter's lover regarding the approval of the family of the latter to the young man's engagement, and he accordingly wrote a very gentlemanly letter, saying that of course he trusted that Ralph had informed his father of his engagement; that Mr Corbet was well known to Mr Wilkins by reputation, holding the position which he did in Shropshire, but that, as Mr Wilkins did not pretend to be in the same station of life, Mr Corbet might possibly never even have heard of his name, although in his own county it was well known as having been for generations that of the principal conveyancer and land agent of ——shire; that his wife had been a member of the old knightly family of Holsters, and that he himself was descended from a younger branch of the South Wales De Wintons, or Wilkins; that Ellinor, as his only child, would naturally inherit all his property, but that, in the meantime, of course some settlement upon her would be made, the nature of which might be decided nearer the time of the marriage.

It was a very good straightforward letter, and well fitted for the purpose to which Mr Wilkins knew it would be applied—of being forwarded to the young man's father. One would have thought that it was not an engagement so disproportioned in point of station as to cause any great opposition on that score; but unluckily, Captain Corbet, the heir and eldest son, had just formed a similar engagement with Lady Maria Brabant, the daughter of one of the proudest earls in ——shire, who had always resented Mr Wilkins's appearance on the field as an insult to the county, and ignored his presence at every dinner-table where they met. Lady Maria was visiting the Corbets at the very time when Ralph's letter, enclosing Mr Wilkins's, reached the paternal halls, and she merely repeated her father's opinions when Mrs Corbet and her daughters naturally questioned her as to who these Wilkinses were; they remembered the name in Ralph's letters formerly; the father was some friend of Mr Ness's, the clergyman with whom Ralph had read; they believed Ralph used to dine with these Wilkinses, sometimes along with Mr Ness.

Lady Maria was a good-natured girl, and meant no harm in repeating her father's words; touched up, it is true, by some of the dislike she herself felt to the intimate alliance proposed, which would make her sister-in-law to the daughter of an 'upstart attorney,' 'not received in the county,' 'always trying to push his way into the set above him,' 'claiming connection with the De Wintons of —— Castle, who, as she well knew, only laughed when he was spoken of, and said they were more rich in relations than they were aware of'—'not people papa would ever like her to know, whatever might be the family connection.'

These little speeches told in a way which the girl who uttered them did not intend they should. Mrs Corbet and her daughters set themselves violently against this foolish entanglement of Ralph's; they would not call it an engagement. They argued, and they urged, and they pleaded, till the squire, anxious for peace at any price, and always more under the sway of the people who were with him, however unreasonable they might be, than of the absent, even though these had the wisdom of Solomon* or the prudence and sagacity of his son Ralph, wrote an angry letter, saying that, as Ralph was of age, of course he had a right to please himself, therefore all his father could say was, that the engagement was not at all what either he or Ralph's mother had expected or hoped; that it was a degradation to the family just going to ally themselves with a peer of James the First's creation;* that of course Ralph must do what he liked, but that if he married this girl he must never expect to have her received by the Corbets of Corbet Hall as a daughter. The squire was rather satisfied with his production, and took it to show it to his wife; but she did not think it was strong enough, and added a little postscript:—

'DEAR RALPH,—Though, as second son, you are entitled to Bromley at my death, yet I can do much to make the estate worthless. Hitherto, regard for you has prevented my taking steps as to sale of timber, &c., which would materially increase your sisters' portions*; this just measure I shall infallibly take if I find you persevere in keeping to this silly engagement. Your father's disapproval is always a sufficient reason to allege.'

Ralph was annoyed at the receipt of these letters, though he only smiled as he locked them up in his desk.

'Dear old father! how he blusters! As to my mother, she is reasonable when I talk to her. Once give her a definite idea of what Ellinor's fortune will be, and let her, if she chooses, cut down her timber—a threat she has held over me ever since I knew what a rocking-horse was, and which I have known to be illegal these ten years past—and she'll come round. I know better than they do how Reginald has run up post-obits,* and as for that vulgar highborn Lady Maria they are all so full of, why, she is a Flanders mare* to my Ellinor, and has not a silver penny to cross herself with,* besides! I bide my time, you dear good people!'

He did not think it necessary to reply to these letters immediately, nor did he even allude to their contents in his to Ellinor.

Mr Wilkins, who had been very well satisfied with his own letter to the young man, and had thought that it must be equally agreeable to everyone, was not at all suspicious of any disapproval, because the fact of a distinct sanction on the part of Mr Ralph Corbet's friends to his engagement was not communicated to him.

As for Ellinor, she trembled all over with happiness. Such a summer for the blossoming of flowers and ripening of fruit had not been known for years; it seemed to her as if bountiful loving Nature wanted to fill the cup of Ellinor's joy to overflowing, and as if everything, animate and inanimate, sympathised with her happiness. Her father was well, and apparently content. Miss Monro was very kind. Dixon's lameness was quite gone off. Only Mr Dunster came creeping about the house, on pretence of business, seeking out her father, and disturbing all his leisure with his dust-coloured parchment-skinned careworn face, and seeming to disturb the smooth current of her daily life whenever she saw him.

Ellinor made her appearance at the Hamley assemblies, but with less *éclat** than either her father or her lover expected. Her beauty and natural grace were admired by those who could discriminate; but to the greater number there was (what they called) 'a want of style'—want of elegance there certainly was not, for her figure was perfect, and though she moved shyly, she moved well. Perhaps it was not a good place for a correct appreciation of Miss Wilkins; some of the old dowagers thought it a piece of presumption in her to be there at all—but the Lady Holster of the day (who remembered her husband's quarrel with Mr Wilkins, and looked away whenever Ellinor came near) resented this opinion. 'Miss Wilkins is descended from Sir Frank's family, one of the oldest in the county; the objection might have been made years ago to the father, but as he had been received, she did not know why Miss Wilkins was to be alluded to as out of her place.' Ellinor's greatest enjoyment in the evening was to hear her father say, after all was over, and they were driving home,

'Well, I thought my Nelly the prettiest girl there, and I think I know some other people who would have said the same if they could have spoken out.'

'Thank you, papa,' said Ellinor, squeezing his hand, which she held. She thought he alluded to the absent Ralph as the person who would have agreed with him, had he had the opportunity of seeing her; but no, he seldom thought much of the absent; but had been rather flattered by seeing Lord Hildebrand take up his glass for the apparent purpose of watching Ellinor.

'Your pearls, too, were as handsome as any in the room, child—but we must have them re-set; the sprays are old-fashioned now. Let me have them tomorrow to send up to Hancock.'

'Papa, please, I had rather keep them as they are—as mamma wore them.'

He was touched in a minute.

'Very well, darling. God bless you for thinking of it.'

But he ordered her a set of sapphires instead, for the next assembly.

These balls were not such as to intoxicate Ellinor with success, and make her in love with gaiety. Large parties came from the different country-houses in the neighbourhood, and danced with each other. When they had exhausted the resources they brought with them, they had generally a few dances to spare for friends of the same standing with whom they were most intimate. Ellinor came with her father, and joined an old card-playing dowager, by way of a chaperone—the said dowager being under old business obligations to the firm of Wilkins and Son, and apologizing to all her acquaintances for her own weak condescension to Mr Wilkins's foible in wishing to introduce his daughter into society above her natural sphere. It was upon this lady, after she had uttered some such speech as the one I have just mentioned, that Lady Holster had come down with the pedigree of Ellinor's mother. But though the old dowager had drawn back a little discomfited at my lady's reply, she was not more attentive to Ellinor in consequence. She allowed Mr Wilkins to bring in his daughter and place her on the crimson sofa beside her; spoke to her occasionally in the interval that elapsed before the rubbers could be properly arranged in the card-room; invited the girl to accompany her to that sober amusement, and on Ellinor's declining, and preferring to remain with her father, the dowager left her with a sweet smile on her plump countenance, and an approving conscience somewhere within her portly frame, assuring her that she had done all that could possibly have been expected from her towards 'that good Wilkins's daughter.' Ellinor stood by her father, watching the dances, and thankful for the occasional chance of a dance. While she had been sitting by her chaperone, Mr Wilkins had made the tour of the room, dropping out the little fact of his daughter's being present wherever he thought the seed likely to bring forth the fruit of partners. And some came because they liked Mr Wilkins, and some asked Ellinor because they had done their duty dances to their own party, and might please themselves. So that she usually had an average of one invitation to every three dances; and this principally towards the end of the evening.

But considering her real beauty, and the care which her father always took about her appearance, she met with far less than her due of admiration. Admiration she did not care for; partners she did; and sometimes felt mortified when she had to sit or stand quiet during all the first part of the evening. If it had not been for her father's wishes she would much rather have stayed at home; but, nevertheless, she talked even to the irresponsive old dowager, and fairly chattered to her father when she got beside him, because she did not like him to fancy that she was not enjoying herself.

And, indeed, she had so much happiness in the daily course of this part of her life, that, on looking back upon it afterwards, she could not imagine anything brighter than it had been. The delight of receiving her lover's letters—the anxious happiness of replying to them (always a little bit fearful lest she should not express herself and her love in the precisely happy medium becoming a maiden)—the father's love and satisfaction in her—the calm prosperity of the whole household—was delightful at the time, and, looking back upon it, it was dreamlike.

Occasionally Mr Corbet came down to see her. He always slept on these occasions at Mr Ness's; but he was at Ford Bank the greater part of the one day between two nights that he allowed himself for the length of his visits. And even these short peeps were not frequently taken. He was working hard at law: fagging at it tooth and nail; arranging his whole life so as best to promote the ends of his ambition; feeling a delight in surpassing and mastering his fellows—those who started in the race at the same time. He read Ellinor's letters over and over again; nothing else beside law-books. He perceived the repressed love hidden away in subdued expressions in her communications, with an amused pleasure at the attempt at concealment. He was glad that her gaieties were not more gay: he was glad that she was not too much admired, although a little indignant at the want of taste on the part of the ——shire gentlemen. But if other admirers had come prominently forward, he would have had to take some more decided steps to assert his rights than he had hitherto done; for he had caused Ellinor to express a wish to her father that her engagement should not be too much talked about until nearer the time when it would be prudent for him to marry her. He thought that the knowledge of this, the only imprudently hasty step he ever meant to take in his life, might go against his character for wisdom, if the fact became known while he was as yet only a student. Mr Wilkins wondered a little; but acceded, as he always did, to any of Ellinor's requests. Mr Ness was a confidant, of course, and some of Lady Maria's connections heard of it, and forgot it again very soon; and, as it happened, no one else was sufficiently interested in Ellinor to care to ascertain the fact.

All this time, Mr Ralph Corbet maintained a very quietly decided attitude towards his own family. He was engaged to Miss Wilkins; and all he could say was he felt sorry that they disapproved of it. He was not able to marry just at present, and before the time for his marriage arrived, he trusted that his family would take a more reasonable view of things, and be willing to receive her as his wife with all becoming respect or affection. This was the substance of what he repeated in different forms in reply to his father's angry letters. At length, his invariable determination made way with his father; the paternal thunderings were subdued to a distant rumbling in the sky; and presently the inquiry was broached as to how much fortune Miss Wilkins would have; how much down on her marriage; what were the eventual probabilities. Now this was a point which Mr Ralph Corbet himself wished to be informed upon. He had not thought much about it in making the engagement; he had been too young, or too much in love. But an only child of a wealthy attorney ought to have something considerable; and an allowance so as to enable the young couple to start housekeeping in a moderately good part of town, would be an advantage to him in his profession. So he replied to his father, adroitly suggesting that a letter containing certain modifications of the inquiry which had been rather roughly put in Mr Corbet's last, should be sent to him, in order that he might himself ascertain from Mr Wilkins what were Ellinor's prospects as regarded fortune.

The desired letter came; but not in such a form that he could pass it on to Mr Wilkins; he preferred to make quotations, and even these quotations were a little altered and dressed before he sent them on. The gist of his letter to Mr Wilkins was this. He stated that he hoped soon to be in a position to offer Ellinor a home; that he anticipated a steady progress in his profession, and consequently in his income; but that contingencies might arise, as his father suggested, which would deprive him of the power of earning a livelihood, perhaps when it might be more required than it would be at first; that it was true that, after his mother's death, a small estate in Shropshire would come to him as second son, and of course Ellinor would receive the benefit of this property, secured to her legally as Mr Wilkins thought best—that being a matter for after discussion—but that at present his father was anxious, as might be seen from the extract, to ascertain whether Mr Wilkins could secure him from the contingency of having his son's widow and possible children thrown upon his hands, by giving Ellinor a dowry; and if so, it was gently insinuated, what would be the amount of the same.

When Mr Wilkins received this letter it startled him out of a happy day-dream. He liked Ralph Corbet and the whole connection quite well enough to give his consent to an engagement; and sometimes even he was glad to think that Ellinor's future was assured, and that she would have a protector and friends after he was dead and gone. But he did not want them to assume their responsibilities so soon. He had not distinctly contemplated her marriage as an event likely to happen before his death. He could not understand how his own life would go on without her: or indeed, why she and Ralph Corbet could not continue just as they were at present. He came down to breakfast with the letter in his hand. By Ellinor's blushes, as she glanced at the handwriting, he knew that she had heard from her lover by the same post; by her tender caresses—caresses given as if to make up for the pain which the prospect of her leaving him was sure to cause him—he was certain that she was aware of the contents of the letter. Yet he put it in his pocket, and tried to forget it.

He did this not merely from his reluctance to complete any arrangements which might facilitate Ellinor's marriage. There was a further annoyance connected with the affair. His money matters had been for some time in an involved state; he had been living beyond his income, even reckoning that, as he always did, at the highest point which it ever touched. He kept no regular accounts, reasoning with himself—or, perhaps, I should rather say persuading himself—that there was no great occasion for regular accounts, when he had a steady income arising from his profession, as well as the interest of a good sum of money left him by his father; and when, living in his own house near a country town where provisions were cheap, his expenditure for his small family—only one child—could never amount to anything like his incomings from the above-mentioned sources. But servants and horses, and choice wines and rare fruit-trees, and a habit of purchasing any book or engraving that may take the fancy, irrespective of the price, run away with money, even though there be but one child. A year or two ago, Mr Wilkins had been startled into a system of exaggerated retrenchment—retrenchment which only lasted about six weeks—by the sudden bursting of a bubble speculation, in which he had invested a part of his father's savings. But as soon as the change in his habits, necessitated by his new economies, became irksome, he had comforted himself for his relapse into his former easy extravagance of living, by remembering the fact that Ellinor was engaged to the son of a man of large property; and that though Ralph was only the second son, yet his mother's estate must come to him, as Mr Ness had already mentioned, on first hearing of her engagement.

Mr Wilkins did not doubt that he could easily make Ellinor

a fitting allowance, or even pay down a requisite dowry; but the doing so would involve an examination into the real state of his affairs, and this involved distasteful trouble. He had no idea how much more than mere temporary annoyance would arise out of the investigation. Until it was made, he decided in his own mind that he would not speak to Ellinor on the subject of her lover's letter. So, for the next few days, she was kept in suspense, seeing little of her father; and during the short times she was with him, she was made aware that he was nervously anxious to keep the conversation engaged on general topics rather than on the one which she had at heart. As I have already said, Mr Corbet had written to her by the same post as that on which he sent the letter to her father, telling her of its contents, and begging her (in all those sweet words which lovers know how to use) to urge her father to compliance for his sake—his, her lover's—who was pining and lonely in all the crowds of London, since her loved presence was not there. He did not care for money, save as a means of hastening their marriage; indeed, if there were only some income fixed, however small; some time for their marriage fixed, however distant, he could be patient. He did not want superfluity of wealth; his habits were simple, as she well knew; and money enough would be theirs in time, both from her share of contingencies, and the certainty of his finally possessing Bromley.

Ellinor delayed replying to this letter until her father should have spoken to her on the subject. But as she perceived that he avoided all such conversation, the young girl's heart failed her. She began to blame herself for wishing to leave him, to reproach herself for being accessory to any step which made him shun being alone with her, and look distressed and full of care as he did now. It was the usual struggle between father and lover for the possession of love, instead of the natural and graceful resignation of the parent to the prescribed course of things; and, as usual, it was the poor girl who bore the suffering for no fault of her own: although she blamed herself for being the cause of the disturbance in the previous order of affairs. Ellinor had no one to speak to confidentially but her father and her lover, and when they were at issue she could talk openly to neither, so she brooded over Mr Corbet's unanswered letter, and her father's silence, and became pale and dispirited. Once or twice she looked up suddenly, and caught her father's eye gazing upon her with a certain wistful anxiety; but the instant she saw this he pulled himself up, as it were, and would begin talking gaily about the small topics of the day.

At length Mr Corbet grew impatient at not hearing either from Mr Wilkins or Ellinor, and wrote urgently to the former, making known to him a new proposal suggested to him by his father, which was, that a certain sum should be paid down by Mr Wilkins, to be applied, under the management of trustees, to the improvement of the Bromley estate, out of the profits of which, or other sources in the elder Mr Corbet's hands, a heavy rate of interest should be paid on this advance, which would secure an income to the young couple immediately, and considerably increase the value of the estate upon which Ellinor's settlement was to be made. The terms offered for this laying down of ready money were so advantageous that Mr Wilkins was strongly tempted to accede to them at once; as Ellinor's pale cheek and want of appetite had only that very morning smote upon his conscience, and this immediate transfer of ready money was as a sacrifice, a soothing balm to his self-reproach, and laziness and dislike to immediate unpleasantness of action had its counterbalancing weakness in imprudence. Mr Wilkins made some rough calculations on a piece of paper—deeds, and all such tests of accuracy being down at the office; discovered that he could pay down the sum required; wrote a letter agreeing to the proposal, and before he sealed it called Ellinor into his study, and bade her read what he had been writing, and tell him what she thought of it. He watched the colour come rushing into her white face, her lips quiver and tremble, and even before the letter was ended she was in his arms, kissing him, and thanking him with blushing caresses rather than words.

'There, there!' said he, smiling and sighing; 'that will do. Why, I do believe you took me for a hard-hearted father, just like a heroine's father in a book. You've looked as woe-begone this week past as Ophelia.* One can't make up one's mind in a day about such sums of money as this, little woman; and you should have let your old father have time to consider.'

'Oh, papa! I was only afraid you were angry.'

'Well, if I was a bit perplexed, seeing you look so ill and pining was not the way to bring me round. Old Corbet, I must say, is trying to make a good bargain for his son. It is well for me that I have never been an extravagant man.'

'But, papa, we don't want all this much.'

'Yes, yes! it is all right. You shall go into their family as a well-portioned girl, if you can't go as a Lady Maria. Come, don't trouble your little head any more about it. Give me one more kiss, and then we'll go and order the horses, and have a ride together, by way of keeping holiday. I deserve a holiday, don't I, Nelly?'

Some country people at work at the roadside, as the father and daughter passed along, stopped to admire their bright happy looks, and one spoke of the hereditary handsomeness of the Wilkins family (for the old man, the present Mr Wilkins's father, had been fine-looking in his drab breeches and gaiters,* and usual assumption of a yeoman's dress). Another said it was easy for the rich to be handsome; they had always plenty to eat, and could ride when they were tired of walking, and had no care for the morrow to keep them from sleeping at nights. And in sad acquiescence with their contrasted lot, the men went on with their hedging and ditching in silence.

And yet, if they had known—if the poor did know—the troubles and temptations of the rich; if those men had foreseen the lot darkening over the father, and including the daughter in its cloud; if Mr Wilkins himself had even imagined such a future possible . . . . Well, there was truth in the old heathen saying, 'Let no man be envied till his death.'*

Ellinor had no more rides with her father; no, not ever again; though they had stopped that afternoon at the summit of a breezy common, and looked at a ruined hall, not so very far off, and discussed whether they could reach it that day, and decided that it was too far away for anything but a hurried inspection, and that some day soon they would make the old place into the principal object of an excursion. But a rainy time came on, when no rides were possible; and whether it was the influence of the weather, or some other care or trouble that oppressed him, Mr Wilkins seemed to lose all wish for much active exercise, and rather sought a stimulus to his spirits and circulation in wine. But of this Ellinor was innocently unaware. He seemed dull and weary, and sat long, drowsing and drinking after dinner. If the servants had not been so fond of him for much previous generosity and kindness, they would have complained now, and with reason, of his irritability, for all sorts of things seemed to annoy him.

'You should get the master to take a ride with you, miss,' said Dixon, one day, as he was putting Ellinor on her horse. 'He's not looking well. He's studying too much at the office.'

But when Ellinor named it to her father, he rather hastily replied that it was all very well for women to ride out whenever they liked—men had something else to do; and then, as he saw her look grave and puzzled, he softened down his abrupt saying by adding that Dunster had been making a fuss about his partner's non-attendance, and altogether taking a good deal upon himself in a very offensive way, so that he thought it better to go pretty regularly to the office, in order to show him who was master—senior partner, and head of the business, at any rate.

Ellinor sighed a little over her disappointment at her father's preoccupation, and then forgot her own little regret in anger at Mr Dunster, who had seemed all along to be a thorn in her father's side,* and had latterly gained some power and authority over him, the exercise of which, Ellinor could not help thinking, was a very impertinent line of conduct from a junior partner, so lately only a paid clerk, to his superior. There was a sense of something wrong in the Ford Bank household for many weeks about this time. Mr Wilkins was not like himself, and his cheerful ways and careless genial speeches were missed, even on the days when he was not irritable, and evidently uneasy with himself and all about him. The spring was late in coming, and cold rain and sleet made any kind of outdoor exercise a trouble and discomfort rather than a bright natural event in the course of the day. All sound of winter gaieties, of assemblies and meets, and jovial dinners, had died away, and the summer pleasures were as yet unthought of. Still Ellinor had a secret perennial source of sunshine in her heart; whenever she thought of Ralph she could not feel much oppression from the present unspoken and indistinct gloom. He loved her; and oh, how she loved him! and perhaps this very next autumn—but that depended on his own success in his profession. After all, if it was not this autumn it would be the next; and with the letters that she received weekly, and the occasional visits that her lover ran down to Hamley to pay Mr Ness, Ellinor felt as if she would almost prefer the delay of the time when she must leave her father's for a husband's roof.

CHAPTER VI

AT Easter—just when the heavens and earth were looking their dreariest, for Easter fell very early this year—Mr Corbet came down. Mr Wilkins was too busy to see much of him; they were together even less than usual, although not less friendly when they did meet. But to Ellinor the visit was one of unmixed happiness. Hitherto she had always had a little fear mingled up with her love of Mr Corbet; but his manners were softened, his opinions less decided and abrupt, and his whole treatment of her showed such tenderness that the young girl basked and revelled in it. One or two of their conversations had reference to their future married life in London; and she then perceived, although it did not jar against her, that her lover had not forgotten his ambition in his love. He tried to inoculate her with something of his own craving for success in life; but it was all in vain: she nestled to him and told him she did not care to be the Lord Chancellor's wife—wigs and woolsacks* were not in her line; only if he wished it, she would wish it.

The last two days of his stay the weather changed. Sudden heat burst forth, as it does occasionally for a few hours even in our chilly English spring. The grey-brown bushes and trees started almost with visible progress into the tender green shade which is the forerunner of the bursting leaves. The sky was of full cloudless blue. Mr Wilkins was to come home pretty early from the office to ride out with his daughter and her lover; but, after waiting some time for him, it grew too late, and they were obliged to give up the project. Nothing would serve Ellinor, then, but that she must carry out a table and have tea in the garden, on the sunny side of the tree, among the roots of which she used to play when a child. Miss Monro objected a little to this caprice of Ellinor's, saying that it was too early for out-of-door meals; but Mr Corbet overruled all objections, and helped her in her gay preparations. She always kept to the early hours of her childhood, although she, as then, regularly sat with her father at his late dinner; and this meal, *al fresco*, was to be a reality to her and Miss Monro. There was a place arranged for her father, and she seized upon him as he was coming from the stable-yard, by the shrubbery-path, to his study, and with merry playfulness made him a prisoner, accusing him of disappointing them of their ride, and drawing him, more than half unwilling, to his chair by the table. But he was silent, and almost sad: his presence damped them all; they could hardly tell why, for he did not object to anything, though he seemed to enjoy nothing, and only to force a smile at Ellinor's occasional sallies. These became more and more rare as she perceived her father's depression. She watched him anxiously. He perceived it, and said—shivering in that strange, unaccountable manner which is popularly explained by the expression that someone is passing over the earth that will one day form your grave—

'Ellinor! this is not a day for out-of-door tea. I never felt so chilly a spot in my life. I cannot keep from shaking where I sit. I must leave this place, my dear, in spite of all your good tea.'

'Oh, papa! I am so sorry. But look how full that hot sun's rays come on this turf. I thought I had chosen such a capital spot!'

But he got up and persisted in leaving the table, although he was evidently sorry to spoil the little party. He walked up and down the gravel walk, close by them, talking to them as he kept passing by, and trying to cheer them up.

'Are you warmer now, papa?' asked Ellinor.

'Oh yes! All right. It's only that place that seems so chilly and damp. I'm as warm as a toast now.'

The next morning Mr Corbet left them. The unseasonably fine weather passed away too, and all things went back to their rather grey and dreary aspect; but Ellinor was too happy to feel this much, knowing what absent love existed for her alone, and from this knowledge unconsciously trusting in the sun behind the clouds.

I have said that few or none in the immediate neighbourhood of Hamley, beside their own household and Mr Ness, knew of Ellinor's engagement. At one of the rare dinner-parties to which she accompanied her father—it was at the old lady's house who chaperoned her to the assemblies—she was taken into dinner by a young clergyman staying in the neighbourhood. He had just had a small living* given to him in his own county, and he felt as if this was a great step in his life. He was good, innocent, and rather boyish in appearance. Ellinor was happy and at her ease, and chatted away to this Mr Livingstone on many little points of interest which they found they had in common: church music, and the difficulty they had in getting people to sing in parts; Salisbury Cathedral, which they had both seen; styles of church architecture, Ruskin's works,* and parish schools, in which Mr Livingstone was somewhat shocked to find that Ellinor took no great interest. When the gentlemen came in from the dining-room, it struck Ellinor, for the first time in her life, that her father had taken more wine than was good for him. Indeed, this had rather become a habit with him of late; but as he always tried to go quietly off to his own room when such had been the case, his daughter had never been aware of it before, and the perception of it now made her cheeks hot with shame. She thought that everyone must be as conscious of his altered manner and way of speaking as she was, and after a pause of sick silence, during which she could not say a word, she set to and talked to Mr Livingstone about parish schools, anything, with redoubled vigour and apparent interest, in order to keep one or two of the company, at least, from noticing what was to her so painfully obvious.

The effect of her behaviour was far more than she had intended. She kept Mr Livingstone, it is true, from observing her father; but she also riveted his attention on herself. He had thought her very pretty and agreeable during dinner; but after dinner he considered her bewitching, irresistible. He dreamed of her all night, and wakened up the next morning to a calculation of how far his income would allow him to furnish his pretty new parsonage with that crowning blessing, a wife. For a day or two he did up little sums, and sighed, and thought of Ellinor, her face listening with admiring interest to his sermons, her arm passed into his as they went together round the parish; her sweet voice instructing classes in his schools—turn where he would, in his imagination Ellinor's presence rose up before him.

The consequence was that he wrote an offer, which he found a far more perplexing piece of composition than a sermon; a real hearty expression of love, going on, over all obstacles, to a straightforward explanation of his present prospects and future hopes, and winding up with the information that on the succeeding morning he would call to know whether he might speak to Mr Wilkins on the subject of this letter. It was given to Ellinor in the evening, as she was sitting with Miss Monro in the library. Mr Wilkins was dining out, she hardly knew where, as it was a sudden engagement, of which he had sent word from the office—a gentleman's dinner-party, she supposed, as he had dressed in Hamley without coming home. Ellinor turned over the letter when it was brought to her, as some people do when they cannot recognize the handwriting, as if to discover from paper or seal what two moments would assure them of, if they opened the letter and looked at the signature. Ellinor could not guess who had written it by any outward sign; but the moment she saw the name 'Herbert Livingstone,' the meaning of the letter flashed upon her, and she coloured all over. She put the letter away, unread, for a few minutes, and then made some excuse for leaving the room and going upstairs. When safe in her bedchamber, she read the young man's eager words with a sense of self-reproach. How must she, engaged to one man, have been behaving to another, if this was the result of a single evening's interview? The self-reproach was unjustly bestowed; but with that we have nothing to do. She made herself very miserable; and at last went down with a heavy heart to go on with Dante,* and rummage up words in the dictionary. All the time she seemed to Miss Monro to be plodding on with her Italian more diligently and sedately than usual, she was planning in her own mind to speak to her father as soon as he returned (and he had said that he should not be late), and beg him to undo the mischief she had done by seeing Mr Livingstone the next morning, and frankly explaining the real state of affairs to him. But she wanted to read her letter again, and think it all over in peace; and so, at an early hour, she wished Miss Monro good-night, and went up into her own room above the drawing-room, and overlooking the flower-garden and shrubbery-path to the stable-yard, by which her father was sure to return. She went upstairs and studied her letter well, and tried to recall all her speeches and conduct on that miserable evening—as she thought it then—not knowing what true misery was. Her head ached, and she put out the candle, and went and sat on the window-seat, looking out into the moonlit garden, watching for her father. She opened the window; partly to cool her forehead, partly to enable her to call down softly when she should see him coming along. By-and-by the door from the stable-yard into the shrubbery clicked and opened, and in a moment she saw Mr Wilkins moving through the bushes; but not alone, Mr Dunster was with him, and the two were talking together in rather excited tones, immediately lost to hearing, however, as they entered Mr Wilkins's study by the outer door.

'They have been dining together somewhere. Probably at Mr Hanbury's' (the Hamley brewer), thought Ellinor. 'But how provoking that he should have come home with papa this night of all nights!'

Two or three times before Mr Dunster had called on Mr Wilkins in the evening, as Ellinor knew; but she was not quite aware of the reason for such late visits, and had never put together the two facts—(as cause and consequence)—that on such occasions her father had been absent from the office all day, and that there might be necessary business for him to transact, the urgency of which was the motive for Mr Dunster's visits. Mr Wilkins always seemed to be annoyed by his coming at so late an hour, and spoke of it, resenting the intrusion upon his leisure; and Ellinor, without consideration, adopted her father's mode of speaking and thinking on the subject, and was rather more angry than he was whenever the obnoxious partner came on business in the evening. This night was, of all nights, the most ill-purposed time (so Ellinor thought) for a *tête-à-tête* with her father! However, there was no doubt in her mind as to what she had to do. So late as it was, the unwelcome visitor could not stop long; and then she would go down and have her little confidence with her father, and beg him to see Mr Livingstone when he came the next morning, and dismiss him as gently as might be.

She sat on in the window-seat; dreaming waking dreams of future happiness. She kept losing herself in such thoughts, and became almost afraid of forgetting why she sat there. Presently she felt cold, and got up to fetch a shawl, in which she muffled herself and resumed her place. It seemed to her growing very late; the moonlight was coming fuller and fuller into the garden, and the blackness of the shadow was more concentrated and stronger. Surely Mr Dunster could not have gone away along the dark shrubbery-path so noiselessly but what she must have heard him? No! there was the swell of voices coming up through the window from her father's study: angry voices they were; and her anger rose sympathetically, as she knew that her father was being irritated. There was a sudden movement, as of chairs pushed hastily aside, and then a mysterious unaccountable noise—heavy, sudden; and then a slight movement as of chairs again; and then a profound stillness. Ellinor leaned her head against the side of the window to listen more intently, for some mysterious instinct made her sick and faint. No sound—no noise. Only by-and-by she heard, what we have all heard at such times of intent listening, the beating of the pulses of her heart, and then the whirling rush of blood through her head. How long did this last? She never knew. By-and-by she heard her father's hurried footstep in his bedroom, next to hers; but when she ran thither to speak to him, and ask him what was amiss—if anything had been—if she might come to him now about Mr Livingstone's letter, she found that he had gone down again to his study, and almost at the same moment she heard the little private outer door of that room open; someone went out, and then there were hurried footsteps along the shrubbery-path. She thought, of course, that it was Mr Dunster leaving the house; and went back for Mr Livingstone's letter. Having found it, she passed through her father's room to the private staircase, thinking that if she went by the more regular way, she would have run the risk of disturbing Miss Monro, and perhaps of being questioned in the morning. Even in passing down this remote staircase, she trod softly for fear of being overheard.

When she entered the room, the full light of the candles dazzled her for an instant, coming out of the darkness. They were flaring wildly in the draught that came in through the open door, by which the outer air was admitted; for a moment there seemed to be no one in the room; and then she saw, with strange sick horror, the legs of someone lying on the carpet behind the table. As if compelled, even while she shrank from doing it, she went round to see who it was that lay there, so still and motionless as never to stir at her sudden coming. It was Mr Dunster; his head propped on chair-cushions, his eyes open, staring, distended. There was a strong smell of brandy and hartshorn* in the room; a smell so powerful as not to be neutralized by the free current of night air that blew through the two open doors. Ellinor could not have told whether it was reason or instinct that made her act as she did during this awful night. In thinking of it afterwards, with shuddering avoidance of the haunting memory that would come and overshadow her during many, many years of her life, she grew to believe that the powerful smell of the spilt brandy absolutely intoxicated her—an unconscious Rechabite* in practice. But something gave her a presence of mind and a courage not her own. And though she learnt to think afterwards that she had acted unwisely, if not wrongly and wickedly, yet she marvelled, in recalling that time, how she could have then behaved as she did. First of all she lifted herself up from her fascinated gaze at the dead man, and went to the staircase door, by which she had entered the study, and shut it softly. Then she went back—looked again; took the brandy-bottle and knelt down, and tried to pour some into the mouth; but this she found she could not do. Then she wetted her handkerchief with the spirit, and moistened the lips; all to no purpose; for, as I have said before, the man was dead—killed by a rupture of a vessel of the brain; how occasioned I must tell by-and-by. Of course, all Ellinor's little cares and efforts produced no effect; her father had tried them before—vain endeavours all, to bring back the precious breath of life! The poor girl could not bear the look of those open eyes, and softly, tenderly, tried to close them, although unconscious that in so doing she was rendering the pious offices of some beloved hand to a dead man. She was sitting by the body on the floor when she heard steps coming with rushing and yet cautious tread, through the shrubbery; she had no fear, although it might be the tread of robbers and murderers. The awfulness of the hour raised her above common fears; though she did not go through the usual process of reasoning, and by it feel assured that the feet which were coming so softly and swiftly along were the same which she had heard leaving the room in like manner only a quarter of an hour before.

Her father entered, and started back, almost upsetting some one behind him by his recoil, on seeing his daughter in her motionless attitude by the dead man.

'My God, Ellinor! what has brought you here?' he said, almost fiercely.

But she answered as one stupefied,

'I don't know. Is he dead?'

'Hush, hush, child; it cannot be helped.'

She raised her eyes to the solemn, pitying, awestricken face behind her father's—the countenance of Dixon.

'Is he dead?' she asked of him.

The man stepped forwards, respectfully pushing his master on one side as he did so. He bent down over the corpse, and looked, and listened, and then, reaching a candle off the table, he signed Mr Wilkins to close the door. And Mr Wilkins obeyed, and looked with an intensity of eagerness almost amounting to faintness on the experiment, and yet he could not hope. The flame was steady—steady and pitilessly unstirred, even when it was adjusted close to mouth and nostril; the head was raised up by one of Dixon's stalwart arms, while he held the candle in the other hand. Ellinor fancied that there was some trembling on Dixon's part, and grasped his wrist tightly in order to give it the requisite motionless firmness.

All in vain. The head was placed again on the cushions, the servant rose and stood by his master, looking sadly on the dead man, whom, living, none of them had liked or cared for, and Ellinor sat on, quiet and tearless, as one in a trance.

'How was it, father?' at length she asked.

He would fain have had her ignorant of all, but so questioned by her lips, so adjured by her eyes, in the very presence of death, he could not choose but speak the truth; he spoke it in convulsive gasps, each sentence an effort:

'He taunted me—he was insolent, beyond my patience—I could not bear it. I struck him—I can't tell how it was. He must have hit his head in falling. Oh, my God! one little hour ago I was innocent of this man's blood!' He covered his face with his hands.

Ellinor took the candle again; kneeling behind Mr Dunster's head, she tried the futile experiment once more.

'Could not a doctor do some good?' she asked of Dixon, in a low hopeless voice.

'No!' said he, shaking his head, and looking with a sidelong glance at his master, who seemed to shrivel up and to shrink away at the bare suggestion. 'Doctors can do nought, I'm afeard. All that a doctor could do, I take it, would be to open a vein, and that I could do along with the best of them, if I had but my fleam here.' He fumbled in his pockets as he spoke, and, as chance would have it, the 'fleam' (or cattle-lancet) was somewhere about his dress. He drew it out, smoothed and tried it on his finger. Ellinor tried to bare the arm, but turned sick as she did so. Her father started eagerly forwards, and did what was necessary with hurried, trembling hands. If they had cared less about the result, they might have been more afraid of the consequences of the operation in the hands of one so ignorant as Dixon. But, vein or artery, it signified little; no living blood gushed out; only a little watery moisture followed the cut of the fleam. They laid him back on his strange sad death-couch. Dixon spoke next.

'Master Ned!' said he—for he had known Mr Wilkins in his days of bright careless boyhood, and almost was carried back to them by the sense of charge and protection which the servant's presence of mind and sharpened senses gave him over his master on this dreary night—'Master Ned! we must do summut.'

No one spoke. What was to be done?

'Did any folk see him come here?' Dixon asked, after a time. Ellinor looked up to hear her father's answer, a wild hope coming into her mind that all might be concealed, somehow; she did not know how, nor did she think of any consequences except saving her father from the vague dread, trouble and punishment that she was aware would await him if all were known.

Mr Wilkins did not seem to hear; in fact, he did not hear anything but the unspoken echo of his own last words, that went booming through his heart:

'An hour ago I was innocent of this man's blood! Only an hour ago!'

Dixon got up and poured out half a tumblerful of raw spirit from the brandy-bottle that stood on the table.

'Drink this, Master Ned!' putting it to his master's lips. 'Nay'—to Ellinor—'it will do him no harm; only bring back his senses, which, poor gentleman, are scared away. We shall need all our wits. Now, sir, please, answer my question. Did anyone see Measter Dunster come here?'

'I don't know,' said Mr Wilkins, recovering his speech. 'It all seems in a mist. He offered to walk home with me; I did not want him. I was almost rude to him to keep him off. I did not want to talk of business; I had taken too much wine to be very clear, and some things at the office were not quite in order, and he had found it out. If anyone heard our conversation, they must know I did not want him to come with me. Oh! why would he come? He was as obstinate—he would come—and here it has been his death!'

'Well, sir, what's done can't be undone, and I'm sure we'd any of us bring him back to life if we could, even by cutting off our hands, though he was a mighty plaguy chap while he'd breath in him. But what I'm thinking is this: it'll maybe go awkward with you, sir, if he's found here. One can't say. But don't you think, miss, as he's neither kith nor kin to miss him, we might just bury him away before morning, somewhere? There's better nor four hours of dark. I wish we could put him i' the churchyard, but that can't be; but to my mind, the sooner we set about digging a place for him to lie in, poor fellow, and the better it'll be for us all in the end. I can pare a piece of turf up where it'll never be missed, and if master'll take one spade, and I another, why, we'll lay him softly down, and cover him up, and no one'll be the wiser.'

There was no reply from either for a minute or so. Then Mr. Wilkins said:

'If my father could have known of my living to this! Why, they will try me as a criminal; and you, Ellinor! Dixon, you are right. We must conceal it, or I must cut my throat, for I never could live through it. One minute of passion, and my life blasted!'

'Come along, sir,' said Dixon; 'there's no time to lose.' And they went out in search of tools; Ellinor following them, shivering all over, but begging that she might be with them, and not have to remain in the study with ——

She would not be bidden into her own room; she dreaded inaction and solitude. She made herself busy with carrying heavy baskets of turf, and straining her strength to the utmost; fetching all that was wanted, with soft swift steps.

Once, as she passed near the open study door, she thought that she heard a rustling, and a flash of hope came across her. Could he be reviving? She entered, but a moment was enough to undeceive her; it had only been a night rustle among the trees. Of hope, life, there was none.

They dug the hole deep and well; working with fierce energy to quench thought and remorse. Once or twice her father asked for brandy, which Ellinor, reassured by the apparently good effect of the first dose, brought to him without a word; and once at her father's suggestion she brought food, such as she could find in the dining-room without disturbing the household, for Dixon.

When all was ready for the reception of the body in its unblessed grave, Mr Wilkins bade Ellinor go up to her own room—she had done all she could to help them; the rest must be done by them alone. She felt that it must; and indeed both her nerves and her bodily strength were giving way. She would have kissed her father, as he sat wearily at the head of the grave—Dixon had gone in to make some arrangement for carrying the corpse—but he pushed her away quietly, but resolutely—

'No, Nelly, you must never kiss me again; I am a murderer.'

'But I will, my own darling papa,' said she, throwing her arms passionately round his neck, and covering his face with kisses. 'I love you, and I don't care what you are, if you were twenty times a murderer, which you are not; I am sure it was only an accident.'

'Go in my child, go in, and try to get some rest. But go in, for we must finish as fast as we can. The moon is down; it will soon be daylight. What a blessing there are no rooms on one side of the house. Go, Nelly.' And she went; straining herself up to move noiselessly, with eyes averted, through the room which she shuddered at as the place of hasty and unhallowed death.

Once in her own room she bolted the door on the inside, and then stole to the window, as if some fascination impelled her to watch all the proceedings to the end. But her aching eyes could hardly penetrate through the thick darkness, which, at the time of the year of which I am speaking, so closely precedes the dawn. She could discern the tops of the trees against the sky, and could single out the well-known one, at a little distance from the stem of which the grave was made, in the very piece of turf over which so lately she and Ralph had had their merry little tea-making; and where her father, as she now remembered, had shuddered and shivered, as if the ground on which his seat had then been placed, was fateful and ominous to him.

Those below moved softly and quietly in all they did; but every sound had a significant and terrible interpretation to Ellinor's ears. Before they had ended, the little birds had begun to pipe out their gay *reveillée* to the dawn. Then doors closed, and all was profoundly still.

Ellinor threw herself, in her clothes, on the bed; and was thankful for the intense weary physical pain which took off something of the anguish of thought—anguish that she fancied from time to time was leading to insanity.

By-and-by the morning cold made her instinctively creep between the blankets; and, once there, she fell into a dead heavy sleep.

CHAPTER VII

ELLINOR was awakened by a rapping at her door: it was her maid.

She was fully aroused in a moment, for she had fallen asleep with one clearly defined plan in her mind, only one, for all thoughts and cares having no relation to the terrible event were as though they had never been. All her purpose was to shield her father from suspicion. And to do this she must control herself—heart, mind, and body must be ruled to this one end.

So she said to Mason:

'Let me lie half an hour longer; and beg Miss Monro not to wait breakfast for me; but in half an hour bring me up a cup of strong tea, for I have a bad headache.'

Mason went away. Ellinor sprang up; rapidly undressed herself, and got into bed again, so that when her maid returned with her breakfast, there was no appearance of the night having been passed in any unusual manner.

'How ill you do look, miss!' said Mason. 'I am sure you had better not get up yet.'

Ellinor longed to ask if her father had yet shown himself; but this question—so natural at any other time—seemed to her so suspicious under the circumstances, that she could not bring her lips to frame it. At any rate, she must get up and struggle to make the day like all other days. So she rose, confessing that she did not feel very well, but trying to make light of it, and when she could think of anything but the one awe, to say a trivial sentence or two. But she could not recollect how she behaved in general, for her life hitherto had been simple, and led without any consciousness of effect.

Before she was dressed, a message came up to say that Mr Livingstone was in the drawing-room.

Mr Livingstone! He belonged to the old life of yesterday! The billows of the night had swept over his mark on the sands of her memory; and it was only by a strong effort that she could remember who he was—what he wanted. She sent Mason down to inquire from the servant who admitted him whom it was that he had asked for.

'He asked for master first. But master has not rung for his water yet, so James told him he was not up. Then he took thought for a while, and asked could he speak to you, he would wait if you were not at liberty; but that he wished particular to see either master, or you. So James asked him to sit down in the drawing-room, and he would let you know.'

'I must go,' thought Ellinor. 'I will send him away directly; to come, thinking of marriage to a house like this—today, too!'

And she went down hastily, and in a hard unsparing mood towards a man, whose affection for her she thought was like a gourd, grown up in a night, and of no account, but as a piece of foolish, boyish excitement.

She never thought of her own appearance—she had dressed without looking in the glass. Her only object was to dismiss her would-be suitor as speedily as possible. All feelings of shyness, awkwardness, or maiden modesty, were quenched and overcome. In she went.

He was standing by the mantelpiece as she entered. He made a step or two forward to meet her; and then stopped, petrified, as it were, at the sight of her hard white face.

'Miss Wilkins, I am afraid you are ill! I have come too early. But I have to leave Hamley in half an hour, and I thought—Oh, Miss Wilkins! what have I done?'

For she sank into the chair nearest to her, as if overcome by his words; but, indeed, it was by the oppression of her own thoughts: she was hardly conscious of his presence.

He came a step or two nearer, as if he longed to take her in his arms and comfort and shelter her; but she stiffened herself and arose, and by an effort walked towards the fireplace, and there stood, as if awaiting what he would say next. But he was overwhelmed by her aspect of illness. He almost forgot his own wishes, his own suit, in his desire to relieve her from the pain, physical as he believed it, under which she was suffering. It was she who had to begin the subject.

'I received your letter yesterday, Mr Livingstone. I was anxious to see you today, in order that I might prevent you from speaking to my father. I do not say anything of the kind of affection you can feel for me—me, whom you have only seen once. All I shall say is, that the sooner we both forget what I must call folly, the better.'

She took the airs of a woman considerably older and more experienced than himself. He thought her haughty; she was only miserable.

'You are mistaken,' said he, more quietly and with more dignity than was likely from his previous conduct. 'I will not allow you to characterize as folly what might be presumptuous on my part—I had no business to express myself so soon—but which in its foundation was true and sincere. That I can answer for most solemnly. It is a possible, though it may not be a usual thing, for a man to feel so strongly attracted by the charms and qualities of a woman, even at first sight, as to feel sure that she, and she alone, can make his happiness. My folly consisted—there you are right—in even dreaming that you could return my feelings in the slightest degree, when you had only seen me once. And I am most truly ashamed of myself. I cannot tell you how sorry I am, when I see how you have compelled yourself to come and speak to me when you are so ill.'

She staggered into a chair, for with all her wish for his speedy dismissal, she was obliged to be seated. His hand was upon the bell.

'No, don't!' she said. 'Wait a minute.'

His eyes, bent upon her with a look of deep anxiety, touched her at that moment, and she was on the point of shedding tears; but she checked herself, and rose again.

'I will go,' said he. 'It is the kindest thing I can do. Only, may I write? May I venture to write and urge what I have to say more coherently?'

'No!' said she. 'Don't write. I have given you my answer. We are nothing, and can be nothing to each other. I am engaged to be married. I should not have told you if you had not been so kind. Thank you. But go now.'

The poor young man's face fell, and he became almost as white as she was for the instant. After a moment's reflection, he took her hand in his, and said:

'May God bless you, and him too, whoever he be. But if you want a friend, I may be that friend, may I not? and try to prove that my words of regard were true, in a better and higher sense than I used them at first.' And kissing her passive hand, he was gone, and she was left sitting alone.

But solitude was not what she could bear. She went quickly upstairs, and took a strong dose of sal-volatile, even while she heard Miss Monro calling to her.

'My dear, who was that gentleman that has been closeted with you in the drawing-room all this time?'

And then, without listening to Ellinor's reply, she went on:

'Mrs Jackson has been here' (it was at Mrs Jackson's house

that Mr Dunster lodged), wanting to know if we could tell her where Mr Dunster was, for he never came home last night at all. And you were in the drawing-room with—who did you say he was?—that Mr Livingstone, who might have come at a better time to bid goodbye; and he had never dined here, had he? so I don't see any reason he had to come calling, and P. P. C.-ing,* and your papa *not* up. So I said to Mrs Jackson, "I'll send and ask Mr Wilkins, if you like, but I don't see any use in it, for I can tell you just as well as anybody, that Mr Dunster is not in this house, wherever he may be." Yet nothing would satisfy her but that someone must go and waken up your papa, and ask if he could tell where Mr Dunster was.'

'And did papa?' inquired Ellinor, her dry throat huskily forming the inquiry that seemed to be expected from her.

'No! to be sure not. How should Mr Wilkins know? As I said to Mrs Jackson, "Mr Wilkins is not likely to know where Mr Dunster spends his time when he is not in the office, for they do not move in the same rank of life, my good woman;" and Mrs Jackson apologised, but said that yesterday they had both been dining at Mr Hodgson's together, she believed; and somehow she had got it into her head that Mr Dunster might have missed his way in coming along Moor Lane, and might have slipped into the canal; so she just thought she would step up and ask Mr Wilkins if they had left Mr Hodgson's together, or if your papa had driven home. I asked her why she had not told me all these particulars before, for I could have asked your papa myself all about when he last saw Mr Dunster; and I went up to ask him a second time, but he did not like it at all, for he was busy dressing, and I had to shout my questions through the door, and he could not always hear me at first.'

'What did he say?'

'Oh! he had walked part of the way with Mr Dunster, and then cut across by the short path through the fields, as far as I could understand him through the door. He seemed very much annoyed to hear that Mr Dunster had not been at home all night; but he said I was to tell Mrs Jackson that he would go to the office as soon as he had had his breakfast, which he ordered to be sent up directly into his own room, and he had no doubt it would all turn out right; but that she had better go home at once. And, as I told her, she might find Mr Dunster there by the time she got there. There, there is your papa going out! He has not lost any time over his breakfast!'

Ellinor had taken up the *Hamley Examiner*, a daily paper, which lay on the table, to hide her face in the first instance; but it served a second purpose, as she glanced languidly over the columns of the advertisements.

'Oh! here are Colonel Macdonald's orchideous plants to be sold. All the stock of hothouse and stove-plants at Hartwell Priory. I must send James over to Hartwell to attend the sale. It is to last for three days.'

'But can he be spared for so long?'

'Oh yes; he had better stay at the little inn there, to be on the spot. Three days,' and as she spoke, she ran out to the gardener, who was sweeping up the newly-mown grass in the front of the house. She gave him hasty and unlimited directions, only seeming intent—if anyone had been suspiciously watching her words and actions—to hurry him off to the distant village, where the auction was to take place.

When he was once gone she breathed more freely. Now, no one but the three cognizant of the terrible reason of the disturbance of the turf under the trees in a certain spot in the belt round the flower-garden, would be likely to go into the place. Miss Monro might wander round with a book in her hand; but she never noticed anything, and was short-sighted into the bargain. Three days of this moist, warm, growing weather, and the green grass would spring, just as if life—was what it had been twenty-four hours before.

When all this was done and said, it seemed as if Ellinor's strength and spirit sank down at once. Her voice became feeble, her aspect wan; and although she told Miss Monro that nothing was the matter, yet it was impossible for anyone who loved her not to perceive that she was far from well. The kind governess placed her pupil on the sofa, covered her feet up warmly, darkened the room, and then stole out on tiptoe, fancying that Ellinor would sleep. Her eyes were, indeed, shut; but try as much as she would to be quiet, she was up in less than five minutes after Miss Monro had left the room, and walking up and down in all the restless agony of body that arises from an overstrained mind. But soon Miss Monro reappeared, bringing with her a dose of soothing medicine of her own concocting, for she was great in domestic quackery. What the medicine was Ellinor did not care to know; she drank it without any sign of her usual merry resistance to physic of Miss Monro's ordering; and, as the latter took up a book, and showed a set purpose of remaining with her patient, Ellinor was compelled to lie still, and presently fell asleep.

She wakened late in the afternoon with a start. Her father was standing over her, listening to Miss Monro's account of her indisposition. She only caught one glimpse of his strangely altered countenance, and hid her head in the cushions—hid it from memory, not from him. For in an instant she must have conjectured the interpretation he was likely to put upon her shrinking action, and she had turned towards him, and had thrown her arms round his neck, and was kissing his cold, passive face. Then she fell back. But all this time their sad eyes never met—they dreaded the look of recollection that must be in each other's gaze.

'There, my dear!' said Miss Monro. 'Now you must lie still till I fetch you a little broth. You are better now, are not you?'

'You need not go for the broth, Miss Monro,' said Mr Wilkins, ringing the bell. 'Fletcher can surely bring it.' He dreaded the being left alone with his daughter—nor did she fear it less. She heard the strange alteration in her father's voice, hard and hoarse, as if it was an effort to speak. The physical signs of his suffering cut her to the heart; and yet she wondered how it was that they could both be alive, or, if alive, that they were not rending their garments and crying aloud.* Mr Wilkins seemed to have lost the power of careless action and speech, it is true. He wished to leave the room now his anxiety about his daughter was relieved, but hardly knew how to set about it. He was obliged to think about the veriest trifle, in order that by an effort of reason he might understand how he should have spoken or acted if he had been free from blood-guiltiness. Ellinor understood all by intuition. But henceforward the unspoken comprehension of each other's hidden motions made their mutual presence a burdensome anxiety to each. Miss Monro was a relief; they were glad of her as a third person, unconscious of the secret which constrained them. This afternoon her unconsciousness gave present pain, although on after reflection each found in her speeches a cause of rejoicing.

'And Mr Dunster, Mr Wilkins, has he come home yet?'

A moment's pause, in which Mr Wilkins pumped the words out of his husky throat:

'I have not heard. I have been riding. I went on business to Mr Estcourt's. Perhaps you will be so kind as to send and inquire at Mrs Jackson's.'

Ellinor sickened at the words. She had been all her life a truthful, plain-spoken girl. She held herself high above deceit. Yet, here came the necessity for deceit—a snare spread around her. She had not revolted so much from the deed which brought unpremeditated death, as she did from these words of her father's. The night before, in her mad fever of affright, she had fancied that to conceal the body was all that would be required; she had not looked forward to the long, weary course of small lies, to be done and said, involved in that one mistaken action. Yet, while her father's words made her soul revolt, his appearance melted her heart, as she caught it, half-turned away from her, neither looking straight at Miss Monro, nor at anything materially visible. His hollow sunken eye seemed, to Ellinor, to have a vision of the dead man before it. His cheek was livid and worn, and its healthy colouring, gained by years of hearty outdoor exercise, was all gone into the wanness of age. His hair even, to Ellinor, seemed greyer for the past night of wretchedness. He stooped, and looked dreamily earthward, where formerly he had stood erect. It needed all the pity called forth by such observation to quench Ellinor's passionate contempt for the course on which she and her father were embarked, when she heard him repeat his words to the servant who came with her broth.

'Fletcher! go to Mrs Jackson's, and inquire if Mr Dunster is come home yet. I want to speak to him.'

'To him!' lying dead where he had been laid; killed by the man who now asked for his presence. Ellinor shut her eyes, and lay back in despair. She wished she might die, and be out of this horrible tangle of events.

Two minutes after, she was conscious of her father and Miss

Monro stealing softly out of the room. They thought that she slept.

She sprang off the sofa and knelt down.

'Oh, God,' she prayed, 'Thou knowest! Help me! There is none other help but Thee!'

I suppose she fainted. For, an hour or more afterwards, Miss Monro, coming in, found her lying insensible by the side of the sofa.

She was carried to bed. She was not delirious, she was only in a stupor, which they feared might end in delirium. To obviate this, her father sent far and wide for skilful physicians, who tended her, almost at the rate of a guinea the minute.

People said how hard it was upon Mr Wilkins, that scarcely had that wretch Dunster gone off, with no one knows how much out of the trusts of the firm, before his only child fell ill. And, to tell the truth, he himself looked burnt and scared with affliction.* He had a startled look, they said, as if he never could tell, after such experience, from which side the awful proofs of the uncertainty of earth would appear, the terrible phantoms of unforeseen dread. Both rich and poor, town and country, sympathized with him. The rich cared not to press their claims, or their business, at such a time; and only wondered, in their superficial talk after dinner, how such a good fellow as Wilkins could ever have been deceived by a man like Dunster. Even Sir Frank Holster and his lady forgot their old quarrel, and came to inquire after Ellinor, and sent her hothouse fruit by the bushel.

Mr Corbet behaved as an anxious lover should do. He wrote daily to Miss Monro to beg for the most minute bulletins; he procured everything in town that any doctor even fancied might be of service. He came down as soon as there was the slightest hint of permission that Ellinor might see him. He overpowered her with tender words and caresses, till at last she shrank away from them, as from something too bewildering, and past all right comprehension.

But one night before this, when all windows and doors stood open to admit the least breath that stirred the sultry July air, a servant on velvet tiptoe had stolen up to Ellinor's open door, and had beckoned out of the chamber of the sleeper the ever watchful nurse, Miss Monro.

'A gentleman wants you,' were all the words the housemaid dared to say so close to the bedroom. And softly, softly Miss Monro stepped down the stairs, into the drawing-room; and there she saw Mr Livingstone. But she did not know him; she had never seen him before.

'I have travelled all day. I heard she was ill—was dying. May I just have one more look at her? I will not speak; I will hardly breathe. Only let me see her once again!'

'I beg your pardon, sir, but I don't know who you are; and if you mean Miss Wilkins, by "her," she is very ill, but we hope not dying. She was very ill, indeed, yesterday; very dangerously ill, I may say, but she is having a good sleep, in consequence of a soporific medicine, and we are really beginning to hope ——'

But just here Miss Monro's hand was taken, and, to her infinite surprise, was kissed before she could remember how improper such behaviour was.

'God bless you, madam, for saying so. But if she sleeps, will you let me see her; it can do no harm, for I will tread as if on egg-shells; and I have come so far—if I might just look on her sweet face. Pray, madam, let me just have one sight of her. I will not ask for more.'

But he did ask for more, after he had had his wish. He stole upstairs after Miss Monro, who looked round reproachfully at him if even a nightingale sang, or an owl hooted in the trees outside the open windows, yet who paused to say herself, outside Mr Wilkins's chamber-door,

'Her father's room; he has not been in bed for six nights, till tonight; pray do not make a noise to waken him.' And on into the deep stillness of the hushed room, where one clear ray of hidden lamplight shot athwart the floor, where a watcher, breathing softly, sat beside the bed—where Ellinor's dark head lay motionless on the white pillow, her face almost as white, her form almost as still. You might have heard a pin fall. After a while he moved to withdraw. Miss Monro, jealous of every sound, followed him, with steps all the more heavy because they were taken with so much care, down the stairs, back into the drawing-room. By the bed-candle flaring in the draught, she saw that there was the glittering mark of wet tears on his cheek; and she felt, as she said afterwards, 'sorry for the young man.'

And yet she urged him to go, for she knew that she might be wanted upstairs. He took her hand, and wrung it hard.

'Thank you. She looked so changed—oh! she looked as though she were dead. You will write—Herbert Livingstone, Langham Vicarage, Yorkshire; you will promise me to write. If I could do anything for her, but I can but pray. Oh, my darling; my darling! and I have no right to be with her.'

'Go away, there's a good young man,' said Miss Monro, all the more pressing to hurry him out by the front door, because she was afraid of his emotion overmastering him, and making him noisy in his demonstrations. 'Yes, I will write; I will write, never fear!' and she bolted the door behind him, and was thankful.

Two minutes afterwards there was a low tap; she undid the fastenings, and there he stood, pale in the moonlight.

'Please don't tell her I came to ask about her; she might not like it.'

'No, no! not I! Poor creature, she's not likely to care to hear anything this long while. She never roused at Mr Corbet's name.'

'Mr Corbet's!' said Livingstone, below his breath, and he turned and went away; this time for good. But Ellinor recovered. She knew she was recovering, when day after day she felt involuntary strength and appetite return. Her body seemed stronger than her will; for that would have induced her to creep into her grave, and shut her eyes for ever on this world, so full of troubles.

She lay, for the most part, with her eyes closed, very still and quiet; but she thought with the intensity of one who seeks for lost peace, and cannot find it. She began to see that if in the mad impulses of that mad nightmare of horror, they had all strengthened each other, and dared to be frank and open, confessing a great fault, a greater disaster, a greater woe—which in the first instance was hardly a crime—their future course, though sad and sorrowful, would have been a simple and straightforward one to tread. But it was not for her to undo what was done, and to reveal the error and shame of a father. Only she, turning anew to God, in the solemn and quiet watches of the night, made a covenant, that in her conduct, her own personal individual life, she would act loyally and truthfully. And as for the future, and all the terrible chances involved in it, she would leave it in His hands—if, indeed (and here came in the Tempter), He would watch over one whose life hereafter must seem based upon a lie. Her only plea, offered 'standing afar off,'* was, 'The lie is said and done and over—it was not for my own sake. Can filial piety be so overcome by the rights of justice and truth, as to demand of me that I should reveal my father's guilt?'

Her father's severe, sharp punishment began. He knew why she suffered, what made her young strength falter and tremble, what made her life seen nigh about to be quenched in death. Yet he could not take his sorrow and care in the natural manner. He was obliged to think how every word and deed would be construed. He fancied that people were watching him with suspicious eyes, when nothing was further from their thoughts. For once let the 'public' of any place be possessed by an idea, it is more difficult to dislodge it than anyone imagines who has not tried. If Mr Wilkins had gone into Hamley market-place, and proclaimed himself guilty of the manslaughter of Mr Dunster—nay, if he had detailed all the circumstances—the people would have exclaimed, 'Poor man, he is crazed by this discovery of the unworthiness of the man he trusted so; and no wonder—it was such a thing to have done—to have defrauded his partner to such an extent, and then have made off to America!'

For many small circumstances, which I do not stop to detail here, went far to prove this, as we know, unfounded supposition; and Mr Wilkins, who was known, from his handsome boyhood, through his comely manhood, up to the present time, by all the people in Hamley, was an object of sympathy and respect to everyone who saw him, as he passed by, old, and lorn, and haggard before his time, all through the evil conduct of one, London-bred, who was as a hard, unlovely stranger to the popular mind of this little country town.

Mr Wilkins's own servants liked him. The workings of his temptations were such as they could understand. If he had been hot-tempered, he had also been generous, or I should rather say careless and lavish with his money. And now that he was cheated and impoverished by his partner's delinquency, they thought it no wonder that he drank long and deep in the solitary evenings which he passed at home. It was not that he was without invitations. Everyone came forward to testify their respect for him by asking him to their houses. He had probably never been so universally popular since his father's death. But, as he said, he did not care to go into society while his daughter was so ill—he had no spirits for company.

But if anyone had cared to observe his conduct at home, and to draw conclusions from it, they could have noticed that, anxious as he was about Ellinor, he rather avoided than sought her presence, now that her consciousness and memory were restored. Nor did she ask for, or wish for him. The presence of each was a burden to the other. Oh, sad and woeful night of May—overshadowing the coming summer months with gloom and bitter remorse!

CHAPTER VIII

STILL youth prevailed over all. Ellinor got well, as I have said, even when she would fain have died. And the afternoon came when she left her room. Miss Monro would gladly have made a festival of her recovery, and have had her conveyed into the unused drawing-room. But Ellinor begged that she might be taken into the library—into the schoolroom—anywhere (thought she) not looking on the side of the house on the flower-garden, which she had felt in all her illness as a ghastly pressure, lying within sight of those very windows, through which the morning sun streamed right upon her bed—like the accusing angel, bringing all hidden things to light.

And when Ellinor was better still, when the Bath-chair* had been sent up for her use, by some kindly old maid, out of Hamley, she still petitioned that it might be kept on the lawn or town side of the house, away from the flower-garden.

One day she almost screamed, when, as she was going to the front door, she saw Dixon standing ready to draw her, instead of Fletcher, the servant who usually went. But she checked all demonstration of feeling; although it was the first time she had seen him since he and she and one more had worked their hearts out in hard bodily labour.

He looked so stern and ill! Cross, too, which she had never seen him before.

As soon as they were out of immediate sight of the windows, she asked him to stop, forcing herself to speak to him.

'Dixon, you look very poorly,' she said, trembling as she spoke.

'Ay!' said he. 'We didn't think much of it at the time, did we, Miss Nelly? But it'll be the death on us, I'm thinking. It has aged me above a bit. All my fifty years afore were but as a forenoon of child's play to that night. Measter, too—I could a-bear a good deal, but measter cuts through the stable-yard, and past me, wi'out a word, as if I was poison, or a stinking foumart.* It's that as is worst, Miss Nelly, it is.'

And the poor man brushed some tears from his eyes with the back of his withered, furrowed hand. Ellinor caught the infection, and cried outright, sobbed like a child, even while she held out her little white thin hand to his grasp. For as soon as he saw her emotion, he was penitent for what he had said.

'Don't now—don't,' was all he could think of to say.

'Dixon!' said she at length, 'you must not mind it. You must try not to mind it. I see he does not like to be reminded of that, even by seeing me. He tries never to be alone with me. My poor old Dixon, it has spoilt my life for me; for I don't think he loves me any more.'

She sobbed as if her heart would break; and now it was Dixon's turn to be comforter.

'Ah, dear, my blessing, he loves you above everything. It's only he can't a-bear the sight of us, as is but natural. And if he doesn't fancy being alone with you, there's always one as does, and that's a comfort at the worst of times. And don't ye fret about what I said a minute ago. I were put out because measter all but pushed me out of his way this morning, without never a word. But I were an old fool for telling ye. And I've really forgotten why I told Fletcher I'd drag ye a bit about today. Th' gardener is beginning for to wonder as you don't want to see th' annuals and bedding-out things as you were so particular about in May. And I thought I'd just have a word wi' ye, and then if you'd let me, we'd go together just once round th' flower-garden, just to say you've been, you know, and to give them chaps a bit of praise. You'll only have to look on the beds, my pretty, and it must be done some time. So come along!'

He began to pull resolutely in the direction of the flower-garden. Ellinor bit her lips to keep in the cry of repugnance that rose to them. As Dixon stopped to unlock the door, he said:

'It's not hardness, nothing like it; I've waited till I heerd you were better; but it's in for a penny in for a pound wi' us all; and folk may talk; and bless your little brave heart, you'll stand a deal for your father's sake, and so will I, though I do feel it above a bit, when he puts out his hand as if to keep me off, and I only going to speak to him about Clipper's knees; though I'll own I had wondered many a day when I was to have the good-morrow master never missed sin' he were a boy till——

'Well! and now you've seen the beds, and can say they looked mighty pretty, and is done all as you wished; and we're got out again, and breathing fresher air than yon sun-baked hole, with its smelling flowers, not half so wholesome to snuff at as good stable-dung.'

So the good man chattered on; not without the purpose of giving Ellinor time to recover herself; and partly also to drown his own cares, which lay heavier on his heart than he could say. But he thought himself rewarded by Ellinor's thanks, and warm pressure of his hard hand as she got out at the front door, and bade him goodbye.

The break to her days of weary monotony was the letters she constantly received from Mr Corbet. And yet, here again lurked the sting. He was all astonishment and indignation at Mr Dunster's disappearance, or rather flight to America. And now that she was growing stronger, he did not scruple to express curiosity respecting the details, never doubting but that she was perfectly acquainted with much that he wanted to know; although he had too much delicacy to question her on the point which was most important of all in his eyes, namely, how far it had affected Mr Wilkins's worldly prospects; for the report prevalent in Hamley had reached London, that Mr Dunster had made away with, or carried off, trust-property to a considerable extent, for all which Mr Wilkins would of course be liable.

It was hard work for Ralph Corbet to keep from seeking direct information on this head from Mr Ness, or, indeed, from Mr Wilkins himself. But he restrained himself, knowing that in August he should be able to make all these inquiries personally. Before the end of the Long Vacation he had hoped to marry Ellinor; that was the time which had been planned by them when they had met in the early spring before her illness and all this misfortune happened. But now, as he wrote to his father, nothing could be definitively arranged until he had paid his visit to Hamley, and seen the state of affairs.

Accordingly, one Saturday in August, he came to Ford Bank, this time as a visitor to Ellinor's home, instead of to his old quarters at Mr Ness's.

The house was still as if asleep in the full heat of the afternoon sun, as Mr Corbet drove up. The window-blinds were down; the front door wide open, great stands of heliotrope and roses and geraniums stood just within the shadow of the hall; but through all the silence his approach seemed to excite no commotion. He thought it strange that he had not been watched for, that Ellinor did not come running out to meet him, that she allowed Fletcher to come and attend to his luggage, and usher him into the library just like any common visitor, any morning-caller. He stiffened himself up into a moment's indignant coldness of manner. But it vanished in an instant when, on the door being opened, he saw Ellinor standing, holding by the table, looking for his appearance with almost panting anxiety. He thought of nothing then but her evident weakness, her changed looks, for which no account of her illness had prepared him. For she was deadly white, lips and all; and her dark eyes seemed unnaturally enlarged, while the caves in which they were set were strangely deep and hollow. Her hair, too, had been cut off pretty closely; she did not usually wear a cap, but with some faint idea of making herself look better in his eye, she had put one on this day, and the effect was that she seemed to be forty years of age; but one instant after he had come in, her pale face was flooded with crimson, and her eyes were full of tears. She had hard work to keep herself from going into hysterics, but she instinctively knew how much he would hate a scene, and she checked herself in time.

'Oh,' she murmured, 'I am so glad to see you; it is such a comfort, such an infinite pleasure.' And so she went on, cooing out words over him, and stroking his hair with her thin fingers. While he rather tried to avert his eyes, he was so much afraid of betraying how much he thought her altered.

But when she came down, dressed for dinner, this sense of her change was diminished to him. Her short brown hair had already a little wave, and was ornamented by some black lace; she wore a large black lace shawl—it had been her mother's of old—over some delicate-coloured muslin dress; her face was slightly flushed, and had the tints of a wild rose; her lips kept pale and trembling with involuntary motion, it is true; and as the lovers stood together, hand in hand, by the window, he was aware of a little convulsive twitching at every noise, even while she seemed gazing in tranquil pleasure on the long smooth slope of the newly-mown lawn, stretching down to the little brook that prattled merrily over the stones on its merry course to Hamley town.

He felt a stronger twitch than ever before; even while his ear, less delicate than hers, could distinguish no peculiar sound. About two minutes after Mr Wilkins entered the room. He came up to Mr Corbet with warm welcome: some of it real, some of it assumed. He talked volubly to him, taking little or no notice of Ellinor, who dropped into the background, and sat down on the sofa by Miss Monro; for on this day they were all to dine together. Ralph Corbet thought that Mr Wilkins was aged; but no wonder, after all his anxiety of various kinds: Mr Dunster's flight and reported defalcations, Ellinor's illness, of the seriousness of which her lover was now convinced by her appearance.

He would fain have spoken more to her during the dinner that ensued, but Mr Wilkins absorbed all his attention, talking and questioning on subjects that left the ladies out of the conversation almost perpetually. Mr Corbet recognized his host's fine tact, even while his persistence in talking annoyed him. He was quite sure that Mr Wilkins was anxious to spare his daughter any exertion beyond that—to which, indeed, she seemed scarcely equal—of sitting at the head of the table. And the more her father talked—so fine an observer was Mr

Corbet—the more silent and depressed Ellinor appeared. But by-and-by he accounted for this inverse ratio of gaiety, as he perceived how quickly Mr Wilkins had his glass replenished. And here, again, Mr Corbet drew his conclusions, from the silent way in which, without a word or a sign from his master, Fletcher gave him more wine continually—wine that was drained off at once.

'Six glasses of sherry before dessert,' thought Mr Corbet to himself. 'Bad habit—no wonder Ellinor looks grave.' And when the gentlemen were left alone, Mr Wilkins helped himself even still more freely; yet without the slightest effect on the clearness and brilliancy of his conversation. He had always talked well and racily, that Ralph knew, and in this power he now recognized a temptation to which he feared that his future father-in-law had succumbed. And yet, while he perceived that this gift led into temptation, he coveted it for himself; for he was perfectly aware that this fluency, this happy choice of epithets, was the one thing he should fail in when he began to enter into the more active career of his profession. But after some time spent in listening, and admiring, with this little feeling of envy lurking in the background, Mr Corbet became aware of Mr Wilkins's increasing confusion of ideas, and rather unnatural merriment; and, with a sudden revulsion from admiration to disgust, he rose up to go into the library, where Ellinor and Miss Monro were sitting. Mr Wilkins accompanied him, laughing and talking somewhat loudly. Was Ellinor aware of her father's state? Of that Mr Corbet could not be sure. She looked up with grave sad eyes as they came into the room, but with no apparent sensation of surprise, annoyance, or shame. When her glance met her father's, Mr Corbet noticed that it seemed to sober the latter immediately. He sat down near the open window, and did not speak, but sighed heavily from time to time. Miss Monro took up a book, in order to leave the young people to themselves; and after a little low murmured conversation, Ellinor went upstairs to put on her things for a stroll through the meadows, by the riverside.

They were sometimes sauntering along in the lovely summer twilight, now resting on some grassy hedgerow bank, or standing still, looking at the great barges, with their crimson sails, lazily floating down the river, making ripples on the glassy opal surface of the water. They did not talk very much; Ellinor seemed disinclined for the exertion; and her lover was thinking over Mr Wilkins's behaviour, with some surprise and distaste of the habit so evidently growing upon him.

They came home, looking serious and tired: yet they could not account for their fatigue by the length of their walk; and Miss Monro, forgetting Autolycus's song,* kept fidgeting about Ellinor, and wondering how it was she looked so pale, if she had only been as far as the Ash meadow. To escape from this wonder, Ellinor went early to bed. Mr Wilkins was gone, no one knew where, and Ralph and Miss Monro were left to a half-hour's *tête-à-tête*. He thought he could easily account for Ellinor's languor, if, indeed, she had perceived as much as he had done of her father's state, when they had come into the library after dinner. But there were many details which he was anxious to hear from a comparatively indifferent person, and as soon as he could, he passed on from the conversation about Ellinor's health, to inquiries as to the whole affair of Mr Dunster's disappearance.

Next to her anxiety about Ellinor, Miss Monro liked to dilate on the mystery connected with Mr Dunster's flight; for that was the word she employed without hesitation, as she gave him the account of the event universally received and believed in by the people of Hamley. How Mr Dunster had never been liked by anyone; how everybody remembered that he could never look them straight in the face; how he always seemed to be hiding something that he did not want to have known; how he had drawn a large sum (exact quantity unknown) out of the county bank, only the day before he left Hamley, doubtless in preparation for his escape; how someone had told Mr Wilkins he had seen a man just like Dunster lurking about the docks at Liverpool, about two days after he had left his lodgings, but that this someone, being in a hurry, had not cared to stop and speak to the man; how that the affairs in the office were discovered to be in such a sad state; that it was no wonder that Mr Dunster had absconded—he that had been so trusted by poor dear Mr Wilkins. Money gone no one knew how or where.'

'But has he no friends who can explain his proceedings, and

account for the missing money, in some way?' asked Mr Corbet.

'No, none. Mr Wilkins has written everywhere, right and left, I believe. I know he had a letter from Mr Dunster's nearest relation—a tradesman in the City—a cousin, I think, and he could give no information in any way. He knew that about ten years ago Mr Dunster had had a great fancy for going to America, and had read a great many travels—all just what a man would do before going off to a country.'

'Ten years is a long time beforehand,' said Mr Corbet, half smiling; 'shows malice prepense* with a vengeance.' But then, turning grave, he said: 'Did he leave Hamley in debt?'

'No; I never heard of that,' said Miss Monro, rather unwillingly, for she considered it as a piece of loyalty to the Wilkinses, whom Mr Dunster had injured (as she thought), to blacken his character as much as was consistent with any degree of truth.

'It is a strange story,' said Mr Corbet, musing.

'Not at all,' she replied, quickly; 'I am sure, if you had seen the man, with one or two side-locks of hair combed over his baldness, as if he were ashamed of it, and his eyes that never looked at you, and his way of eating with his knife when he thought he was not observed—oh, and numbers of things!—you would not think it strange.'

Mr Corbet smiled.

'I only meant that he seems to have had no extravagant or vicious habits which would account for his embezzlement of the money that is missing—but, to be sure, money in itself is a temptation—only he, being a partner, was in a fair way of making it without risk to himself. Has Mr Wilkins taken any steps to have him arrested in America? He might easily do that.'

'Oh, my dear Mr Ralph, you don't know our good Mr Wilkins! He would rather bear the loss, I am sure, and all this trouble and care which it has brought upon him, than be revenged upon Mr Dunster.'

'Revenged! What nonsense! It is simple justice—justice to himself and to others—to see that villainy is so sufficiently punished as to deter others from entering upon such courses. But I have little doubt Mr Wilkins has taken the right steps: he is not the man to sit down quietly under such a loss.'

'No, indeed! He had him advertised in *The Times* and in the county papers, and offered a reward of twenty pounds for information concerning him.'

'Twenty pounds was too little.'

'So I said. I told Ellinor that I would give twenty pounds myself to have him apprehended, and she, poor darling! fell a-trembling, and said, "I would give all I have—I would give my life." And then she was in such distress, and sobbed so, I promised her I would never name it to her again.'

'Poor child—poor child! she wants change of scene. Her nerves have been sadly shaken by her illness.'

The next day was Sunday; Ellinor was to go to church for the first time since her illness. Her father had decided it for her, or else she would fain have stayed away—she would hardly acknowledge why, even to herself, but it seemed to her as if the very words and presence of God must there search her and find her out.

She went early, leaning on the arm of her lover, and trying to forget the past in the present. They walked slowly along between the rows of waving golden corn ripe for the harvest. Mr Corbet gathered blue and scarlet flowers, and made up a little rustic nosegay for her. She took and stuck it in her girdle, smiling faintly as she did so.

Hamley Church had, in former days, been collegiate,* and was, in consequence, much larger and grander than the majority of country-town churches. The Ford Bank pew was a square one, downstairs; the Ford Bank servants sat in a front pew in the gallery, right before their master. Ellinor was 'hardening her heart'* not to listen, not to hearken to what might disturb the wound which was just being skinned over, when she caught Dixon's face up above. He looked worn, sad, soured, and anxious to a miserable degree; but he was straining eyes and ears, heart and soul, to hear the solemn words read from the pulpit, as if in them alone he could find help in his strait. Ellinor felt rebuked and humbled.

She was in a tumultuous state of mind when they left church; she wished to do her duty, yet could not ascertain what it was. Who was to help her with wisdom and advice? Assuredly he to whom her future life was to be trusted. But the case must be stated in an impersonal form. No one, not even her husband, must ever know anything against her father from her. Ellinor was so artless herself, that she had little idea how quickly and easily some people can penetrate motives, and combine disjointed sentences. She began to speak to Ralph on their slow sauntering walk homewards through the quiet meadows:

'Suppose, Ralph, that a girl was engaged to be married ——'

'I can very easily suppose that, with you by me,' said he, filling up her pause.

'Oh! but I don't mean myself at all,' replied she, reddening. 'I am only thinking of what might happen; and suppose that this girl knew of someone belonging to her—we will call it a brother—who had done something wrong, that would bring disgrace upon the whole family if it was known—though, indeed, it might not have been so very wrong as it seemed, and as it would look to the world—ought she to break off her engagement for fear of involving her lover in the disgrace?'

'Certainly not, without telling him her reason for doing so.'

'Ah! but suppose she could not. She might not be at liberty to do so.'

'I can't answer supposititious cases. I must have the facts—if facts there are—more plainly before me before I can give an opinion. Who are you thinking of, Ellinor?' asked he, rather abruptly.

'Oh, of no one,' she answered, in affright. 'Why should I be thinking of anyone? I often try to plan out what I should do, or what I ought to do, if such and such a thing happened, just as you recollect I used to wonder if I should have presence of mind in case of fire.'

'Then, after all, you yourself are the girl who is engaged, and who has the imaginary brother who gets into disgrace?'

'Yes, I suppose so,' said she, a little annoyed at having betrayed any personal interest in the affair.

He was silent, meditating.

'There is nothing wrong in it,' said she, timidly, 'is there?'

'I think you had better tell me fully out what is in your mind,' he replied, kindly. 'Something has happened which has suggested these questions. Are you putting yourself in the place of anyone about whom you have been hearing lately? I know you used to do so formerly, when you were a little girl.'

'No; it was a very foolish question of mine, and I ought not to have said anything about it. See! here is Mr Ness overtaking us.'

The clergyman joined them on the broad walk that ran by the riverside, and the talk became general. It was a relief to Ellinor, who had not attained her end, but who had gone far towards betraying something of her own individual interest in the question she had asked. Ralph had been more struck even by her manner than her words. He was sure that something lurked behind, and had an idea of his own that it was connected with Dunster's disappearance. But he was glad that Mr Ness's joining them gave him leisure to consider a little. The end of his reflections was, that the next day, Monday, he went into the town, and artfully learnt all he could hear about Mr Dunster's character and mode of going on; and with still more skill he extracted the popular opinion as to the embarrassed nature of Mr Wilkins's affairs—embarrassment which was generally attributed to Dunster's disappearance with a good large sum belonging to the firm in his possession. But Mr Corbet thought otherwise; he had accustomed himself to seek out the baser motives for men's conduct, and to call the result of these researches wisdom. He imagined that Dunster had been well paid by Mr Wilkins for his disappearance, which was an easy way of accounting for the derangement of accounts and loss of money that arose, in fact, from Mr Wilkins's extravagance of habits and growing intemperance.

On the Monday afternoon he said to Ellinor, 'Mr Ness interrupted us yesterday in a very interesting conversation. Do you remember, love?'

Ellinor reddened, and kept her head still more intently bent over a sketch she was making.

'Yes; I recollect.'

'I have been thinking about it. I still think she ought to tell her lover that such disgrace hung over him—I mean, over the family with whom he was going to connect himself. Of course, the only effect would be to make him stand by her still more for her frankness.'

'Oh! but, Ralph, it might perhaps be something she ought not to tell, whatever came of her silence.'

'Of course there might be all sorts of cases. Unless I knew more I could not pretend to judge.'

This was said rather more coolly. It had the desired effect. Ellinor laid down her brush, and covered her face with her hand. After a pause, she turned towards him and said:

'I will tell you this; and more you must not ask of me. I know you are as safe as can be. I am the girl, you are the lover, and possible shame hangs over my father, if something—oh, so dreadful' (here she blanched), 'but not so very much his fault, is ever found out.'

Though this was nothing more than he expected; though Ralph thought that he was aware what the dreadful something might be, yet, when it was acknowledged in words, his heart contracted, and for a moment he forgot the intent, wistful, beautiful face creeping close to his to read his expression aright. But after that his presence of mind came in aid. He took her in his arms and kissed her; murmuring fond words of sympathy, and promises of faith, nay, even of greater love than before, since greater need she might have of that love. But somehow he was glad when the dressing-bell rang, and in the solitude of his own room he could reflect on what he had heard; for the intelligence had been a great shock to him, although he had fancied that his morning's inquiries had prepared him for it.

CHAPTER IX

RALPH CORBET found it a very difficult thing to keep down his curiosity during the next few days. It was a miserable thing to have Ellinor's unspoken secret severing them like a phantom. But he had given her his word that he would make no further inquiries from her. Indeed, he thought he could well enough make out the outline of past events; still, there was too much left to conjecture for his mind not to be always busy on the subject. He felt inclined to probe Mr Wilkins, in their after-dinner conversation, in which his host was frank and lax enough on many subjects. But once touch on the name of Dunster and Mr Wilkins sank into a kind of suspicious depression of spirits; talking little, and with evident caution; and from time to time shooting furtive glances at his interlocutor's face. Ellinor was resolutely impervious to any attempts of his to bring his conversation with her back to the subject which more and more engrossed Ralph Corbet's mind. She had done her duty, as she understood it; and had received assurances which she was only too glad to believe fondly with all the tender faith of her heart. Whatever came to pass, Ralph's love would still be hers; nor was he unwarned of what might come to pass in some dread future day. So she shut her eyes to what might be in store for her (and, after all, the chances were immeasurably in her favour); and she bent herself with her whole strength into enjoying the present. Day by day, Mr Corbet's spirits flagged. He was, however, so generally uniform in the tenor of his talk—never very merry, and always avoiding any subject that might call out deep feeling either on his own or anyone else's part, that few people were aware of his changes of mood. Ellinor felt them, though she would not acknowledge them: it was bringing her too much face to face with the great terror of her life.

One morning he announced the fact of his brother's approaching marriage; the wedding was hastened on account of some impending event in the duke's family; and the home letter he had received that day was to bid his presence at Stokely Castle, and also to desire him to be at home by a certain time, not very distant, in order to look over the requisite legal papers, and to give his assent to some of them. He gave many reasons why this unlooked-for departure of his was absolutely necessary; but no one doubted it. He need not have alleged such reiterated excuses. The truth was, he was restrained and uncomfortable at Ford Bank ever since Ellinor's confidence. He could not rightly calculate on the most desirable course for his own interests, while his love for her was constantly being renewed by her sweet presence. Away from her, he could judge more wisely. Nor did he allege any false reasons for his departure; but the sense of relief to himself was so great at his recall home, that he was afraid of having it perceived by others; and so took the very way which, if others had been as penetrating as himself, would have betrayed him.

Mr Wilkins, too, had begun to feel the restraint of Ralph's grave watchful presence. Ellinor was not strong enough to be married; nor was the promised money forthcoming if she had been. And to have a fellow dawdling about the house all day, sauntering into the flower-garden, peering about everywhere, and having a kind of right to put all manner of unexpected questions, was anything but agreeable. It was only Ellinor that clung to his presence—clung as though some shadow of what might happen before they met again had fallen on her spirit. As soon as he had left the house she flew up to a spare bedroom window, to watch for the last glimpse of the fly* which was taking him into the town. And then she kissed the part of the pane on which his figure, waving an arm out of the carriage window, had last appeared; and went down slowly to gather together all the things he had last touched—the pen he had mended, the flower he had played with, and to lock them up in the little quaint cabinet that had held her treasures since she was a tiny child.

Miss Monro was, perhaps, very wise in proposing the translation of a difficult part of Dante for a distraction to Ellinor. The girl went meekly, if reluctantly, to the task set her by her good governess, and by-and-by her mind became braced by the exertion.

Ralph's people were not very slow in discovering that something had not gone on quite smoothly with him at Ford Bank. They knew his ways and looks with family intuition, and could easily be certain thus far. But not even his mother's skilfulest wiles, nor his favourite sister's coaxing, could obtain a word or a hint; and when his father, the squire, who had heard the opinions of the female part of the family on this head, began, in his honest blustering way, in their *tête-à-têtes* after dinner, to hope that Ralph was thinking better than to run his head into that confounded Hamley attorney's noose, Ralph gravely required Mr Corbet to explain his meaning, which he professed not to understand so worded. And when the squire had, with much perplexity, put it into the plain terms of hoping that his son was thinking of breaking off his engagement to Miss Wilkins, Ralph coolly asked him if he was aware that, in that case, he should lose all title to being a man of honour, and might have an action brought against him for breach of promise?*

Yet not the less for all this was the idea in his mind as a future possibility.

Before very long the Corbet family moved *en masse* to Stokely Castle for the wedding. Of course, Ralph associated on equal terms with the magnates of the county, who were the employers of Ellinor's father, and spoke of him always as 'Wilkins,' just as they spoke of the butler as 'Simmons.' Here, too, among a class of men high above local gossip, and thus unaware of his engagement, he learnt the popular opinion respecting his future father-in-law; an opinion not entirely respectful, though intermingled with a good deal of personal liking. 'Poor Wilkins,' as they called him, 'was sadly extravagant for a man in his position; had no right to spend money, and act as if he were a man of independent fortune.' His habits of life were criticized; and pity, not free from blame, was bestowed upon him for the losses he had sustained from his late clerk's disappearance and defalcation. But what could be expected, if a man did not choose to attend to his own business?

The wedding went by, as grand weddings do, without let or hindrance, according to the approved pattern. A cabinet minister honoured it with his presence, and, being a distant relation of the Brabants, remained for a few days after the grand occasion. During this time he became rather intimate with Ralph Corbet; many of their tastes were in common. Ralph took a great interest in the manner of working out political questions; in the balance and state of parties; and had the right appreciation of the exact qualities on which the minister piqued himself. In return, the latter was always on the look-out for promising young men, who, either by their capability of speech-making, or article-writing, might advance the views of his party. Recognizing the powers he most valued in Ralph, he spared no pains to attach him to his own political set. When they separated, it was with the full understanding that they were to see a good deal of each other in London.

The holiday Ralph allowed himself was passing rapidly away; but, before he returned to his chambers and his hard work, he had promised to spend a few more days with Ellinor; and it suited him to go straight from the duke's to Ford Bank. He left the castle soon after breakfast—the luxurious, elegant breakfast, served by domestics who performed their work with the accuracy and perfection of machines. He arrived at Ford Bank before the man-servant had quite finished the dirtier part of his morning's work, and he came to the glass-door in his striped cotton jacket, a little soiled, and rolling up his working apron. Ellinor was not yet strong enough to get up and go out and gather flowers for the rooms, so those left from yesterday were rather faded; in short, the contrast from entire completeness and exquisite freshness of arrangement struck forcibly upon Ralph's perceptions, which were critical rather than appreciative; and, as his affections were always subdued to his intellect, Ellinor's lovely face and graceful figure flying to meet him did not gain his full approval, because her hair was dressed in an old-fashioned way, her waist was either too long or too short, her sleeves too full or too tight for the standard of fashion to which his eye had been accustomed while scanning the bridesmaids and various high-born ladies at Stokely Castle.

But, as he had always piqued himself upon being able to put on one side all superficial worldliness in his chase after power, it did not do for him to shrink from seeing and facing the incompleteness of moderate means. Only marriage upon moderate means was gradually becoming more distasteful to him.

Nor did his subsequent intercourse with Lord Bolton, the cabinet minister before mentioned, tend to reconcile him to early matrimony. At Lord Bolton's house he met polished and intellectual society, and all that smoothness in ministering to the lower wants in eating and drinking which seems to provide that the right thing shall always be at the right place at the right time, so that the want of it shall never impede for an instant the feast of wit or reason;* while, if he went to the houses of his friends, men of the same college and standing as himself, who had been seduced into early marriages, he was uncomfortably aware of numerous inconsistencies and hitches in their *ménages*.* Besides, the idea of the possible disgrace that might befall the family with which he thought of allying himself haunted him with the tenacity and also with the exaggeration of a nightmare, whenever he had overworked himself in his search after available and profitable knowledge, or had a fit of indigestion after the exquisite dinners he was learning so well to appreciate.

Christmas was, of course, to be devoted to his own family; it was an unavoidable necessity, as he told Ellinor, while, in reality, he was beginning to find absence from his betrothed something of a relief. Yet the wranglings and folly of his home, even blessed by the presence of a Lady Maria, made him look forward to Easter at Ford Bank with something of the old pleasure.

Ellinor, with the fine tact which love gives, had discovered his annoyance at various little incongruities in the household at the time of his second visit in the previous autumn, and had laboured to make all as perfect as she could before his return. But she had much to struggle against. For the first time in her life there was a great want of ready money; she could scarcely obtain the servants' wages; and the bill for the spring seeds was a heavy weight on her conscience. For Miss Monro's methodical habits had taught her pupil great exactitude as to all money matters.

Then, her father's temper had become very uncertain. He avoided being alone with her whenever he possibly could; and the consciousness of this, and of the terrible mutual secret which was the cause of this estrangement, were the reasons why Ellinor never recovered her pretty youthful bloom after her illness. Of course it was to this that the outside world attributed her changed appearance. They would shake their heads and say, 'Ah, poor Miss Wilkins! What a lovely creature she was before that fever!'

But youth is youth, and will assert itself in a certain elasticity of body and spirits; and at times Ellinor forgot that fearful night for several hours together. Even when her father's averted eye brought it all once more before her, she had learnt to form excuses, and palliations, and to regard Mr Dunster's death as only the consequence of an unfortunate accident. But she tried to put the miserable remembrance entirely out of her mind; to go on from day to day thinking only of the day, and how to arrange it so as to cause the least irritation to her father. She would so gladly have spoken to him on the one subject which overshadowed all their intercourse; she fancied that by speaking she might have been able to banish the phantom, or reduce its terror to what she believed to be the due proportion. But her father was evidently determined to show that he was never more to be spoken to on that subject; and all she could do was to follow his lead on the rare occasions that they fell into something like the old confidential intercourse. As yet, to her, he had never given way to anger; but before her he had often spoken in a manner which both pained and terrified her. Sometimes his eye in the midst of his passion caught on her face of affright and dismay, and then he would stop, and make such an effort to control himself as sometimes ended in tears. Ellinor did not understand that both these phases were owing to his increasing habit of drinking more than he ought to have done. She set them down as the direct effects of a sorely burdened conscience; and strove more and more to plan for his daily life at home, how it should go on with oiled wheels, neither a jerk nor a jar. It was no wonder she looked wistful, and careworn, and old. Miss Monro was her great comfort; the total unconsciousness on that lady's part of anything below the surface, and yet her full and delicate recognition of all the little daily cares and trials, made her sympathy most valuable to Ellinor, while there was no need to fear that it would ever give Miss Monro that power of seeing into the heart of things which it frequently confers upon imaginative people, who are deeply attached to someone in sorrow.

There was a strong bond between Ellinor and Dixon, although they scarcely ever exchanged a word save on the most commonplace subjects; but their silence was based on different feelings from that which separated Ellinor from her father. Ellinor and Dixon could not speak freely, because their hearts were full of pity for the faulty man whom they both loved so well, and tried so hard to respect.

This was the state of the household to which Ralph Corbet came down at Easter. He might have been known in London as a brilliant diner-out by this time; but he could not afford to throw his life away in fireworks; he calculated his forces, and condensed their power as much as might be, only visiting where he was likely to meet men who could help in his future career. He had been invited to spend the Easter vacation at a certain country house, which would be full of such human steppingstones; and he declined in order to keep his word to Ellinor, and go to Ford Bank. But he could not help looking upon himself a little in the light of a martyr to duty; and perhaps this view of his own merits made him chafe under his future father-in-law's irritability of manner, which now showed itself even to him. He found himself distinctly regretting that he had suffered himself to be engaged so early in life; and having become conscious of the temptation and not having repelled it at once, of course it returned and returned, and gradually obtained the mastery over him. What was to be gained by keeping to his engagement with Ellinor? He should have a delicate wife to look after, and even more than the common additional expenses of married life. He should have a father-in-law whose character at best had had only a local and provincial respectability; which it was now daily losing by habits which were both sensual and vulgarizing; a man, too, who was strangely changing from joyous geniality into moody surliness. Besides, he doubted if, in the evident change in the prosperity of the family, the fortune to be paid down on the occasion of his marriage to Ellinor could be forthcoming. And above all, and around all, there hovered the shadow of some unrevealed disgrace, which might come to light at any time, and involve him in it. He thought he had pretty well ascertained the nature of this possible shame, and had little doubt it would turn out to be that Dunster's disappearance to America, or elsewhere, had been an arranged plan with Mr Wilkins. Although Mr Ralph Corbet was capable of suspecting him of this mean crime (so far removed from the impulsive commission of the past sin, which was dragging him daily lower and lower down), it was of a kind that was peculiarly distasteful to the acute lawyer, who foresaw how such base conduct would taint all whose names were ever mentioned, even by chance, in connection with it. He used to lie miserably tossing on his sleepless bed, turning over these things in the night season. He was tormented by all these thoughts; he would bitterly regret the past events that connected him with Ellinor, from the day when he first came to read with Mr Ness, up to the present time. But when he came down in the morning, and saw the faded Ellinor flash into momentary beauty at his entrance into the dining-room, and when she blushingly drew near with the one single flower freshly gathered, which it had been her custom to place in his button-hole when he came down to breakfast, he felt as if his better self was stronger than temptation, and as if he must be an honest man and honourable lover, even against his wish.

As the day wore on the temptation gathered strength. Mr Wilkins came down, and while he was on the scene Ellinor seemed always engrossed by her father, who apparently cared little enough for all her attentions. Then there was a complaining of the food, which did not suit the sickly palate of a man who had drunk hard the night before; and possibly these complaints were extended to the servants, and their incompleteness or incapacity was thus brought prominently before the eyes of Ralph, who would have preferred to eat a dry crust in silence, or to have gone without breakfast altogether, if he could have had intellectual conversation of some high order, to having the greatest dainties with the knowledge of the care required in their preparation thus coarsely discussed before him. By the time such breakfasts were finished, Ellinor looked thirty, and her spirits were gone for the day. It had become difficult for Ralph to contract his mind to her small domestic interests, and she had little else to talk to him about, now that he responded but curtly to all her questions about himself, and was weary of professing a love which he was ceasing to feel, in all the passionate nothings which usually make up so much of lovers' talk. The books she had been reading were old classics, whose place in literature no longer admitted of keen discussion; the poor whom she cared for were all very well in their way; and, if they could have been brought in to illustrate a theory, hearing about them might have been of some use; but, as it was, it was simply tiresome to hear day after day of Betty Palmer's rheumatism and Mrs Kay's baby's fits. There was no talking politics with her, because she was so ignorant that she always agreed with everything he said.

He even grew to find luncheon and Miss Monro not unpleasant varieties to his monotonous *tête-à-têtes*. Then came the walk, generally to the town to fetch Mr Wilkins from his office; and once or twice it was pretty evident how he had been employing his hours. One day in particular his walk was so unsteady and his speech so thick, that Ralph could only wonder how it was that Ellinor did not perceive the cause; but she was too openly anxious about the headache of which her father complained to have been at all aware of the previous self-indulgence which must have brought it on. This very afternoon, as ill-luck would have it, the Duke of Hinton and a gentleman whom Ralph had met in town at Lord Bolton's, rode by, and recognized him; saw Ralph supporting a tipsy man with such quiet friendly interest as must show all passers-by that they were previous friends. Mr Corbet chafed and fumed inwardly all the way home after this unfortunate occurrence; he was in a thoroughly evil temper before they reached Ford Bank, but he had too much self-command to let this be very apparent. He turned into the shrubbery-paths, leaving Ellinor to take her father into the quietness of his own room, there to lie down and shake off his headache.

Ralph walked along, ruminating in gloomy mood as to what was to be done; how he could best extricate himself from the miserable relation in which he had placed himself by giving way to impulse. Almost before he was aware, a little hand stole within his folded arms, and Ellinor's sweet sad eyes looked into his.

'I have put papa down for an hour's rest before dinner,' said she. 'His head seems to ache terribly.'

Ralph was silent and unsympathizing, trying to nerve himself up to be disagreeable, but finding it difficult in face of such sweet trust.

'Do you remember our conversation last autumn, Ellinor?' he began at length.

Her head sunk. They were near a garden-seat, and she quietly sat down, without speaking.

'About some disgrace which you then fancied hung over you?' No answer. 'Does it still hang over you?'

'Yes!' she whispered, with a heavy sigh.

'And your father knows of this, of course?'

'Yes!' again, in the same tone; and then silence.

'I think it is doing him harm,' at length Ralph went on, decidedly.

'I am afraid it is,' she said, in a low tone.

'I wish you would tell me what it is,' he said, a little impatiently. 'I might be able to help you about it.'

'No! you could not,' replied Ellinor. 'I was sorry to my very heart to tell you what I did; I did not want help; all that is past. But I wanted to know if you thought that a person situated as I was, was justified in marrying anyone ignorant of what might happen; what I do hope and trust never will.'

'But if I don't know what you are alluding to in this mysterious way, you must see—don't you see, love?—I am in the position of the ignorant man, whom I think you said you could not feel it right to marry. Why don't you tell me straight out what it is?' He could not help his irritation betraying itself in his tones and manner of speaking. She bent a little forward, and looked full into his face, as though to pierce to the very heart's truth of him. Then she said, as quietly as she ever had spoken in her life,—

'You wish to break off our engagement?'

He reddened and grew indignant in a moment. 'What nonsense! Just because I ask a question and make a remark! I think your illness must have made you fanciful, Ellinor. Surely nothing I said deserves such an interpretation. On the contrary, have I not shown the sincerity and depth of my affection to you by clinging to you through—through everything?'

He was going to say 'through the wearying opposition of my family,' but he stopped short, for he knew that the very fact of his mother's opposition had only made him the more determined to have his own way in the first instance; and even now he did not intend to let out what he had concealed up to this time, that his friends all regretted his imprudent engagement.

Ellinor sat silently gazing out upon the meadows, but seeing nothing. Then she put her hand into his. 'I quite trust you, Ralph. I was wrong to doubt. I am afraid I have grown fanciful and silly.'

He was rather put to it for the right words, for she had precisely divined the dim thought that had overshadowed his mind when she had looked so intently at him. But he caressed her, and reassured her with fond words, as incoherent as lovers' words generally are.

By-and-by they sauntered homewards. When they reached the house, Ellinor left him, and flew up to see how her father was. When Ralph went into his own room he was vexed with himself, both for what he had said and what he had not said. His mental look-out was not satisfactory.

Neither he nor Mr Wilkins was in good humour with the world in general at dinner-time, and it needs little in such cases to condense and turn the lowering tempers into one particular direction. As long as Ellinor and Miss Monro stayed in the dining-room, a sort of moody peace had been kept up, the ladies talking incessantly to each other about the trivial nothings of their daily life, with an instinctive consciousness that if they did not chatter on, something would be said by one of the gentlemen which would be distasteful to the other.

As soon as Ralph had shut the door behind them, Mr Wilkins went to the sideboard, and took out a bottle which had not previously made its appearance.

'Have a little cognac?' he asked, with an assumption of carelessness, as he poured out a wineglassful. 'It's a capital thing for the headache: and this nasty lowering weather has given me a racking headache all day.'

'I am sorry for it,' said Ralph, 'for I wanted particularly to speak to you about business—about my marriage, in fact.'

'Well! speak away, I'm as clear-headed as any man, if that's what you mean?'

Ralph bowed, a little contemptuously.

'What I wanted to say was, that I am anxious to have all things arranged for my marriage in August. Ellinor is so much better now; in fact, so strong, that I think we may reckon upon her standing the change to a London life pretty well.'

Mr Wilkins stared at him rather blankly; but did not immediately speak.

'Of course I may have the deeds drawn up in which, as by previous arrangement, you advance a certain portion of Ellinor's fortune for the purposes therein to be assigned; as we settled last year when I hoped to have been married in August?'

A thought flitted through Mr Wilkins's confused brain that he should find it impossible to produce the thousands required without having recourse to the money-lenders, who were already making difficulties, and charging him usurious interest for the advances they had lately made; and he unwisely tried to obtain a diminution in the sum he had originally proposed to give Ellinor. 'Unwisely,' because he might have read Ralph's character better than to suppose he would easily consent to any diminution without good and sufficient reason being given; or without some promise of compensating advantages in the future for the present sacrifice asked from him. But, perhaps, Mr Wilkins, dulled as he was by wine, thought he could allege a good and sufficient reason, for he said:

'You must not be hard upon me, Ralph. That promise was made before—before I exactly knew the state of my affairs!'

'Before Dunster's disappearance, in fact,' said Mr Corbet, fixing his steady penetrating eyes on Mr Wilkins's countenance.

'Yes—exactly—before Dunster's ——' mumbled out Mr Wilkins, red and confused, and not finishing his sentence.

'By the way,' said Ralph (for with careful carelessness of manner he thought he could extract something of the real nature of the impending disgrace from his companion, in the state in which he then was; and if he only knew more about this danger he could guard against it; guard others: perhaps himself). 'By the way, have you ever heard anything of Dunster since he went off to—America, isn't it thought?'

He was startled beyond his power of self-control by the instantaneous change in Mr Wilkins which his question produced. Both started up; Mr Wilkins white, shaking, and trying to say something, but unable to form a sensible sentence.

'Good God! sir, what is the matter?' said Ralph, alarmed at these signs of physical suffering.

Mr Wilkins sat down, and repelled his nearer approach without speaking.

'It is nothing, only this headache which shoots through me at times. Don't look at me, sir, in that way. It is very unpleasant to find another man's eyes perpetually fixed upon you.'

'I beg your pardon,' said Ralph, coldly; his short-lived sympathy thus repulsed, giving way to his curiosity. But he waited for a minute or two without daring to renew the conversation at the point where they had stopped: whether interrupted by bodily or mental discomfort on the part of his companion he was not quite sure. While he hesitated how to begin again on the subject, Mr Wilkins pulled the bottle of brandy to himself and filled his glass again, tossing off the spirit as if it had been water. Then he tried to look Mr Corbet full in the face, with a stare as pertinacious as he could make it, but very different from the keen observant gaze which was trying to read him through.

'What were we talking about?' said Ralph, at length, with the most natural air in the world, just as if he had really been forgetful of some half-discussed subject of interest.

'Of what you'd a d——d deal better hold your tongue about,' growled out Mr Wilkins, in a surly thick voice.

'Sir!' said Ralph, starting to his feet with real passion at being so addressed by 'Wilkins the attorney.'

'Yes,' continued the latter, 'I'll manage my own affairs, and allow of no meddling and no questioning. I said so once before, and I was not minded, and bad came of it; and now I say it again. And if you're to come here and put impertinent questions, and stare at me as you've been doing this half-hour past, why, the sooner you leave this house the better!'

Ralph half turned to take him at his word, and go at once; but then he 'gave Ellinor another chance,' as he worded it in his thoughts; but it was in no spirit of conciliation that he said:

'You've taken too much of that stuff, sir. You don't know what you're saying. If you did, I should leave your house at once, never to return.'

'You think so, do you?' said Mr Wilkins, trying to stand up, and look dignified and sober. 'I say, sir, that if you ever venture again to talk and look as you have done tonight, why, sir, I will ring the bell and have you shown the door by my servants. So now you're warned, my fine fellow!' He sat down, laughing a foolish tipsy laugh of triumph. In another minute his arm was held firmly but gently by Ralph.

'Listen, Mr Wilkins!' he said, in a low hoarse voice. 'You shall never have to say to me twice what you have said tonight. Henceforward we are as strangers to each other. As to Ellinor'—his tones softened a little, and he sighed in spite of himself—'I do not think we should have been happy. I believe our engagement was formed when we were too young to know our own minds, but I would have done my duty and kept to my word; but you, sir, have yourself severed the connection between us by your insolence tonight. I, to be turned out of your house by your servants!—I, a Corbet, of Westley, who would not submit to such threats from a peer of the realm, let him be ever so drunk!' He was out of the room, almost out of the house, before he had spoken the last words.

Mr Wilkins sat still, first fiercely angry, then astonished, and lastly dismayed into sobriety. 'Corbet, Corbet! Ralph!' he called in vain; then he got up and went to the door, opened it, looked into the fully-lighted hall; all was so quiet there that he could hear the quiet voices of the women in the drawing-room talking together. He thought for a moment, went to the hat-stand, and missed Ralph's low-crowned straw hat.

Then he sat down once more in the dining-room, and endeavoured to make out exactly what had passed; but he could not believe that Mr Corbet had come to any enduring or final resolution to break off his engagement, and he had almost reasoned himself back into his former state of indignation at impertinence and injury, when Ellinor came in, pale, hurried, and anxious.

'Papa! what does this mean?' said she, putting an open note into his hand. He took up his glasses, but his hand shook so that he could hardly read. The note was from the parsonage, to Ellinor; only three lines sent by Mr Ness's servant, who had come to fetch Mr Corbet's things. He had written three lines with some consideration for Ellinor, even when he was in his first flush of anger against her father, and it must be confessed of relief at his own freedom, thus brought about by the act of another, and not of his own working out, which partly saved his conscience. The note ran thus:

'DEAR ELLINOR,—Words have passed between your father and me which have obliged me to leave his house, I fear, never to return to it. I will write more fully tomorrow. But do not grieve too much, for I am not, and never have been, good enough for you. God bless you, my dearest Nelly, though I call you so for the last time.—R.C.'

'Papa, what is it?' Ellinor cried, clasping her hands together, as her father sat silent, vacantly gazing into the fire, after finishing the note.

'I don't know!' said he, looking up at her piteously; 'it's the world, I think. Everything goes wrong with me and mine: it went wrong before THAT night—so it can't be that, can it, Ellinor?'

'Oh, papa!' said she, kneeling down by him, her face hidden on his breast.

He put one arm languidly round her. 'I used to read of Orestes and the Furies* at Eton when I was a boy, and I thought it was all a heathen fiction. Poor little motherless girl!' said he, laying his other hand on her head, with the caressing gesture he had been accustomed to use when she had been a little child. 'Did you love him so very dearly, Nelly?' he whispered, his cheek against her; 'for somehow of late he has not seemed to me good enough for thee. He has got an inkling that something has gone wrong; and he was very inquisitive—I may say, he questioned me in a relentless kind of way.'

'Oh, papa, it was my doing, I am afraid. I said something long ago about possible disgrace.'

He pushed her away; he stood up, and looked at her with the eyes dilated, half in fear, half in fierceness, of an animal at bay; he did not heed that his abrupt movement had almost thrown her prostrate on the ground.

'You, Ellinor! You—you ——'

'Oh, darling father, listen!' said she, creeping to his knees, and clasping them with her hands. 'I said it, as if it were a possible case, of someone else—last August—but he immediately applied it, and asked me if it was over me the disgrace, or shame—I forget the words we used—hung; and what could I say?'

'Anything—anything to put him off the scent. God help me, I am a lost man, betrayed by my child!'

Ellinor let go his knees, and covered her face. Everyone stabbed at that poor heart. In a minute or so her father spoke again.

'I don't mean what I say. I often don't mean it now. Ellinor, you must forgive me, my child!' He stooped, and lifted her up, and sat down, taking her on his knee, and smoothing her hair off her hot forehead. 'Remember, child, how very miserable I am, and have forgiveness for me. He had none, and yet he must have seen I had been drinking.'

'Drinking, papa!' said Ellinor, raising her head, and looking at him with sorrowful surprise.

'Yes. I drink now to try and forget,' said he, blushing and confused.

'Oh, how miserable we are!' cried Ellinor, bursting into tears—'how very miserable! It seems almost as if God had forgotten to comfort us!'

'Hush! hush!' said he. 'Your mother said once she did so pray that you might grow up religious; you must be religious, child, because she prayed for it so often. Poor Lettice, how glad I am that you are dead!' Here he began to cry like a child. Ellinor comforted him with kisses rather than words. He pushed her away, after a while, and said, sharply: 'How much does he know? I must make sure of that. How much did you tell him, Ellinor?'

'Nothing—nothing, indeed, papa, but what I told you just now!'

'Tell it me again—the exact words!'

'I will, as well as I can; but it was last August. I only said, "Was it right for a woman to marry, knowing that disgrace hung over her, and keeping her lover in ignorance of it?"'

'That was all, you are sure?'

'Yes. He immediately applied the case to me—to ourselves.'

'And he never wanted to know what was the nature of the threatened disgrace?'

'Yes, he did.'

'And you told him?'

'No, not a word more. He referred to the subject again today, in the shrubbery; but I told him nothing more. You quite believe me, don't you, papa?'

He pressed her to him, but did not speak. Then he took the note up again, and read it with as much care and attention as he could collect in his agitated state of mind.

'Nelly,' said he, at length, 'he says true; he is not good enough for thee. He shrinks from the thought of the disgrace. Thou must stand alone, and bear the sins of thy father.'*

He shook so much as he said this, that Ellinor had to put any suffering of her own on one side, and try to confine her thoughts to the necessity of getting her father immediately up to bed. She sat by him till he went to sleep and she could leave him, and go to her own room, to forgetfulness and rest, if she could find those priceless blessings.

CHAPTER X

MR CORBET was so well known at the parsonage by the two old servants, that he had no difficulty, on reaching it, after his departure from Ford Bank, in having the spare bed-chamber made ready for him, late as it was, and in the absence of the master, who had taken a little holiday, now that Lent and Easter were over, for the purpose of fishing. While his room was getting ready, Ralph sent for his clothes, and by the same messenger he despatched the little note to Ellinor. But there was the letter he had promised her in it still to be written; and it was almost his night's employment to say enough, yet not too much; for, as he expressed it to himself, he was half way over the stream, and it would be folly to turn back, for he had given nearly as much pain both to himself and Ellinor by this time as he should do by making the separation final. Besides, after Mr Wilkins's speeches that evening—but he was candid enough to acknowledge that, bad and offensive as they had been, if they had stood alone they might have been condoned.

His letter ran as follows:

'DEAREST ELLINOR, for dearest you are, and I think will ever be, my judgment has consented to a step which is giving me great pain, greater than you will readily believe. I am convinced that it is better that we should part; for circumstances have occurred since we formed our engagement which, although I am unaware of their exact nature, I can see weigh heavily upon you, and have materially affected your father's behaviour. Nay, I think, after tonight, I may almost say have entirely altered his feelings towards me. What these circumstances are I am ignorant, any further than that I know from your own admission, that they may lead to some future disgrace. Now, it may be my fault, it may be in my temperament, to be anxious, above all things earthly, to obtain and possess a high reputation. I can only say that it is so, and leave you to blame me for my weakness as much as you like. But anything that might come in between me and this object would, I own, be ill tolerated by me; the very dread of such an obstacle intervening would paralyse me. I should become irritable, and, deep as my affection is, and always must be, towards you, I could not promise you a happy, peaceful life. I should be perpetually haunted by the idea of what might happen in the way of discovery and shame. I am the more convinced of this from my observation of your father's altered character—an alteration which I trace back to the time when I conjecture that the secret affairs took place to which you have alluded. In short, it is for your sake, my dear Ellinor, even more than for my own, that I feel compelled to affix a final meaning to the words which your father addressed to me last night, when he desired me to leave his house for ever. God bless you, my Ellinor, for the last time my Ellinor. Try to forget as soon as you can the unfortunate tie which has bound you for a time to one so unsuitable—I believe I ought to say so unworthy of you—as—RALPH CORBET.'

Ellinor was making breakfast when this letter was given her. According to the wont of the servants of the respective households of the parsonage and Ford Bank, the man asked if there was any answer. It was only custom; for he had not been desired to do so. Ellinor went to the window to read her letter; the man waiting all the time respectfully for her reply. She went to the writing-table, and wrote:

'It is all right—quite right. I ought to have thought of it all last August. I do not think you will forget me easily, but I entreat you never at any future time to blame yourself. I hope you will be happy and successful. I suppose I must never write to you again: but I shall always pray for you. Papa was very sorry last night for having spoken angrily to you. You must forgive him—there is great need for forgiveness in this world.—ELLINOR.'

She kept putting down thought after thought, just to prolong the last pleasure of writing to him. She sealed the note and gave it to the man. Then she sat down and waited for Miss Monro, who had gone to bed on the previous night without awaiting Ellinor's return from the dining-room.

'I am late, my dear,' said Miss Monro, on coming down, 'but I have a bad headache, and I knew you had a pleasant companion.' Then, looking round, she perceived Ralph's absence.

'Mr Corbet not down yet!' she exclaimed. And then Ellinor had to tell her the outline of the facts so soon likely to be made public; that Mr Corbet and she had determined to break off their engagement; and that Mr Corbet had accordingly betaken himself to the parsonage; and that she did not expect him to return to Ford Bank. Miss Monro's astonishment was unbounded. She kept going over and over all the little circumstances she had noticed during the last visit, only on yesterday, in fact, which she could not reconcile with the notion that the two, apparently so much attached to each other but a few hours before, were now to be for ever separated and estranged. Ellinor sickened under the torture; which yet seemed like torture in a dream, from which there must come an awakening and a relief. She felt as if she could not bear any more; yet there was more to bear. Her father, as it turned out, was very ill, and had been so all night long; he had evidently had some kind of attack on the brain, whether apoplectic or paralytic it was for the doctors to decide. In the hurry and anxiety of this day of misery succeeding to misery, she almost forgot to wonder whether Ralph were still at the parsonage—still in Hamley; it was not till the evening visit of the physician that she learnt that he had been seen by Dr Moore as he was taking his place in the morning mail* to London. Dr Moore alluded to his name as to a thought that would cheer and comfort the fragile girl during her night-watch by her father's bedside. But Miss Monro stole out after the doctor to warn him off the subject for the future, crying bitterly over the forlorn position of her darling as she spoke—crying as Ellinor had never yet been able to cry: though all the time, in the pride of her sex, she was endeavouring to persuade the doctor it was entirely Ellinor's doing, and the wisest and best thing she could have done, as he was not good enough for her, only a poor barrister struggling for a livelihood. Like many other kindhearted people, she fell into the blunder of lowering the moral character of those whom it is their greatest wish to exalt. But Dr Moore knew Ellinor too well to believe the whole of what Miss Monro said; she would never act from interested motives, and was all the more likely to cling to a man because he was down, and unsuccessful. No! there had been a lovers' quarrel; and it could not have happened at a sadder time.

Before the June roses were in full bloom, Mr Wilkins was dead. He had left his daughter to the guardianship of Mr Ness by some will made years ago; but Mr Ness had caught a rheumatic fever with his Easter fishings, and been unable to be moved home from the little Welsh inn where he had been staying when he was taken ill. Since his last attack, Mr Wilkins's mind had been much affected; he often talked strangely and wildly; but he had rare intervals of quietness and full possession of his senses. At one of these times he must have written a half-finished pencil note, which his nurse found under his pillow after his death, and brought to Ellinor. Through her tear-blinded eyes she read the weak, faltering words:

'I am very ill. I sometimes think I shall never get better, so I wish to ask your pardon for what I said the night before I was taken ill. I am afraid my anger made mischief between you and Ellinor, but I think you will forgive a dying man. If you will come back and let all be as it used to be, I will make any apology you may require. If I go, she will be so very friendless; and I have looked to you to care for her ever since you first ——' Then came some illegible and incoherent writing, ending with, 'From my death-bed I adjure you to stand her friend; I will beg pardon on my knees for anything ——'

And there strength had failed; the paper and pencil had been laid aside to be resumed at some time when the brain was clearer, the hand stronger. Ellinor kissed the letter, reverently folded it up, and laid it among her sacred treasures, by her mother's half-finished sewing, and a little curl of her baby sister's golden hair.

Mr Johnson, who had been one of the trustees for Mrs Wilkins's marriage-settlement, a respectable solicitor in the county town, and Mr Ness, had been appointed executors of his will, and guardians to Ellinor. The will itself had been made several years before, when he imagined himself the possessor of a handsome fortune, the bulk of which he bequeathed to his only child. By her mother's marriage-settlement, Ford Bank was held in trust for the children of the marriage; the trustees being Sir Frank Holster and Mr Johnson. There were legacies to his executors; a small annuity to Miss Monro, with the expression of a hope that it might be arranged for her to continue living with Ellinor as long as the latter remained unmarried; all his servants were remembered, Dixon especially, and most liberally.

What remained of the handsome fortune once possessed by the testator? The executors asked in vain; there was nothing. They could hardly make out what had become of it, in such utter confusion were all the accounts, both personal and official. Mr Johnson was hardly restrained by his compassion for the orphan from throwing up the executorship in disgust. Mr Ness roused himself from his scholar-like abstraction to labour at the examination of books, parchments, and papers, for Ellinor's sake. Sir Frank Holster professed himself only a trustee for Ford Bank.

Meanwhile she went on living at Ford Bank, quite unconscious of the state of her father's affairs, but sunk into a deep, plaintive melancholy, which affected her looks and the tones of her voice in such a manner as to distress Miss Monro exceedingly. It was not that the good lady did not quite acknowledge the great cause her pupil had for grieving—deserted by her lover, her father dead—but that she could not bear the outward signs of how much these sorrows had told on Ellinor. Her love for the poor girl was infinitely distressed by seeing the daily wasting away, the constant heavy depression of spirits, and she grew impatient of the continual pain of sympathy. If Miss Monro could have done something to relieve Ellinor of her woe she would have been less inclined to scold her for giving way to it.

The time came when Miss Monro could act; and after that, there was no more irritation on her part. When all hope of Ellinor's having anything beyond the house and grounds of Ford Bank was gone; when it was proved that of all the legacies bequeathed by Mr Wilkins not one farthing could ever be paid; when it came to be a question how far the beautiful pictures and other objects of art in the house were not legally the property of unsatisfied creditors, the state of her father's affairs was communicated to Ellinor as delicately as Mr Ness knew how.

She was drooping over her work—she always drooped now—and she left off sewing to listen to him, leaning her head on the arm which rested on the table. She did not speak when he had ended his statement. She was silent for whole minutes afterwards; he went on speaking out of very agitation and awkwardness.

'It was all the rascal Dunster's doing, I've no doubt,' said he, trying to account for the entire loss of Mr Wilkins's fortune.

To his surprise she lifted up her white stony face, and said slowly and faintly, but with almost solemn calmness:

'Mr Ness, you must never allow Mr Dunster to be blamed for this!'

'My dear Ellinor, there can be no doubt about it. Your father himself always referred to the losses he had sustained by Dunster's disappearance.'

Ellinor covered her face with her hands. 'God forgive us all,' she said, and relapsed into the old unbearable silence. Mr Ness had undertaken to discuss her future plans with her, and he was obliged to go on.

'Now, my dear child—I have known you since you were quite a little girl, you know—we must try not to give way to feeling'—he himself was choking; she was quite quiet—'but think what is to be done. You will have the rent of this house; and we have a very good offer for it—a tenant on lease of seven years at a hundred and twenty pounds a year ——'

'I will never let this house,' said she, standing up suddenly, and as if defying him.

'Not let Ford Bank! Why? I don't understand it—I can't have been clear—Ellinor, the rent of this house is all you will have to live on!'

'I can't help it, I can't leave this house. Oh, Mr Ness, I can't leave this house.'

'My dear child, you shall not be hurried—I know how hardly all these things are coming upon you (and I wish I had never seen Corbet, with all my heart I do!)'—this was almost to himself, but she must have heard it, for she quivered all over—'but leave this house you must. You must eat, and the rent of this house must pay for your food; you must dress, and there is nothing but the rent to clothe you. I will gladly have you to stay at the parsonage as long as ever you like; but, in fact, the negotiations with Mr Osbaldistone, the gentleman who offers to take the house, are nearly completed ——'

'It is my house!' said Ellinor, fiercely. 'I know it is settled on me.'

'No, my dear. It is held in trust for you by Sir Frank Holster and Mr Johnson; you to receive all moneys and benefits accruing from it'—he spoke gently, for he almost thought her head was turned—'but you remember you are not of age, and Mr Johnson and I have full power.'

Ellinor sat down, helpless.

'Leave me,' she said, at length. 'You are very kind, but you don't know all. I cannot stand any more talking now,' she added faintly.

Mr Ness bent over her and kissed her forehead, and withdrew without another word. He went to Miss Monro.

'Well! and how did you find her?' was her first inquiry, after the usual greetings had passed between them. 'It is really quite sad to see how she gives way; I speak to her, and speak to her, and tell her how she is neglecting all her duties, and it does no good.'

'She has had to bear a still further sorrow today,' said Mr Ness. 'On the part of Mr Johnson and myself I have a very painful duty to perform to you as well as to her. Mr Wilkins has died insolvent. I grieve to say there is no hope of your ever receiving any of your annuity!'

Miss Monro looked very blank. Many happy little visions faded away in those few moments; then she roused up and said, 'I am but forty;* I have a good fifteen years of work in me left yet, thank God. Insolvent! Do you mean he has left no money?'

'Not a farthing. The creditors may be thankful if they are fully paid.'

'And Ellinor?'

'Ellinor will have the rent of this house, which is hers by right of her mother's settlement, to live on.'

'How much will that be?'

'One hundred and twenty pounds.'

Miss Monro's lips went into a form prepared for whistling. Mr Ness continued:

'She is at present unwilling enough to leave this house, poor girl. It is but natural; but she has no power in the matter, even were there any other course open to her. I can only say how glad, how honoured, I shall feel by as long a visit as you and she can be prevailed upon to pay me at the parsonage.'

'Where is Mr Corbet?' said Miss Monro.

'I do not know. After breaking off his engagement he wrote me a long letter, explanatory, as he called it; exculpatory, as I termed it. I wrote back, curtly enough, saying that I regretted the breaking off of an intercourse which had always been very pleasant to me, but that he must be aware that, with my intimacy with the family at Ford Bank, it would be both awkward and unpleasant to all parties if he and I remained on our previous footing. Who is that going past the window? Ellinor riding?'

Miss Monro went to the window. 'Yes! I am thankful to see her on horseback again. It was only this morning I advised her to have a ride!'

'Poor Dixon! he will suffer, too; his legacy can no more be paid than the others; and it is not many young ladies who will be as content to have so old-fashioned a groom riding after them as Ellinor seems to be.'

As soon as Mr Ness had left, Miss Monro went to her desk and wrote a long letter to some friends she had at the cathedral town of East Chester, where she had spent some happy years of her former life. Her thoughts had gone back to this time even while Mr Ness had been speaking; for it was there her father had lived, and it was after his death that her cares in search of a subsistence had begun. But the recollections of the peaceful years spent there were stronger than the remembrance of the weeks of sorrow and care; and, while Ellinor's marriage had seemed a probable event, she had made many a little plan of returning to her native place, and obtaining what daily teaching she could there meet with, and the friends to whom she was now writing had promised her their aid. She thought that as Ellinor had to leave Ford Bank, a home at a distance might be more agreeable to her, and she went on to plan that they should live together, if possible, on her earnings, and the small income that would be Ellinor's. Miss Monro loved her pupil so dearly, that, if her own pleasure only were to be consulted, this projected life would be more agreeable to her than if Mr Wilkins's legacy had set her in independence, with Ellinor away from her, married, and with interests in which her former governess had but little part.

As soon as Mr Ness had left her, Ellinor rang the bell, and startled the servant who answered it by her sudden sharp desire to have the horses at the door as soon as possible, and to tell Dixon to be ready to go out with her.

She felt that she must speak to him, and in her nervous state she wanted to be out on the free broad common, where no one could notice or remark their talk. It was long since she had ridden, and much wonder was excited by the sudden movement in kitchen and stable-yard. But Dixon went gravely about his work of preparation, saying nothing.

They rode pretty hard till they reached Monk's Heath, six or seven miles away from Hamley. Ellinor had previously determined that here she would talk over the plan Mr Ness had proposed to her with Dixon, and he seemed to understand her without any words passing between them. When she reined in he rode up to her, and met the gaze of her sad eyes with sympathetic, wistful silence.

'Dixon,' said she, 'they say I must leave Ford Bank.'

'I was afeared on it, from all I've heerd say i' the town since the master's death.'

'Then you've heard—then you know—that papa has left hardly any money—my poor dear Dixon, you won't have your legacy, and I never thought of that before!'

'Never heed, never heed,' said he, eagerly; 'I couldn't have touched it if it had been there, for the taking it would ha' seemed too like ——' Blood-money, he was going to say, but he stopped in time. She guessed the meaning, though not the word he would have used.

'No, not that,' said she; 'his will was dated years before. But oh, Dixon, what must I do? They will make me leave Ford Bank, I see. I think the trustees have half let it already.'

'But you'll have the rent on't, I reckon?' asked he, anxiously.

'I've many a time heerd 'em say as it was settled on the missus first, and then on you.'

'Oh, yes, it is not that; but, you know, under the beech-tree ——'

'Ay!' said he, heavily. 'It's been oftentimes on my mind, waking, and I think there's ne'er a night as I don't dream of it.'

'But how can I leave it?' Ellinor cried. 'They may do a hundred things—may dig up the shrubbery. Oh! Dixon, I feel as if it was sure to be found out! Oh! Dixon, I cannot bear any more blame on papa—it will kill me—and such a dreadful thing, too!'

Dixon's face fell into the lines of habitual pain that it had always assumed of late years whenever he was thinking or remembering anything.

'They must ne'er ha' reason to speak ill of the dead, that's for certain,' said he. 'The Wilkinses have been respected in Hamley all my lifetime, and all my father's before me, and—surely, missy, there's ways and means of tying tenants up from alterations both in the house and out of it, and I'd beg the trustees, or whatever they's called, to be very particular, if I was you, and not have a thing touched either in the house, or the gardens, or the meadows, or the stables. I think, wi' a word from you, they'd maybe keep me on i' the stables, and I could look after things a bit; and the Day o' Judgment will come at last, when all our secrets will be made known wi'out our having the trouble and the shame o' telling 'em. I'm getting rayther tired o' this world, Miss Ellinor.'

'Don't talk so,' said Ellinor, tenderly. 'I know how sad it is, but, oh! remember how I shall want a friend when you're gone, to advise me as you have done today. You're not feeling ill, Dixon, are you?' she continued, anxiously.

'No! I'm hearty enough, and likely for t' live. Father was eighty-one, and mother above the seventies, when they died. It's only my heart as is got to feel so heavy; and as for that matter, so is yours, I'll be bound. And it's a comfort to us both if we can serve him as is dead by any care of ours, for he were such a bright handsome lad, with such a cheery face, as never should ha' known shame.'

They rode on without much more speaking. Ellinor was

silently planning for Dixon, and he, not caring to look forward to the future, was bringing up before his fancy the time, thirty years ago, when he had first entered the elder Mr Wilkins's service as stable-lad, and pretty Molly, the scullery-maid, was his daily delight. Pretty Molly lay buried in Hamley churchyard, and few living, except Dixon, could have gone straight to her grave.

CHAPTER XI

In a few days Miss Monro obtained a most satisfactory reply to her letter of inquiries as to whether a daily governess could find employment in East Chester. For once, the application seemed to have come just at the right time. The canons* were most of them married men, with young families; those at present in residence welcomed the idea of such instruction as Miss Monro could offer for their children, and could almost answer for their successors in office. This was a great step gained. Miss Monro, the daughter of the precentor* to this very cathedral, had a secret unwillingness to being engaged as a teacher by any wealthy tradesman there; but, to be received into the canons' families in almost any capacity, was like going home. Moreover, besides the empty honour of the thing, there were many small pieces of patronage in the gift of the chapter*—such as a small house opening on to the Close, which had formerly belonged to the verger, but which was now vacant, and was offered to Miss Monro at a nominal rent.

Ellinor had once more sunk into her old depressed passive state; Mr Ness and Miss Monro, modest and undecided as they both were in general, had to fix and arrange everything for her. Her great interest seemed to be in the old servant Dixon, and her great pleasure to lie in seeing him, and talking over old times; so her two friends talked about her, little knowing what a bitter, stinging pain her 'pleasure' was. In vain Ellinor tried to plan how they could take Dixon with them to East Chester. If he had been a woman it would have been a feasible step; but they were only to keep one servant, and Dixon, capable and versatile as he was, would not do for that servant. All this was what passed through Ellinor's mind: it is still a question whether Dixon would have felt his love of his native place, with all its associations and remembrances, or his love for Ellinor, the stronger. But he was not put to the proof; he was only told that he must leave, and, seeing Ellinor's extreme grief at the idea of their separation, he set himself to comfort her by every means in his power, reminding her, with tender choice of words, how necessary it was that he should remain on the spot, in Mr Osbaldistone's service, in order to frustrate, by any small influence he might have, every project of alteration in the garden that contained the dreadful secret. He persisted in this view, though Ellinor repeated, with pertinacious anxiety, the care which Mr Johnson had taken, in drawing up the lease, to provide against any change or alteration being made in the present disposition of the house or grounds.

People in general were rather astonished at the eagerness Miss Wilkins showed to sell all the Ford Bank furniture. Even Miss Monro was a little scandalized at this want of sentiment, although she said nothing about it; indeed justified the step, by telling everyone how wisely Ellinor was acting, as the large, handsome tables and chairs would be very much out of place and keeping with the small, oddly-shaped rooms of their future home in East Chester Close. None knew how strong was the instinct of self-preservation, it may almost be called, which impelled Ellinor to shake off, at any cost of present pain, the incubus of a terrible remembrance. She wanted to go into an unhaunted dwelling in a free, unknown country—she felt as if it was her only chance of sanity. Sometimes she thought her senses would not hold together till the time when all these arrangements were ended. But she did not speak to anyone about her feelings, poor child—to whom could she speak on the subject but to Dixon? Nor did she define them to herself. All she knew was, that she was as nearly going mad as possible; and if she did, she feared that she might betray her father's guilt. All this time she never cried, or varied from her dull, passive demeanour. And they were blessed tears of relief that she shed when Miss Monro, herself weeping bitterly, told her to put her head out of the post-chaise window, for at the next turning of the road they would catch the last glimpse of Hamley church spire.

Late one October evening, Ellinor had her first sight of East Chester Close, where she was to pass the remainder of her life. Miss Monro had been backwards and forwards between Hamley and East Chester more than once, while Ellinor remained at the parsonage; so she had not only the pride of proprietorship in the whole of the beautiful city, but something of the desire of hospitably welcoming Ellinor to their joint future home.

'Look! the fly must take us a long round, because of our luggage; but behind these high old walls are the canons' gardens. That high-pitched roof, with the clumps of stonecrop on the walls near it, is Canon Wilson's, whose four little girls I am to teach. Hark! the great cathedral clock. How proud I used to be of its great boom when I was a child! I thought all the other church clocks in the town sounded so shrill and poor after that, which I considered mine especially. There are rooks flying home to the elms in the Close. I wonder if they are the same that used to be there when I was a girl. They say the rook is a very long-lived bird, and I feel as if I could swear to the way they are cawing. Ay, you may smile, Ellinor, but I understand now those lines of Gray's you used to say so prettily—

> I feel the gales that from ye blow,
> A momentary bless bestow,
> And breathe a second spring.*

Now, dear, you must get out. This flagged walk leads to our front door; but our back rooms, which are the pleasantest, look on to the Close, and the cathedral, and the lime-tree walk, and the deanery, and the rookery.'

It was a mere slip of a house; the kitchen being wisely placed close to the front door, and so reserving the pretty view for the little dining-room, out of which a glass-door opened into a small walled-in garden, which had again an entrance into the Close. Upstairs was a bedroom to the front, which Miss Monro had taken for herself, because, as she said, she had old associations with the back of every house in the High Street, while Ellinor mounted to the pleasant chamber above the tiny drawing-room, both of which looked on to the vast and solemn cathedral, and the peaceful dignified Close. East Chester Cathedral is Norman, with a low, massive tower, a grand, majestic nave, and a choir full of stately historic tombs. The whole city is so quiet and decorous a place, that the perpetual daily chants and hymns of praise seemed to sound far and wide over the roofs of the houses. Ellinor soon became a regular attendant at all the morning and evening services. The sense of worship calmed and soothed her aching weary heart, and to be punctual to the cathedral hours she roused and exerted herself, when probably nothing else would have been sufficient to this end.

By-and-by Miss Monro formed many acquaintances; she picked up, or was picked up by, old friends, and the descendants of old friends. The grave and kindly canons, whose children she taught, called upon her with their wives, and talked over the former deans and chapters, of whom she had both a personal and traditional knowledge, and as they walked away they talked about her silent, delicate-looking friend Miss Wilkins, and perhaps planned some little present out of their fruitful garden or bounteous stores, which should make Miss Monro's table a little more tempting to one apparently so frail as Ellinor, for the household was always spoken of as belonging to Miss Monro, the active and prominent person. By-and-by, Ellinor herself won her way to their hearts, not by words or deeds, but by her sweet looks, and meek demeanour, as they marked her regular attendance at cathedral service: and when they heard of her constant visits to a certain parochial school, and of her being sometimes seen carrying a little covered basin to the cottages of the poor, they began to try, and tempt her with more urgent words, to accompany Miss Monro in her frequent tea-drinkings at their houses. The old dean, that courteous gentleman and good Christian, had early become great friends with Ellinor. He would watch at the windows of his great vaulted library till he saw her emerge from the garden into the Close, and then open the deanery door, and join her, she softly adjusting the measure of her pace to his. The time of his departure from East Chester became a great blank in her life, although she would never accept, or allow Miss Monro to accept, his repeated invitations to go and pay him a visit at his country-place. Indeed, having once tasted comparative peace again in East Chester Cathedral Close, it seemed as though she was afraid of ever venturing out of those calm precincts. All Mr Ness's invitations to visit him at his parsonage at Hamley were declined, although he was welcomed at Miss Monro's, on the occasion of his annual visit, by every means in their power. He slept at one of the canon's vacant houses, and lived with his two friends, who made a yearly festivity, to the best of their means, in his honour, inviting such of the cathedral clergy as were in residence; or, if they failed, condescending to the town clergy. Their friends knew well that no presents were so acceptable as those sent while Mr Ness was with them; and from the dean, who would send them a hamper of choice fruit and flowers from Oxton Park, down to the curate, who worked in the same schools as Ellinor, and who was a great fisher, and caught splendid trout—all did their best to help them to give a welcome to the only visitor they ever had. The only visitor they ever had, as far as the stately gentry knew. There was one, however, who came as often as his master could give him a holiday long enough to undertake a journey to so distant a place; but few knew of his being a guest at Miss Monro's, though his welcome there was not less hearty than Mr Ness's—this was Dixon. Ellinor had convinced him that he could give her no greater pleasure at any time than by allowing her to frank* him to and from East Chester. Whenever he came they were together the greater part of every day; she taking him hither and thither to see all the sights that she thought would interest or please him; but they spoke very little to each other during all this companionship. Miss Monro had much more to say to him. She questioned him right and left whenever Ellinor was out of the room. She learnt that the house at Ford Bank was splendidly furnished, and no money spared on the garden; that the eldest Miss Hanbury was very well married; that Brown had succeeded to Jones in the haberdasher's shop. Then she hesitated a little before making her next inquiry:

'I suppose Mr Corbet never comes to the parsonage now?'

'No, not he. I don't think as how Mr Ness would have him; but they write letters to each other by times. Old Job—you'll recollect old Job, ma'am, he that gardened for Mr Ness, and waited in the parlour when there was company—did say as one day he heerd them speaking about Mr Corbet; and he's a grand counsellor now—one of them as goes about at assize-time, and speaks in a wig.'

'A barrister you mean,' said Miss Monro.

'Ay; and he's something more than that, though I can't rightly remember what.'

Ellinor could have told them both. They had *The Times* lent to them on the second day after publication by one of their friends in the Close, and Ellinor, watching till Miss Monro's eyes were otherwise engaged, always turned with trembling hands and a beating heart to the reports of the various courts of law. In them she found—at first rarely—the name she sought for, the name she dwelt upon, as if every letter were a study. Mr Losh and Mr Duncombe appeared for the plaintiff, Mr Smythe and Mr Corbet for the defendant. In a year or two that name appeared more frequently, and generally took precedence of the other, whatever it might be; then on special occasions his speeches were reported at full length, as if his words were accounted weighty; and by-and-by she saw that he had been appointed a Queen's Counsel.* And this was all she ever heard or saw about him; his once familiar name never passed her lips except in hurried whispers to Dixon, when he came to stay with them. Ellinor had had no idea when she parted from Mr Corbet how total the separation between them was henceforward to be, so much seemed left unfinished, unexplained. It was so difficult, at first, to break herself of the habit of constant mental reference to him; and for many a long year she kept thinking that surely some kind fortune would bring them together again, and all this heart-sickness and melancholy estrangement from each other would then seem to both only as an ugly dream that had passed away in the morning light.

The dean was an old man, but there was a canon who was older still, and whose death had been expected by many, and speculated upon by some, anytime for ten years at least. Canon Holdsworth was too old to show active kindness to anyone; the good dean's life was full of thoughtful and benevolent deeds. But he was taken, and the other left. Ellinor looked out at the vacant deanery with tearful eyes, the last thing at night, the first in the morning. But it is pretty nearly the same with church dignitaries as with kings; the dean is dead, long live the dean! A clergyman from a distant county was appointed, and all the Close was astir to learn and hear every particular connected with him. Luckily he came in at the tag-end of one of the noble families in the peerage; so, at any rate, all his future associates could learn with tolerable certainty that he was forty-two years of age, married, and with eight daughters and one son. The deanery, formerly so quiet and sedate a dwelling of the one old man, was now to be filled with noise and merriment. Iron railings were being placed before three windows, evidently to be the nursery. In the summer publicity of open windows and doors, the sound of the busy carpenters was perpetually heard all over the Close; and by-and-by waggon-loads of furniture and carriage-loads of people began to arrive. Neither Miss Monro nor Ellinor felt themselves of sufficient importance or station to call on the newcomers, but they were as well acquainted with the proceedings of the family as if they had been in daily intercourse; they knew that the eldest Miss Beauchamp was seventeen, and very pretty, only one shoulder was higher than the other; that she was dotingly fond of dancing, and talked a great deal in a *tête-à-tête*, but not much if her mamma was by, and never opened her lips at all if the dean was in the room; that the next sister was wonderfully clever, and was supposed to know all the governess could teach her, and to have private lessons in Greek and mathematics from her father; and so on down to the little boy at the preparatory school and the baby girl in arms. Moreover, Miss Monro, at any rate, could have stood an examination as to the number of servants at the deanery, their division of work, and the hours of their meals. Presently, a very beautiful, haughty-looking young lady made her appearance in the Close, and in the dean's pew. She was said to be his niece, the orphan daughter of his brother, General Beauchamp, come to East Chester to reside for the necessary time before her marriage, which was to be performed in the cathedral by her uncle, the new dignitary. But as callers at the deanery did not see this beautiful bride-elect, and as the Beauchamps had not as yet fallen into habits of intimacy with any of their new acquaintances, very little was known of the circumstances of this approaching wedding beyond the particulars given above.

Ellinor and Miss Monro sat at their drawing-room window, a little shaded by the muslin curtains, watching the busy preparations for the marriage, which was to take place the next day. All morning long hampers of fruit and flowers, boxes from the railway—for by this time East Chester had got a railway*—shop-messengers, hired assistants, kept passing backwards and forwards in the busy Close. Towards afternoon the bustle subsided, the scaffolding was up, the materials for the next day's feast carried out of sight. It was to be concluded that the bride-elect was seeing to the packing of her trousseau, helped by the merry multitude of cousins, and that the servants were arranging the dinner for the day, or the breakfast for the morrow. So Miss Monro had settled it, discussing every detail and every probability as though she were a chief actor, instead of only a distant, uncared-for spectator of the coming event. Ellinor was tired, and now that there was nothing interesting going on, she had fallen back to her sewing, when she was startled by Miss Monro's exclamation:

'Look, look! here are two gentlemen coming along the lime-tree walk! it must be the bridegroom and his friend.' Out of much sympathy, and some curiosity, Ellinor bent forward, and saw just emerging from the shadow of the trees on to the full afternoon sun-lit pavement, Mr Corbet and another gentleman; the former changed, worn, aged, though with still the same fine intellectual face, leaning on the arm of the younger taller man, and talking eagerly. The other gentleman was doubtless the bridegroom, Ellinor said to herself; and yet her prophetic heart did not believe her words. Even before the bright beauty at the deanery looked out of the great oriel-window of the drawing-room, and blushed, and smiled, and kissed her hand—a gesture replied to by Mr Corbet with much *empressement*,* while the other man only took off his hat, almost as if he saw her there for the first time—Ellinor's greedy eyes watched him till he was hidden from sight in the deanery, unheeding Miss Monro's eager incoherent sentences, in turn entreating, apologizing, comforting, and upbraiding. Then she slowly turned her painful eyes upon Miss Monro's face, and moved her lips without a sound being heard, and fainted dead away. In all her life she had never done so before, and when she came round she was not like herself: in all probability the persistence and wilfulness she, who was usually so meek and docile, showed during the next twenty-four hours, was the consequence of fever. She resolved to be present at the wedding: numbers were going; she would be unseen, unnoticed in the crowd; but whatever befell, go she would, and neither the tears nor the prayers of Miss Monro could keep her back. She gave no reason for this determination; indeed, in all probability she had none to give; so there was no arguing the point. She was inflexible to entreaty, and no one had any authority over her, except, perhaps, distant Mr Ness. Miss Monro had all sorts of forebodings as to the possible scenes that might come to pass. But all went on as quietly, as though the fullest sympathy pervaded every individual of the great numbers assembled. No one guessed that the muffled veiled figure, sitting in the shadow behind one of the great pillars, was that of one who had once hoped to stand at the altar with the same bridegroom, who now cast tender looks at the beautiful bride; her veil white and fairy-like, Ellinor's black and shrouding as that of any nun.

Already Mr Corbet's name was known through the country as that of a great lawyer; people discussed his speeches and character far and wide; and the well-informed in legal gossip spoke of him as sure to be offered a judgeship at the next vacancy. So he, though grave, and middle-aged, and somewhat grey, divided attention and remark with his lovely bride, and her pretty train of cousin bridesmaids. Miss Monro need not have feared for Ellinor: she saw and heard all things as in a mist—a dream; as something she had to go through, before she could waken up to a reality of brightness in which her youth, and the hopes of her youth, should be restored, and all these weary years of dreaminess and woe should be revealed as nothing but the nightmare of a night. She sat motionless enough, still enough, Miss Monro by her, watching her as intently as a keeper watches a madman, and with the same purpose—to prevent any outburst even by bodily strength, if such restraint be needed. When all was over, when the principal personages of the ceremony had filed into the vestry to sign their names; when the swarm of townspeople were going out as swiftly as their individual notions of the restraints of the sacred edifice permitted; when the great chords of the 'Wedding March'* clanged out from the organ, and the loud bells pealed overhead, Ellinor laid her hand in Miss Monro's. 'Take me home,' she said softly. And Miss Monro led her home as one leads the blind.

CHAPTER XII

THERE are some people who imperceptibly float away from their youth into middle age, and thence pass into declining life with the soft and gentle motion of happy years. There are others who are whirled, in spite of themselves, down dizzy rapids of agony away from their youth at one great bound, into old age with another sudden shock; and thence into the vast calm ocean where there are no shore-marks to tell of time.

This last, it seemed, was to be Ellinor's lot. Her youth had gone in a single night, fifteen years ago, and now she appeared to have become an elderly woman; very still and hopeless in look and movement, but as sweet and gentle in speech and smile as ever she had been in her happiest days. All young people, when they came to know her, loved her dearly, though at first they might call her dull, and heavy to get on with; and as for children and old people, her ready watchful sympathy in their joys as well as their sorrows was an unfailing passage to their hearts. After the first great shock of Mr Corbet's marriage was over, she seemed to pass into a greater peace than she had known for years; the last faint hope of happiness was gone; it would, perhaps, be more accurate to say, of the bright happiness she had planned for herself in her early youth. Unconsciously, she was being weaned from self-seeking in any shape, and her daily life became, if possible, more innocent and pure and holy. One of the canons used to laugh at her for her constant attendance at all the services, and for her devotion to good works, and call her always the reverend sister. Miss Monro was a little annoyed at this faint clerical joke; Ellinor smiled quietly. Miss Monro disapproved of Ellinor's grave ways and sober severe style of dress.

'You may be as good as you like, my dear, and yet go dressed in some pretty colour, instead of those perpetual blacks and greys, and then there would be no need for me to be perpetually telling people you are only four-and-thirty (and they don't believe me, though I tell them so till I am black in the face). Or, if you would but wear a decent-shaped bonnet, instead of always wearing those of the poky shape in fashion when you were seventeen.'

The old canon died, and someone was to be appointed in his stead. These clerical preferments and appointments were the all-important interests to the inhabitants of the Close, and the discussion of probabilities came up invariably if any two met together, in street or house, or even in the very cathedral itself. At length it was settled and announced by the higher powers. An energetic, hard-working clergyman from a distant part of the diocese, Livingstone by name, was to have the vacant canonry.

Miss Monro said that the name was somehow familiar to her, and by degrees she recollected the young curate, who had come to inquire after Ellinor in that dreadful illness she had had at Hamley in the year 1829.* Ellinor knew nothing of that visit; no more than Miss Monro did of what had passed between the two before that anxious night. Ellinor just thought it possible it might be the same Mr Livingstone, and would rather it were not, because she did not feel as if she could bear the frequent though not intimate intercourse she must needs have, if such were the case, with one so closely associated with that great time of terror which she was striving to bury out of sight by every effort in her power. Miss Monro, on the contrary, was busy weaving a romance for her pupil; she thought of the passionate interest displayed by the fair young clergyman fifteen years ago, and believed that occasionally men could be constant, and hoped that, if Mr Livingstone were the new canon, he might prove the *rara avis** which exists but once in a century. He came, and it was the same. He looked a little stouter, a little older, but had still the gait and aspect of a young man. His smooth fair face was scarcely lined at all with any marks of care; the blue eyes looked so kindly and peaceful, that Miss Monro could scarcely fancy they were the same which she had seen fast filling with tears; the bland calm look of the whole man needed the ennoblement of his evident devoutness to be raised into the type of holy innocence which some of the Romanists call the 'sacerdotal face.'* His entire soul was in his work, and he looked as little likely to step forth in the character of either a hero of romance or a faithful lover as could be imagined. Still Miss Monro was not discouraged; she remembered the warm passionate feeling she had once seen break through the calm exterior, and she believed that what had happened once might occur again.

Of course, while all eyes were directed on the new canon, he had to learn who the possessors of those eyes were one by one; and it was probably some time before the idea came into his mind that Miss Wilkins, the lady in black, with the sad pale face, so constant an attendant at service, so regular a visitor at the school, was the same Miss Wilkins as the bright vision of his youth. It was her sweet smile at a painstaking child that betrayed her—if, indeed, betrayal it might be called—where there was no wish or effort to conceal anything. Canon Livingstone left the schoolroom almost directly, and, after being for an hour or so in his house, went out to call on Mrs Randall, the person who knew more of her neighbours' affairs than anyone in East Chester.

The next day he called on Miss Wilkins herself. She would have been very glad if he had kept on in his ignorance; it was so keenly painful to be in the company of one the sight of whom, even at a distance, had brought her such a keen remembrance of past misery; and when told of his call, as she was sitting at her sewing in the dining-room, she had to nerve herself for the interview before going upstairs into the drawing-room, where he was being entertained by Miss Monro with warm demonstrations of welcome. A little contraction of the brow, a little compression of the lips, an increased pallor on Ellinor's part, was all that Miss Monro could see in her, though she had put on her glasses with foresight and intention to observe. She turned to the canon; his colour had certainly deepened as he went forwards with outstretched hand to meet Ellinor. That was all that was to be seen; but on the slight foundation of that blush, Miss Monro built many castles; and when they faded away, one after one, she recognized that they were only baseless visions. She used to put the disappointment of her hopes down to Ellinor's unvaried calmness of demeanour, which might be taken for coldness of disposition; and to her steady refusal to allow Miss Monro to invite Canon Livingstone to the small teas they were in the habit of occasionally giving. Yet he persevered in his calls; about once every fortnight he came, and would sit an hour or more, looking covertly at his watch, as if, as Miss Monro shrewdly observed to herself, he did not go away at last because he wished to do so, but because he ought. Sometimes Ellinor was present, sometimes she was away; in this latter case Miss Monro thought she could detect a certain wistful watching of the door every time a noise was heard outside the room. He always avoided any reference to former days at Hamley, and that, Miss Monro feared, was a bad sign.

After this long uniformity of years without any event closely touching on Ellinor's own individual life, with the one great exception of Mr Corbet's marriage, something happened which much affected her. Mr Ness died suddenly at his parsonage, and Ellinor learnt it first from Mr Brown, a clergyman, whose living was near Hamley, and who had been sent for by the parsonage servants as soon as they discovered that it was not sleep, but death, that made their master so late in rising.

Mr Brown had been appointed executor by his late friend, and wrote to tell Ellinor that after a few legacies were paid, she was to have a life-interest in the remainder of the small property which Mr Ness had left, and that it would be necessary for her, as the residuary legatee, to come to Hamley Parsonage as soon as convenient, to decide upon certain courses of action with regard to furniture, books, &c.

Ellinor shrank from this journey, which her love and duty towards her dead friend rendered necessary. She had scarcely left East Chester since she first arrived there, sixteen or seventeen years ago, and she was timorous about the very mode of travelling; and then to go back to Hamley, which she thought never to have seen again! She never spoke much about any feelings of her own, but Miss Monro could always read her silence, and interpreted it into pretty just and forcible words that afternoon when Canon Livingstone called. She liked to talk about Ellinor to him, and suspected that he liked to hear. She was almost annoyed this time by the comfort he would keep giving her; there was no greater danger in travelling by railroad than by coach, a little care about certain things was required, that was all, and the average number of deaths by accidents on railroads were not greater than the average number when people travelled by coach, if you took into consideration the far greater number of travellers. Yes! returning to the deserted scenes of one's youth was very painful. . . . . Had Miss Wilkins made any provision for another lady to take her place as visitor at the school? He believed it was her week. Miss Monro was out of all patience at his entire calmness and reasonableness. Later in the day she became more at peace with him, when she received a kind little note from Mrs Forbes, a great friend of hers, and the mother of the family she was now teaching, saying that Canon Livingstone had called and told her that Ellinor had to go on a very painful journey, and that Mrs Forbes was quite sure Miss Monro's companionship upon it would be a great comfort to both, and that she could perfectly be set at liberty for a fortnight or so, for it would fall in admirably with the fact that 'Jeanie was growing tall, and the doctor had advised sea air this spring; so a month's holiday would suit them now even better than later on.' Was this going straight to Mrs Forbes, to whom she should herself scarcely have liked to name it, the act of a good, thoughtful man, or of a lover? questioned Miss Monro; but she could not answer her own inquiry, and had to be very grateful for the deed, without accounting for the motives.

A coach met the train at a station about ten miles from Hamley, and Dixon was at the inn where the coach stopped, ready to receive them.

The old man was almost in tears at the sight of them again in the familiar place. He had put on his Sunday clothes to do them honour; and to conceal his agitation he kept up a pretended bustle about their luggage. To the indignation of the inn-porters, who were of a later generation, he would wheel it himself to the parsonage, though he broke down from fatigue once or twice on the way, and had to stand and rest, his ladies waiting by his side, and making remarks on the alterations of houses and the places of trees, in order to give him ample time to recruit himself, for there was no one to wait for them and give them a welcome to the parsonage, which was to be their temporary home. The respectful servants, in deep mourning, had all prepared, and gave Ellinor a note from Mr Brown, saying that he purposely refrained from disturbing them that day after their long journey, but would call on the morrow, and tell them of the arrangements he had thought of making, always subject to Miss Wilkins's approval.

These were simple enough; certain legal forms to be gone through, any selections from books or furniture to be made, and the rest to be sold by auction as speedily as convenient, as the successor to the living might wish to have repairs and alterations effected in the old parsonage. For some days Ellinor employed herself in business in the house, never going out except to church. Miss Monro, on the contrary, strolled about everywhere, noticing all the alterations in place and people, which were never improvements in her opinion. Ellinor had plenty of callers (her tenants, Mr and Mrs Osbaldistone among others), but, excepting in rare cases—most of them belonged to humble life—she declined to see everyone, as she had business enough on her hands: sixteen years makes a great difference in any set of people. The old acquaintances of her father in his better days were almost all dead or removed; there were one or two remaining, and these Ellinor received; one or two more, old and infirm, confined to their houses, she planned to call upon before leaving Hamley. Every evening, when Dixon had done his work at Mr Osbaldistone's, he came up to the parsonage, ostensibly to help her in moving or packing books, but really because these two clung to each other—were bound to each other by a bond never to be spoken about. It was understood between them that once before Ellinor left she should go and see the old place, Ford Bank. Not to go into the house, though Mr and Mrs Osbaldistone had begged her to name her own time for revisiting it when they and their family would be absent, but to see all the gardens and grounds once more; a solemn, miserable visit, which, because of the very misery it involved, appeared to Ellinor to be an imperative duty.

Dixon and she talked together as she sat making a catalogue one evening in the old low-browed library; the casement windows were open into the garden, and the May showers had brought out the scents of the new-leaved sweetbriar bush just below. Beyond the garden-hedge the grassy meadows sloped away down to the river; the parsonage was so much raised that sitting in the house you could see over the boundary hedge. Men with instruments were busy in the meadow. Ellinor, pausing in her work, asked Dixon what they were doing.

'Them's the people for the new railway,' said he. 'Nought would satisfy the Hamley folk but to have a railway all to themselves—coaches isn't good enough nowadays.'

He spoke with a tone of personal offence natural to a man who had passed all his life among horses, and considered railway-engines as their despicable rivals, conquering only by stratagem.

By-and-by Ellinor passed on to a subject the consideration of which she had repeatedly urged upon Dixon, and entreated him to come and form one of their household at East Chester. He was growing old, she thought, older even in looks and feelings than in years, and she would make him happy and comfortable in his declining years if he would but come and pass them under her care. The addition which Mr Ness's bequest made to her income would enable her to do not only this, but to relieve Miss Monro of her occupation of teaching; which, at the years she had arrived at, was becoming burdensome. When she proposed the removal to Dixon he shook his head.

'It's not that I don't thank you, and kindly, too; but I'm too old to go chopping and changing.'

'But it would be no change to come back to me, Dixon,' said Ellinor.

'Yes, it would. I were born i' Hamley, and it's i' Hamley I reckon to die.'

On her urging him a little more, it came out that he had a strong feeling that if he did not watch the spot where the dead man lay buried, the whole would be discovered; and that this dread of his had often poisoned the pleasure of his visit to East Chester.

'I don't rightly know how it is, for I sometimes think if it wasn't for you, missy, I should be glad to have made it all clear before I go; and yet at times I dream, or it comes into my head as I lie awake with the rheumatics, that someone is there, digging; or that I hear 'em cutting down the tree; and then I get up and look out of the loft window—you'll mind the window over the stables, as looks into the garden, all covered over wi' the leaves of the jargonelle pear-tree? That were my room when first I come as stable-boy, and tho' Mr Osbaldistone would fain give me a warmer one, I allays tell him I like th' old place best. And by times I've getten up five or six times a-night to make sure as there was no one at work under the tree.'

Ellinor shivered a little. He saw it, and restrained himself in the relief he was receiving from imparting his superstitious fancies.

'You see, missy, I could never rest a-nights if I didn't feel as if I kept the secret in my hand, and held it tight day and night, so as I could open my hand at any minute and see as it was there. No! my own little missy will let me come and see her now and again, and I know as I can allays ask her for what I want: and if it please God to lay me by, I shall tell her so, and she'll see as I want for nothing. But somehow I could ne'er bear leaving Hamley. You shall come and follow me to my grave when my time comes.'

'Don't talk so, please, Dixon,' said she.

'Nay, it'll be a mercy when I can lay me down and sleep in peace: though I sometimes fear as peace will not come to me even there.' He was going out of the room, and was now more talking to himself than to her. 'They say blood will out,* and if it weren't for her part in it, I could wish for a clear breast before I die.'

She did not hear the latter part of this mumbled sentence. She was looking at a letter just brought in and requiring an immediate answer. It was from Mr Brown. Notes from him were of daily occurrence, but this contained an open letter the writing of which was strangely familiar to her—it did not need the signature, 'Ralph Corbet,' to tell her whom the letter came from. For some moments she could not read the words. They expressed a simple enough request, and were addressed to the auctioneer who was to dispose of the rather valuable library of the late Mr Ness, and whose name had been advertised in connection with the sale, in the *Athenaeum*,* and other similar papers. To him Mr Corbet wrote, saying that he should be unable to be present when the books were sold, but that he wished to be allowed to buy in, at any price decided upon, a certain rare folio edition of *Virgil*,* bound in parchment, and with notes in Italian. The book was fully described. Though no

Latin scholar, Ellinor knew the book well—remembered its look from old times, and could instantly have laid her hand upon it. The auctioneer had sent the request on to his employer, Mr Brown. That gentleman applied to Ellinor for her consent. She saw that the fact of the intended sale must be all that Mr Corbet was aware of, and that he could not know to whom the books belonged. She chose out the book, and wrapped and tied it up with trembling hands. *He* might be the person to untie the knot. It was strangely familiar to her love, after so many years, to be brought into thus much contact with him. She wrote a short note to Mr Brown, in which she requested him to say, as though from himself, and without any mention of her name, that he, as executor, requested Mr Corbet's acceptance of the *Virgil*, as a remembrance of his former friend and tutor. Then she rang the bell, and gave the letter and parcel to the servant.

Again alone, and Mr Corbet's open letter on the table. She took it up and looked at it till the letters dazzled crimson on the white paper. Her life rolled backwards, and she was a girl again. At last she roused herself; but instead of destroying the note—it was long years since all her love-letters from him had been returned to the writer—she unlocked her little writing-case again, and placed this letter carefully down at the bottom, among the dead rose-leaves which embalmed the note from her father, found after his death under his pillow, the little golden curl of her sister's, the half-finished sewing of her mother.

The shabby writing-case itself was given her by her father long ago, and had since been taken with her everywhere. To be sure, her changes of places had been but few; but if she had gone to Nova Zembla,* the sight of that little leather box on awaking from her first sleep, would have given her a sense of home. She locked the case up again, and felt all the richer for that morning.

A day or two afterwards she left Hamley. Before she went she compelled herself to go round the gardens and grounds of Ford Bank. She had made Mrs Osbaldistone understand that it would be painful to her to re-enter the house; but Mr Osbaldistone accompanied her in her walk.

'You see how literally we have obeyed the clause in the lease which ties us out from any alterations,' said he, smiling. 'We are living in a tangled thicket of wood. I must confess that I should have liked to cut down a good deal; but we do not do even the requisite thinnings without making the proper application for leave to Mr Johnson. In fact, your old friend Dixon is jealous of every pea-stick the gardener cuts. I never met with so faithful a fellow. A good enough servant, too, in his way; but somewhat too old-fashioned for my wife and daughters, who complain of his being surly now and then.'

'You are not thinking of parting with him?' said Ellinor, jealous for Dixon.

'Oh, no; he and I are capital friends. And I believe Mrs Osbaldistone herself would never consent to his leaving us. But some ladies, you know, like a little more subserviency in manner than our friend Dixon can boast.'

Ellinor made no reply. They were entering the painted flower-garden, hiding the ghastly memory. She could not speak. She felt as if, with all her striving, she could not move—just as one does in a nightmare—but she was past the place even as this terror came to its acme; and when she came to herself, Mr Osbaldistone was still blandly talking, and saying—

'It is now a reward for our obedience to your wishes, Miss Wilkins, for if the projected railway passes through the ash-field yonder, we should have been perpetually troubled with the sight of the trains; indeed, the sound would have been much more distinct than it will be now coming through the interlacing branches. Then you will not go in, Miss Wilkins? Mrs Osbaldistone desired me to say how happy—Ah! I can understand such feelings—Certainly, certainly; it is so much the shortest way to the town, that we elder ones always go through the stable-yard; for young people, it is perhaps not quite so desirable. Ha! Dixon,' he continued, 'on the watch for the Miss Ellinor we so often hear of! This old man,' he continued to Ellinor, 'is never satisfied with the seat of our young ladies, always comparing their way of riding with that of a certain missy ——'

'I cannot help it, sir; they've quite a different style of hand, and sit all lumpish-like. Now, Miss Ellinor, there ——'

'Hush, Dixon,' she said, suddenly aware of why the old servant was not popular with his mistress. 'I suppose I may be allowed to ask for Dixon's company for an hour or so; we have something to do together before we leave.'

The consent given, the two walked away, as by previous appointment, to Hamley churchyard, where he was to point out to her the exact spot where he wished to be buried. Trampling over the long, rank grass, but avoiding passing directly over any of the thickly-strewn graves, he made straight for one spot,—a little space of unoccupied ground close by, where Molly, the pretty scullery-maid, lay:

Sacred to the Memory of
MARY GREAVES.
Born 1797. Died 1818.
'We part to meet again.'

'I put this stone up over her with my first savings,' said he, looking at it; and then pulling out his knife, he began to clean out the letters. I said then as I would lie by her. And it'll be a comfort to think you'll see me laid here. I trust no one'll be so crabbed as to take a fancy to this here spot of ground.'

Ellinor grasped eagerly at the only pleasure which her money enabled her to give to the old man; and promised him that she would take care and buy the right to that particular piece of ground. This was evidently a gratification Dixon had frequently yearned after; he kept saying, 'I'm greatly obleeged to ye, Miss Ellinor. I may say I'm truly obleeged.' And when he saw them off by the coach the next day, his last words were, 'I cannot justly say how greatly I'm obleeged to you for that matter o' the churchyard.' It was a much more easy affair to give Miss Monro some additional comforts; she was as cheerful as ever; still working away at her languages in any spare time, but confessing that she was tired of the perpetual teaching in which her life had been spent during the last thirty years. Ellinor was now enabled to set her at liberty from this, and she accepted the kindness from her former pupil with as much simple gratitude as that with which a mother receives a favour from a child. 'If Ellinor were but married to Canon Livingstone, I should be happier than I have ever been since my father died,' she used to say to herself in the solitude of her bedchamber, for talking aloud had become her wont in the early years of her isolated life as a governess. 'And yet,' she went on, 'I don't know what I should do without her; it is lucky for me that things are not in my hands, for a pretty mess I should make of them, one way or another. Dear! how old Mrs Cadogan used to hate that word "mess," and correct her grand-daughters for using it right before my face, when I knew I had said it myself only the moment before! Well! those days are all over now. God be thanked!'

In spite of being glad that 'things were not in her hands,' Miss Monro tried to take affairs into her charge by doing all she could to persuade Ellinor to allow her to invite the canon to their 'little sociable teas.' The most provoking part was, that she was sure he would have come if he had been asked; but she could never get leave to do so. 'Of course no man could go on for ever and ever without encouragement,' as she confided to herself in a plaintive tone of voice; and by-and-by many people were led to suppose that the bachelor canon was paying attention to Miss Forbes, the eldest daughter of the family to which the delicate Jeanie belonged. It was, perhaps, with the Forbeses that both Miss Monro and Ellinor were the most intimate of all the families in East Chester. Mrs Forbes was a widow lady of good means, with a large family of pretty, delicate daughters. She herself belonged to one of the great houses in ——shire, but had married into Scotland; so, after her husband's death, it was the most natural thing in the world that she should settle in East Chester; and one after another of her daughters had become first Miss Monro's pupil and afterwards her friend. Mrs Forbes herself had always been strongly attracted by Ellinor, but it was long before she could conquer the timid reserve by which Miss Wilkins was hedged round. It was Miss Monro, who was herself incapable of jealousy, who persevered in praising them to one another, and in bringing them together; and now Ellinor was as intimate and familiar in Mrs Forbes's household as she ever could be with any family not her own.

Mrs Forbes was considered to be a little fanciful as to illness; but it was no wonder, remembering how many sisters she had lost by consumption. Miss Monro had often grumbled at the way in which her pupils were made irregular for very trifling causes. But no one so alarmed as she, when, in the autumn succeeding Mr Ness's death, Mrs Forbes remarked to her on Ellinor's increased delicacy of appearance, and shortness of breathing. From that time forwards she worried Ellinor (if anyone so sweet and patient could ever have been worried) with respirators and precautions. Ellinor submitted to all her friend's wishes and cares, sooner than make her anxious, and remained a prisoner in the house through the whole of November. Then Miss Monro's anxiety took another turn. Ellinor's appetite and spirits failed her—not at all an unnatural consequence of so many weeks' confinement to the house. A plan was started, quite suddenly, one morning in December, that met with approval from everyone but Ellinor, who was, however, by this time too languid to make much resistance.

Mrs Forbes and her daughters were going to Rome for three or four months, so as to avoid the trying east winds of spring; why should not Miss Wilkins go with them? They urged it, and Miss Monro urged it, though with a little private sinking of the heart at the idea of the long separation from one who was almost like a child to her. Ellinor was, as it were, lifted off her feet and borne away by the unanimous opinion of others—the doctor included—who decided that such a step was highly desirable, if not absolutely necessary. She knew that she had only a life interest both in her father's property and in that bequeathed to her by Mr Ness. Hitherto she had not felt much troubled by this, as she had supposed that in the natural course of events she should survive Miss Monro and Dixon, both of whom she looked upon as dependent upon her. All she had to bequeath to the two, was the small savings, which would not nearly suffice for both purposes, especially considering that Miss Monro had given up her teaching, and that both she and Dixon were passing into years.

Before Ellinor left England she had made every arrangement for the contingency of her death abroad that Mr Johnson could suggest. She had written and sent a long letter to Dixon; and a shorter one was left in charge of Canon Livingstone (she dared not hint at the possibility of her dying to Miss Monro) to be sent to the old man.

As they drove out of the King's Cross station, they passed a gentleman's carriage entering. Ellinor saw a bright, handsome lady, a nurse, and baby inside, and a gentleman sitting by them whose face she could never forget. It was Mr Corbet taking his wife and child to the railway. They were going on a Christmas visit to East Chester deanery. He had been leaning back, not noticing the passers-by, not attending to the other inmates of the carriage, probably absorbed in the consideration of some law case. Such were the casual glimpses Ellinor had of one, with whose life she had once thought herself bound up.

Who so proud as Miss Monro when a foreign letter came? Her correspondent was not particularly graphic in her descriptions, nor were there any adventures to be described, nor was the habit of mind of Ellinor such as to make her clear and definite in her own impressions of what she saw, and her natural reserve kept her from being fluent in communicating them even to Miss Monro. But that lady would have been pleased to read aloud these letters to the assembled dean and canons, and would not have been surprised if they had invited her to the chapter-house for that purpose. To her circle of untravelled ladies, ignorant of Murray,* but laudably desirous of information, all Ellinor's historical reminiscences, and rather formal details were really interesting. There was no railroad in those days between Lyons and Marseilles, so their progress was slow, and the passage of letters to and fro, when they had arrived in Rome, long and uncertain. But all seemed going on well. Ellinor spoke of herself as in better health; and Canon Livingstone (between whom and Miss Monro great intimacy had sprung up since Ellinor had gone away, and Miss Monro could ask him to tea) confirmed this report of Miss Wilkins's health from a letter which he had received from Mrs Forbes. Curiosity about that letter was Miss Monro's torment. What could they have had to write to each other about! It was a very odd proceeding; although the Livingstones and Forbeses were distantly related, after the manner of Scotland. Could it have been that he had offered to Euphemia, after all, and that her mother had answered; or, possibly, there was a letter from Effie herself, enclosed? It was a pity for Miss Monro's peace of mind that she did not ask him straight away. She would then have learnt what Canon Livingstone had no thought of concealing, that Mrs Forbes had written solely to give him some fuller directions about certain charities than she had had time to think about in the hurry of starting. As it was, and when a little later on, she heard him speak of the possibility of his going himself to Rome, as soon as his term of residence was over, in time for the Carnival,* she gave up her fond project in despair, and felt very much like a child whose house of bricks has been knocked down by the unlucky waft of some passing petticoat.

Meanwhile, the entire change of scene brought on the exquisite refreshment of entire change of thought. Ellinor had not been able so completely to forget her past life for many years; it was like a renewing of her youth; cut so suddenly short by the shears of fate. Ever since that night, she had had to rouse herself on awakening in the morning into a full comprehension of the great cause she had for much fear and heavy grief. Now, when she wakened in her little room, fourth piano, No. 36, Babuino,* she saw the strange, pretty things around her, and her mind went off into pleasant wonder and conjecture, happy recollections of the day before, and pleasant anticipations of the day to come. Latent in Ellinor was her father's artistic temperament; everything new and strange was a picture and a delight; the merest group in the street, a Roman *facchino*,* with his cloak draped over his shoulder, a girl going to market or carrying her pitcher back from the fountain, everything and every person that presented it or himself to her senses, gave them a delicious shock, as if it were something strangely familiar from Pinelli,* but unseen by her mortal eyes before. She forgot her despondency, her ill health disappeared as if by magic; the Misses Forbes, who had taken the pensive, drooping invalid as a companion out of kindness of heart, found themselves amply rewarded by the sight of her amended health, and her keen enjoyment of everything, and the half-quaint, half-naïve expressions of her pleasure.

So March came round; Lent was late that year. The great nosegays of violets and camellias were for sale at the corner of the Condotti,* and the revellers had no difficulty in procuring much rarer flowers for the belles of the Corso. The embassies had their balconies; the attachés of the Russian embassy threw their light and lovely presents at every pretty girl, or suspicion of a pretty girl, who passed slowly in her carriage, covered over with her white *domino*,* and holding her wire mask as a protection to her face from the showers of lime *confetti*,* which otherwise would have been enough to blind her; Mrs Forbes had her own hired balcony as became a wealthy and respectable Englishwoman. The girls had a great basket full of bouquets with which to pelt their friends in the crowd below; a store of *moccoletti** lay piled on the table behind, for it was the last day of Carnival, and as soon as dusk came on the tapers were to be lighted, to be as quickly extinguished by every means in everyone's power. The crowd below was at its wildest pitch; the rows of stately *contadini** alone sitting immovable as their possible ancestors, the senators who received Brennus and his Gauls.* Masks and white *dominoes*, foreign gentlemen, and the riffraff of the city, slow-driving carriages, showers of flowers, most of them faded by this time, everyone shouting and struggling at that wild pitch of excitement which may so soon turn into fury. The Forbes girls had given place at the window to their mother and Ellinor, who were gazing half amused, half terrified, at the mad parti-coloured movement below; when a familiar face* looked up, smiling a recognition; and 'How shall I get to you?' was asked in English, by the well-known voice of Canon Livingstone. They saw him disappear under the balcony on which they were standing, but it was some time before he made his appearance in their room. And when he did, he was almost overpowered with greetings; so glad were they to see an East Chester face.

'When did you come? Where are you? What a pity you did not come sooner! It is so long since we have heard anything; do tell us everything! It is three weeks since we have had any letters; those tiresome boats have been so irregular because of the weather.' 'How was everybody—Miss Monro in particular?' Ellinor asks.

He, quietly smiling, replied to their questions by slow degrees. He had only arrived the night before, and had been hunting for them all day; but no one could give him any distinct intelligence as to their whereabouts in all the noise and confusion of the place, especially as they had their only English servant with them, and the canon was not strong in his Italian.

He was not sorry he had missed all but this last day of Carnival, for he was half blinded, and wholly deafened, as it was. He was at the Angleterre;* he had left East Chester about a week ago; he had letters for all of them, but had not dared to bring them through the crowd for fear of having his pocket picked. Miss Monro was very well, but very uneasy at not having heard from Ellinor for so long; the irregularity of the boats must be telling both ways, for their English friends were full of wonder at not hearing from Rome. And then followed some well deserved abuse of the Roman post, and some suspicion of the carelessness with which Italian servants posted English letters. All these answers were satisfactory enough, yet Mrs Forbes thought she saw a latent uneasiness in Canon Livingstone's manner, and fancied once or twice that he hesitated in replying to Ellinor's questions. But there was no being quite sure in the increasing darkness, which prevented countenances from being seen; nor in the constant interruptions and screams which were going on in the small crowded room, as wafting handkerchiefs, puffs of wind, or veritable extinguishers, fastened to long sticks, and coming from nobody knew where, put out taper after taper as fast as they were lighted.

'You will come home with us,' said Mrs Forbes. 'I can only offer you cold meat with tea; our cook is gone out, this being a universal *festa*; but we cannot part with an old friend for any scruples as to the commissariat.'

'Thank you. I should have invited myself if you had not been good enough to ask me.'

When they had all arrived at their apartment in the Babuino (Canon Livingstone had gone round to fetch the letters with which he was entrusted), Mrs Forbes was confirmed in her supposition that he had something particular and not very pleasant to say to Ellinor, by the rather grave and absent manner in which he awaited her return from taking off her out-of-door things. He broke off, indeed, in his conversation with Mrs Forbes to go and meet Ellinor, and to lead her into the most distant window before he delivered her letters.

'From what you said in the balcony yonder, I fear you have not received your home letters regularly?'

'No!' replied she, startled and trembling, she hardly knew why.

'No more has Miss Monro heard from you; nor, I believe, has someone else who expected to hear. Your man of business—I forget his name.'

'My man of business! Something has gone wrong, Mr Livingstone. Tell me—I want to know. I have been expecting it—only tell me.' She sat down suddenly, as white as ashes.

'Dear Miss Wilkins, I'm afraid it is painful enough, but you are fancying it worse than it is. All your friends are quite well; but an old servant ——'

'Well!' she said, seeing his hesitation, and leaning forwards and griping* at his arm.

'Is taken up on a charge of manslaughter or murder.—Oh! Mrs Forbes, come here!'

For Ellinor had fainted, falling forwards on the arm she had held. When she came round she was lying half-undressed on her bed; they were giving her tea in spoonfuls.

'I must get up,' she moaned. 'I must go home.'

'You must lie still,' said Mrs Forbes, firmly.

'You don't know. I must go home,' she repeated; and she tried to sit up, but fell back helpless. Then she did not speak, but lay and thought. 'Will you bring me some meat?' she whispered. 'And some wine?' They brought her meat and wine; she ate, though she was choking. 'Now, please, bring me my letters, and leave me alone; and after that I should like to speak to Canon Livingstone. Don't let him go, please. I won't be long—half an hour, I think. Only let me be alone.'

There was a hurried feverish sharpness in her tone that made Mrs Forbes very anxious, but she judged it best to comply with her requests.

The letters were brought, the lights were arranged so that she could read them lying on her bed; and they left her. Then she got up and stood on her feet, dizzy enough, her arms clasped at the top of her head, her eyes dilated and staring as if looking at some great horror. But after a few minutes she sat down suddenly, and began to read. Letters were evidently missing. Some had been sent by an opportunity that had been delayed on the journey, and had not yet arrived in Rome. Others had been despatched by the post, but the severe weather, the unusual snow, had, in those days, before the railway was made between Lyons and Marseilles, put a stop to many a traveller's plans, and had rendered the transmission of the mail extremely uncertain; so, much of that intelligence which Miss Monro had evidently considered as certain to be known to Ellinor was entirely matter of conjecture, and could only be guessed at from what was told in these letters. One was from Mr Johnson, one from Mr Brown, one from Miss Monro; of course the last mentioned was the first read. She spoke of the shock of the discovery of Mr Dunster's body, found in the cutting of the new line of railroad from Hamley to the nearest railway station; the body so hastily buried long ago, in its clothes, by which it was now recognized—a recognition confirmed by one or two more personal and indestructible things, such as his watch and seal with his initials; of the shock to everyone, the Osbaldistones in particular, on the further discovery of a fleam, or horse-lancet, having the name of Abraham Dixon engraved on the handle; how Dixon had gone on Mr Osbaldistone's business to a horse-fair in Ireland some weeks before this, and had had his leg broken by a kick from an unruly mare, so that he was barely able to move about when the officers of justice went to apprehend him in Tralee.

At this point Ellinor cried out loud and shrill.

'Oh, Dixon! Dixon! and I was away enjoying myself.'

They heard her cry, and came to the door, but it was bolted inside.

'Please, go away,' she said; 'please, go. I will be very quiet, only, please, go.'

She could not bear just then to read any more of Miss Monro's letter; she tore open Mr Johnson's—the date was a fortnight earlier than Miss Monro's; he also expressed his wonder at not hearing from her, in reply to his letter of January 9; but he added, that he thought that her trustees had judged rightly; the handsome sum the railway company had offered for the land when their surveyor decided on the alteration of the line, Mr Osbaldistone, &c. &c., she could not read any more; it was Fate pursuing her. Then she took the letter up again and tried to read; but all that reached her understanding was the fact that Mr Johnson had sent his present letter to Miss Monro, thinking that she might know of some private opportunity safer than the post. Mr Brown's was just such a letter as he occasionally sent her from time to time; a correspondence that arose out of their mutual regard for their dead friend Mr Ness. It, too, had been sent to Miss Monro to direct. Ellinor was on the point of putting it aside entirely, when the name of Corbet caught her eye: 'You will be interested to hear that the old pupil of our departed friend who was so anxious to obtain the folio Virgil with the Italian notes, is appointed the new judge in room of Mr Justice Jenkin. At least I conclude that Mr Ralph Corbet, Q.C., is the same as the Virgil fancier.'

'Yes,' said Ellinor, bitterly; 'he judged well; it would never have done.' They were the first words of anything like reproach which she ever formed in her own mind during all these years. She thought for a few moments of the old times; it seemed to steady her brain to think of them. Then she took up and finished Miss Monro's letter. That excellent friend had done all which she thought Ellinor would have wished without delay. She had written to Mr Johnson, and charged him to do everything he could to defend Dixon, and to spare no expense. She was thinking of going to the prison in the county town, to see the old man herself, but Ellinor could perceive that all these endeavours and purposes of Miss Monro's were based on love for her own pupil, and a desire to set her mind at ease as far as she could, rather than from any idea that Dixon himself could be innocent. Ellinor put down the letters, and went to the door, then turned back, and locked them up in her writing-case with trembling hands; and after that she entered the drawing-room, looking liker to a ghost than to a living woman.

'Can I speak to you for a minute alone?' Her still, tuneless voice made the words into a command. Canon Livingstone arose and followed her into the little dining-room. 'Will you tell me all you know—all you have heard about my—you know what.'

'Miss Monro was my informant—at least at first—it was in *The Times* the day before I left. Miss Monro says it could only have been done in a moment of anger if the old servant is really guilty; that he was as steady and good a man as she ever knew, and she seems to have a strong feeling against Mr Dunster, as always giving your father much unnecessary trouble; in fact, she hints that his disappearance at the time was supposed to be the cause of a considerable loss of property to Mr Wilkins.'

'No!' said Ellinor, eagerly, feeling that some justice ought to be done to the dead man; and then she stopped short, fearful of saying anything that should betray her full knowledge. 'I mean this,' she went on; 'Mr Dunster was a very disagreeable man personally—and papa—we none of us liked him; but he was quite honest—please remember that.'

The canon bowed, and said a few acquiescing words. He waited for her to speak again.

'Miss Monro says she is going to see Dixon in ——'

'Oh, Mr Livingstone, I can't bear it!'

He let her alone, looking at her pitifully, as she twisted and wrung her hands together in her endeavour to regain the quiet manner she had striven to maintain through the interview. She looked up at him with a poor attempt at an apologetic smile:

'It is so terrible to think of that good old man in prison.'

'You do not believe him guilty!' said Canon Livingstone, in some surprise. 'I am afraid, from all I heard and read, there is but little doubt that he did kill the man; I trust in some moment of irritation, with no premeditated malice.'

Ellinor shook her head.

'How soon can I get to England?' asked she. 'I must start at once.'

'Mrs Forbes sent out while you were lying down. I am afraid there is no boat to Marseilles till Thursday, the day after tomorrow.'

'But I must go sooner!' said Ellinor, starting up. 'I must go; please help me. He may be tried before I can get there!'

'Alas! I fear that will be the case, whatever haste you make. The trial was to come on at the Hellingford Assizes, and that town stands first on the Midland Circuit list. Today is the 27th of February; the assizes begin on the 6th of March.'

'I will start tomorrow morning early for Civita;* there may be a boat there they do not know of here. At any rate, I shall be on my way. If he dies, I must die too. Oh! I don't know what I am saying, I am so utterly crushed down! It would be such a kindness if you would go away, and let no one come to me. I know Mrs Forbes is so good, she will forgive me. I will say goodbye to you all before I go tomorrow morning; but I must think now.'

For one moment he stood looking at her as if he longed to comfort her by more words. He thought better of it, however, and silently left the room.

For a long time Ellinor sat still; now and then taking up Miss Monro's letter, and re-reading the few terrible details. Then she bethought her that possibly the canon might have brought a copy of *The Times*, containing the examination of Dixon before the magistrates, and she opened the door and called to a passing servant to make the inquiry. She was quite right in her conjecture; Dr Livingstone* had had the paper in his pocket during his interview with her; but he thought the evidence so conclusive, that the perusal of it would only be adding to her extreme distress by accelerating the conviction of Dixon's guilt, which he believed she must arrive at, sooner or later.

He had been reading the report over with Mrs Forbes and her daughters, after his return from Ellinor's room, and they were all participating in his opinion upon it, when her request for *The Times* was brought. They had reluctantly agreed, saying there did not appear to be a shadow of doubt on the fact of Dixon's having killed Mr Dunster, only hoping there might prove to be some extenuating circumstances, which Ellinor had probably recollected, and which she was desirous of producing on the approaching trial.

CHAPTER XIII

Ellinor, having read the report of Dixon's examination in the newspaper, bathed her eyes and forehead in cold water, and tried to still her poor heart's beating, that she might be clear and collected enough to weigh the evidence.

Every line of it was condemnatory. One or two witnesses spoke of Dixon's unconcealed dislike of Dunster, a dislike which Ellinor knew had been entertained by the old servant out of a species of loyalty to his master, as well as from personal distaste. The fleam was proved beyond all doubt to be Dixon's; and a man, who had been stable-boy in Mr Wilkins's service, swore that on the day when Mr Dunster was missed, and when the whole town was wondering what had become of him, a certain colt of Mr Wilkins's had needed bleeding, and that he had been sent by Dixon to the farrier's for a horse-lancet—an errand which he had remarked upon at the time, as he knew that Dixon had a fleam of his own.

Mr Osbaldistone was examined. He kept interrupting himself perpetually to express his surprise at the fact of so steady and well-conducted a man as Dixon being guilty of so heinous a crime, and was willing enough to testify to the excellent character which he had borne during all the many years he had been in his (Mr Osbaldistone's) service; but he appeared to be quite convinced by the evidence previously given of the prisoner's guilt in the matter, and strengthened the case against him materially by stating the circumstance of the old man's dogged unwillingness to have the slightest interference by cultivation with that particular piece of ground.

Here Ellinor shuddered. Before her, in that Roman bedchamber, rose the fatal oblong she knew by heart—a little green moss or lichen, and thinly-growing blades of grass scarcely covering the caked and undisturbed soil under the old tree. Oh, that she had been in England when the surveyors of the railway between Ashcombe and Hamley had altered their line; she would have entreated, implored, compelled her trustees not to have sold that piece of ground for any sum of money whatever. She would have bribed the surveyors, done she knew not what—but now it was too late; she would not let her mind wander off to what might have been; she would force herself again to attend to the newspaper columns. There was little more: the prisoner had been asked if he could say anything to clear himself, and properly cautioned not to say anything to incriminate himself. The poor old man's person was described, and his evident emotion. 'The prisoner was observed to clutch at the rail before him to steady himself, and his colour changed so much at this part of the evidence that one of the turnkeys offered him a glass of water, which he declined. He is a man of a strongly-built frame, and with rather a morose and sullen cast of countenance.'

'My poor, poor Dixon!' said Ellinor, laying down the paper for an instant, and she was near crying, only she had resolved to shed no tears till she had finished all, and could judge of the chances. There were but a few lines more: 'At one time the prisoner seemed to be desirous of alleging something in his defence, but he changed his mind, if such had been the case, and in reply to Mr Gordon (the magistrate) he only said, "You've made a pretty strong case out again me, gentlemen, and it seems for to satisfy you; so I think I'll not disturb your minds by saying anything more." Accordingly, Dixon now stands committed for trial for murder at the next Hellingford Assizes, which commence on March the sixth, before Baron Rushton and Mr Justice Corbet.'

'Mr Justice Corbet!' The words ran through Ellinor as though she had been stabbed with a knife, and by an irrepressible movement she stood up rigid. The young man, her lover in her youth, the old servant who in those days was perpetually about her—the two who had so often met in familiar if not friendly relations, now to face each other as judge and accused! She could not tell how much Mr Corbet had conjectured from the partial revelation she had made to him of the impending shame that hung over her and hers. A day or two ago, she could have remembered the exact words she had used in that memorable interview; but now, strive as she would, she could only recall facts, not words. After all, the Mr Justice Corbet might not be Ralph. There was one chance in a hundred against the identity of the two.

While she was weighing probabilities in her sick dizzy mind, she heard soft steps outside her bolted door, and low voices whispering. It was the bedtime of happy people with hearts at ease. Some of the footsteps passed lightly on; but there was a gentle rap at Ellinor's door. She pressed her two hot hands hard against her temples for an instant before she went to open the door. There stood Mrs Forbes in her handsome evening dress, holding a lighted lamp in her hand.

'May I come in, my dear?' she asked. Ellinor's stiff dry lips refused to utter the words of assent which indeed did not come readily from her heart.

'I am so grieved at this sad news which the canon brings. I can well understand what a shock it must be to you; we have just been saying it must be as bad for you as it would be to us if our old Donald should turn out to have been a hidden murderer all these years that he has lived with us; I really could have as soon suspected Donald as that white-haired respectable old man who used to come and see you at East Chester.'

Ellinor felt that she must say something. 'It is a terrible shock—poor old man! and no friend near him, even Mr Osbaldistone giving evidence against him. Oh, dear, dear! why did I ever come to Rome?'

'Now, my dear, you must not let yourself take an exaggerated view of the case. Sad and shocking as it is to have been so deceived, it is what happens to many of us, though not to so terrible a degree; and as to your coming to Rome having anything to do with it ——'

(Mrs Forbes almost smiled at the idea, so anxious was she to banish the idea of self-reproach from Ellinor's sensitive mind, but Ellinor interrupted her abruptly:)

'Mrs Forbes! did he—did Canon Livingstone tell you that I must leave tomorrow? I must go to England as fast as possible to do what I can for Dixon.'

'Yes, he told us you were thinking of it, and it was partly that made me force myself in upon you tonight. I think, my love, you are mistaken in feeling as if you were called upon to do more than what the canon tells me Miss Monro has already done in your name—engaged the best legal advice, and spared no expense to give the suspected man every chance. What could you do more even if you were on the spot? And it is very possible that the trial may have come on before you get home. Then what could you do? He would either have been acquitted or condemned; if the former, he would find public sympathy all in his favour; it always is for the unjustly accused. And if he turns out to be guilty, my dear Ellinor, it will be far better for you to have all the softening which distance can give to such a dreadful termination to the life of a poor man whom you have respected so long.'

But Ellinor spoke again with a kind of irritated determination, very foreign to her usual soft docility:

'Please just let me judge for myself this once. I am not ungrateful. God knows I don't want to vex one who has been so kind to me as you have been, dear Mrs Forbes; but I must go—and every word you say to dissuade me only makes me more convinced. I am going to Civita tomorrow. I shall be that much on the way. I cannot rest here.'

Mrs Forbes looked at her in grave silence. Ellinor could not bear the consciousness of that fixed gaze. Yet its fixity only arose from Mrs Forbes's perplexity as to how best to assist Ellinor, whether to restrain her by further advice—of which the first dose had proved so useless—or to speed her departure. Ellinor broke in on her meditations:

'You have always been so kind and good to me,—go on being so—please, do! Leave me alone now, dear Mrs Forbes, for I cannot bear talking about it, and help me to go tomorrow, and you do not know how I will pray to God to bless you!'

Such an appeal was irresistible. Mrs Forbes kissed her very tenderly, and went to rejoin her daughters, who were clustered together in their mother's bedroom, awaiting her coming.

'Well, mamma, how is she? What does she say?'

'She is in a very excited state, poor thing! and has got so strong an impression that it is her duty to go back to England and do all she can for this wretched old man, that I am afraid we must not oppose her. I am afraid she really must go on Thursday.'

Although Mrs Forbes secured the services of a travelling-maid, Dr Livingstone insisted on accompanying Ellinor to England, and it would have required more energy than she possessed at this time to combat a resolution which both words and manner expressed as determined. She would much rather have travelled alone with her maid; she did not feel the need of the services he offered; but she was utterly listless and broken down; all her interest was centred in the thought of Dixon and his approaching trial, and perplexity as to the mode in which she must do her duty.

They embarked late that evening in the tardy *Santa Lucia*, and Ellinor immediately went to her berth. She was not sea-sick; that might possibly have lessened her mental sufferings, which all night long tormented her. High-perched in an upper berth, she did not like disturbing the other occupants of the cabin till daylight appeared. Then she descended and dressed, and went on deck; the vessel was just passing the rocky coast of Elba, and the sky was flushed with rosy light, that made the shadows on the island of the most exquisite purple. The sea still heaved with yesterday's storm, but the motion only added to the beauty of the sparkles and white foam that dimpled and curled on the blue waters. The air was delicious, after the closeness of the cabin, and Ellinor only wondered that more people were not on deck to enjoy it. One or two stragglers came up, time after time, and began pacing the deck. Dr Livingstone came up before very long; but he seemed to have made a rule of not obtruding himself on Ellinor, excepting when he could be of some use. After a few words of commonplace morning greeting, he, too, began to walk backwards and forwards, while Ellinor sat quietly watching the lovely island receding fast from her view—a beautiful vision never to be seen again by her mortal eyes.

Suddenly there was a shock and stound* all over the vessel, her progress was stopped, and a rocking vibration was felt everywhere. The quarter-deck was filled with blasts of steam, which obscured everything. Sick people came rushing up out of their berths in strange undress; the steerage passengers—a motley and picturesque set of people, in many varieties of gay costume—took refuge on the quarter-deck, speaking loudly in all varieties of French and Italian *patois*. Ellinor stood up in silent, wondering dismay. Was the *Santa Lucia* going down on the great deep, and Dixon unaided in his peril? Dr Livingstone was by her side in a moment. She could scarcely see him for the vapour, nor hear him for the roar of the escaping steam.

'Do not be unnecessarily frightened,' he repeated, a little louder. 'Some accident has occurred to the engines. I will go and make instant inquiry, and come back to you as soon as I can. Trust to me.'

He came back to where she sat trembling.

'A part of the engine is broken,* through the carelessness of these Neapolitan engineers; they say we must make for the nearest port—return to Civita, in fact.'

'But Elba is not many miles away,' said Ellinor. 'If this steam were but away, you could see it still.'

'And if we were landed there we might stay on the island for many days; no steamer touches there; but if we return to Civita, we shall be in time for the Sunday boat.'

'Oh, dear, dear!' said Ellinor. 'Today is the second—Sunday will be the fourth—the assizes begin on the seventh; how miserably unfortunate!'

'Yes!' he said, 'it is. And these things always appear so doubly unfortunate when they hinder our serving others! But it does not follow that because the assizes begin at Hellingford on the seventh, Dixon's trial will come on so soon. We may still get to Marseilles on Monday evening; on by *diligence** to Lyons; it will—it must, I fear, be Thursday, at the earliest, before we reach Paris—Thursday, the eighth—and I suppose you know of some exculpatory evidence that has to be hunted up?'

He added this unwillingly; for he saw that Ellinor was jealous of the secrecy she had hitherto maintained as to her reasons for believing Dixon innocent; but he could not help thinking that she, a gentle, timid woman, unaccustomed to action or business, would require some of the assistance which he would have been so thankful to give her; especially as this untoward accident would increase the press of time in which what was to be done would have to be done.

But no. Ellinor scarcely replied to his half-inquiry as to her reasons for hastening to England. She yielded to all his directions, agreed to his plans, but gave him none of her confidence, and he had to submit to this exclusion from sympathy in the exact causes of her anxiety.

Once more in the dreary *sala*,* with the gaudy painted ceiling, the bare dirty floor, the innumerable rattling doors and windows! Ellinor was submissive and patient in demeanour, because so sick and despairing at heart. Her maid was ten times as demonstrative of annoyance and disgust; she who had no particular reason for wanting to reach England, but who thought it became her dignity to make it seem as though she had.

At length the weary time was over; and again they sailed past Elba, and arrived at Marseilles. Now Ellinor began to feel how much assistance it was to her to have Dr Livingstone for a 'courier,' as he had several times called himself.

CHAPTER XIV

'WHERE now?' said the canon, as they approached the London Bridge station.

'To the Great Western,' said she; 'Hellingford is on that line, I see. But, please, now we must part.'

'Then I may not go with you to Hellingford? At any rate, you will allow me to go with you to the railway station, and do my last office as courier in getting you your ticket and placing you in the carriage.'

So they went together to the station, and learnt that no train was leaving for Hellingford for two hours. There was nothing for it but to go to the hotel close by, and pass away the time as best they could.

Ellinor called for her maid's accounts, and dismissed her. Some refreshment that the canon had ordered was eaten, and the table cleared. He began walking up and down the room, his arms folded, his eyes cast down. Every now and then he looked at the clock on the mantelpiece. When that showed that it only wanted a quarter of an hour to the time appointed for the train to start, he came up to Ellinor, who sat leaning her head upon her hand, her hand resting on the table.

'Miss Wilkins,' he began—and there was something peculiar in his tone which startled Ellinor—'I am sure you will not scruple to apply to me if in any possible way I can help you in this sad trouble of yours?'

'No, indeed I won't!' said Ellinor, gratefully, and putting out her hand as a token. He took it, and held it; she went on, a little more hastily than before: 'You know you were so good as to say you would go at once and see Miss Monro, and tell her all you know, and that I will write to her as soon as I can.'

'May I not ask for one line?' he continued, still holding her hand.

'Certainly: so kind a friend as you shall hear all I can tell; that is, all I am at liberty to tell.'

'A friend! Yes, I am a friend; and I will not urge any other claim just now. Perhaps ——'

Ellinor could not affect to misunderstand him. His manner implied even more than his words.

'No!' she said, eagerly. 'We are friends. That is it. I think we shall always be friends, though I will tell you now—something—this much—it is a sad secret. God help me! I am as guilty as poor Dixon, if, indeed, he is guilty—but he is innocent—indeed he is!'

'If he is no more guilty than you, I am sure he is! Let me be more than your friend, Ellinor—let me know all, and help you all that I can, with the right of an affianced husband.'

'No, no!' said she, frightened both at what she had revealed, and his eager, warm, imploring manner. 'That can never be. You do not know the disgrace that may be hanging over me.'

'If that is all,' said he, 'I take my risk—if that is all—if you only fear that I may shrink from sharing any peril you may be exposed to.'

'It is not peril—it is shame and obloquy ——' she murmured.

'Well! shame and obloquy. Perhaps, if I knew all, I could shield you from it.'

'Don't, pray, speak any more about it now; if you do, I must say "No." '

She did not perceive the implied encouragement in these words; but he did, and they sufficed to make him patient. The time was up, and he could only render her his last services as 'courier,' and none other but the necessary words at starting passed between them. But he went away from the station with a cheerful heart; while she sitting alone and quiet, and at last approaching near to the place where so much was to be decided, felt sadder and sadder, heavier and heavier.

All the intelligence she had gained since she had seen the *Galignani** in Paris, had been from the waiter at the Great Western Hotel, who, after returning from a vain search for an unoccupied *Times*, had volunteered the information that there was an unusual demand for the paper because of Hellingford Assizes, and the trial there for murder that was going on.

There was no electric telegraph in those days;* at every station Ellinor put her head out, and inquired if the murder trial at Hellingford was ended. Some porters told her one thing, some another, in their hurry; she felt that she could not rely on them.

'Drive to Mr Johnson's in the High Street—quick, quick. I will give you half-a-crown if you will go quick.'

For, indeed, her endurance, her patience, was strained almost to snapping; yet at Hellingford station, where doubtless they could have told her the truth, she dared not ask the question. It was past eight o'clock at night. In many houses in the little country town there were unusual lights and sounds. The inhabitants were showing their hospitality to such of the strangers brought by the assizes, as were lingering there now that the business which had drawn them was over. The judges had left the town that afternoon, to wind up the circuit by the short list of a neighbouring county town.

Mr Johnson was entertaining a dinner-party of attorneys when he was summoned from dessert by the announcement of a 'lady who wanted to speak to him immediate and particular.'

He went into his study in not the best of tempers. There he found his client, Miss Wilkins, white and ghastly, standing by the fireplace, with her eyes fixed on the door.

'It is you, Miss Wilkins! I am very glad ——'

'Dixon!' said she. It was all she could utter.

Mr Johnson shook his head.

'Ah! that's a sad piece of business, and I'm afraid it has shortened your visit at Rome.'

'Is he ——?'

'Ay, I am afraid there's no doubt of his guilt. At any rate, the jury found him guilty, and ——'

'And!' she repeated, quickly, sitting down, the better to hear the words that she knew were coming ——

'He is condemned to death.'

'When?'

'The Saturday but one after the judges left the town, I suppose—it's the usual time.'

'Who tried him?'

'Judge Corbet; and, for a new judge, I must say I never knew one who got through his business so well. It was really as much as I could stand to hear him condemning the prisoner to death. Dixon was undoubtedly guilty, and he was as stubborn as could be—a sullen old fellow who would let no one help him through. I am sure I did my best for him at Miss Monro's desire and for your sake. But he would furnish me with no particulars, help us to no evidence. I had the hardest work to keep him from confessing all before witnesses, who would have been bound to repeat it as evidence against him. Indeed, I never thought he would have pleaded "Not Guilty." I think it was only with a desire to justify himself in the eyes of some old Hamley acquaintances. Good God, Miss Wilkins! What's the matter? You're not fainting!' He rang the bell till the rope remained in his hands. 'Here, Esther! Jerry! Whoever you are, come quick! Miss Wilkins has fainted! Water! Wine! Tell Mrs Johnson to come here directly!'

Mrs Johnson, a kind, motherly woman, who had been excluded from the 'gentleman's dinner-party,' and had devoted her time to superintending the dinner her husband had ordered, came in answer to his call for assistance, and found Ellinor lying back in her chair white and senseless.

'Bessy, Miss Wilkins has fainted; she has had a long journey, and is in a fidget about Dixon, the old fellow who was sentenced to be hung for that murder, you know. I can't stop here, I must go back to those men. You bring her round, and see her to bed. The blue room is empty since Horner left. She must stop here, and I'll see her in the morning. Take care of her, and keep her mind as easy as you can, will you, for she can do no good by fidgeting.'

And, knowing that he left Ellinor in good hands, and with plenty of assistance about her, he returned to his friends.

Ellinor came to herself before long.

'It was very foolish of me, but I could not help it,' said she, apologetically.

'No; to be sure not, dear. Here, drink this; it is some of Mr Johnson's best port wine that he has sent out on purpose for you. Or would you rather have some white soup*—or what? We've had everything you could think of at dinner, and you've only to ask and have. And then you must go to bed, my dear—Mr Johnson says you must; and there's a well-aired room, for Mr Horner only left us this morning.'

'I must see Mr Johnson again, please.'

'But indeed you must not. You must not worry your poor

head with business now; and Johnson would only talk to you on business. No; go to bed, and sleep soundly, and then you'll get up quite bright and strong, and fit to talk about business.'

'I cannot sleep—I cannot rest till I have asked Mr Johnson one or two more questions; indeed I cannot,' pleaded Ellinor.

Mrs Johnson knew that her husband's orders on such occasions were peremptory, and that she should come in for a good conjugal scolding if, after what he had said, she ventured to send for him again. Yet Ellinor looked so entreating and wistful that she could hardly find in her heart to refuse her. A bright thought struck her.

'Here is pen and paper, my dear. Could you not write the questions you wanted to ask? and he'll just jot down the answers upon the same piece of paper. I'll send it in by Jerry. He has got friends to dinner with him, you see.'

Ellinor yielded. She sat, resting her weary head on her hand, and wondering what were the questions which would have come so readily to her tongue could she have been face to face with him. As it was, she only wrote this:

'How early can I see you tomorrow morning? Will you take all the necessary steps for my going to Dixon as soon as possible? Could I be admitted to him tonight?'

The pencilled answers were:

'Eight o'clock. Yes. No.'

'I suppose he knows best,' said Ellinor, sighing, as she read the last word. 'But it seems wicked in me to be going to bed—and he so near, in prison.'

When she rose up and stood she felt the former dizziness return, and that reconciled her to seeking rest before she entered upon the duties which were becoming clearer before her, now that she knew all and was on the scene of action. Mrs Johnson brought her white-wine whey* instead of the tea she had asked for; and perhaps it was owing to this that she slept so soundly.

CHAPTER XV

WHEN Ellinor awoke the clear light of dawn was fully in the room. She could not remember where she was; for so many mornings she had wakened up in strange places that it took her several minutes before she could make out the geographical whereabouts of the heavy blue moreen* curtains, the print of the lord-lieutenant of the county on the wall, and all the handsome ponderous mahogany furniture that stuffed up the room. As soon as full memory came into her mind, she started up; nor did she go to bed again, although she saw by her watch on the dressing-table that it was not yet six o'clock. She dressed herself with the dainty completeness so habitual to her that it had become an unconscious habit, and then—the instinct was irrepressible—she put on her bonnet and shawl, and went down, past the servant on her knees cleaning the door step, out into the fresh open air; and so she found her way down the High Street to Hellingford Castle, the building in which the courts of assize were held—the prison in which Dixon lay condemned to die. She almost knew she could not see him; yet it seemed like some amends to her conscience for having slept through so many hours of the night if she made the attempt. She went up to the porter's lodge, and asked the little girl sweeping out the place if she might see Abraham Dixon. The child stared at her, and ran into the house, bringing out her father, a great burly man, who had not yet donned either coat or waistcoat, and who, consequently, felt the morning air as rather nipping. To him Ellinor repeated her question.

'Him as is to be hung come Saturday se'nnight?* Why, ma'am, I've nought to do with it. You may go to the governor's house and try; but, if you'll excuse me, you'll have your walk for your pains. Them in the condemned cells is never seen by nobody without the sheriff's order. You may go up to the governor's house, and welcome; but they'll only tell you the same. Yon's the governor's house.'

Ellinor fully believed the man, and yet she went on to the house indicated, as if she still hoped that in her case there might be some exception to the rule, which she now remembered to have heard of before, in days when such a possible desire as to see a condemned prisoner was treated by her as a wish that some people might have, did have—people as far removed from her circle of circumstances as the inhabitants of the moon. Of course she met with the same reply, a little more abruptly given, as if every man was from his birth bound to know such an obvious regulation.

She went out past the porter, now fully clothed. He was sorry for her disappointment, but could not help saying, with a slight tone of exultation: 'Well, you see I was right, ma'am!'

She walked as nearly round the castle as ever she could, looking up at the few high-barred windows she could see, and wondering in what part of the building Dixon was confined. Then she went into the adjoining churchyard, and sitting down upon a tombstone, she gazed idly at the view spread below her—a view which was considered as the lion of the place,* to be shown to all strangers by the inhabitants of Hellingford. Ellinor did not see it, however. She only saw the blackness of that fatal night. The hurried work—the lanterns glancing to and fro. She only heard the hard breathing of those who are engaged upon unwonted labour; the few hoarse muttered words; the swaying of the branches to and fro. All at once the church clock above her struck eight, and then pealed out for distant labourers to cease their work for a time. Such was the old custom of the place. Ellinor rose up, and made her way back to Mr Johnson's house in High Street. The room felt close and confined in which she awaited her interview with Mr Johnson, who had sent down an apology for having overslept himself, and at last made his appearance in a hurried, half-awakened state, in consequence of his late hospitality of the night before.

'I am so sorry I gave you all so much trouble last night,' said Ellinor, apologetically. 'I was overtired, and much shocked by the news I heard.'

'No trouble, no trouble, I am sure. Neither Mrs Johnson nor I felt it in the least a trouble. Many ladies, I know, feel such things very trying, though there are others that can stand a judge's putting on the black cap better than most men. I'm sure I saw some as composed as could be under Judge Corbet's speech.'

'But about Dixon? He must not die, Mr Johnson.'

'Well, I don't know that he will,' said Mr Johnson, in something of the tone of voice he would have used in soothing a child. 'Judge Corbet said something about the possibility of a pardon. The jury did not recommend him to mercy: you see, his looks went so much against him, and all the evidence was so strong, and no defence, so to speak, for he would not furnish any information on which we could base defence. But the judge did give some hope, to my mind, though there are others that think differently.'

'I tell you, Mr Johnson, he must not die, and he shall not. To whom must I go?'

'Whew! Have you got additional evidence?' with a sudden sharp glance of professional inquiry.

'Never mind,' Ellinor answered. 'I beg your pardon . . . . only tell me into whose hands the power of life and death has passed.'

'Into the Home Secretary's—Sir Philip Homes; but you cannot get access to him on such an errand. It is the judge who tried the case that must urge a reprieve—Judge Corbet.'

'Judge Corbet?'

'Yes; and he was rather inclined to take a merciful view of the whole case. I saw it in his charge. He'll be the person for you to see. I suppose you don't like to give me your confidence, or else I could arrange and draw up what will have to be said?'

'No. What I have to say must be spoken to the arbiter—to no one else. I am afraid I answered you impatiently just now. You must forgive me; if you knew all, I am sure you would.'

'Say no more, my dear lady. We will suppose you have some evidence not adduced at the trial. Well; you must go up and see the judge, since you don't choose to impart it to anyone, and lay it before him. He will, doubtless, compare it with his notes of the trial, and see how far it agrees with them. Of course you must be prepared with some kind of proof; for Judge Corbet will have to test your evidence.'

'It seems strange to think of him as the judge,' said Ellinor, almost to herself.

'Why, yes. He's but a young judge. You knew him at Hamley, I suppose? I remember his reading there with Mr Ness.'

'Yes: but do not let us talk more about that time. Tell me, when can I see Dixon? I have been to the castle already, but they said I must have a sheriff's order.'

'To be sure. I desired Mrs Johnson to tell you so last night. Old Ormerod was dining here; he is clerk to the magistrates, and I told him of your wish. He said he would see Sir Henry

Croper, and have the order here before ten. But all this time Mrs Johnson is waiting breakfast for us. Let me take you into the dining-room.'

It was very hard work for Ellinor to do her duty as a guest, and to allow herself to be interested and talked to on local affairs by her host and hostess. But she felt as if she had spoken shortly and abruptly to Mr Johnson in their previous conversation, and that she must try and make amends for it; so she attended to all the details about the restoration of the church, and the difficulty of getting a good music-master for the three little Miss Johnsons, with all her usual gentle good breeding and patience, though no one can tell how her heart and imagination were full of the coming interview with poor old Dixon.

By-and-by Mr Johnson was called out of the room to see Mr Ormerod, and receive the order of admission from him. Ellinor clasped her hands tight together as she listened with apparent composure to Mrs Johnson's never-ending praise of the Hullah system.* But, when Mr Johnson returned she could not help interrupting her eulogy, and saying,

'Then, I may go now?'

Yes, the order was there—she might go, and Mr Johnson would accompany her, to see that she met with no difficulty or obstacle.

As they walked thither, he told her that someone—a turnkey, or someone—would have to be present at the interview; that such was always the rule in the case of condemned prisoners; but that if this third person was 'obliging,' he would keep out of earshot. Mr Johnson quietly took care to see that the turnkey who accompanied Ellinor was 'obliging.'

The man took her across high-walled courts, along stone corridors, and through many locked doors, before they came to the condemned cells.

'I've had three at a time in here,' said he, unlocking the final door, 'after Judge Morton had been here. We always called him the "Hanging Judge." But it's five years since he died, and now there's never more than one in at a time; though once it was a woman for poisoning her husband. Mary Jones was her name.'

The stone passage out of which the cells opened was light, and bare, and scrupulously clean. Over each door was a small barred window, and an outer window of the same description was placed high up in the cell, which the turnkey now opened.

Old Abraham Dixon was sitting on the side of his bed, doing nothing. His head was bent, his frame sunk, and he did not seem to care to turn round and see who it was that entered.

Ellinor tried to keep down her sobs while the man went up to him, and laying his hand on his shoulder, and lightly shaking him, he said:

'Here's a friend come to see you, Dixon.' Then, turning to Ellinor, he added, 'There's some as takes it in this kind o' stunned way, while others are as restless as a wild beast in a cage, after they're sentenced.' And then he withdrew into the passage, leaving the door open, so that he could see all that passed if he chose to look, but ostentatiously keeping his eyes averted, and whistling to himself, so that he could not hear what they said to each other.

Dixon looked up at Ellinor, but then let his eyes fall on the ground again; the increasing trembling of his shrunk frame was the only sign he gave that he had recognized her.

She sat down by him, and took his large horny hand in hers. She wanted to overcome her inclination to sob hysterically before she spoke. She stroked the bony shrivelled fingers, on which her hot scalding tears kept dropping.

'Dunnot do that,' said he, at length, in a hollow voice. 'Dunnot take on about it; it's best as it is, missy.'

'No, Dixon, it's not best. It shall not be. You know it shall not—cannot be.'

'I'm rather tired of living. It's been a great strain and labour for me. I think I'd as lief* be with God as with men. And you see, I were fond on him ever sin' he were a little lad, and told me what hard times he had at school, he did, just as if I were his brother! I loved him next to Molly Greaves. Dear! and I shall see her again, I reckon, come next Saturday week! They'll think well on me, up there, I'll be bound; though I cannot say as I've done all as I should do here below.'

'But Dixon,' said Ellinor, 'you know who did this—this ——'

'Guilty o' murder,' said he. 'That's what they called it. Murder. And that it never were, choose who did it.'

'My poor, poor father did it. I am going up to London this

afternoon; I am going to see the judge, and tell him all.'

'Don't you demean yourself to that fellow, missy. It's him as left you in the lurch as soon as sorrow and shame came nigh you.'

He looked up at her now, for the first time; but she went on as if she had not noticed those wistful, weary eyes.

'Yes! I shall go to him. I know who it is; and I am resolved. After all, he may be better than a stranger, for real help; and I shall never remember any—anything else, when I think of you, good faithful friend.'

'He looks but a wizened old fellow in his grey wig. I should hardly ha' known him. I gave him a look, as much as to say, "I could tell tales o' you, my lord judge, if I chose." I don't know if he heeded me, though. I suppose it were for a sign of old acquaintance that he said he'd recommend me to mercy. But I'd sooner have death nor mercy, by long odds. Yon man out there says mercy means Botany Bay.* It 'ud be like killing me by inches, that would. It would. I'd liefer go straight to Heaven, than live on, among the black folk.'

He began to shake again: this idea of transportation, from its very mysteriousness, was more terrifying to him than death. He kept on saying plaintively, 'Missy, you'll never let 'em send me to Botany Bay; I couldn't stand that.'

'No, no!' said she. 'You shall come out of this prison, and go home with me to East Chester; I promise you, you shall. I promise you. I don't yet quite know how, but trust in my promise. Don't fret about Botany Bay. If you go there, I go too. I am so sure you will not go. And you know if you have done anything against the law in concealing that fatal night's work, I did too, and if you are to be punished, I will be punished too. But I feel sure it will be right; I mean, as right as anything can be, with the recollection of that time present to us, as it must always be.' She almost spoke these last words to herself. They sat on, hand in hand, for a few minutes more in silence.

'I thought you'd come to me. I knowed you were far away in foreign parts. But I used to pray to God. "Dear Lord God!" I used to say, "let me see her again." I told the chaplain as I'd begin to pray for repentance, at after I'd done praying that I might see you once again: for it just seemed to take all my strength to say those words as I've named. And I thought as how God knew what was in my heart better than I could tell Him. How I was main and sorry* for all as I'd ever done wrong; I allays were, at after it was done; but I thought as no one could know how bitter-keen I wanted to see you.'

Again they sank into silence. Ellinor felt as if she would fain be away and active in procuring his release; but she also perceived how precious her presence was to him; and she did not like to leave him a moment before the time allowed her. His voice had changed to a weak piping old man's quaver, and between the times of his talking he seemed to relapse into a dreamy state; but through it all he held her hand tight, as though afraid that she would leave him.

So the hour elapsed, with no more spoken words than those above. From time to time Ellinor's tears dropped down upon her lap; she could not restrain them, though she scarce knew why she cried just then.

At length the turnkey said that the time allowed for the interview was ended. Ellinor spoke no word; but rose, and bent down and kissed the old man's forehead, saying,

'I shall come back tomorrow. God keep and comfort you.'

So, almost without an articulate word from him in reply (he rose up, and stood on his shaking legs, as she bade him farewell, putting his hand to his head with the old habitual mark of respect), she went her way, swiftly out of the prison, swiftly back with Mr Johnson to his house, scarcely patient or strong enough in her hurry to explain to him fully all that she meant to do. She only asked him a few absolutely requisite questions; and informed him of her intention to go straight to London to see Judge Corbet.

Just before the railway carriage in which she was seated started on the journey, she bent forward and put out her hand once more to Mr Johnson. 'Tomorrow I will thank you for all,' she said. 'I cannot now.'

It was about the same time that she had reached Hellingford on the previous night, that she arrived at the Great Western station on this evening—past eight o'clock. On the way she had remembered and arranged many things: one important question she had omitted to ask Mr Johnson; but that was easily remedied. She had not inquired where she could find Judge Corbet; if she had, Mr Johnson could probably have given her his professional address. As it was, she asked for a Post-Office Directory at the hotel, and looked out for his private dwelling—128, Hyde Park Gardens.

She rang for a waiter.

'Can I send a messenger to Hyde Park Gardens,' she said, hurrying on to her business, tired and worn-out as she was. 'It is only to ask if Judge Corbet is at home this evening. If he is, I must go and see him.'

The waiter was a little surprised, and would gladly have had her name to authorize the inquiry; but she could not bear to send it; it would be bad enough that first meeting, without the feeling that he, too, had had time to recall all the past days. Better to go in upon him unprepared, and plunge into the subject.

The waiter returned with the answer while she yet was pacing up and down the room restlessly, nerving herself for the interview.

'The messenger has been to Hyde Park Gardens, ma'am. The Judge and Lady Corbet are gone out to dinner.'

Lady Corbet! Of course Ellinor knew that he was married. Had she not been present at the wedding in East Chester Cathedral; but, somehow, these recent events had so carried her back to old times, that the intimate association of the names, 'the Judge and Lady Corbet,' seemed to awaken her out of some dream.

'Oh, very well,' she said, just as if these thoughts were not passing rapidly through her mind. 'Let me be called at seven tomorrow morning, and let me have a cab at the door to Hyde Park Gardens at eight.'

And so she went to bed; but scarcely to sleep. All night long she had the scenes of those old times, the happy, happy days of her youth, the one terrible night that cut all happiness short, present before her. She could almost have fancied that she heard the long-silent sounds of her father's step, her father's way of breathing, the rustle of his newspaper as he hastily turned it over, coming through the lapse of years; the silence of the night. She knew that she had the little writing-case of her girlhood with her, in her box. The treasures of the dead that it contained, the morsel of dainty sewing, the little sister's golden curl, the half-finished letter to Mr Corbet, were all there. She took them out, and looked at each separately; looked at them long—long and wistfully. 'Will it be of any use to me?' she questioned of herself, as she was about to put her father's letter back into its receptacle. She read the last words over again, once more: 'From my death-bed I adjure you to stand her friend; I will beg pardon on my knees for anything.'

'I will take it,' thought she. 'I need not bring it out; most likely there will be no need for it, after what I shall have to say. All is so altered, so changed between us, as utterly as if it never had been, that I think I shall have no shame in showing it him for my own part of it. While, if he sees poor papa's, dear, dear papa's suffering humility, it may make him think more gently of one who loved him once, though they parted in wrath with each other, I'm afraid.'

So she took the letter with her when she drove to Hyde Park Gardens.

Every nerve in her body was in such a high state of tension that she could have screamed out at the cabman's boisterous knock at the door. She got out hastily, before anyone was ready or willing to answer such an untimely summons; paid the man double what he ought to have had; and stood there, sick, trembling, and humble.

CHAPTER XVI AND LAST

'Is Judge Corbet at home? Can I see him?' she asked of the footman, who at length answered the door.

He looked at her curiously, and a little familiarly, before he replied,

'Why, yes! He's pretty sure to be at home at this time of day; but whether he'll see you is quite another thing.'

'Would you be so good as to ask him? It is on very particular business.'

'Can you give me a card? your name, perhaps, will do, if you have not a card. I say, Simmons' (to a lady's-maid crossing the hall), 'is the judge up yet?'

'Oh, yes! he's in his dressing-room this half-hour. My lady is coming down directly. It is just breakfast time.'

'Can't you put it off, and come again, a little later?' said he, turning once more to Ellinor—white Ellinor! trembling Ellinor!

'No! please let me come in. I will wait. I am sure Judge Corbet will see me, if you will tell him I am here. Miss Wilkins. He will know the name.'

'Well, then; will you wait here till I have got breakfast in?' said the man, letting her into the hall, and pointing to the bench there. He took her, from her dress, to be a lady's-maid or governess, or at most a tradesman's daughter; and besides, he was behindhand with all his preparations. She came in and sat down.

'You will tell him I am here,' she said, faintly.

'Oh, yes, never fear: I'll send up word, though I don't believe he'll come to you before breakfast.'

He told a page, who ran upstairs, and, knocking at the judge's door, said that a Miss Jenkins wanted to speak to him.

'Who?' asked the judge from the inside.

'Miss Jenkins. She said you would know the name, sir.'

'Not I. Tell her to wait.'

So Ellinor waited. Presently down the stairs, with slow deliberate dignity, came the handsome Lady Corbet, in her rustling silks and ample petticoats, carrying her fine boy, and followed by her majestic nurse. She was ill-pleased that anyone should come and take up her husband's time when he was at home, and supposed to be enjoying domestic leisure; and her imperious, inconsiderate nature did not prompt her to any civility towards the gentle creature sitting down weary and heart-sick in her house. On the contrary, she looked her over as she slowly descended, till Ellinor shrank abashed from the steady gaze of the large black eyes. Then she, her baby and nurse, disappeared into the large dining-room, into which all the preparations for breakfast had been carried.

The next person to come down would be the judge. Ellinor instinctively put down her veil. She heard his quick decided step; she had known it well of old.

He gave one of his sharp, shrewd glances at the person sitting in the hall and waiting to speak to him, and his practised eye recognized the lady at once, in spite of her travel-worn dress.

'Will you just come into this room,' said he, opening the door of his study, to the front of the house: the dining-room was to the back; they communicated by folding-doors.

The astute lawyer placed himself with his back to the window; it was the natural position of the master of the apartment; but it also gave him the advantage of seeing his companion's face in full light. Ellinor lifted her veil; it had only been a dislike to a recognition in the hall, which had made her put it down.

Judge Corbet's countenance changed more than hers; she had been prepared for the interview; he was not. But he usually had the full command of the expression on his face.

'Ellinor! Miss Wilkins! is it you?' And he went forwards, holding out his hand with cordial greeting, under which the embarrassment, if he felt any, was carefully concealed. She could not speak all at once in the way she wished.

'That stupid Henry told me Jenkins! I beg your pardon. How could they put you down to sit in the hall? You must come in and have some breakfast with us; Lady Corbet will be delighted, I'm sure.' His sense of the awkwardness of the meeting with the woman who was once to have been his wife, and of the probable introduction which was to follow to the woman who was his actual wife, grew upon him, and made him speak a little hurriedly. Ellinor's next words were a wonderful relief; and her soft, gentle way of speaking was like the touch of a cooling balsam.

'Thank you, you must excuse me. I am come strictly on business, otherwise I should never have thought of calling on you at such an hour. It is about poor Dixon.'

'Ah! I thought as much!' said the judge, handing her a chair, and sitting down himself. He tried to compose his mind to business, but, in spite of his strength of character, and his present efforts, the remembrance of old times would come back at the sound of her voice. He wondered if he was as much changed in appearance as she struck him as being in that first look of recognition; after that first glance he rather avoided meeting her eyes.

'I knew how much you would feel it. Someone at Hellingford told me you were abroad, in Rome, I think. But you must not distress yourself unnecessarily; the sentence is sure to be commuted to transportation, or something equivalent. I was talking to the Home Secretary about it only last night. Lapse of time and subsequent good character quite preclude any idea of capital punishment.' All the time that he said this he had other thoughts at the back of his mind—some curiosity, a little regret, a touch of remorse, a wonder how the meeting (which, of course, would have to be some time) between Lady Corbet and Ellinor would go off; but he spoke clearly enough on the subject in hand, and no outward mark of distraction from it appeared.

Ellinor answered:

'I came to tell you, what I suppose may be told to any judge, in confidence and full reliance on his secrecy, that Abraham Dixon was not the murderer.' She stopped short, and choked a little.

The judge looked sharply at her.

'Then you know who was?' said he.

'Yes,' she replied, with a low, steady voice, looking him full in the face, with sad, solemn eyes.

The truth flashed into his mind. He shaded his face, and did not speak for a minute or two. Then he said, not looking up, a little hoarsely, 'This, then, was the shame you told me of long ago?'

'Yes,' said she.

Both sat quite still; quite silent for some time. Through the silence a sharp, clear voice was heard speaking through the folding-doors.

'Take the kedgeree down, and tell the cook to keep it hot for the judge. It is so tiresome people coming on business here, as if the judge had not his proper hours for being at chambers.'

He got up hastily, and went into the dining-room; but he had audibly some difficulty in curbing his wife's irritation.

When he came back, Ellinor said:

'I am afraid I ought not to have come here, now.'

'Oh! it's all nonsense!' said he, in a tone of annoyance. 'You've done quite right.' He seated himself where he had been before; and again half-covered his face with his hand.

'And Dixon knew of this. I believe I must put the fact plainly to you—your father was the guilty person? He murdered Dunster?'

'Yes. If you call it murder. It was done by a blow, in the heat of passion. No one can ever tell how Dunster always irritated papa,' said Ellinor, in a stupid, heavy way; and then she sighed.

'How do you know this?' There was a kind of tender reluctance in the judge's voice, as he put all these questions. Ellinor had made up her mind beforehand that something like them must be asked, and must also be answered; but she spoke like a sleep-walker.

'I came into papa's room just after he had struck Mr Dunster the blow. He was lying insensible, as we thought—dead, as he really was.'

'What was Dixon's part in it? He must have known a good deal about it. And the horse-lancet that was found with his name upon it?'

'Papa went to wake Dixon, and he brought his fleam—I suppose to try and bleed him. I have said enough, have I not? I seem so confused. But I will answer any question to make it appear that Dixon is innocent.'

The judge had been noting all down. He sat still now without replying to her. Then he wrote rapidly, referring to his previous paper, from time to time. In five minutes or so he read the facts which Ellinor had stated, as he now arranged them, in a legal and connected form. He just asked her one or two trivial questions as he did so. Then he read it over to her, and asked her to sign it. She took up the pen, and held it, hesitating.

'This will never be made public?' said she.

'No! I shall take care that no one but the Home Secretary sees it.'

'Thank you. I could not help it, now it has come to this.'

'There are not many men like Dixon,' said the judge, almost to himself, as he sealed the paper in an envelope.

'No!' said Ellinor. 'I never knew anyone so faithful.'

And just at the same moment the reflection on a less faithful person that these words might seem to imply struck both of them, and each instinctively glanced at the other.

'Ellinor!' said the judge, after a moment's pause, 'we are friends, I hope?'

'Yes; friends,' said she, quietly and sadly.

He felt a little chagrined at her answer. Why, he could hardly tell. To cover any sign of his feeling he went on talking.

'Where are you living now?'

'At East Chester.'

'But you come sometimes to town, don't you? Let us know always—whenever you come; and Lady Corbet shall call on you. Indeed, I wish you'd let me bring her to see you today.'

'Thank you. I am going straight back to Hellingford; at least, as soon as you can get me the pardon for Dixon.'

He half smiled at her ignorance.

'The pardon must be sent to the sheriff, who holds the warrant for his execution. But, of course, you may have every assurance that it shall be sent as soon as possible. It is just the same as if he had it now.'

'Thank you very much,' said Ellinor, rising.

'Pray don't go without breakfast. If you would rather not see Lady Corbet just now, it shall be sent in to you in this room, unless you have already breakfasted.'

'No, thank you; I would rather not. You are very kind, and I am very glad to have seen you once again. There is just one thing more,' said she, colouring a little and hesitating. 'This note to you was found under papa's pillow after his death; some of it refers to past things; but I should be glad if you could think as kindly as you can of poor papa—and so—if you will read it ——'

He took it and read it, not without emotion. Then he laid it down on his table, and said,

'Poor man! he must have suffered a great deal for that night's work. And you, Ellinor, you have suffered too.'

Yes, she had suffered; and he who spoke had been one of the instruments of her suffering, although he seemed forgetful of it. She shook her head a little for reply. Then she looked up at him—they were both standing at the time—and said:

'I think I shall be happier now. I always knew it must be found out. Once more, goodbye, and thank you. I may take this letter, I suppose?' said she, casting envious loving eyes at her father's note, lying unregarded on the table.

'Oh! certainly, certainly,' said he; and then he took her hand; he held it, while he looked into her face. He had thought it changed when he had first seen her, but it was now almost the same to him as of yore. The sweet shy eyes, the indicated dimple in the cheek, and something of fever had brought a faint pink flush into her usually colourless cheeks. Married judge though he was, he was not sure if she had not more charms for him still in her sorrow and her shabbiness than the handsome stately wife in the next room, whose looks had not been of the pleasantest when he left her a few minutes before. He sighed a little regretfully as Ellinor went away. He had obtained the position he had struggled for, and sacrificed for; but now he could not help wishing that the slaughtered creature laid on the shrine of his ambition were alive again.

The kedgeree was brought up again, smoking hot, but it remained untasted by him; and though he appeared to be reading *The Times*, he did not see a word of the distinct type. His wife, meanwhile, continued her complaints of the untimely visitor, whose name he did not give to her in its corrected form, as he was not anxious that she should have it in her power to identify the call of this morning with a possible future acquaintance.

When Ellinor reached Mr Johnson's house in Hellingford that afternoon, she found Miss Monro was there, and that she had been with much difficulty restrained by Mr Johnson from following her to London.

Miss Monro fondled and purred inarticulately through her tears over her recovered darling, before she could speak intelligibly enough to tell her that Canon Livingstone had come straight to see her immediately on his return to East Chester, and had suggested her journey to Hellingford, in order that she might be of all the comfort she could to Ellinor. She did not at first let out that he had accompanied her to Hellingford; she was a little afraid of Ellinor's displeasure at his being there; Ellinor had always objected so much to any advance towards intimacy with him that Miss Monro had wished to make. But Ellinor was different now.

'How white you are, Nelly!' said Miss Monro. 'You have been

travelling too much and too fast, my child.'

'My head aches!' said Ellinor, wearily. 'But I must go to the castle, and tell my poor Dixon that he is reprieved,—I am so tired! Will you ask Mr Johnson to get me leave to see him? He will know all about it.'

She threw herself down on the bed in the spare room; the bed with the heavy blue curtains. After an unheeded remonstrance, Miss Monro went to do her bidding. But it was now late afternoon, and Mr Johnson said that it would be impossible for him to get permission from the sheriff that night.

'Besides,' said he, courteously, 'one scarcely knows whether Miss Wilkins may not give the old man false hopes,—whether she has not been excited to have false hopes herself; it might be a cruel kindness to let her see him, without more legal certainty as to what his sentence, or reprieve, is to be. By tomorrow morning, if I have properly understood her story, which was a little confused ——'

'She is so dreadfully tired, poor creature,' put in Miss Monro, who never could bear the shadow of a suspicion that Ellinor was not wisest, best,* in all relations and situations of life.

Mr Johnson went on, with a deprecatory bow: 'Well then—it really is the only course open to her besides,—persuade her to rest for this evening. By tomorrow morning I will have obtained the sheriff's leave, and he will most likely have heard from London.'

'Thank you! I believe that will be best.'

'It is the only course,' said he.

When Miss Monro returned to the bedroom, Ellinor was in a heavy feverish slumber: so feverish and so uneasy did she appear, that, after the hesitation of a moment or two, Miss Monro had no scruple in wakening her.

But she did not appear to understand the answer to her request; she did not seem even to remember that she had made any request.

The journey to England, the misery, the surprises, had been too much for her. The morrow morning came, bringing the formal free pardon for Abraham Dixon. The sheriff's order for her admission to see the old man lay awaiting her wish to use it; but she knew nothing of all this.

For days, nay weeks, she hovered between life and death, tended, as of old, by Miss Monro, while good Mrs Johnson was ever willing to assist.

One summer evening in early June she wakened into memory.

Miss Monro heard the faint piping voice, as she kept her watch by the bedside.

'Where is Dixon?' asked she.

'At the canon's house at Bromham.' This was the name of Dr Livingstone's country parish.

'Why?'

'We thought it better to get him into country air and fresh scenes at once.'

'How is he?'

'Much better. Get strong, and he shall come to see you.'

'You are sure all is right?' said Ellinor.

'Sure, my dear. All is quite right.'

Then Ellinor went to sleep again out of very weakness and weariness.

From that time she recovered pretty steadily. Her great desire was to return to East Chester as soon as possible. The associations of grief, anxiety, and coming illness, connected with Hellingford, made her wish to be once again in the solemn, quiet, sunny close of East Chester.

Canon Livingstone came over to assist Miss Monro in managing the journey with her invalid. But he did not intrude himself upon Ellinor, any more than he had done in coming from home.*

The morning after her return, Miss Monro said:

'Do you feel strong enough to see Dixon?'

'Yes. Is he here?'

'He is at the canon's house. He sent for him from Bromham, in order that he might be ready for you to see him when you wished.'

'Please let him come directly,' said Ellinor, flushing and trembling.

She went to the door to meet the tottering old man; she led him to the easy-chair that had been placed and arranged for herself; she knelt down before him, and put his hands on her head, he trembling and shaking all the while.

'Forgive me all the shame and misery, Dixon. Say you forgive me; and give me your blessing. And then let never a word of the terrible past be spoken between us.'

'It's not for me to forgive you as never did harm to no one ——'

'But say you do—it will ease my heart.'

'I forgive thee!' said he. And then he raised himself to his feet with effort, and, standing up above her, he blessed her solemnly.

After that he sat down, she by him, gazing at him.

'Yon's a good man, missy,' he said, at length, lifting his slow eyes and looking at her. 'Better nor t'other ever was.'

'He is a good man,' said Ellinor.

But no more was spoken on the subject. The next day, Canon Livingstone made his formal call. Ellinor would fain have kept Miss Monro in the room, but that worthy lady knew better than to stop.

They went on, forcing talk on indifferent subjects. At last he could speak no longer on everything but that which he had most at heart. 'Miss Wilkins!' (he had got up, and was standing by the mantelpiece, apparently examining the ornaments upon it)—'Miss Wilkins! is there any chance of your giving me a favourable answer now—you know what I mean—what we spoke about at the Great Western Hotel, that day?'

Ellinor hung her head.

'You know that I was once engaged before?'

'Yes! I know; to Mr Corbet—he that is now the judge; you cannot suppose that would make any difference, if that is all. I have loved you, and you only, ever since we met eighteen years ago, Miss Wilkins—Ellinor—put me out of suspense.'

'I will!' said she, putting out her thin white hand for him to take and kiss, almost with tears of gratitude, but she seemed frightened at his impetuosity, and tried to check him. 'Wait—you have not heard all—my poor, poor father, in a fit of anger, irritated beyond his bearing, struck the blow that killed Mr Dunster—Dixon and I knew of it, just after the blow was struck—we helped to hide it—we kept the secret—my poor father died of sorrow and remorse—you now know all—can you still love me? It seems to me as if I had been an accomplice in such a terrible thing!'

'Poor, poor Ellinor!' said he, now taking her in his arms as a shelter. 'How I wish I had known of all this years and years ago: I could have stood between you and so much!'

Those who pass through the village of Bromham, and pause to look over the laurel-hedge that separates the rectory garden from the road, may often see, on summer days, an old, old man, sitting in a wicker-chair, out upon the lawn. He leans upon his stick, and seldom raises his bent head; but for all that his eyes are on a level with the two little fairy children who come to him in all their small joys and sorrows, and who learnt to lisp his name, almost as soon as they did that of their father and mother.

Nor is Miss Monro often absent; and although she prefers to retain the old house in the Close for winter quarters, she generally makes her way across to Canon Livingstone's residence every evening.

SO ENDS 'A DARK NIGHT'S WORK'

LIBBIE MARSH'S THREE ERAS

ERA I

VALENTINE'S DAY

Last November but one, there was a flitting in our neighbourhood; hardly a flitting, after all, for it was only a single person changing her place of abode from one lodging to another; and instead of a cartload of drawers and baskets, dressers and beds, with old king clock at the top of all, it was only one large wooden chest to be carried after the girl, who moved slowly and heavily along the streets, listless and depressed, more from the state of her mind than of her body. It was Libbie Marsh, who had been obliged to quit her room in Dean Street, because the acquaintances whom she had been living with were leaving Manchester. She tried to think herself fortunate in having met with lodgings rather more out of the town, and with those who were known to be respectable; she did indeed try to be contented, but in spite of her reason, the old feeling of desolation came over her, as she was now about to be thrown again entirely among strangers.

No. 2, —— Court, Albemarle Street, was reached at last, and the pace, slow as it was, slackened as she drew near the spot where she was to be left by the man who carried her box, for, trivial as her acquaintance with him was, he was not quite a stranger, as everyone else was, peering out of their open doors, and satisfying themselves it was only 'Dixon's new lodger.'

Dixon's house was the last on the left-hand side of the court. A high dead brick wall connected it with its opposite neighbour. All the dwellings were of the same monotonous pattern, and one side of the court looked at its exact likeness opposite, as if it were seeing itself in a looking-glass.

Dixon's house was shut up, and the key left next door; but the woman in whose charge it was left knew that Libbie was expected, and came forward to say a few explanatory words, to unlock the door, and stir the dull grey ashes that were lazily burning in the grate: and then she returned to her own house, leaving poor Libbie standing alone with the great big chest in the middle of the house-place* floor, with no one to say a word to (even a commonplace remark would have been better than this dull silence), that could help her to repel the fast-coming tears.

Dixon and his wife, and their eldest girl, worked in factories, and were absent all day from the house: the youngest child, also a little girl, was boarded out on the week-days at the neighbour's where the door-key was deposited, but although busy making dirt-pies, at the entrance to the court, when Libbie came in, she was too young to care much about her parents' new lodger. Libbie knew that she was to sleep with the elder girl in the front bedroom, but, as you may fancy, it seemed a liberty even to go upstairs to take off her things, when no one was at home to marshal the way up the ladder-like steps. So she could only take off her bonnet, and sit down, and gaze at the now blazing fire, and think sadly on the past, and on the lonely creature she was in this wide world—father and mother gone, her little brother long since dead—he would have been more than nineteen had he been alive, but she only thought of him as the darling baby; her only friends (to call friends) living far away at their new house; her employers, kind enough people in their way, but too rapidly twirling round on this bustling earth to have leisure to think of the little work-woman, excepting when they wanted gowns turned, carpets mended, or household linen darned; and hardly even the natural though hidden hope of a young girl's heart, to cheer her on with the bright visions of a home of her own at some future day, where, loving and beloved, she might fulfil a woman's dearest duties.

For Libbie was very plain, as she had known so long that the consciousness of it had ceased to mortify her. You can hardly live in Manchester without having some idea of your personal appearance: the factory lads and lasses take good care of that; and if you meet them at the hours when they are pouring out of the mills, you are sure to hear a good number of truths, some of them combined with such a spirit of impudent fun, that you can scarcely keep from laughing, even at the joke against yourself. Libbie had often and often been greeted by such questions as—'How long is it since you were a beauty?'—'What would you take a day to stand in the fields to scare away the birds?' &c., for her to linger under any impression as to her looks.

While she was thus musing, and quietly crying, under the pictures her fancy had conjured up, the Dixons came dropping in, and surprised her with her wet cheeks and quivering lips.

She almost wished to have the stillness again that had so oppressed her an hour ago, they talked and laughed so loudly and so much, and bustled about so noisily over everything they did. Dixon took hold of one iron handle of her box, and helped her to bump it upstairs, while his daughter Anne followed to see the unpacking, and what sort of clothes 'little sewing body had gotten.' Mrs Dixon rattled out her tea-things, and put the kettle on, fetched home her youngest child, which added to the commotion. Then she called Anne downstairs, and sent her for this thing and that: eggs to put to the cream, it was so thin; ham, to give a relish to the bread and butter; some new bread, hot, if she could get it. Libbie heard all these orders, given at full pitch of Mrs Dixon's voice, and wondered at their extravagance, so different from the habits of the place where she had last lodged. But they were fine spinners, in the receipt of good wages; and confined all day in an atmosphere ranging from seventy-five to eighty degrees. They had lost all natural, healthy appetite for simple food, and, having no higher tastes, found their greatest enjoyment in their luxurious meals.

When tea was ready, Libbie was called downstairs, with a rough but hearty invitation, to share their meal; she sat mutely at the corner of the tea-table, while they went on with their own conversation about people and things she knew nothing about, till at length she ventured to ask for a candle, to go and finish her unpacking before bedtime, as she had to go out sewing for several succeeding days. But once in the comparative peace of her bedroom, her energy failed her, and she contented herself with locking her Noah's ark of a chest, and put out her candle, and went to sit by the window, and gaze out at the bright heavens; for ever and ever 'the blue sky, that bends over all,'* sheds down a feeling of sympathy with the sorrowful at the solemn hours when the ceaseless stars are seen to pace its depths.

By-and-by her eye fell down to gazing at the corresponding window to her own, on the opposite side of the court. It was lighted, but the blind was drawn down: upon the blind she saw, first unconsciously, the constant weary motion of a little spectral shadow, a child's hand and arm—no more; long, thin fingers hanging down from the wrist, while the arm moved up and down, as if keeping time to the heavy pulses of dull pain. She could not help hoping that sleep would soon come to still that incessant, feeble motion: and now and then it did cease, as if the little creature had dropped into a slumber from very weariness; but presently the arm jerked up with the fingers clenched, as if with a sudden start of agony. When Anne came up to bed, Libbie was still sitting, watching the shadow, and she directly asked to whom it belonged.

'It will be Margaret Hall's lad. Last summer, when it was so hot, there was no biding with the window shut at night, and theirs was open too: and many's the time he has waked me with his moans; they say he's been better sin' cold weather came.'

'Is he always in bed? Whatten ails him?' asked Libbie.

'Summat's amiss wi' his backbone, folks say; he's better and worse, like. He's a nice little chap enough, and his mother's not that bad either; only my mother and her had words, so now we don't speak.'

Libbie went on watching, and when she next spoke, to ask who and what his mother was, Anne Dixon was fast asleep.

Time passed away, and as usual unveiled the hidden things. Libbie found out that Margaret Hall was a widow, who earned her living as a washerwoman; that the little suffering lad was her only child, her dearly beloved. That while she scolded, pretty nearly, everybody else, 'till her name was up'* in the neighbourhood for a termagant, to him she was evidently most tender and gentle. He lay alone on his little bed, near the window, through the day, while she was away toiling for a livelihood. But when Libbie had plain sewing to do at her lodgings, instead of going out to sew, she used to watch from her bedroom window for the time when the shadows opposite, by their mute gestures, told that the mother had returned to bend over her child, to smooth his pillow, to alter his position, to get him his nightly cup of tea. And often in the night Libbie could not help rising gently from bed, to see if the little arm was waving up and down, as was his accustomed habit when sleepless from pain.

Libbie had a good deal of sewing to do at home that winter, and whenever it was not so cold as to benumb her fingers, she took it upstairs, in order to watch the little lad in her few odd moments of pause. On his better days he could sit up enough to peep out of his window, and she found he liked to look at her. Presently she ventured to nod to him across the court; and his faint smile, and ready nod back again, showed that this gave him pleasure. I think she would have been encouraged by this smile to have proceeded to a speaking acquaintance, if it had not been for his terrible mother, to whom it seemed to be irritation enough to know that Libbie was a lodger at the Dixons' for her to talk at her whenever they encountered each other, and to live evidently in wait for some good opportunity of abuse.

With her constant interest in him, Libbie soon discovered his great want of an object on which to occupy his thoughts, and which might distract his attention, when alone through the long day, from the pain he endured. He was very fond of flowers. It was November when she had first removed to her lodgings, but it had been very mild weather, and a few flowers yet lingered in the gardens, which the country people gathered into nosegays, and brought on market-days into Manchester. His mother had bought him a bunch of Michaelmas daisies the very day Libbie had become a neighbour, and she watched their history. He put them first in an old teapot, of which the spout was broken off and the lid lost; and he daily replenished the teapot from the jug of water his mother left near him to quench his feverish thirst. By-and-by, one or two of the constellation of lilac stars faded, and then the time he had hitherto spent in admiring, almost caressing them, was devoted to cutting off those flowers whose decay marred the beauty of the nosegay. It took him half the morning, with his feeble, languid motions, and his cumbrous old scissors, to trim up his diminished darlings. Then at last he seemed to think he had better preserve the few that remained by drying them; so they were carefully put between the leaves of the old Bible; and then, whenever a better day came, when he had strength enough to lift the ponderous book, he used to open the pages to look at his flower friends. In winter he could have no more living flowers to tend.

Libbie thought and thought, till at last an idea flashed upon her mind, that often made a happy smile steal over her face as she stitched away, and that cheered her through the solitary winter—for solitary it continued to be, though the Dixons were very good sort of people, never pressed her for payment, if she had had but little work to do that week; never grudged her a share of their extravagant meals, which were far more luxurious than she could have met with anywhere else, for her previously agreed payment in case of working at home; and they would fain have taught her to drink rum in her tea, assuring her that she should have it for nothing and welcome. But they were too touchy, too prosperous, too much absorbed in themselves, to take off Libbie's feeling of solitariness; not half as much as the little face by day, and the shadow by night, of him with whom she had never yet exchanged a word.

Her idea was this: her mother came from the east of England, where, as perhaps you know, they have the pretty custom of sending presents on St Valentine's day,* with the donor's name unknown, and, of course, the mystery constitutes half the enjoyment. The fourteenth of February was Libbie's birthday too, and many a year, in the happy days of old, had her mother delighted to surprise her with some little gift, of which she more than half-guessed the giver, although each Valentine's day the manner of its arrival was varied. Since then the fourteenth of February had been the dreariest of all the year, because the most haunted by memory of departed happiness. But now, this year, if she could not have the old gladness of heart herself, she would try and brighten the life of another. She would save, and she would screw, but she would buy a canary and a cage for that poor little laddie opposite, who wore out his monotonous life with so few pleasures, and so much pain.

I doubt I may not tell you here of the anxieties and the fears, of the hopes and the self-sacrifices—all, perhaps small in the tangible effect as the widow's mite,* yet not the less marked by the viewless angels who go about continually among us—which varied Libbie's life before she accomplished her purpose. It is enough to say it was accomplished. The very day before the fourteenth she found time to go with her half-guinea to a barber's who lived near Albemarle Street, and who was famous for his stock of singing-birds. There are enthusiasts about all sorts of things, both good and bad, and many of the weavers in Manchester know and care more about birds than anyone would easily credit. Stubborn, silent, reserved men on many things, you have only to touch on the subject of birds to light up their faces with brightness. They will tell you who won the prizes at the last canary show, where the prize birds may be seen, and give you all the details of those funny, but pretty and interesting mimicries of great people's cattle shows. Among these amateurs, Emanuel Morris the barber was an oracle.

He took Libbie into his little back room, used for private shaving of modest men, who did not care to be exhibited in the front shop decked out in the full glories of lather; and which was hung round with birds in rude wicker cages, with the exception of those who had won prizes, and were consequently honoured with gilt-wire prisons. The longer and thinner the body of the bird was, the more admiration it received, as far as external beauty went; and when, in addition to this, the colour was deep and clear, and its notes strong and varied, the more did Emanuel dwell upon its perfections. But these were all prize birds; and, on inquiry, Libbie heard, with some little sinking at heart, that their price ran from one to two guineas.

'I'm not over-particular as to shape and colour,' said she, 'I should like a good singer, that's all!'

She dropped a little in Emanuel's estimation. However, he showed her his good singers, but all were above Libbie's means.

'After all, I don't think I care so much about the singing very loud; it's but a noise after all, and sometimes noise fidgets folks.'

'They must be nesh* folks as is put out with the singing o' birds,' replied Emanuel, rather affronted.

'It's for one who is poorly,' said Libbie, deprecatingly.

'Well,' said he, as if considering the matter, 'folk that are cranky, often take more to them as shows 'em love, than to them as is clever and gifted. Happen yo'd rather have this'n,' opening a cage-door, and calling to a dull-coloured bird, sitting moped up in a corner, 'Here—Jupiter, Jupiter!'

The bird smoothed its feathers in an instant, and, uttering a little note of delight, flew to Emanuel, putting his beak to his lips, as if kissing him, and then, perching on his head, it began a gurgling warble of pleasure, not by any means so varied or so clear as the song of the others, but which pleased Libbie more; for she was always one to find out she liked the gooseberries that were accessible, better than the grapes that were beyond her reach.* The price too was just right, so she gladly took possession of the cage, and hid it under her cloak, preparatory to carrying it home. Emanuel meanwhile was giving her directions as to its food, with all the minuteness of one loving his subject.

'Will it soon get to know anyone?' asked she.

'Give him two days only, and you and he'll be as thick as him and me are now. You've only to open his door, and call him, and he'll follow you round the room; but he'll first kiss you, and then perch on your head. He only wants larning, which I've no time to give him, to do many another accomplishment.'

'What's his name? I did not rightly catch it.'

'Jupiter,—it's not common; but the town's o'errun with Bobbies and Dickies, and as my birds are thought a bit out o' the way, I like to have better names for 'em, so I just picked a few out o' my lad's school books. It's just as ready, when you're used to it, to say Jupiter as Dicky.'

'I could bring my tongue round to Peter better; would he answer to Peter?' asked Libbie, now on the point of departing.

'Happen he might; but I think he'd come readier to the three syllables.'

On Valentine's day, Jupiter's cage was decked round with ivy leaves, making quite a pretty wreath on the wicker work; and to one of them was pinned a slip of paper, with these words, written in Libbie's best round hand:—

'From your faithful Valentine. Please take notice his name is Peter, and he'll come if you call him, after a bit.'

But little work did Libbie do that afternoon, she was so engaged in watching for the messenger who was to bear her present to her little valentine, and run away as soon as he had delivered up the canary, and explained to whom it was sent.

At last he came; then there was a pause before the woman of the house was at liberty to take it upstairs. Then Libbie saw the little face flush up into a bright colour, the feeble hands tremble with delighted eagerness, the head bent down to try and make out the writing (beyond his power, poor lad, to read), the rapturous turning round of the cage in order to see the canary in every point of view, head, tail, wings, and feet; an intention in which Jupiter, in his uneasiness at being again among strangers, did not second, for he hopped round so as continually to present a full front to the boy. It was a source of never wearying delight to the little fellow, till daylight closed in; he evidently forgot to wonder who had sent it him, in his gladness at his possession of such a treasure; and when the shadow of his mother darkened on the blind, and the bird had been exhibited, Libbie saw her do what, with all her tenderness, seemed rarely to have entered into her thoughts—she bent down and kissed her boy, in a mother's sympathy with the joy of her child.

The canary was placed for the night between the little bed and window; and when Libbie rose once, to take her accustomed peep, she saw the little arm put fondly round the cage, as if embracing his new treasure even in his sleep. How Jupiter slept this first night is quite another thing.

So ended the first day in Libbie's three eras in last year.

ERA II

WHITSUNTIDE*

THE brightest, fullest daylight poured down into No. 2, —— Court, Albemarle Street, and the heat, even at the early hour of five, as at the noontide on the June days of many years past.

The court seemed alive, and merry with voices and laughter. The bedroom windows were open wide, and had been so all night, on account of the heat; and every now and then you might see a head and a pair of shoulders, simply encased in shirt sleeves, popped out, and you might hear the inquiry passed from one to the other,—'Well, Jack, and where art thee bound for?'

'Dunham!'*

'Why, what an old-fashioned chap thou be'st. Thy grandad afore thee went to Dunham: but thou wert always a slow coach. I'm off to Alderley,*—me and my missis.'

'Ay, that's because there's only thee and thy missis. Wait till thou hast gotten four childer, like me, and thou'lt be glad enough to take 'em to Dunham, oud-fashioned way, for fourpence apiece.'

'I'd still go to Alderley; I'd not be bothered with my children; they should keep house at home.'

A pair of hands, the person to whom they belonged invisible, boxed his ears on this last speech, in a very spirited, though playful, manner, and the neighbours all laughed at the surprised look of the speaker, at this assault from an unseen foe. The man who had been holding conversation with him cried out,—

'Sarved him right, Mrs Slater: he knows nought about it yet; but when he gets them he'll be as loth to leave the babbies at home on a Whitsuntide as any on us. We shall live to see him in Dunham Park yet, wi' twins in his arms, and another pair on 'em clutching at daddy's coat-tails, let alone your share of youngsters, missis.'

At this moment our friend Libbie appeared at her window, and Mrs Slater, who had taken her discomfited husband's place, called out,—

'Elizabeth Marsh, where are Dixons and you bound to?'

'Dixons are not up yet; he said last night he'd take his holiday out in lying in bed. I'm going to the old-fashioned place, Dunham.'

'Thou art never going by thyself, moping!'

'No. I'm going with Margaret Hall and her lad,' replied Libbie, hastily withdrawing from the window, in order to avoid hearing any remarks on the associates she had chosen for her day of pleasure—the scold of the neighbourhood, and her sickly, ailing child!

But Jupiter might have been a dove,* and his ivy leaves an olive branch, for the peace he had brought, the happiness he had caused, to three individuals at least. For of course it could not long be a mystery who had sent little Frank Hall his valentine; nor could his mother long entertain her hard manner towards one who had given her child a new pleasure. She was shy, and she was proud, and for some time she struggled against the natural desire of manifesting her gratitude; but one evening, when Libbie was returning home, with a bundle of work half as large as herself, as she dragged herself along through the heated streets, she was overtaken by Margaret Hall, her burden gently pulled from her, and her way home shortened, and her weary spirits soothed and cheered, by the outpourings of Margaret's heart; for the barrier of reserve once broken down, she had much to say, to thank her for days of amusement and happy employment for her lad, to speak of his gratitude, to tell of her hopes and fears,—the hopes and fears that made up the dates of her life. From that time, Libbie lost her awe of the termagant in interest for the mother, whose all was ventured in so frail a bark. From this time, Libbie was a fast friend with both mother and son, planning mitigations for the sorrowful days of the latter as eagerly as poor Margaret Hall, and with far more success. His life had flickered up under the charm and excitement of the last few months. He even seemed strong enough to undertake the journey to Dunham, which Libbie had arranged as a Whitsuntide treat, and for which she and his mother had been hoarding up for several weeks. The canal boat left Knott Mill at six, and it was now past five; so Libbie let herself out very gently, and went across to her friends. She knocked at the door of their lodging-room, and, without waiting for an answer, entered.

Franky's face was flushed, and he was trembling with excitement,—partly with pleasure, but partly with some eager wish not yet granted.

'He wants sore to take Peter with him,' said his mother to Libbie, as if referring the matter to her. The boy looked imploringly at her.

'He would like it, I know; for one thing, he'd miss me sadly, and chirrup for me all day long, he'd be so lonely. I could not be half so happy a-thinking on him, left alone here by himself. Then, Libbie, he's just like a Christian, so fond of flowers and green leaves, and them sort of things. He chirrups to me so when mother brings me a pennyworth of wallflowers to put round his cage. He would talk if he could, you know; but I can tell what he means quite as one as if he spoke. Do let Peter go, Libbie; I'll carry him in my own arms.'

So Jupiter was allowed to be of the party. Now Libbie had overcome the great difficulty of conveying Franky to the boat, by offering to 'slay'* for a coach, and the shouts and exclamations of the neighbours told them that their conveyance awaited them at the bottom of the court. His mother carried Franky, light in weight, though heavy in helplessness, and he would hold the cage, believing that he was thus redeeming his pledge, that Peter should be a trouble to no one. Libbie proceeded to arrange the bundle containing their dinner, as a support in the corner of the coach. The neighbours came out with many blunt speeches, and more kindly wishes, and one or two of them would have relieved Margaret of her burden, if she would have allowed it. The presence of that little crippled fellow seemed to obliterate all the angry feelings which had existed between his mother and her neighbours, and which had formed the politics of that little court for many a day.

And now they were fairly off! Franky bit his lips in attempted endurance of the pain the motion caused him; he winced and shrank, until they were fairly on a Macadamized* thoroughfare, when he closed his eyes, and seemed desirous of a few minutes' rest. Libbie fell very shy, and very much afraid of being seen by her employers, 'set up in a coach!' and so she hid herself in a corner, and made herself as small as possible; while Mrs Hall had exactly the opposite feeling, and was delighted to stand up, stretching out of the window, and nodding to pretty nearly everyone they met or passed on the footpaths; and they were not a few, for the streets were quite gay, even at that early hour, with parties going to this or that railway station, or to the boats which crowded the canals on this bright holiday week; and almost everyone they met seemed to enter into Mrs Hall's exhilaration of feeling, and had a smile or nod in return. At last she plumped down by Libbie, and exclaimed, 'I never was in a coach but once afore, and that was when I was a-going to be married. It's like heaven; and all done over with such beautiful gimp,* too!' continued she, admiring the lining of the vehicle. Jupiter did not enjoy it so much.

As if the holiday time, the lovely weather, and the 'sweet hour of prime'* had a genial influence, as no doubt they have, everybody's heart seemed softened towards poor Franky. The driver lifted him out with the tenderness of strength, and bore him carefully down to the boat; the people then made way, and gave him the best seat in their power,—or rather I should call it a couch, for they saw he was weary, and insisted on his lying down,—an attitude he would have been ashamed to assume without the protection of his mother and Libbie, who now appeared, bearing their baskets and carrying Peter.

Away the boat went, to make room for others, for every conveyance, both by land and water, is in requisition in Whitsun-week, to give the hard-worked crowds the opportunity of enjoying the charms of the country. Even every standing-place in the canal packets was occupied, and as they glided along, the banks were lined with people, who seemed to find it object enough to watch the boats go by, packed close and full with happy beings brimming with anticipations of a day's pleasure. The country through which they passed is as uninteresting as can well be imagined; but still it is the country: and the screams of delight from the children, and the low laughs of pleasure from the parents, at every blossoming tree that trailed its wreath against some cottage wall, or at the tufts of late primroses which lingered in the cool depths of grass along the canal banks, the thorough relish of everything, as if dreading to let the least circumstance of this happy day pass over without its due appreciation, made the time seem all too short, although it took two hours to arrive at a place only eight miles from Manchester. Even Franky, with all his impatience to see Dunham woods (which I think he confused with London, believing both to be paved with gold), enjoyed the easy motion of the boat so much, floating along, while pictures moved before him, that he regretted when the time came for landing among the soft, green meadows, that came sloping down to the dancing water's brim. His fellow-passengers carried him to the park, and refused all payment, although his mother had laid by sixpence on purpose, as a recompense for this service.

'Oh, Libbie, how beautiful! Oh, mother, mother! is the whole world out of Manchester as beautiful as this? I did not know trees were like this! Such green homes for birds! Look, Peter! would not you like to be there, up among those boughs? But I can't let you go, you know, because you're my little bird brother, and I should be quite lost without you.'

They spread a shawl upon the fine mossy turf, at the root of a beech-tree, which made a sort of natural couch, and there they laid him, and bade him rest, in spite of the delight which made him believe himself capable of any exertion. Where he lay,—always holding Jupiter's cage, and often talking to him as to a playfellow,—he was on the verge of a green area, shut in by magnificent trees, in all the glory of their early foliage, before the summer heats had deepened their verdure into one rich, monotonous tint. And hither came party after party; old men and maidens, young men and children,*—whole families trooped along after the guiding fathers, who bore the youngest in their arms, or astride upon their backs, while they turned round occasionally to the wives, with whom they shared some fond local remembrance. For years has Dunham Park been the favourite resort of the Manchester workpeople; for more years than I can tell; probably ever since 'the Duke,'* by his canals, opened out the system of cheap travelling. Its scenery, too, which presents such a complete contrast to the whirl and turmoil of Manchester; so thoroughly woodland, with its ancestral trees (here and there lightning blanched); its 'verdurous walls;'* its grassy walks, leading far away into some glade, where you start at the rabbit rustling among the last year's fern, and where the wood-pigeon's call seems the only fitting and accordant sound. Depend upon it, this complete sylvan repose, this accessible quiet, this lapping the soul in green images of the country, forms the most complete contrast to a town's-person, and consequently has over such the greatest power to charm.

Presently Libbie found out she was very hungry. Now they were but provided with dinner, which was, of course, to be eaten as near twelve o'clock as might be; and Margaret Hall, in her prudence, asked a working-man near to tell her what o'clock it was.

'Nay,' said he, 'I'll ne'er look at clock or watch today. I'll not spoil my pleasure by finding out how fast it's going away. If thou'rt hungry, eat. I make my own dinner hour, and I have eaten mine an hour ago.'

So they had their veal pies, and then found out it was only about half-past ten o'clock; by so many pleasurable events had that morning been marked. But such was their buoyancy of spirits, that they only enjoyed their mistake, and joined in the general laugh against the man who had eaten his dinner somewhere about nine. He laughed most heartily of all, till, suddenly stopping, he said,—

'I must not go on at this rate; laughing gives one such an appetite.'

'Oh! if that's all,' said a merry-looking man, lying at full length, and brushing the fresh scent out of the grass, while two or three little children tumbled over him, and crept about him, as kittens or puppies frolic with their parents, 'if that's all, we'll have a subscription of eatables for them improvident folk as have eaten their dinner for their breakfast. Here's a sausage pasty and a handful of nuts for my share. Bring round a hat, Bob, and see what the company will give.'

Bob carried out the joke, much to little Franky's amusement; and no one was so churlish as to refuse, although the contributions varied from a peppermint drop up to a veal pie and a sausage pasty.

'It's a thriving trade,' said Bob, as he emptied his hatful of provisions on the grass by Libbie's side. 'Besides, it's tiptop, too, to live on the public. Hark! what is that?'

The laughter and the chat were suddenly hushed, and mothers told their little ones to listen,—as, far away in the distance, now sinking and falling, now swelling and clear, came a ringing peal of children's voices, blended together in one of those psalm tunes which we are all of us familiar with, and which bring to mind the old, old days, when we, as wondering children, were first led to worship 'Our Father,' by those beloved ones who have since gone to the more perfect worship. Holy was that distant choral praise, even to the most thoughtless; and when it, in fact, was ended, in the instant's pause, during which the ear awaits the repetition of the air, they caught the noontide hum and buzz of the myriads of insects who danced away their lives in the glorious day; they heard the swaying of the mighty woods in the soft but resistless breeze, and then again once more burst forth the merry jests and the shouts of childhood; and again the elder ones resumed their happy talk, as they lay or sat 'under the greenwood tree.'* Fresh parties came dropping in; some laden with wild flowers—almost with branches of hawthorn, indeed; while one or two had made prizes of the earliest dog-roses, and had cast away campion, stitchwort, ragged robin, all to keep the lady of the hedges from being obscured or hidden by the community.

One after another drew near to Franky, and looked on with interest as he lay sorting the flowers given to him. Happy parents stood by, with their household bands around them, in health and comeliness, and felt the sad prophecy of those shrivelled limbs, those wasted fingers, those lamp-like eyes, with their bright, dark lustre. His mother was too eagerly watching his happiness to read the meaning of those grave looks, but Libbie saw them and understood them; and a chill shudder went through her, even on that day, as she thought on the future.

'Ay! I thought we should give you a start!'

A start they did give, with their terrible slap on Libbie's back, as she sat idly grouping flowers, and following out her sorrowful thoughts. It was the Dixons. Instead of keeping their holiday by lying in bed, they and their children had roused themselves, and had come by the omnibus to the nearest point. For an instant the meeting was an awkward one, on account of the feud between Margaret Hall and Mrs Dixon, but there was no long resisting of kindly mother Nature's soothings, at that holiday time, and in that lovely tranquil spot; or if they could have been unheeded, the sight of Franky would have awed every angry feeling into rest, so changed was he since the Dixons had last seen him; and since he had been the Puck or Robin Goodfellow* of the neighbourhood, whose marbles were always rolling under other people's feet, and whose top-strings* were always hanging in nooses to catch the unwary. Yes, he, the feeble, mild, almost girlish-looking lad, had once been a merry, happy rogue, and as such often cuffed by Mrs Dixon, the very Mrs Dixon who now stood gazing with the tears in her eyes. Could she, in sight of him, the changed, the fading, keep up a quarrel with his mother?

'How long hast thou been here?' asked Dixon.

'Welly* on for all day,' answered Libbie.

'Hast never been to see the deer, or the king and queen oaks? Lord, how stupid.'

His wife pinched his arm, to remind him of Franky's helpless condition, which of course tethered the otherwise willing feet. But Dixon had a remedy. He called Bob, and one or two others, and each taking a corner of the strong plaid shawl, they slung Franky as in a hammock, and thus carried him merrily along, down the wood paths, over the smooth, grassy turf, while the glimmering shine and shadow fell on his upturned face. The women walked behind, talking, loitering along, always in sight of the hammock; now picking up some green treasure from the ground, now catching at the low hanging branches of the horse-chestnut. The soul grew much on this day, and in these woods, and all unconsciously, as souls do grow. They followed Franky's hammock-bearers up a grassy knoll, on the top of which stood a group of pine trees, whose stems looked like dark red gold in the sunbeams. They had taken Franky there to show him Manchester, far away in the blue plain, against which the woodland foreground cut with a soft clear line. Far, far away in the distance on that flat plain, you might see the motionless cloud of smoke hanging over a great town, and that was Manchester,—ugly, smoky Manchester, dear, busy, earnest, noble-working Manchester; where their children had been born, and where, perhaps, some lay buried; where their homes were, and where God had cast their lives, and told them to work out their destiny.

'Hurrah! for oud smoke-jack!'* cried Bob, putting Franky softly down on the grass, before he whirled his hat round, preparatory to a shout. 'Hurrah! hurrah!' from all the men. 'There's the rim of my hat lying like a quoit yonder,' observed Bob quietly, as he replaced his brimless hat on his head with the gravity of a judge.

'Here's the Sunday-school children a-coming to sit on this shady side, and have their buns and milk. Hark! they're singing the infant-school grace.'

They sat close at hand, so that Franky could hear the words they sang, in rings of children, making, in their gay summer prints, newly donned for that week, garlands of little faces, all happy and bright upon that green hillside. One little 'Dot'* of a girl came shyly behind Franky, whom she had long been watching, and threw her half-bun at his side, and then ran away and hid herself, in very shame at the boldness of her own sweet impulse. She kept peeping from her screen at Franky all the time; and he meanwhile was almost too much pleased and happy to eat; the world was so beautiful, and men, women, and children all so tender and kind; so softened, in fact, by the beauty of this earth, so unconsciously touched by the spirit of love, which was the Creator of this lovely earth. But the day drew to an end; the heat declined; the birds once more began their warblings; the fresh scents again hung about plant, and tree, and grass, betokening the fragrant presence of the reviving dew, and—the boat time was near. As they trod the meadow-path once more, they were joined by many a party they had encountered during the day, all abounding in happiness, all full of the day's adventures. Long-cherished quarrels had been forgotten, new friendships formed. Fresh tastes and higher delights had been imparted that day. We have all of us our look, now and then, called up by some noble or loving thought (our highest on earth), which will be our likeness in heaven. I can catch the glance on many a face, the glancing light of the cloud of glory from heaven, 'which is our home.'* That look was present on many a hard-worked, wrinkled countenance, as they turned backwards to catch a longing, lingering look at Dunham woods, fast deepening into blackness of night, but whose memory was to haunt, in greenness and freshness, many a loom, and workshop, and factory, with images of peace and beauty.

That night, as Libbie lay awake, revolving the incidents of the day, she caught Franky's voice through the open windows. Instead of the frequent moan of pain, he was trying to recall the burden of one of the children's hymns,—

Here we suffer grief and pain,*
Here we meet to part again;
In Heaven we part no more.
Oh! that will be joyful, &c.

She recalled his question, the whispered question, to her, in the happiest part of the day. He asked Libbie, 'Is Dunham like heaven? the people here are as kind as angels, and I don't want heaven to be more beautiful than this place. If you and mother would but die with me, I should like to die, and live always there!' She had checked him, for she feared he was impious; but now the young child's craving for some definite idea of the land to which his inner wisdom told him he was hastening, had nothing in it wrong, or even sorrowful, for—

In Heaven we part no more.

ERA III

MICHAELMAS*

THE church clocks had struck three; the crowds of gentlemen returning to business, after their early dinners, had disappeared within offices and warehouses; the streets were clear and quiet, and ladies were venturing to sally forth for their afternoon shoppings and their afternoon calls.

Slowly, slowly, along the streets, elbowed by life at every turn, a little funeral wound its quiet way. Four men bore along a child's coffin; two women with bowed heads followed meekly.

I need not tell you whose coffin it was, or who were those two mourners. All was now over with little Frank Hall: his romps, his games, his sickening, his suffering, his death. All was now over, but the Resurrection and the Life.

His mother walked as in a stupor. Could it be that he was dead! If he had been less of an object of her thoughts, less of a motive for her labours, she could sooner have realized it. As it was, she followed his poor, cast-off, worn-out body as if she were borne along by some oppressive dream. If he were really dead, how could she be still alive?

Libbie's mind was far less stunned, and consequently far more active, than Margaret Hall's. Visions, as in a phantasmagoria, came rapidly passing before her—recollections of the time (which seemed now so long ago) when the shadow of the feebly-waving arm first caught her attention; of the bright, strangely isolated day at Dunham Park, where the world had seemed so full of enjoyment, and beauty, and life; of the long-continued heat, through which poor Franky had panted away his strength in the little close room, where there was no escaping the hot rays of the afternoon sun; of the long nights when his mother and she had watched by his side, as he moaned continually, whether awake or asleep; of the fevered moaning slumber of exhaustion; of the pitiful little self-upbraidings for his own impatience of suffering, only impatient in his own eyes—most true and holy patience in the sight of others; and then the fading away of life, the loss of power, the increased unconsciousness, the lovely look of angelic peace, which followed the dark shadow on the countenance, where was he—what was he now?

And so they laid him in his grave, and heard the solemn funeral words; but far off in the distance, as if not addressed to them.

Margaret Hall bent over the grave to catch one last glance—she had not spoken, nor sobbed, nor done aught but shiver now and then, since the morning; but now her weight bore more heavily on Libbie's arm, and without sigh or sound she fell an unconscious heap on the piled-up gravel. They helped Libbie to bring her round; but long after her half-opened eyes and altered breathings showed that her senses were restored, she lay, speechless and motionless, without attempting to rise from her strange bed, as if the earth contained nothing worth even that trifling exertion.

At last Libbie and she left that holy, consecrated spot, and bent their steps back to the only place more consecrated still; where he had rendered up his spirit; and where memories of him haunted each common, rude piece of furniture that their eyes fell upon. As the woman of the house opened the door, she pulled Libbie on one side, and said—

'Anne Dixon has been across to see you; she wants to have a word with you.'

'I cannot go now,' replied Libbie, as she pushed hastily along, in order to enter the room (*his* room), at the same time with the childless mother: for, as she had anticipated, the sight of that empty spot, the glance at the uncurtained open window, letting in the fresh air, and the broad, rejoicing light of day, where all had so long been darkened and subdued, unlocked the waters of the fountain, and long and shrill were the cries for her boy that the poor woman uttered.

'Oh! dear Mrs Hall,' said Libbie, herself drenched in tears, 'do not take on so badly; I'm sure it would grieve *him* sore if he were alive, and you know he is—Bible tells us so; and maybe he's here watching how we go on without him, and hoping we don't fret over-much.'

Mrs Hall's sobs grew worse and more hysterical.

'Oh! listen,' said Libbie, once more struggling against her own increasing agitation. 'Listen! there's Peter chirping as he always does when he's put about, frightened like; and you know he that's gone could never abide to hear the canary chirp in that shrill way.'

Margaret Hall did check herself, and curb her expressions of agony, in order not to frighten the little creature he had loved; and as her outward grief subsided, Libbie took up the large old Bible, which fell open at the never-failing comfort of the fourteenth chapter of St John's Gospel.*

How often these large family Bibles do open at that chapter! as if, unused in more joyous and prosperous times, the soul went home to its words of loving sympathy when weary and sorrowful, just as the little child seeks the tender comfort of its mother in all its griefs and cares.

And Margaret put back her wet, ruffled, grey hair from her heated, tear-stained, woeful face, and listened with such earnest eyes, trying to form some idea of the 'Father's house,'* where her boy had gone to dwell.

They were interrupted by a low tap at the door. Libbie went. 'Anne Dixon has watched you home, and wants to have a word with you,' said the woman of the house, in a whisper. Libbie went back and closed the book, with a word of explanation to Margaret Hall, and then ran downstairs, to learn the reason of Anne's anxiety to see her.

'Oh, Libbie!' she burst out with, and then, checking herself with the remembrance of Libbie's last solemn duty, 'how's Margaret Hall? But, of course, poor thing, she'll fret a bit at first; she'll be some time coming round, mother says, seeing it's as well that poor lad is taken; for he'd always ha' been a cripple, and a trouble to her—he was a fine lad once, too.'

She had come full of another and a different subject; but the sight of Libbie's sad, weeping face, and the quiet, subdued tone of her manner, made her feel it awkward to begin on any other theme than the one which filled up her companion's mind. To her last speech Libbie answered sorrowfully—

'No doubt, Anne, it's ordered for the best; but oh! don't call him, don't think he could ever ha' been, a trouble to his mother, though he were a cripple. She loved him all the more for each thing she had to do for him—I am sure I did.' Libbie cried a little behind her apron. Anne Dixon felt still more awkward in introducing the discordant subject.

'Well! "flesh is grass," Bible says,'* and having fulfilled the etiquette of quoting a text if possible, if not of making a moral observation on the fleeting nature of earthly things, she thought she was at liberty to pass on to her real errand.

'You must not go on moping yourself, Libbie Marsh. What I wanted special for to see you this afternoon, was to tell you, you must come to my wedding tomorrow. Nanny Dawson has fallen sick, and there's none as I should like to have bridesmaid in her place as well as you.'

'Tomorrow! Oh, I cannot!—indeed I cannot!'

'Why not?'

Libbie did not answer, and Anne Dixon grew impatient.

'Surely, in the name o' goodness, you're never going to baulk yourself of a day's pleasure for the sake of yon little cripple that's dead and gone!'

'No,—it's not baulking myself of—don't be angry, Anne Dixon, with him, please; but I don't think it would be a pleasure to me,—I don't feel as if I could enjoy it; thank you all the same. But I did love that little lad very dearly—I did,' sobbing a little, 'and I can't forget him and make merry so soon.'

'Well—I never!' exclaimed Anne, almost angrily.

'Indeed, Anne, I feel your kindness, and you and Bob have my best wishes,—that's what you have; but even if I went, I should be thinking all day of him, and of his poor, poor mother, and they say it's bad to think very much on them that's dead, at a wedding.'

'Nonsense,' said Anne, 'I'll take the risk of the ill-luck. After all, what is marrying? Just a spree, Bob says. He often says he does not think I shall make him a good wife, for I know nought about house matters, wi' working in a factory; but he says he'd rather be uneasy wi' me than easy wi' anybody else. There's love for you! And I tell him I'd rather have him tipsy than anyone else sober.'

'Oh! Anne Dixon, hush! you don't know yet what it is to have a drunken husband. I have seen something of it: father used to get fuddled, and, in the long run, it killed mother, let alone—oh! Anne, God above only knows what the wife of a drunken man has to bear. Don't tell,' said she, lowering her voice, 'but father killed our little baby in one of his bouts; mother never looked up again, nor father either, for that matter, only his was in a different way. Mother will have gotten to little Jemmie* now, and they'll be so happy together,—and perhaps Franky too. Oh!' said she, recovering herself from her train of thought, 'never say aught lightly of the wife's lot whose husband is given to drink!'

'Dear, what a preachment. I tell you what, Libbie, you're as born an old maid as ever I saw. You'll never be married to either drunken or sober.'

Libbie's face went rather red, but without losing its meek expression.

'I know that as well as you can tell me; and more reason, therefore, as God has seen fit to keep me out of woman's natural work, I should try and find work for myself. I mean,' seeing Anne Dixon's puzzled look, 'that as I know I'm never likely to have a home of my own, or a husband that would look to me to make all straight, or children to watch over or care for, all which I take to be woman's natural work, I must not lose time in fretting and fidgetting after marriage, but just look about me for somewhat else to do. I can see many a one misses it in this. They will hanker after what is ne'er likely to be theirs, instead of facing it out, and settling down to be old maids; and, as old maids, just looking round for the odd jobs God leaves in the world for such as old maids to do. There's plenty of such work, and there's the blessing of God on them as does it.' Libbie was almost out of breath at this outpouring of what had long been her inner thoughts.

'That's all very true, I make no doubt, for them as is to be old maids; but as I'm not, please God tomorrow comes, you might have spared your breath to cool your porridge. What I want to know is, whether you'll be bridesmaid tomorrow or not. Come, now do; it will do you good, after all your working, and watching, and slaving yourself for that poor Franky Hall.'

'It was one of my odd jobs,' said Libbie, smiling, though her eyes were brimming over with tears; 'but, dear Anne,' said she, recovering herself, 'I could not do it tomorrow, indeed I could not.'

'And I can't wait,' said Anne Dixon, almost sulkily, 'Bob and I put it off from today, because of the funeral, and Bob had set his heart on its being on Michaelmas Day; and mother says the goose won't keep beyond tomorrow. Do come: father finds eatables, and Bob finds drink, and we shall be so jolly! and after we've been to church, we're to walk round the town in pairs, white satin ribbon in our bonnets, and refreshments at any public-house we like, Bob says. And after dinner there's to be a dance. Don't be a fool; you can do no good by staying. Margaret Hall will have to go out washing, I'll be bound.'

'Yes, she must go to Mrs Wilkinson's, and, for that matter, I must go working too. Mrs Williams has been after me to make her girl's winter things ready; only I could not leave Franky, he clung so to me.'

'Then you won't be bridesmaid! is that your last word?'

'It is; you must not be angry with me, Anne Dixon,' said Libbie, deprecatingly.

But Anne was gone without a reply.

With a heavy heart Libbie mounted the little staircase, for she felt how ungracious her refusal of Anne's kindness must appear, to one who understood so little the feelings which rendered her acceptance of it a moral impossibility.

On opening the door she saw Margaret Hall, with the Bible open on the table before her. For she had puzzled out the place where Libbie was reading, and, with her finger under the line, was spelling out the words of consolation, piecing the syllables together aloud, with the earnest anxiety of comprehension with which a child first learns to read. So Libbie took the stool by her side, before she was aware that anyone had entered the room.

'What did she want you for?' asked Margaret. 'But I can guess; she wanted you to be at th' wedding that is to come off this week, they say. Ay, they'll marry, and laugh, and dance, all as one as if my boy was alive,' said she, bitterly. 'Well, he was neither kith nor kin of yours, so I maun try and be thankful for what you've done for him, and not wonder at your forgetting him afore he's well settled in his grave.'

'I never can forget him, and I'm not going to the wedding,' said Libbie, quietly, for she understood the mother's jealousy of her dead child's claims.

'I must go work at Mrs Williams' tomorrow,' she said, in explanation, for she was unwilling to boast of her tender, fond regret, which had been her principal motive for declining Anne's invitation.

'And I mun go washing, just as if nothing had happened,' sighed forth Mrs Hall, 'and I mun come home at night, and find his place empty, and all still where I used to be sure of hearing his voice ere ever I got up the stair: no one will ever call me mother again.' She fell crying pitifully, and Libbie could not speak for her own emotion for some time. But during this silence she put the keystone in the arch of thoughts she had been building up for many days; and when Margaret was again calm in her sorrow, Libbie said, 'Mrs Hall, I should like—would you like me to come for to live here altogether?'

Margaret Hall looked up with a sudden light in her countenance, which encouraged Libbie to go on.

'I could sleep with you, and pay half, you know; and we should be together in the evenings; and her as was home first would watch for the other, and' (dropping her voice) 'we could talk of him at nights, you know.'

She was going on, but Mrs Hall interrupted her.

'Oh, Libbie Marsh! and can you really think of coming to live wi' me. I should like it above—but no! it must not be; you've no notion on what a creature I am, at times; more like a mad one when I'm in a rage, and I cannot keep it down. I seem to get out of bed wrong side in the morning, and I must have my passion out with the first person I meet. Why, Libbie,' said she, with a doleful look of agony on her face, 'I even used to fly out on him, poor sick lad as he was, and you may judge how little you can keep it down frae that. No, you must not come. I must live alone now,' sinking her voice into the low tones of despair.

But Libbie's resolution was brave and strong. 'I'm not afraid,' said she, smiling. 'I know you better than you know yourself, Mrs Hall. I've seen you try of late to keep it down, when you've been boiling over, and I think you'll go on a-doing so. And at any rate, when you've had your fit out, you're very kind, and I can forget if you've been a bit put out. But I'll try not to put you out. Do let me come: I think *he* would like us to keep together. I'll do my very best to make you comfortable.'

'It's me! it's me as will be making your life miserable with my temper; or else, God knows, how my heart clings to you. You and me is folk alone in the world, for we both loved one who is dead, and who had none else to love him. If you will live with me, Libbie, I'll try as I never did afore to be gentle and quiet-tempered. Oh! will you try me, Libbie Marsh?' So out of the little grave there sprang a hope and a resolution, which made life an object to each of the two.

When Elizabeth Marsh returned home the next evening from her day's labours, Anne (Dixon no longer) crossed over, all in her bridal finery, to endeavour to induce her to join the dance going on in her father's house.

'Dear Anne, this is good of you, a-thinking of me tonight,' said Libbie, kissing her, 'and though I cannot come,—I've promised Mrs Hall to be with her,—I shall think on you, and I trust you'll be happy. I have got a little needle-case I have looked out for you; stay, here it is,—I wish it were more—only ——'

'Only, I know what. You've been a-spending all your money in nice things for poor Franky. Thou'rt a real good un, Libbie, and I'll keep your needle-book to my dying day, that I will.' Seeing Anne in such a friendly mood, emboldened Libbie to tell her of her change of place; of her intention of lodging henceforward with Margaret Hall.

'Thou never will! Why father and mother are as fond of thee as can be; they'll lower thy rent if that's what it is—and thou knowst they never grudge thee bit or drop. And Margaret Hall, of all folk, to lodge wi'! She's such a Tartar! Sooner than not have a quarrel, she'd fight right hand against left. Thou'lt have no peace of thy life. What on earth can make you think of such a thing, Libbie Marsh?'

'She'll be so lonely without me,' pleaded Libbie. 'I'm sure I could make her happier, even if she did scold me a bit now and then, than she'd be a living alone, and I'm not afraid of her; and I mean to do my best not to vex her: and it will ease her heart, maybe, to talk to me at times about Franky. I shall often see your father and mother, and I shall always thank them for their kindness to me. But they have you and little Mary, and poor Mrs Hall has no one.'

Anne could only repeat, 'Well, I never!' and hurry off to tell the news at home.

But Libbie was right. Margaret Hall is a different woman to the scold of the neighbourhood she once was; touched and softened by the two purifying angels, Sorrow and Love. And it is beautiful to see her affection, her reverence, for Libbie Marsh. Her dead mother could hardly have cared for her more tenderly than does the hard-hearted washerwoman, not long ago so fierce and unwomanly. Libbie, herself, has such peace shining on her countenance, as almost makes it beautiful, as she tenders the services of a daughter to Franky's mother, no longer the desolate lonely orphan, a stranger on the earth.

Do you ever read the moral, concluding sentence of a story? I never do, but I once (in the year 1811, I think) heard of a deaf old lady, living by herself, who did; and as she may have left some descendants with the same amiable peculiarity, I will put in, for their benefit, what I believe to be the secret of Libbie's peace of mind, the real reason why she no longer feels oppressed at her own loneliness in the world,—

She has a purpose in life; and that purpose is a holy one.

SIX WEEKS AT HEPPENHEIM

After I left Oxford, I determined to spend some months in travel before settling down in life. My father had left me a few thousands, the income arising from which would be enough to provide for all the necessary requirements of a lawyer's education; such as lodgings in a quiet part of London, fees and payment to the distinguished barrister with whom I was to read; but there would be small surplus left over for luxuries or amusements; and as I was rather in debt on leaving college, since I had forestalled my income, and the expenses of my travelling would have to be defrayed out of my capital, I determined that they should not exceed fifty pounds. As long as that sum would last me I would remain abroad; when it was spent my holiday should be over, and I would return and settle down somewhere in the neighbourhood of Russell Square, in order to be near Mr ——'s chambers in Lincoln's Inn.* I had to wait in London for one day while my passport was being made out, and I went to examine the streets in which I purposed to live; I had picked them out, from studying a map, as desirable; and so they were, if judged entirely by my reason; but their aspect was very depressing to one country-bred, and just fresh from the beautiful street-architecture of Oxford. The thought of living in such a monotonous grey district for years made me all the more anxious to prolong my holiday by all the economy which could eke out my fifty pounds. I thought I could make it last for one hundred days at least. I was a good walker, and had no very luxurious tastes in the matter of accommodation or food; I had as fair a knowledge of German and French as any untravelled Englishman can have; and I resolved to avoid expensive hotels such as my own countrymen frequented.

I have stated this much about myself to explain how I fell in with the little story that I am going to record, but with which I had not much to do,—my part in it being little more than that of a sympathizing spectator. I had been through France into Switzerland, where I had gone beyond my strength in the way of walking, and I was on my way home, when one evening I came to the village of Heppenheim, on the Berg-Strasse.* I had strolled about the dirty town of Worms all morning, and dined in a filthy hotel; and after that I had crossed the Rhine, and walked through Lorsch to Heppenheim. I was unnaturally tired and languid as I dragged myself up the rough-paved and irregular village street to the inn recommended to me. It was a large building, with a green court before it. A cross-looking but scrupulously clean hostess received me, and showed me into a large room with a dinner-table in it, which, though it might have accommodated thirty or forty guests, only stretched down half the length of the eating-room. There were windows at each end of the room; two looked to the front of the house, on which the evening shadows had already fallen; the opposite two were partly doors, opening into a large garden full of trained fruit-trees and beds of vegetables, amongst which rose-bushes and other flowers seemed to grow by permission, not by original intention. There was a stove at each end of the room, which, I suspect, had originally been divided into two. The door by which I had entered was exactly in the middle, and opposite to it was another, leading to a great bedchamber, which my hostess showed me as my sleeping quarters for the night.

If the place had been much less clean and inviting, I should have remained there; I was almost surprised myself at my *vis inertiae**; once seated in the last warm rays of the slanting sun by the garden window, I was disinclined to move, or even to speak. My hostess had taken my orders as to my evening meal, and had left me. The sun went down, and I grew shivery. The vast room looked cold and bare; the darkness brought out shadows that perplexed me, because I could not fully make out the objects that produced them after dazzling my eyes by gazing out into the crimson light.

Someone came in; it was the maiden to prepare for my supper. She began to lay the cloth at one end of the large table. There was a smaller one close by me. I mustered up my voice, which seemed a little as if it was getting beyond my control, and called to her,—

'Will you let me have my supper here on this table?'

She came near; the light fell on her while I was in shadow. She was a tall young woman, with a fine strong figure, a pleasant face, expressive of goodness and sense, and with a good deal of comeliness about it, too, although the fair complexion was bronzed and reddened by weather, so as to have lost much of its delicacy, and the features, as I had afterwards opportunity enough of observing, were anything but regular. She had white teeth, however, and well-opened blue eyes—grave-looking eyes which had shed tears for past sorrow—plenty of light-brown hair, rather elaborately plaited, and fastened up by two great silver pins. That was all—perhaps more than all—I noticed that first night. She began to lay the cloth where I had directed. A shiver passed over me: she looked at me, and then said,—

'The gentleman is cold: shall I light the stove?'

Something vexed me—I am not usually so impatient: it was the coming-on of serious illness—I did not like to be noticed so closely; I believed that food would restore me, and I did not want to have my meal delayed, as I feared it might be by the lighting of the stove; and most of all I was feverishly annoyed by movement. I answered sharply and abruptly,—

'No; bring supper quickly; that is all I want.'

Her quiet, sad eyes met mine for a moment; but I saw no change in their expression, as if I had vexed her by my rudeness: her countenance did not for an instant lose its look of patient sense, and that is pretty nearly all I can remember of Thekla that first evening at Heppenheim.

I suppose I ate my supper, or tried to do so, at any rate; and I must have gone to bed, for days after I became conscious of lying there, weak as a new-born babe, and with a sense of past pain in all my weary limbs. As is the case in recovering from fever, one does not care to connect facts, much less to reason upon them; so how I came to be lying in that strange bed, in that large, half-furnished room; in what house that room was; in what town, in what country, I did not take the trouble to recall. It was of much more consequence to me then to discover what was the well-known herb that gave the scent to the clean, coarse sheets in which I lay. Gradually I extended my observations, always confining myself to the present. I must have been well cared-for by someone, and that lately, too, for the window was shaded, so as to prevent the morning sun from coming in upon the bed; there was the crackling of fresh wood in the great white china stove, which must have been newly replenished within a short time.

By-and-by the door opened slowly. I cannot tell why, but my impulse was to shut my eyes as if I were still asleep. But I could see through my apparently closed eyelids. In came, walking on tip-toe, with a slow care that defeated its object, two men. The first was aged from thirty to forty, in the dress of a Black Forest peasant,—old-fashioned coat and knee-breeches of strong blue cloth, but of a thoroughly good quality; he was followed by an older man, whose dress, of more pretension as to cut and colour (it was all black), was, nevertheless, as I had often the opportunity of observing afterwards, worn threadbare.

Their first sentences, in whispered German, told me who they were: the landlord of the inn where I was lying a helpless log, and the village doctor who had been called in. The latter felt my pulse, and nodded his head repeatedly in approbation. I had instinctively known that I was getting better, and hardly cared for this confirmation; but it seemed to give the truest pleasure to the landlord, who shook the hand of the doctor, in a pantomime expressive of as much thankfulness as if I had been his brother. Some low-spoken remarks were made, and then some question was asked, to which, apparently, my host was unable to reply. He left the room, and in a minute or two returned, followed by Thekla, who was questioned by the doctor, and replied with a quiet clearness, showing how carefully the details of my illness had been observed by her. Then she left the room, and, as if every minute had served to restore to my brain its power of combining facts, I was suddenly prompted to open my eyes, and ask in the best German I could muster what day of the month it was; not that I clearly remembered the date of my arrival at Heppenheim, but I knew it was about the beginning of September.

Again the doctor conveyed his sense of extreme satisfaction in a series of rapid pantomimic nods, and then replied in deliberate but tolerable English, to my great surprise,—

'It is the 29th of September, my dear sir. You must thank the dear God. Your fever has made its course of twenty-one days. Now patience and care must be practised. The good host and his household will have the care; you must have the patience. If you have relations in England, I will do my endeavours to tell them the state of your health.'

'I have no near relations,' said I, beginning in my weakness to cry, as I remembered, as if it had been a dream, the days when I had father, mother, sister.

'Chut, chut!' said he; then, turning to the landlord, he told him in German to make Thekla bring me one of her good *bouillons*; after which I was to have certain medicines, and to sleep as undisturbedly as possible. For days, he went on, I should require constant watching and careful feeding; every twenty minutes I was to have something, either wine or soup, in small quantities.

A dim notion came into my hazy mind that my previous husbandry of my fifty pounds, by taking long walks and scanty diet, would prove in the end very bad economy; but I sank into dozing unconsciousness before I could quite follow out my idea. I was roused by the touch of a spoon on my lips; it was Thekla feeding me. Her sweet, grave face had something approaching to a mother's look of tenderness upon it, as she gave me spoonful after spoonful with gentle patience and dainty care: and then I fell asleep once more. When next I wakened it was night; the stove was lighted, and the burning wood made a pleasant crackle, though I could only see the outlines and edges of red flame through the crevices of the small iron door. The uncurtained window on my left looked into the purple, solemn night. Turning a little, I saw Thekla sitting near a table, sewing diligently at some great white piece of household work. Every now and then she stopped to snuff the candle; sometimes she began to ply her needle again immediately; but once or twice she let her busy hands lie idly in her lap, and looked into the darkness, and thought deeply for a moment or two; these pauses always ended in a kind of sobbing sigh, the sound of which seemed to restore her to self-consciousness, and she took to her sewing even more diligently than before. Watching her had a sort of dreamy interest for me; this diligence of hers was a pleasant contrast to my repose; it seemed to enhance the flavour of my rest. I was too much of an animal just then to have my sympathy, or even my curiosity, strongly excited by her look of sad remembrance, or by her sighs.

After a while she gave a little start, looked at a watch lying by her on the table, and came, shading the candle by her hand, softly to my bedside. When she saw my open eyes she went to a porringer placed at the top of the stove, and fed me with soup. She did not speak while doing this. I was half aware that she had done it many times since the doctor's visit, although this seemed to be the first time that I was fully awake. She passed her arm under the pillow on which my head rested, and raised me a very little; her support was as firm as a man's could have been. Again back to her work, and I to my slumbers, without a word being exchanged.

It was broad daylight when I wakened again; I could see the sunny atmosphere of the garden outside stealing in through the nicks at the side of the shawl hung up to darken the room—a shawl which I was sure had not been there when I had observed the window in the night. How gently my nurse must have moved about while doing her thoughtful act!

My breakfast was brought me by the hostess; she who had received me on my first arrival at this hospitable inn. She meant to do everything kindly, I am sure; but a sickroom was not her place; by a thousand little maladroitnesses she fidgeted me past bearing; her shoes creaked, her dress rustled; she asked me questions about myself which it irritated me to answer; she congratulated me on being so much better, while I was faint for want of the food which she delayed giving me in order to talk. My host had more sense in him when he came in, although his shoes creaked as well as hers. By this time I was somewhat revived, and could talk a little; besides, it seemed churlish to be longer without acknowledging so much kindness received.

'I am afraid I have been a great trouble,' said I. 'I can only say that I am truly grateful.'

His good broad face reddened, and he moved a little uneasily.

'I don't see how I could have done otherwise than I—than we, did,' replied he, in the soft German of the district. 'We were all glad enough to do what we could; I don't say it was a pleasure, because it is our busiest time of year,—but then,' said he, laughing a little awkwardly, as if he feared his expression might have been misunderstood, 'I don't suppose it has been a pleasure to you either, sir, to be laid up so far from home.'

'No, indeed.'

'I may as well tell you now, sir, that we had to look over your papers and clothes. In the first place, when you were so ill I would fain have let your kinsfolk know, if I could have found a clue; and besides, you needed linen.'

'I am wearing a shirt of yours though,' said I, touching my sleeve.

'Yes, sir!' said he again, reddening a little. 'I told Thekla to take the finest out of the chest; but I am afraid you find it coarser than your own.'

For all answer I could only lay my weak hand on the great brown paw resting on the bedside. He gave me a sudden squeeze in return that I thought would have crushed my bones.

'I beg your pardon, sir,' said he, misinterpreting the sudden look of pain which I could not repress; 'but watching a man come out of the shadow of death into life makes one feel very friendly towards him.'

'No old or true friend that I have had could have done more for me than you, and your wife, and Thekla, and the good doctor.'

'I am a widower,' said he, turning round the great wedding-ring that decked his third finger. 'My sister keeps house for me, and takes care of the children,—that is to say, she does it with the help of Thekla, the house-maiden. But I have other servants,' he continued. 'I am well to do; the good God be thanked! I have land, and cattle, and vineyards. It will soon be our vintage-time, and then you must go and see my grapes as they come into the village. I have a *chasse*,* too, in the Odenwald;* perhaps one day you will be strong enough to go and shoot the *chevreuil** with me.'

His good, true heart was trying to make me feel like a welcome guest. Some time afterwards I learnt from the doctor that—my poor fifty pounds being nearly all expended—my host and he had been brought to believe in my poverty, as the necessary examination of my clothes and papers showed so little evidence of wealth. But I myself have but little to do with my story; I only name these things, and repeat these conversations, to show what a true, kind, honest man my host was. By the way, I may as well call him by his name henceforward, Fritz Müller. The doctor's name, Wiedermann.

I was tired enough with this interview with Fritz Müller; but when Dr Wiedermann came he pronounced me to be much better; and through the day much the same course was pursued as on the previous one: being fed, lying still, and sleeping, were my passive and active occupations. It was a hot, sunshiny day, and I craved for air. Fresh air does not enter into the pharmacopoeia of a German doctor; but somehow I obtained my wish. During the morning hours the window through which the sun streamed—the window looking on to the front court—was opened a little; and through it I heard the sounds of active life, which gave me pleasure and interest enough. The hen's cackle, the cock's exultant call when he had found the treasure of a grain of corn,—the movements of a tethered donkey, and the cooing and whirring of the pigeons which lighted on the window-sill, gave me just subjects enough for interest. Now and then a cart or carriage drove up,—I could hear them ascending the rough village street long before they stopped at the Halbmond,* the village inn. Then there came a sound of running and haste in the house; and Thekla was always called for in sharp, imperative tones. I heard little children's footsteps, too, from time to time; and once there must have been some childish accident or hurt, for a shrill, plaintive little voice kept calling out, 'Thekla, Thekla, liebe Thekla.'* Yet, after the first early morning hours, when my hostess attended on my wants, it was always Thekla who came to give me my food or my medicine; who redded up* my room; who arranged the degree of light, shifting the temporary curtain with the shifting sun; and always as quietly and deliberately as though her attendance upon me were her sole work. Once or twice my hostess came into the large eating-room (out of which my room opened), and called Thekla away from whatever was her occupation in my room at the time, in a sharp, injured, imperative whisper. Once I remember it was to say that sheets were wanted for some stranger's bed, and to ask where she, the speaker, could have put the keys, in a tone of irritation, as though Thekla were responsible for Fräulein Müller's own forgetfulness.

Night came on; the sounds of daily life died away into silence; the children's voices were no more heard; the poultry were all gone to roost; the beasts of burden to their stables; and travellers were housed. Then Thekla came in softly and quietly, and took up her appointed place, after she had done all in her power for my comfort. I felt that I was in no state to be left all those weary hours which intervened between sunset and sunrise; but I did feel ashamed that this young woman, who had watched by me all the previous night, and for aught I knew, for many before, and had worked hard, been run off her legs, as English servants would say, all day long, should come and take up her care of me again; and it was with a feeling of relief that I saw her head bend forwards, and finally rest on her arms, which had fallen on the white piece of sewing spread before her on the table. She slept; and I slept. When I wakened dawn was stealing into the room, and making pale the lamplight. Thekla was standing by the stove, where she had been preparing the *bouillon* I should require on wakening. But she did not notice my half-open eyes, although her face was turned towards the bed. She was reading a letter slowly, as if its words were familiar to her, yet as though she were trying afresh to extract some fuller or some different meaning from their construction. She folded it up softly and slowly, and replaced it in her pocket with the quiet movement habitual to her. Then she looked before her, not at me, but at vacancy filled up by memories; and as the enchanter brought up the scenes and people which she saw, but I could not, her eyes filled with tears—tears that gathered almost imperceptibly to herself as it would seem—for when one large drop fell on her hands (held slightly together before her as she stood) she started a little, and brushed her eyes with the back of her hand, and then came towards the bed to see if I was awake. If I had not witnessed her previous emotion, I could never have guessed that she had any hidden sorrow or pain from her manner; tranquil, self-restrained as usual. The thought of this letter haunted me, especially as more than once I, wakeful or watchful during the ensuing nights, either saw it in her hands, or suspected that she had been recurring to it from noticing the same sorrowful, dreamy look upon her face when she thought herself unobserved. Most likely everyone has noticed how inconsistently out of proportion some ideas become when one is shut up in any place without change of scene or thought. I really grew quite irritated about this letter. If I did not see it, I suspected it lay *perdu** in her pocket. What was in it? Of course it was a love-letter; but if so, what was going wrong in the course of her love? I became like a spoilt child in my recovery; everyone whom I saw for the time being was thinking only of me, so it was perhaps no wonder that I became my sole object of thought; and at last the gratification of my curiosity about this letter seemed to me a duty that I owed to myself. As long as my fidgety inquisitiveness remained ungratified, I felt as if I could not get well. But to do myself justice, it was more than inquisitiveness. Thekla had tended me with the gentle, thoughtful care of a sister, in the midst of her busy life. I could often hear the Fräulein's sharp voice outside blaming her for something that had gone wrong; but I never heard much from Thekla in reply. Her name was called in various tones by different people, more frequently than I could count, as if her services were in perpetual requisition, yet I was never neglected, or even long uncared-for. The doctor was kind and attentive; my host friendly and really generous; his sister subdued her acerbity of manner when in my room, but Thekla was the one of all to whom I owed my comforts, if not my life. If I could do anything to smooth her path (and a little money goes a great way in these primitive parts of Germany), how willingly would I give it? So one night I began—she was no longer needed to watch by my bedside, but she was arranging my room before leaving me for the night ——

'Thekla,' said I, 'you don't belong to Heppenheim, do you?'

She looked at me, and reddened a little.

'No. Why do you ask?'

'You have been so good to me that I cannot help wanting to know more about you. I must needs feel interested in one who has been by my side through my illness as you have. Where do your friends live? Are your parents alive?'

All this time I was driving at the letter.

'I was borne at Altenahr. My father is an innkeeper there. He owns the Golden Stag. My mother is dead, and he has married again, and has many children.'

'And your stepmother is unkind to you,' said I, jumping to a conclusion.

'Who said so?' asked she, with a shade of indignation in her tone. 'She is a right good woman, and makes my father a good wife.'

'Then why are you here living so far from home?'

Now the look came back to her face which I had seen upon it during the night hours when I had watched her by stealth; a dimming of the grave frankness of her eyes, a light quiver at the corners of her mouth. But all she said was, 'It was better.'

Somehow, I persisted with the wilfulness of an invalid. I am half ashamed of it now.

'But why better, Thekla? Was there ——' How should I put it? I stopped a little, and then rushed blindfold at my object: 'Has not that letter which you read so often something to do with your being here?'

She fixed me with her serious eyes till I believe I reddened far more than she; and I hastened to pour out, incoherently enough, my conviction that she had some secret care, and my desire to help her if she was in any trouble.

'You cannot help me,' said she, a little softened by my explanation, though some shade of resentment at having been thus surreptitiously watched yet lingered in her manner. 'It is an old story; a sorrow gone by, past, at least it ought to be, only sometimes I am foolish'—her tones were softening now—'and it is punishment enough that you have seen my folly.'

'If you had a brother here, Thekla, you would let him give you his sympathy if he could not give you his help, and you would not blame yourself if you had shown him your sorrow, should you? I tell you again, let me be as a brother to you.'

'In the first place, sir'—this 'sir' was to mark the distinction between me and the imaginary brother—'I should have been ashamed to have shown even a brother my sorrow, which is also my reproach and my disgrace.' These were strong words; and I suppose my face showed that I attributed to them a still stronger meaning than they warranted; but *honi soit qui mal y pense**—for she went on dropping her eyes and speaking hurriedly.

'My shame and my reproach is this: I have loved a man who has not loved me'—she grasped her hands together till the fingers made deep white dents in the rosy flesh—'and I can't make out whether he ever did, or whether he did once and is changed now; if only he did once love me, I could forgive myself.'

With hasty, trembling hands she began to rearrange the *tisane** and medicines for the night on the little table at my bedside. But, having got thus far, I was determined to persevere.

'Thekla,' said I, 'tell me all about it, as you would to your mother, if she were alive. There are often misunderstandings which, never set to rights, make the misery and desolation of a lifetime.'

She did not speak at first. Then she pulled out the letter, and said, in a quiet, hopeless tone of voice:—

'You can read German writing? Read that, and see if I have any reason for misunderstanding.'

The letter was signed 'Franz Weber,' and dated from some small town in Switzerland—I forget what—about a month previous to the time when I read it. It began with acknowledging the receipt of some money which had evidently been requested by the writer, and for which the thanks were almost fulsome; and then, by the quietest transition in the world, he went on to consult her as to the desirability of his marrying some girl in the place from which he wrote, saying that this Anna Somebody was only eighteen and very pretty, and her father a well-to-do shopkeeper, and adding, with coarse coxcombry, his belief that he was not indifferent to the maiden herself. He wound up by saying that, if this marriage did take place, he should certainly repay the various sums of money which Thekla had lent him at different times.

I was some time in making out all this. Thekla held the candle for me to read it; held it patiently and steadily, not speaking a word till I had folded up the letter again, and given it back to her. Then our eyes met.

'There is no misunderstanding possible, is there, sir?' asked she, with a faint smile.

'No,' I replied; 'but you are well rid of such a fellow.'

She shook her head a little. 'It shows his bad side, sir. We have all our bad sides. You must not judge him harshly; at least, I cannot. But then we were brought up together.'

'At Altenahr?'

'Yes; his father kept the other inn, and our parents, instead of being rivals, were great friends. Franz is a little younger than I, and was a delicate child. I had to take him to school, and I used to be so proud of it and of my charge. Then he grew strong, and was the handsomest lad in the village. Our fathers used to sit and smoke together, and talk of our marriage, and Franz must have heard as much as I. Whenever he was in trouble, he would come to me for what advice I could give him; and he danced twice as often with me as with any other girl at all the dances, and always brought his nosegay to me. Then his father wished him to travel, and learn the ways at the great hotels on the Rhine before he settled down in Altenahr. You know that is the custom in Germany, sir. They go from town to town as journeymen, learning something fresh everywhere, they say.'

'I knew that was done in trades,' I replied.

'Oh, yes; and among innkeepers, too,' she said. 'Most of the waiters at the great hotels in Frankfurt, and Heidelberg, and Mainz, and, I daresay, at all the other places, are the sons of innkeepers in small towns, who go out into the world to learn new ways, and perhaps to pick up a little English and French; otherwise, they say, they should never get on. Franz went off from Altenahr on his journeyings four years ago next May Day; and before he went, he brought me back a ring from Bonn, where he bought his new clothes. I don't wear it now; but I have got it upstairs, and it comforts me to see something that shows me it was not all my silly fancy. I suppose he fell among bad people, for he soon began to play for money,—and then he lost more than he could always pay—and sometimes I could help him a little, for we wrote to each other from time to time, as we knew each other's addresses; for the little ones grew around my father's hearth, and I thought that I, too, would go forth into the world and earn my own living, so that——well, I will tell the truth—I thought that by going into service, I could lay by enough for buying a handsome stock of household linen, and plenty of pans and kettles against—against what will never come to pass now.'

'Do the German women buy the pots and kettles, as you call them, when they are married?' asked I, awkwardly, laying hold of a trivial question to conceal the indignant sympathy with her wrongs which I did not like to express.

'Oh, yes; the bride furnishes all that is wanted in the kitchen, and all the store of house-linen. If my mother had lived, it would have been laid by for me, as she could have afforded to buy it, but my stepmother will have hard enough work to provide for her own four little girls. However,' she continued, brightening up, 'I can help her, for now I shall never marry; and my master here is just and liberal, and pays me sixty florins a year, which is high wages.' (Sixty florins are about five pounds sterling.) 'And now, good-night, sir. This cup to the left holds the *tisane*, that to the right the acorn-tea.' She shaded the candle, and was leaving the room. I raised myself on my elbow, and called her back.

'Don't go on thinking about this man,' said I. 'He was not good enough for you. You are much better unmarried.'

'Perhaps so,' she answered gravely. 'But you cannot do him justice; you do not know him.'

A few minutes after, I heard her soft and cautious return; she had taken her shoes off, and came in her stockinged feet up to my bedside, shading the light with her hand. When she saw that my eyes were open, she laid down two letters on the table, close by my night-lamp.

'Perhaps, some time, sir, you would take the trouble to read these letters; you would then see how noble and clever Franz really is. It is I who ought to be blamed, not he.'

No more was said that night.

Some time the next morning I read the letters. They were filled with vague, inflated, sentimental descriptions of his inner life and feelings; entirely egotistical, and intermixed with quotations from second-rate philosophers and poets. There was, it must be said, nothing in them offensive to good principle or good feeling, however much they might be opposed to good taste. I was to go into the next room that afternoon for the first time of leaving my sick chamber. All morning I lay and ruminated. From time to time I thought of Thekla and Franz Weber. She was the strong, good, helpful character, he the weak and vain; how strange it seemed that she should have cared for one so dissimilar; and then I remembered the various happy marriages when to an outsider it seemed as if one was so inferior to the other that their union would have appeared a subject for despair if it had been looked at prospectively. My host came in, in the midst of these meditations, bringing a great flowered dressing-gown, lined with flannel, and the embroidered smoking-cap which he evidently considered as belonging to this Indian-looking robe. They had been his father's, he told me; and as he helped me to dress, he went on with his communications on small family matters. His inn was flourishing; the numbers increased every year of those who came to see the church at Heppenheim: the church which was the pride of the place, but which I had never yet seen. It was built by the great Kaiser Karl.* And there was the Castle of Starkenburg, too, which the Abbots of Lorsch* had often defended, stalwart churchmen as they were, against the temporal power of the emperors. And Melibocus* was not beyond a walk either. In fact, it was the work of one person to superintend the inn alone; but he had his farm and his vineyards beyond, which of themselves gave him enough to do. And his sister was oppressed with the perpetual calls made upon her patience and her nerves in an inn; and would rather go back and live at Worms. And his children wanted so much looking after. By the time he had placed himself in a condition for requiring my full sympathy, I had finished my slow toilette; and I had to interrupt his confidences, and accept the help of his good strong arm to lead me into the great eating-room, out of which my chamber opened. I had a dreamy recollection of the vast apartment. But how pleasantly it was changed! There was the bare half of the room, it is true, looking as it had done on that first afternoon, sunless and cheerless, with the long, unoccupied table, and the necessary chairs for the possible visitors; but round the windows that opened on the garden a part of the room was enclosed by the household clothes'-horses hung with great pieces of the blue homespun cloth of which the dress of the Black Forest peasant is made. This shut-in space was warmed by the lighted stove, as well as by the lowering rays of the October sun. There was a little round walnut table with some flowers upon it, and a great cushioned armchair placed so as to look out upon the garden and the hills beyond. I felt sure that this was all Thekla's arrangement; I had rather wondered that I had seen so little of her this day. She had come once or twice on necessary errands into my room in the morning, but had appeared to be in great haste, and had avoided meeting my eye. Even when I had returned the letters, which she had entrusted to me with so evident a purpose of placing the writer in my good opinion, she had never inquired as to how far they had answered her design; she had merely taken them with some low word of thanks, and put them hurriedly into her pocket. I suppose she shrank from remembering how fully she had given me her confidence the night before, now that daylight and actual life pressed close around her. Besides, there surely never was anyone in such constant request as Thekla. I did not like this estrangement, though it was the natural consequence of my improved health, which would daily make me less and less require services which seemed so urgently claimed by others. And, moreover, after my host left me—I fear I had cut him a little short in the recapitulation of his domestic difficulties, but he was too thorough and goodhearted a man to bear malice—I wanted to be amused or interested. So I rang my little hand-bell, hoping that Thekla would answer it, when I could have fallen into conversation with her, without specifying any decided want. Instead of Thekla the Fräulein came, and I had to invent a wish; for I could not act as a baby, and say that I wanted my nurse. However, the Fräulein was better than no one, so I asked her if I could have some grapes, which had been provided for me on every day but this, and which were especially grateful to my feverish palate. She was a good, kind woman, although, perhaps, her temper was not the best in the world; and she expressed the sincerest regret as she told me that there were no more in the house. Like an invalid I fretted at my wish not being granted, and spoke out.

'But Thekla told me the vintage was not till the fourteenth; and you have a vineyard close beyond the garden on the slope of the hill out there, have you not?'

'Yes; and grapes for the gathering. But perhaps the gentleman does not know our laws. Until the vintage—(the day of beginning the vintage is fixed by the Grand Duke,* and advertised in the public papers)—until the vintage, all owners of vineyards may only go on two appointed days in every week to gather their grapes; on those two days (Tuesdays and Fridays this year) they must gather enough for the wants of their families; and if they do not reckon rightly, and gather short measure, why they have to go without. And these two last days the Half-Moon has been besieged with visitors, all of whom have asked for grapes. But tomorrow the gentleman can have as many as he will; it is the day for gathering them.'

'What a strange kind of paternal law,' I grumbled out. 'Why is it so ordained? Is it to secure the owners against pilfering from their unfenced vineyards?'

'I am sure I cannot tell,' she replied. 'Country people in these villages have strange customs in many ways, as I daresay the English gentleman has perceived. If he would come to Worms he would see a different kind of life.'

'But not a view like this,' I replied, caught by a sudden change of light—some cloud passing away from the sun, or something. Right outside of the windows was, as I have so often said, the garden. Trained plum-trees with golden leaves, great bushes of purple Michaelmas daisy, late flowering roses, apple-trees partly stripped of their rosy fruit, but still with enough left on their boughs to require the props set to support the luxuriant burden; to the left an arbour covered over with honey-suckle and other sweet-smelling creepers—all bounded by a low grey stone wall which opened out upon the steep vineyard, that stretched up the hill beyond, one hill of a series rising higher and higher into the purple distance. 'Why is there a rope with a bunch of straw tied in it stretched across the opening of the garden into the vineyard?' I inquired, as my eye suddenly caught upon the object.

'It is the country way of showing that no one must pass along that path. Tomorrow the gentleman will see it removed; and then he shall have the grapes. Now I will go and prepare his coffee.' With a curtsey, after the fashion of Worms gentility, she withdrew. But an under-servant brought me my coffee; and with her I could not exchange a word: she spoke in such an execrable *patois*. I went to bed early, weary, and depressed.

I must have fallen asleep immediately, for I never heard anyone come to arrange my bedside table; yet in the morning I found that every usual want or wish of mine had been attended to.

I was wakened by a tap at my door, and a pretty piping child's voice asking, in broken German, to come in. On giving the usual permission, Thekla entered, carrying a great lovely boy of two years old, or thereabouts, who had only his little night-shirt on, and was all flushed with sleep. He held tight in his hands a great cluster of muscatel and noble grapes. He seemed like a little Bacchus,* as she carried him towards me with an expression of pretty loving pride upon her face as she looked at him. But when he came close to me—the grim, wasted, unshorn—he turned quick away, and hid his face in her neck, still grasping tight his bunch of grapes. She spoke to him rapidly and softly, coaxing him as I could tell full well, although I could not follow her words; and in a minute or two the little fellow obeyed her, and turned and stretched himself almost to overbalancing out of her arms, and half-dropped the fruit on the bed by me. Then he clutched at her again, burying his face in her kerchief, and fastening his little fists in her luxuriant hair.

'It is my master's only boy,' said she, disentangling his fingers with quiet patience, only to have them grasp her braids afresh. 'He is my little Max, my heart's delight, only he must not pull so hard. Say his "to-meet-again," and kiss his hand lovingly, and we will go.' The promise of a speedy departure from my dusky room proved irresistible; he babbled out his *Aufwiedersehen*,* and kissing his chubby hand, he was borne away joyful and chattering fast in his infantile half-language. I did not see Thekla again until late afternoon, when she brought me in my coffee. She was not like the same creature as the blooming, cheerful maiden whom I had seen in the morning; she looked wan and careworn, older by several years.

'What is the matter, Thekla?' said I, with true anxiety as to what might have befallen my good, faithful nurse.

She looked round before answering. 'I have seen him,' she said. 'He has been here, and the Fräulein has been so angry! She says she will tell my master. Oh, it has been such a day!' The poor young woman, who was usually so composed and self-restrained, was on the point of bursting into tears; but by a strong effort she checked herself, and tried to busy herself with rearranging the white china cup, so as to place it more conveniently to my hand.

'Come, Thekla,' said I, 'tell me all about it. I have heard loud voices talking, and I fancied something had put the Fräulein out; and Lottchen looked flurried when she brought me my dinner. Is Franz here? How has he found you out?'

'He is here. Yes, I am sure it is he; but four years makes such a difference in a man; his whole look and manner seemed so strange to me; but he knew me at once, and called me all the old names which we used to call each other when we were children; and he must needs tell me how it had come to pass that he had not married that Swiss Anna. He said he had never loved her; and that now he was going home to settle, and he hoped that I would come too, and ——' There she stopped short.

'And marry him, and live at the inn at Altenahr,' said I, smiling, to reassure her, though I felt rather disappointed about the whole affair.

'No,' she replied. 'Old Weber, his father, is dead; he died in debt, and Franz will have no money. And he was always one that needed money. Some are, you know; and while I was thinking, and he was standing near me, the Fräulein came in; and—and—I don't wonder—for poor Franz is not a pleasant-looking man nowadays—she was very angry, and called me a bold, bad girl, and said she could have no such goings on at the Halbmond, but would tell my master when he came home from the forest.'

'But you could have told her that you were old friends.' I hesitated, before saying the word lovers, but, after a pause, out it came.

'Franz might have said so,' she replied, a little stiffly. 'I could not; but he went off as soon as she bade him. He went to the Adler* over the way, only saying he would come for my answer tomorrow morning. I think it was he that should have told her what we were—neighbours' children and early friends—not have left it all to me. Oh,' said she, clasping her hands tight together, 'she will make such a story of it to my master.'

'Never mind,' said I, 'tell the master I want to see him, as soon as he comes in from the forest, and trust me to set him right before the Fräulein has the chance to set him wrong.'

She looked up at me gratefully, and went away without any more words. Presently the fine burly figure of my host stood at the opening to my enclosed sitting-room. He was there, three-cornered hat in hand, looking tired and heated as a man does after a hard day's work, but as kindly and genial as ever, which is not what every man is who is called to business after such a day, before he has had the necessary food and rest.

I had been reflecting a good deal on Thekla's story; I could not quite interpret her manner today to my full satisfaction; but yet the love which had grown with her growth, must assuredly have been called forth by her lover's sudden reappearance; and I was inclined to give him some credit for having broken off an engagement to Swiss Anna, which had promised so many worldly advantages; and, again, I had considered that if he was a little weak and sentimental, it was Thekla, who would marry him by her own free will, and perhaps she had sense and quiet resolution enough for both. So I gave the heads of the little history I have told you to my good friend and host, adding that I should like to have a man's opinion of this man; but that if he were not an absolute good-for-nothing, and if Thekla still loved him, as I believed, I would try and advance them the requisite money towards establishing themselves in the hereditary inn at Altenahr.

Such was the romantic ending to Thekla's sorrows I had been planning and brooding over for the last hour. As I narrated my tale, and hinted at the possible happy conclusion that might be in store, my host's face changed. The ruddy colour faded, and his look became almost stern—certainly very grave in expression. It was so unsympathetic, that I instinctively cut my words short. When I had done, he paused a little, and then said: 'You would wish me to learn all I can respecting this stranger now at the Adler, and give you the impression I receive of the fellow.'

'Exactly so,' said I; 'I want to learn all I can about him for Thekla's sake.'

'For Thekla's sake I will do it,' he gravely repeated.

'And come to me tonight, even if I am gone to bed?'

'Not so,' he replied. 'You must give me all the time you can in a matter like this.'

'But he will come for Thekla's answer in the morning.'

'Before he comes you shall know all I can learn.'

I was resting during the fatigues of dressing the next day, when my host tapped at my door. He looked graver and sterner than I had ever seen him do before; he sat down almost before I had begged him to do so.

'He is not worthy of her,' he said. 'He drinks brandy right hard; he boasts of his success at play, and'—here he set his teeth hard—'he boasts of the women who have loved him. In a village like this, sir, there are always those who spend their evenings in the gardens of the inns; and this man, after he had drank his fill, made no secrets; it needed no spying to find out what he was, else I should not have been the one to do it.'

'Thekla must be told of this,' said I. 'She is not the woman to love anyone whom she cannot respect.'

Herr Müller laughed a low bitter laugh, quite unlike himself. Then he replied,—

'As for that matter, sir, you are young; you have had no great experience of women. From what my sister tells me there can be little doubt of Thekla's feeling towards him. She found them standing together by the window; his arm round Thekla's waist, and whispering in her ear—and to do the maiden justice she is not the one to suffer such familiarities from everyone. No'—continued he, still in the same contemptuous tone—'you'll find she will make excuses for his faults and vices; or else, which is perhaps more likely, she will not believe your story, though I who tell it you can vouch for the truth of every word I say.' He turned short away and left the room. Presently I saw his stalwart figure in the hillside vineyard, before my windows, scaling the steep ascent with long regular steps, going to the forest beyond. I was otherwise occupied than in watching his progress during the next hour; at the end of that time he re-entered my room, looking heated and slightly tired, as if he had been walking fast, or labouring hard; but with the cloud off his brows, and the kindly light shining once again out of his honest eyes.

'I ask your pardon, sir,' he began, 'for troubling you afresh. I believe I was possessed by the devil this morning. I have been thinking it over. One has perhaps no right to rule for another person's happiness. To have such a'—here the honest fellow choked a little—'such a woman as Thekla to love him ought to raise any man. Besides, I am no judge for him or for her. I have found out this morning that I love her myself, and so the end of it is, that if you, sir, who are so kind as to interest yourself in the matter, and if you think it is really her heart's desire to marry this man—which ought to be his salvation both for earth and heaven—I shall be very glad to go halves with you in any place* for setting them up in the inn at Altenahr; only allow me to see that whatever money we advance is well and legally tied up, so that it is secured to her. And be so kind as to take no notice of what I have said about my having found out that I have loved her; I named it as a kind of apology for my hard words this morning, and as a reason why I was not a fit judge of what was best.' He had hurried on, so that I could not have stopped his eager speaking even had I wished to do so; but I was too much interested in the revelation of what was passing in his brave tender heart to desire to stop him. Now, however, his rapid words tripped each other up, and his speech ended in an unconscious sigh.

'But,' I said, 'since you were here Thekla has come to me, and we have had a long talk. She speaks now as openly to me as she would if I were her brother; with sensible frankness, where frankness is wise, with modest reticence, where confidence would be unbecoming. She came to ask me if I thought it her duty to marry this fellow, whose very appearance, changed for the worse, as she says it is, since she last saw him four years ago, seemed to have repelled her.'

'She could let him put his arm round her waist yesterday,' said Herr Müller, with a return of his morning's surliness.

'And she would marry him now if she could believe it to be her duty. For some reason of his own, this Franz Weber has tried to work upon this feeling of hers. He says it would be the saving of him.'

'As if a man had not strength enough in him—a man who is good for aught—to save himself, but needed a woman to pull him through life!'

'Nay,' I replied, hardly able to keep from smiling. 'You yourself said, not five minutes ago, that her marrying him might be his salvation both for earth and heaven.'

'That was when I thought she loved the fellow,' he answered quick. 'Now—but what did you say to her, sir?'

'I told her, what I believe to be as true as gospel, that as she owned she did not love him any longer now his real self had come to displace his remembrance, that she would be sinning in marrying him; doing evil that possible good might come.* I was clear myself on this point, though I should have been perplexed how to advise, if her love had still continued.'

'And what answer did she make?'

'She went over the history of their lives; she was pleading against her wishes to satisfy her conscience. She said that all along through their childhood she had been his strength; that while under her personal influence he had been negatively good; away from her, he had fallen into mischief ——'

'Not to say vice,' put in Herr Müller.

'And now he came to her penitent, in sorrow, desirous of amendment, asking her for the love she seems to have considered as tacitly plighted to him in years gone by ——'

'And which he has slighted and insulted. I hope you told her of his words and conduct last night in the Adler gardens?'

'No. I kept myself to the general principle, which, I am sure, is a true one. I repeated it in different forms; for the idea of the duty of self-sacrifice had taken strong possession of her fancy. Perhaps, if I had failed in setting her notion of her duty in the right aspect, I might have had recourse to the statement of facts, which would have pained her severely, but would have proved to her how little his words of penitence and promises of amendment were to be trusted to.'

'And it ended?'

'Ended by her being quite convinced that she would be doing wrong instead of right if she married a man whom she had entirely ceased to love, and that no real good could come from a course of action based on wrong-doing.'

'That is right and true,' he replied, his face broadening into happiness again.

'But she says she must leave your service, and go elsewhere.'

'Leave my service she shall; go elsewhere she shall not.'

'I cannot tell what you may have the power of inducing her to do; but she seems to me very resolute.'

'Why?' said he, firing round at me, as if I had made her resolute.

'She says your sister spoke to her before the maids of the household, and before some of the townspeople, in a way that she could not stand; and that you yourself by your manner to her last night showed how she had lost your respect. She added, with her face of pure maidenly truth, that he had come into such close contact with her only the instant before your sister had entered the room.'

'With your leave, sir,' said Herr Müller, turning towards the door, 'I will go and set all that right at once.'

It was easier said than done. When I next saw Thekla, her eyes were swollen up with crying, but she was silent, almost defiant towards me. A look of resolute determination had settled down upon her face. I learnt afterwards that parts of my conversation with Herr Müller had been injudiciously quoted by him in the talk he had had with her. I thought I would leave her to herself, and wait till she unburdened herself of the feeling of unjust resentment towards me. But it was days before she spoke to me with anything like her former frankness. I had heard all about it from my host long before.

He had gone to her straight on leaving me; and like a foolish, impetuous lover, had spoken out his mind and his wishes to her in the presence of his sister, who, it must be remembered, had heard no explanation of the conduct which had given her propriety so great a shock the day before. Herr Müller thought to reinstate Thekla in his sister's good opinion by giving her in the Fräulein's very presence the highest possible mark of his own love and esteem. And there in the kitchen, where the Fräulein was deeply engaged in the hot work of making some delicate preserve on the stove, and ordering Thekla about with short, sharp displeasure in her tones, the master had come in, and possessing himself of the maiden's hand, had, to her infinite surprise—to his sister's infinite indignation—made her the offer of his heart, his wealth, his life; had begged of her to marry him. I could gather from his account that she had been in a state of trembling discomfiture at first; she had not spoken, but had twisted her hand out of his, and had covered her face with her apron. And then the Fräulein had burst forth—'accursed words' he called her speech. Thekla uncovered her face to listen; to listen to the end; to listen to the passionate recrimination between the brother and the sister. And then she went up, close up to the angry Fräulein, and had said quite quietly, but with a manner of final determination which had evidently sunk deep into her suitor's heart, and depressed him into hopelessness, that the Fräulein had no need to disturb herself; that on this very day she had been thinking of marrying another man, and that her heart was not like a room to let, into which as one tenant went out another might enter. Nevertheless, she felt the master's goodness. He had always treated her well from the time when she had entered the house as his servant. And she should be sorry to leave him; sorry to leave the children; very sorry to leave little Max: yes, she should even be sorry to leave the Fräulein, who was a good woman, only a little too apt to be hard on other women. But she had already been that very day and deposited her warning at the police office; the busy time would be soon over, and she should be glad to leave their service on All Saints' Day.* Then (he thought) she had felt inclined to cry, for she suddenly braced herself up, and said, yes, she should be very glad; for somehow, though they had been kind to her, she had been very unhappy at Heppenheim; and she would go back to her home for a time, and see her old father and kind stepmother, and her nursling half-sister Ida, and be among her own people again.

I could see it was this last part that most of all rankled in Herr Müller's mind. In all probability Franz Weber was making his way back to Altenahr too; and the bad suspicion would keep welling up that some lingering feeling for her old lover and disgraced playmate was making her so resolute to leave and return to Altenahr.

For some days after this I was the confidant of the whole household, excepting Thekla. She, poor creature, looked miserable enough; but the hardy, defiant expression was always on her face. Lottchen spoke out freely enough; the place would not be worth having if Thekla left it; it was she who had the head for everything, the patience for everything; who stood between all the under-servants and the Fräulein's tempers. As for the children, poor motherless children! Lottchen was sure that the master did not know what he was doing when he allowed his sister to turn Thekla away—and all for what? for having a lover, as every girl had who could get one. Why, the little boy Max slept in the room which Lottchen shared with Thekla; and she heard him in the night as quickly as if she was his mother; when she had been sitting up with me, when I was so ill, Lottchen had had to attend to him; and it was weary work after a hard day to have to get up and soothe a teething child; she knew she had been cross enough sometimes; but Thekla was always good and gentle with him, however tired she was. And as Lottchen left the room I could hear her repeating that she thought she should leave when Thekla went, for that her place would not be worth having.

Even the Fräulein had her word of regret—regret mingled with self-justification. She thought she had been quite right in speaking to Thekla for allowing such familiarities; how was she to know that the man was an old friend and playmate? He looked like a right profligate good-for-nothing. And to have a servant take up her scolding as an unpardonable offence, and persist in quitting her place, just when she had learnt all her work, and was so useful in the household—so useful that the Fräulein could never put up with any fresh, stupid housemaiden, but, sooner than take the trouble of teaching the new servant where everything was, and how to give out the stores if she was busy, she would go back to Worms. For, after all, housekeeping for a brother was thankless work; there was no satisfying men; and Heppenheim was but a poor ignorant village compared to Worms.

She must have spoken to her brother about her intention of leaving him, and returning to her former home; indeed a feeling of coolness had evidently grown up between the brother and sister during these latter days. When one evening Herr Müller brought in his pipe, and, as his custom had sometimes been, sat down by my stove to smoke, he looked gloomy and annoyed. I let him puff away, and take his own time. At length he began,—

'I have rid the village of him at last. I could not bear to have him here disgracing Thekla with speaking to her whenever she went to the vineyard or the fountain. I don't believe she likes him a bit.'

'No more do I,' I said. He turned on me.

'Then why did she speak to him at all? Why cannot she like an honest man who likes her? Why is she so bent on going home to Altenahr?'

'She speaks to him because she has known him from a child, and has a faithful pity for one whom she has known so innocent, and who is now so lost in all good men's regard. As for not liking an honest man—(though I may have my own opinion about that)—liking goes by fancy, as we say in English; and Altenahr is her home; her father's house is at Altenahr, as you know.'

'I wonder if he will go there,' quoth Herr Müller, after two or three more puffs. 'He was fast at the Adler; he could not pay his score, so he kept on staying here, saying that he should receive a letter from a friend with money in a day or two; lying in wait, too, for Thekla, who is well-known and respected all through Heppenheim: so his being an old friend of hers made him have a kind of standing. I went in this morning and paid his score, on condition that he left the place this day; and he left the village as merrily as a cricket, caring no more for Thekla than for the Kaiser who built our church: for he never looked back at the Halbmond, but went whistling down the road.'

'That is a good riddance,' said I.

'Yes. But my sister says she must return to Worms. And Lottchen has given notice; she says the place will not be worth having when Thekla leaves. I wish I could give notice too.'

'Try Thekla again.'

'Not I,' said he, reddening. 'It would seem now as if I only wanted her for a housekeeper. Besides, she avoids me at every turn, and will not even look at me. I am sure she bears me some ill-will about that ne'er-do-well.'

There was silence between us for some time, which he at length broke.

'The pastor has a good and comely daughter. Her mother is a famous housewife. They often have asked me to come to the parsonage and smoke a pipe. When the vintage is over, and I am less busy, I think I will go there, and look about me.'

'When is the vintage?' asked I. 'I hope it will take place soon, for I am growing so well and strong I fear I must leave you shortly; but I should like to see the vintage first.'

'Oh, never fear! you must not travel yet awhile; and Government has fixed the grape-gathering to begin on the fourteenth.'

'What a paternal Government! How does it know when the grapes will be ripe? Why cannot every man fix his own time for gathering his own grapes?'

'That has never been our way in Germany. There are people employed by the Government to examine the vines, and report when the grapes are ripe. It is necessary to make laws about it; for, as you must have seen, there is nothing but the fear of the law to protect our vineyards and fruit-trees; there are no enclosures along the Berg-Strasse, as you tell me you have in England; but, as people are only allowed to go into the vineyards on stated days, no one, under pretence of gathering his own produce, can stray into his neighbour's grounds and help himself, without some of the Duke's foresters seeing him.'

'Well,' said I, 'to each country its own laws.'*

I think it was on that very evening that Thekla came in for something. She stopped arranging the tablecloth and the flowers, as if she had something to say, yet did not know how to begin. At length I found that her sore, hot heart wanted some sympathy; her hand was against everyone's,* and she fancied everyone had turned against her. She looked up at me, and said, a little abruptly,—

'Does the gentleman know that I go on the fifteenth?'

'So soon?' said I, with surprise. 'I thought you were to remain here till All Saints' Day.'

'So I should have done—so I must have done—if the Fräulein had not kindly given me leave to accept of a place—a very good place too—of housekeeper to a widow lady at Frankfurt. It is just the sort of situation I have always wished for. I expect I shall be so happy and comfortable there.'

'Methinks the lady doth profess too much,'* came into my mind. I saw she expected me to doubt the probability of her happiness, and was in a defiant mood.

'Of course,' said I, 'you would hardly have wished to leave

Heppenheim if you had been happy here; and every new place always promises fair, whatever its performance may be. But wherever you go, remember you have always a friend in me.'

'Yes,' she replied, 'I think you are to be trusted. Though, from my experience, I should say that of very few men.'

'You have been unfortunate,' I answered; 'many men would say the same of women.'

She thought a moment, and then said, in a changed tone of voice, 'The Fräulein here has been much more friendly and helpful of these late days than her brother; yet I have served him faithfully, and have cared for his little Max as though he were my own brother. But this morning he spoke to me for the first time for many days,—he met me in the passage, and, suddenly stopping, he said he was glad I had met with so comfortable a place, and that I was at full liberty to go whenever I liked: and then he went quickly on, never waiting for my answer.'

'And what was wrong in that? It seems to me he was trying to make you feel entirely at your ease, to do as you thought best, without regard to his own interests.'

'Perhaps so. It is silly, I know,' she continued, turning full on me her grave, innocent eyes; 'but one's vanity suffers a little when everyone is so willing to part with one.'

'Thekla! I owe you a great debt—let me speak to you openly. I know that your master wanted to marry you, and that you refused him. Do not deceive yourself. You are sorry for that refusal now?'

She kept her serious look fixed upon me; but her face and throat reddened all over.

'No,' said she, at length; 'I am not sorry. What can you think I am made of; having loved one man ever since I was a little child until a fortnight ago, and now just as ready to love another? I know you do not rightly consider what you say, or I should take it as an insult.'

'You loved an ideal man; he disappointed you, and you clung to your remembrance of him. He came, and the reality dispelled all illusions.'

'I do not understand philosophy,' said she. 'I only know that I think that Herr Müller had lost all respect for me from what his sister had told him; and I know that I am going away; and I trust I shall be happier in Frankfurt than I have been here of late days.' So saying, she left the room.

I was wakened up on the morning of the fourteenth by the merry ringing of church bells, and the perpetual firing and popping off of guns and pistols. But all this was over by the time I was up and dressed, and seated at breakfast in my partitioned room. It was a perfect October day; the dew not yet off the blades of grass, glistening on the delicate gossamer webs, which stretched from flower to flower in the garden, lying in the morning shadow of the house. But beyond the garden, on the sunny hillside, men, women, and children were clambering up the vineyards like ants,—busy, irregular in movement, clustering together, spreading wide apart,—I could hear the shrill merry voices as I sat,—and all along the valley, as far as I could see, it was much the same; for everyone filled his house for the day of the vintage, that great annual festival. Lottchen, who had brought in my breakfast, was all in her Sunday best, having risen early to get her work done and go abroad to gather grapes. Bright colours seemed to abound; I could see dots of scarlet, and crimson, and orange through the fading leaves; it was not a day to languish in the house; and I was on the point of going out by myself, when Herr Müller came in to offer me his sturdy arm, and help me in walking to the vineyard. We crept through the garden scented with late flowers and sunny fruit,—we passed through the gate I had so often gazed at from the easy-chair, and were in the busy vineyard; great baskets lay on the grass already piled nearly full of purple and yellow grapes. The wine made from these was far from pleasant to my taste; for the best Rhine wine is made from a smaller grape, growing in closer, harder clusters; but the larger and less profitable grape is by far the most picturesque in its mode of growth, and far the best to eat into the bargain. Wherever we trod, it was on fragrant, crushed vine-leaves; everyone we saw had his hands and face stained with the purple juice. Presently I sat down on a sunny bit of grass, and my host left me to go farther afield, to look after the more distant vineyards. I watched his progress. After he left me, he took off coat and waistcoat, displaying his snowy shirt and gaily-worked braces; and presently he was as busy as anyone. I looked down on the village; the grey and orange and crimson roofs lay glowing in the noonday sun. I could see down into the streets; but they were all empty—even the old people came toiling up the hillside to share in the general festivity. Lottchen had brought up cold dinners for a regiment of men; everyone came and helped himself. Thekla was there, leading the little Karoline, and helping the toddling steps of Max; but she kept aloof from me; for I knew, or suspected, or had probed too much. She alone looked sad and grave, and spoke so little, even to her friends, that it was evident to see that she was trying to wean herself finally from the place. But I could see that she had lost her short, defiant manner. What she did say was kindly and gently spoken. The Fräulein came out late in the morning, dressed, I suppose, in the latest Worms fashion—quite different to anything I had ever seen before. She came up to me, and talked very graciously to me for some time.

'Here comes the proprietor (squire) and his lady, and their dear children. See, the vintagers have tied bunches of the finest grapes on to a stick, heavier than the children or even the lady can carry. Look! look! how he bows!—one can tell he has been an *attaché* at Vienna. That is the court way of bowing there—holding the hat right down before them, and bending the back at right angles. How graceful! And here is the doctor! I thought he would spare time to come up here. Well, doctor, you will go all the more cheerfully to your next patient for having been up into the vineyards. Nonsense, about grapes making other patients for you. Ah, here is the pastor and his wife, and the Fräulein Anna. Now, where is my brother, I wonder? Up in the far vineyard, I make no doubt. Mr Pastor, the view up above is far finer than what it is here, and the best grapes grow there; shall I accompany you and madame, and the dear Fräulein? The gentleman will excuse me.'

I was left alone. Presently I thought I would walk a little farther, or at any rate change my position. I rounded a corner in the pathway, and there I found Thekla, watching by little sleeping Max. He lay on her shawl; and over his head she had made an arching canopy of broken vine-branches, so that the great leaves threw their cool, flickering shadows on his face. He was smeared all over with grape-juice, his sturdy fingers grasped a half-eaten bunch even in his sleep. Thekla was keeping Lina quiet by teaching her how to weave a garland for her head out of field-flowers and autumn-tinted leaves. The maiden sat on the ground, with her back to the valley beyond, the child kneeling by her, watching the busy fingers with eager intentness. Both looked up as I drew near, and we exchanged a few words.

'Where is the master?' I asked. 'I promised to await his return; he wished to give me his arm down the wooden steps; but I do not see him.'

'He is in the higher vineyard,' said Thekla, quietly, but not looking round in that direction. He will be some time there, I should think. He went with the pastor and his wife; he will have to speak to his labourers and his friends. My arm is strong, and I can leave Max in Lina's care for five minutes. If you are tired, and want to go back, let me help you down the steps; they are steep and slippery.'

I had turned to look up the valley. Three or four hundred yards off, in the higher vineyard, walked the dignified pastor, and his homely, decorous wife. Behind came the Fräulein Anna, in her short-sleeved Sunday gown, daintily holding a parasol over her luxuriant brown hair. Close behind her came Herr Müller, stopping now to speak to his men,—again, to cull out a bunch of grapes to tie on to the Fräulein's stick; and by my feet sat the proud serving-maid in her country dress, waiting for my answer, with serious, upturned eyes, and sad, composed face.

'No, I am much obliged to you, Thekla; and if I did not feel so strong I would have thankfully taken your arm. But I only wanted to leave a message for the master, just to say that I have gone home.'

'Lina will give it to the father when he comes down,' said Thekla.

I went slowly down into the garden. The great labour of the day was over, and the younger part of the population had returned to the village, and were preparing the fireworks and pistol-shootings for the evening. Already one or two of those well-known German carts (in the shape of a V) were standing near the vineyard gates, the patient oxen meekly waiting while basketful after basketful of grapes were being emptied into the leaf-lined receptacle.

As I sat down in my easy-chair close to the open window through which I had entered, I could see the men and women on the hillside drawing to a centre, and all stand round the pastor, bareheaded, for a minute or so. I guessed that some words of holy thanksgiving were being said, and I wished that I had stayed to hear them, and mark my especial gratitude for having been spared to see that day. Then I heard the distant voices, the deep tones of the men, the shriller pipes of women and children, join in the German harvest-hymn,* which is generally sung on such occasions;[1] then silence, while I concluded that a blessing was spoken by the pastor, with outstretched arms; and then they once more dispersed, some to the village, some to finish their labours for the day among the vines. I saw Thekla coming through the garden with Max in her arms, and Lina clinging to her woollen skirts. Thekla made for my open window; it was rather a shorter passage into the house than round by the door. 'I may come through, may I not?' she asked, softly. 'I fear Max is not well; I cannot understand his look, and he wakened up so strange!' She paused to let me see the child's face; it was flushed almost to a crimson look of heat, and his breathing was laboured and uneasy, his eyes half-open and filmy.

'Something is wrong, I am sure,' said I. 'I don't know anything about children, but he is not in the least like himself.'

[1] Wir pflügen und wir streuen,
Den Saamen auf das Land;
Das Wachsen und Gedeihen steht,
In des höchsten Hand.
Er sendet Thau und Regen,
Und Sonn und Mondeschein;
Von Ihm kommt aller Segen,
Von unserm Gott allein:
Alle gute Gabe kommt her
Von Gott dem Herrn,
Drum dankt und hofft auf Ihm.

She bent down and kissed the cheek so tenderly that she would not have bruised the petal of a rose. 'Heart's darling,' she murmured. He quivered all over at her touch, working his fingers in an unnatural kind of way, and ending with a convulsive twitching all over his body. Lina began to cry at the grave, anxious look on our faces.

'You had better call the Fräulein to look at him,' said I. 'I feel sure he ought to have a doctor; I should say he was going to have a fit.'

'The Fräulein and the master are gone to the pastor's for coffee, and Lottchen is in the higher vineyard, taking the men their bread and beer. Could you find the kitchen girl, or old Karl? he will be in the stables, I think. I must lose no time.' Almost without waiting for my reply, she had passed through the room, and in the empty house I could hear her firm, careful footsteps going up the stair; Lina's pattering beside her; and the one voice wailing, the other speaking low comfort.

I was tired enough, but this good family had treated me too much like one of their own for me not to do what I could in such a case as this. I made my way out into the street, for the first time since I had come to the house on that memorable evening six weeks ago. I bribed the first person I met to guide me to the doctor's, and sent him straight down to the Halbmond, not staying to listen to the thorough scolding he fell to giving me; then on to the parsonage, to tell the master and the Fräulein of the state of things at home.

I was sorry to be the bearer of bad news into such a festive chamber as the pastor's. There they sat, resting after heat and fatigue, each in their best gala dress, the table spread with *Dicker-milch*,* potato-salad, cakes of various shapes and kinds—all the dainty cates* dear to the German palate. The pastor was talking to Herr Müller, who stood near the pretty young Fräulein Anna, in her fresh white *chemisette*,* with her round white arms, and her youthful coquettish airs, as she prepared to pour out the coffee; our Fräulein was talking busily to the Frau Mama; the younger boys and girls of the family filling up the room. A ghost would have startled the assembled party less than I did, and would probably have been more welcome, considering the news I brought. As he listened, the master caught up his hat and went forth, without apology or farewell. Our Fräulein made up for both, and questioned me fully; but now she, I could see, was in haste to go, although restrained by her manners, and the kindhearted Frau Pastorin soon set her at liberty to follow her inclination. As for me I was dead-beat, and only too glad to avail myself of the hospitable couple's pressing request that I would stop and share their meal. Other magnates of the village came in presently, and relieved me of the strain of keeping up a German conversation about nothing at all with entire strangers. The pretty Fräulein's face had clouded over a little at Herr Müller's sudden departure; but she was soon as bright as could be, giving private chase and sudden little scoldings to her brothers, as they made raids upon the dainties under her charge. After I was duly rested and refreshed, I took my leave; for I, too, had my quieter anxieties about the sorrow in the Müller family.

The only person I could see at the Halbmond was Lottchen; everyone else was busy about the poor little Max, who was passing from one fit into another. I told Lottchen to ask the doctor to come in and see me before he took his leave for the night, and tired as I was, I kept up till after his visit, though it was very late before he came; I could see from his face how anxious he was. He would give me no opinion as to the child's chances of recovery, from which I guessed that he had not much hope. But when I expressed my fear he cut me very short.

'The truth is, you know nothing about it; no more do I, for that matter. It is enough to try any man, much less a father, to hear his perpetual moans—not that he is conscious of pain, poor little worm; but if she stops for a moment in her perpetual carrying him backwards and forwards, he plains so piteously it is enough to—enough to make a man bless the Lord who never led him into the pit of matrimony. To see the father up there, following her as she walks up and down the room, the child's head over her shoulder, and Müller trying to make the heavy eyes recognize the old familiar ways of play, and the chirruping sounds which he can scarce make for crying—I shall be here tomorrow early, though before that either life or death will have come without the old doctor's help.'

All night long I dreamt my feverish dream—of the vineyard—

the carts, which held little coffins instead of baskets of grapes—of the pastor's daughter, who would pull the dying child out of Thekla's arms; it was a bad, weary night! I slept long into the morning; the broad daylight filled my room, and yet no one had been near to waken me! Did that mean life or death? I got up and dressed as fast as I could; for I was aching all over with the fatigue of the day before. Out into the sitting-room; the table was laid for breakfast, but no one was there. I passed into the house beyond, up the stairs, blindly seeking for the room where I might know whether it was life or death. At the door of a room I found Lottchen crying; at the sight of me in that unwonted place she started, and began some kind of apology, broken both by tears and smiles, as she told me that the doctor said the danger was over—past, and that Max was sleeping a gentle peaceful slumber in Thekla's arms—arms that had held him all through the livelong night.

'Look at him, sir; only go in softly; it is a pleasure to see the child today; tread softly, sir.'

She opened the chamber-door. I could see Thekla sitting, propped up by cushions and stools, holding her heavy burden, and bending over him with a look of tenderest love. Not far off stood the Fräulein, all disordered and tearful, stirring or seasoning some hot soup, while the master stood by her impatient. As soon as it was cooled or seasoned enough he took the basin and went to Thekla, and said something very low; she lifted up her head, and I could see her face; pale, weary with watching, but with a soft peaceful look upon it, which it had not worn for weeks. Fritz Müller began to feed her, for her hands were occupied in holding his child; I could not help remembering Mrs Inchbald's pretty description of Dorriforth's anxiety in feeding Miss Milner;* she compares it, if I remember rightly, to that of a tender-hearted boy, caring for his darling bird, the loss of which would embitter all the joys of his holidays. We closed the door without noise, so as not to waken the sleeping child. Lottchen brought me my coffee and bread; she was ready either to laugh or to weep on the slightest occasion. I could not tell if it was in innocence or mischief. She asked me the following question,—

'Do you think Thekla will leave today, sir?'

In the afternoon I heard Thekla's step behind my extemporary screen. I knew it quite well. She stopped for a moment before emerging into my view.

She was trying to look as composed as usual, but, perhaps because her steady nerves had been shaken by her night's watching, she could not help faint touches of dimples at the corners of her mouth, and her eyes were veiled from any inquisitive look by their drooping lids.

'I thought you would like to know that the doctor says Max is quite out of danger now. He will only require care.'

'Thank you, Thekla; Doctor —— has been in already this afternoon to tell me so, and I am truly glad.'

She went to the window, and looked out for a moment. Many people were in the vineyards again today; although we, in our household anxiety, had paid them but little heed. Suddenly she turned round into the room, and I saw that her face was crimson with blushes. In another instant Herr Müller entered by the window.

'Has she told you, sir?' said he, possessing himself of her hand, and looking all aglow with happiness. 'Hast thou told our good friend?' addressing her.

'No. I was going to tell him, but I did not know how to begin.'

'Then I will prompt thee. Say after me—"I have been a wilful, foolish woman ——" '

She wrenched her hand out of his, half-laughing—'I am a foolish woman, for I have promised to marry him. But he is a still more foolish man, for he wishes to marry me. That is what I say.'

'And I have sent Babette to Frankfurt with the pastor. He is going there, and will explain all to Frau v. Schmidt; and Babette will serve her for a time. When Max is well enough to have the change of air the doctor prescribes for him, thou shalt take him to Altenahr, and thither will I also go; and become known to thy people and thy father. And before Christmas the gentleman here shall dance at our wedding.'

'I must go home to England, dear friends, before many days are over. Perhaps we may travel together as far as Remagen. Another year I will come back to Heppenheim and see you.'

As I planned it, so it was. We left Heppenheim all together on a lovely All Saints' Day. The day before—the day of All Souls*—I had watched Fritz and Thekla lead little Lina up to the Acre of God, the Field of Rest, to hang the wreath of *immortelles** on her mother's grave. Peace be with the dead and the living.

CUMBERLAND SHEEP-SHEARERS

THREE or four years ago* we spent part of a summer in one of the dales in the neighbourhood of Keswick.* We lodged at the house of a small Statesman,* who added to his occupation of a sheep-farmer that of a woollen manufacturer. His own flock was not large, but he bought up other people's fleeces, either on commission, or for his own purposes; and his life seemed to unite many pleasant and various modes of employment, and the great jolly burly man throve upon all, both in body and mind.

One day, his handsome wife proposed to us that we should accompany her to a distant sheep-shearing, to be held at the house of one of her husband's customers, where she was sure we should be heartily welcome, and where we should see an old-fashioned shearing, such as was not often met with now in the Dales. I don't know why it was, but we were lazy, and declined her invitation. It might be that the day was a broiling one, even for July, or it might be a fit of shyness; but whichever was the reason, it very unaccountably vanished soon after she was gone, and the opportunity seemed to have slipped through our fingers. The day was hotter than ever; and we should have twice as much reason to be shy and self-conscious, now that we should not have our hostess to introduce and chaperone us. However, so great was our wish to go, that we blew these obstacles to the winds, if there were any that day; and, obtaining the requisite directions from the farm-servant, we set out on our five mile walk, about one o'clock on a cloudless day in the first half of July.

Our party consisted of two grown up persons and four children, the youngest almost a baby, who had to be carried the greater part of that weary length of way. We passed through Keswick, and saw the groups of sketching, boating tourists, on whom we, as residents for a month in the neighbourhood, looked down with some contempt as mere strangers, who were sure to go about blundering, or losing their way, or being imposed upon by guides, or admiring the wrong things, and never seeing the right things. After we had dragged ourselves through the long straggling town, we came to a part of the highway where it wound between copses sufficiently high to make a green gloom in a green shade;* the branches touched and interlaced overhead, while the road was so straight, that all the quarter-of-an-hour that we were walking we could see the opening of blue light at the other end, and note the quivering of the heated luminous air beyond the dense shade in which we moved. Every now and then, we caught glimpses of the silver lake that shimmered through the trees; and, now and then, in the dead noon-tide stillness, we could hear the gentle lapping of the water on the pebbled shore—the only sound we heard, except the low deep hum of myriads of insects revelling out their summer lives. We had all agreed that talking made us hotter, so we and the birds were very silent. Out again into the hot bright sunny dazzling road, the fierce sun above our heads made us long to be at home, but we had passed the half-way, and to go on was shorter than to return. Now we left the highway, and began to mount. The ascent looked disheartening, but at almost every step we gained increased freshness of air; and the crisp short mountain grass was soft and cool in comparison with the high road. The little wandering breezes, that came every now and then athwart us, were laden with fragrant scents—now of wild thyme—now of the little scrambling creeping white rose, which ran along the ground and pricked our feet with its sharp thorns; and now we came to a trickling streamlet, on whose spongy banks grew great bushes of the bog-myrtle, giving a spicy odour to the air. When our breath failed us during that steep ascent, we had one invariable dodge by which we hoped to escape the 'fat and scant of breath' quotation;* we turned round and admired the lovely views, which from each succeeding elevation became more and more beautiful.

At last, perched on a level which seemed nothing more than a mere shelf of rock, we saw our destined haven—a grey stone farmhouse, high over our heads, high above the lake as we were—with out-buildings enough around it to justify the

Scotch name of a 'town;'* and near it one of those great bossy sycamores, so common in similar situations all through Cumberland and Westmoreland. One more long tug and then we should be there. So, cheering the poor tired little ones, we set off bravely for that last piece of steep rocky path; and we never looked behind till we stood in the coolness of the deep porch, looking down from our natural terrace on the glassy Derwent Water,* far, far below, reflecting each tint of the blue sky, only in darker fuller colours every one. We seemed on a level with the top of Cat Bell;* and the tops of great trees lay deep down—so deep that we felt as if they were close enough together and solid enough to bear our feet if we chose to spring down and walk upon them. Right in front of where we stood, there was a ledge of the rocky field that surrounded the house. We had knocked at the door, but it was evident that we were unheard in the din and merry clatter of voices within, and our old original shyness returned. By and by, someone found us out, and a hearty burst of hospitable welcome ensued. Our coming was all right; it was understood in a minute who we were; our real hostess was hardly less urgent in her civilities than our temporary hostess, and both together bustled us out of the room upon which the outer door entered, into a large bedroom which opened out of it—the state apartment, in all such houses in Cumberland—where the children make their first appearance, and where the heads of the household lie down to die if the Great Conqueror gives them sufficient warning for such decent and composed submission as is best in accordance with the simple dignity of their lives.

Into this chamber we were ushered, and the immediate relief from its dark coolness to our overheated bodies and dazzled eyes was inexpressibly refreshing. The walls were so thick that there was room for a very comfortable window-seat in them, without there being any projection into the room; and the long low shape prevented the sky-line from being unusually depressed, even at that height, and so the light was subdued, and the general tint through the room deepened into darkness, where the eye fell on that stupendous bed, with its posts, and its head-piece, and its foot-board, and its trappings of all kinds of the deepest brown; and the frame itself looked large enough for six or seven people to lie comfortably therein, without even touching each other. In the hearth-place, stood a great pitcher filled with branches of odorous mountain flowers; and little bits of rosemary and lavender were strewed about the room; partly, as I afterwards learnt, to prevent incautious feet from slipping about on the polished oak floor. When we had noticed everything, and rested, and cooled (as much as we could do before the equinox*), we returned to the company assembled in the house-place.*

This house-place was almost a hall in grandeur. Along one side ran an oaken dresser, all decked with the same sweet evergreens, fragments of which strewed the bedroom floor. Over this dresser were shelves, bright with most exquisitely polished pewter. Opposite to the bedroom door was the great hospitable fireplace, ensconced within its proper chimney corners,* and having the 'master's cupboard' on its right hand side. Do you know what a 'master's cupboard' is? Mr Wordsworth could have told you; ay, and have shown you one at Rydal Mount,* too. It is a cupboard about a foot in width, and a foot and a half in breadth, expressly reserved for the use of the master of the household. Here he may keep pipe and tankard, almanac, and what not; and although no door bars the access of any hand, in this open cupboard his peculiar properties rest secure, for is it not 'the master's cupboard'? There was a fire in the house-place, even on this hot day; it gave a grace and a vividness to the room, and being kept within proper limits, it seemed no more than was requisite to boil the kettle. For, I should say, that the very minute of our arrival, our hostess (so I shall designate the wife of the farmer at whose house the sheep-shearing was to be held) proposed tea; and although we had not dined, for it was but little past three, yet, on the principle of 'Do at Rome as the Romans do,'* we assented with a good grace, thankful to have any refreshment offered us, short of water-gruel,* after our long and tiring walk, and rather afraid of our children 'cooling too quickly.'

While the tea was preparing, and it took six comely matrons to do it justice, we proposed to Mrs C. (our real hostess), that we should go and see the sheep-shearing. She accordingly led us away into a back yard, where the process was going on. By a back yard I mean a far different place from what a Londoner would so designate; our back yard, high up on the mountain-side, was a space about forty yards by twenty, overshadowed by the noble sycamore, which might have been the very one that suggested to Coleridge—

> This sycamore (oft musical with bees—
> Such tents the Patriarchs loved) &c., &c.*

And in this deep, cool, green shadow sat two or three grey-haired sires, smoking their pipes, and regarding the proceedings with a placid complacency, which had a savour of contempt in it for the degeneracy of the present times—a sort of 'Ah! they don't know what good shearing is nowadays' look in it. That round shadow of the sycamore tree, and the elders who sat there looking on, were the only things not full of motion and life in the yard. The yard itself was bounded by a grey stone wall, and the moors rose above it to the mountain top; we looked over the low walls on to the spaces bright with the yellow asphodel,* and the first flush of the purple heather. The shadow of the farmhouse fell over this yard, so that it was cool in aspect, save for the ruddy faces of the eager shearers, and the gay-coloured linsey* petticoats of the women, folding the fleeces with tucked-up gowns.

When we first went into the yard, every corner of it seemed as full of motion as an antique frieze, and, like that, had to be studied before I could ascertain the different actions and purposes involved. On the left hand was a walled-in field of small extent, full of sunshine and light, with the heated air quivering over the flocks of panting bewildered sheep, who were penned up therein, awaiting their turn to be shorn. At the gate by which this field was entered from the yard stood a group of eager-eyed boys, panting like the sheep, but not like them from fear, but from excitement and joyous exertion. Their faces were flushed with brown-crimson, their scarlet lips were parted into smiles, and their eyes had that peculiar blue lustre in them, which is only gained by a free life in the pure and blithesome air. As soon as these lads saw that a sheep was wanted by the shearers within, they sprang towards one in the field—the more boisterous and stubborn an old ram the better—and tugging, and pulling, and pushing, and shouting—sometimes mounting astride of the poor obstreperous brute, and holding his horns like a bridle—they gained their point and dragged their captive up to the shearer, like little victors as they were, all glowing and ruddy with conquest. The shearers sat each astride on a long bench, grave and important—the heroes of the day. The flock of sheep to be shorn on this occasion consisted of more than a thousand, and eleven famous shearers had come, walking in from many miles' distance to try their skill one against the other; for sheep-shearings are a sort of rural Olympics.* They were all young men in their prime, strong, and well-made; without coat or waistcoat, and with upturned shirt-sleeves. They sat each across a long bench or narrow table, and caught up the sheep from the attendant boys, who had dragged it in; they lifted it on to the bench, and placing it by a dexterous knack on its back, they began to shear the wool off the tail and under parts; then they tied the two hind legs and the two fore legs together, and laid it first on one side and then on the other, till the fleece came off in one whole piece; the art was to shear all the wool off, and yet not to injure the sheep by any awkward cut: if such an accident did occur, a mixture of tar and butter was immediately applied; but every wound was a blemish on the shearer's fame. To shear well and completely, and yet to do it quickly, shows the perfection of the clippers. Some can finish off as many as six score* sheep in a summer's day; and if you consider the weight and uncouthness of the animal, and the general heat of the weather, you will see that, with justice, clipping or shearing is regarded as harder work than mowing. But most good shearers are content with despatching four or five score; it is only on unusual occasions, or when Greek meets Greek,* that six score are attempted or accomplished.

When the sheep is divided into its fleece and itself, it becomes the property of two persons. The women seize the fleece, and, standing by the side of a temporary dresser (in this case made of planks laid across barrels, beneath what sharp scant shadow could be obtained from the eaves of the house), they fold it up. This again is an art, simple as it may seem; and the farmer's wives and daughters about Langdale Head* are famous for it.

They begin with folding up the legs, and then roll the whole fleece up, tying it with the neck; and the skill consists, not merely in doing this quickly and firmly, but in certain artistic pulls of the wool so as to display the finer parts, and not, by crushing up the fibre, to make it appear coarse to the buyer. Six comely women were thus employed; they laughed, and talked, and sent shafts of merry satire at the grave and busy shearers, who were too earnest in their work to reply, although an occasional deepening of colour, or twinkle of the eye, would tell that the remark had hit. But they reserved their retorts, if they had any, until the evening, when the day's labour would be over, and when, in the licence of country humour, I imagine, some of the saucy speakers would meet with their match. As yet, the applause came from their own party of women; though now and then one of the old men, sitting under the shade of a sycamore, would take his pipe out of his mouth to spit, and, before beginning again to send up the softly curling white wreaths of smoke, he would condescend on a short deep laugh, and a 'Well done, Maggie!' 'Give it him, lass!' for with the not unkindly jealousy of age towards youth, the old grandfathers invariably took part with the women against the young men. These sheared on, throwing the fleeces to the folders, and casting the sheep down on the ground with gentle strength, ready for another troop of boys to haul it to the right hand side of the farmyard, where the great out-buildings were placed; where all sorts of country vehicles were crammed and piled, and seemed to throw up their scarlet shafts into the air, as if imploring relief from the crowd of shandries* and market carts that pressed upon them. Out of the sun, in the dark shadow of the cart-house, a pan of red-hot coals glowed in a trivet; and upon them was placed an iron basin holding tar and raddle, or ruddle.* Hither the right hand troop of boys dragged the poor naked sheep to be 'smitten'—that is to say, marked with the initials or cypher of the owner. In this case, the sign of the possessor was a circle or spot on one side, and a straight line on the other; and after the sheep were thus marked, they were turned out to the moor, and the crowd of bleating lambs that sent up an incessant moan for their lost mothers; each found out the ewe to which it belonged the moment she was turned out of the yard, and the placid contentment of the sheep that wandered away up the hillside, with their little lambs trotting by them, gave just the necessary touch of peace and repose to the scene. There were all the classical elements for the representation of life; there were the 'Old men and maidens, young men and children' of the Psalmist;* there were all the stages and conditions of being that sing forth their farewell to the departing crusaders in the 'Saint's Tragedy.'*

We were very glad indeed that we had seen the sheep-shearing, though the road had been hot, and long, and dusty, and we were as yet unrefreshed and hungry. When we had understood the separate actions of the busy scene, we could begin to notice individuals. I soon picked out a very beautiful young woman as an object of admiration and interest. She stood by a buxom woman of middle age, who had just sufficient likeness to point her out as the mother. Both were folding fleeces, and folding them well; but the mother talked all the time with a rich-toned voice, and a merry laugh and eye, while the daughter hung her head silently over her work; and I could only guess at the beauty of her eyes by the dark sweeping shadow of her eyelashes. She was well dressed, and had evidently got on her Sunday gown, although a good deal for the honour of the thing, as the flowing skirt was tucked up in a bunch behind, in order to be out of her way: beneath the gown, and far more conspicuous—and, possibly, far prettier—was a striped petticoat of full deep blue and scarlet, revealing the blue cotton stockings common in that part of the country, and the pretty, neat leather shoes. The girl had tucked her brown hair back behind her ears; but if she had known how often she would have had occasion to blush, I think she would have kept that natural veil more over her delicate cheek. She blushed deeper and ever deeper, because one of the shearers, in every interval of his work, looked at her and sighed. Neither of them spoke a word, though both were as conscious of the other as could be; and the buxom mother, with a side-long glance, took cognizance of the affair from time to time, with no unpleased expression.

I had got thus far in my career of observation when our hostess for the day came to tell us that tea was ready, and we arose stiffly from the sward on which we had been sitting, and went indoors to the house-place. There, all round, were ranged rows of sedate matrons; some with babies, some without; they had been summoned from over mountains, and beyond wild fells, and across deep dales, to the shearing of that day, just as their ancestors were called out by the Fiery Cross.* We were conducted to a tea-table, at which, in spite of our entreaties, no one would sit down except our hostess, who poured out tea, of which more by-and-by. Behind us, on the dresser, were plates piled up with 'berry-cake' (puff-paste with gooseberries inside), currant and plain bread and butter, hot cakes buttered with honey (if that is not Irish), and great pieces of new cheese to be put in between the honeyed slices, and so toasted impromptu. There were two black teapots on the tray, and taking one of these in her left hand, and one in her right, our hostess held them up both on high, and skilfully poured from each into one and the same cup; the teapots contained green and black tea,* and this was her way of mixing them, which she considered far better, she told us, than if both the leaves had been 'masked' together. The cups of tea were dosed with lump upon lump of the finest sugar, but the rich yellow fragrant cream was dropped in but very sparingly. I reserved many of my inquiries, suggested by this Dale tea-drinking, to be answered by Mrs C., with whom we were lodging: and I asked her why I could neither get cream enough for myself, nor milk sufficient for the children, when both were evidently so abundant, and our entertainers so profusely hospitable. She told me, that my request for each was set down to modesty and a desire to spare the 'grocer's stuff,' which, as costing money, was considered the proper thing to force upon visitors, while the farm produce was reckoned too common and everyday for such a choice festivity and such honoured guests. So I drank tea as strong as brandy and as sweet as syrup, and had to moan in secret over my children's nerves. My children found something else to moan over before the meal was ended; the good farmer's wife would give them each 'sweet butter' on their oat-cake or 'clap-bread;'* and sweet butter is made of butter, sugar, and rum melted together and potted, and is altogether the most nauseous compound in the shape of a dainty I ever tasted. My poor children thought it so, as I could tell by their glistening piteous eyes and trembling lips, as they vainly tried to get through what their stomachs rejected. I got it from them by stealth and ate it myself, in order to spare the feelings of our hostess, who, evidently, considered it as a choice delicacy. But no sooner did she perceive that they were without sweet butter than she urged them to take some more, and bade me not scrimp it, for they had enough and to spare for everybody. This 'sweet butter' is made for express occasions—the clippings, and Christmas; and for these two seasons all christenings in a family are generally reserved. When we had eaten and eaten—and, hungry as we were, we found it difficult to come up to our hostess's ideas of the duty before us—she took me into the real working kitchen, to show me the preparations going on for the refreshment of the seventy people there and then assembled. Rounds of beef, hams, fillets of veal, and legs of mutton bobbed, indiscriminately with plum puddings, up and down in a great boiler, from which a steam arose, when she lifted up the lid, reminding one exceedingly of Camacho's wedding.* The resemblance was increased when we were shown another boiler out of doors, placed over a temporary framework of brick, and equally full with the other, if, indeed, not more so.

Just at this moment—as she and I stood on the remote side of the farm-buildings, within sound of all the pleasant noises which told of merry life so near, and yet out of sight of any of them, gazing forth on the moorland and the rocks, and the purple crest of the mountain, the opposite base of which fell into Watendlath*—the gate of the yard was opened, and my rustic beauty came rushing in, her face all a-fire. When she saw us she stopped suddenly, and was about to turn, when she was followed, and the entrance blocked up by the handsome young shearer. I saw a knowing look on my companion's face, as she quietly led me out by another way.

'Who is that handsome girl?' asked I.

'It's just Isabel Crosthwaite,' she replied. 'Her mother is a cousin of my master's, widow of a statesman near Appleby. She is well to do, and Isabel is her only child.'

'Heiress, as well as beauty,' thought I; but all I said was,

'And who is the young man with her?'

'That,' said she, looking up at me with surprise. 'That's our

Tom. You see, his father and me and Margaret Crosthwaite have fixed that these young ones are to wed each other; and Tom is very willing—but she is young and skittish; but she'll come to—she'll come to. He'll not be best shearer this day anyhow, as he was last year down in Buttermere; but he'll maybe come round for next year.'

So spoke middle age of the passionate loves of the young. I could fancy that Isabel might resent being so calmly disposed of, and I did not like or admire her the less because by-and-by she plunged into the very midst of the circle of matrons, as if in the Eleusinian circle* she could alone obtain a sanctuary against her lover's pursuit. She looked so much and so truly annoyed that I disliked her mother, and thought the young man unworthy of her, until I saw the mother come and take into her arms a little orphan child, whom I learnt she had bought from a beggar on the roadside that was ill-using her. This child hung about the woman, and called her 'Mammy' in such pretty trusting tones, that I became reconciled to the matchmaking widow, for the sake of her warm heart; and as for the young man—the woe-begone face that he presented from time to time at the open door, to be scouted and scolded thence by all the women, while Isabel resolutely turned her back upon him, and pretended to be very busy cutting bread and butter, made me really sorry for him; though we—experienced spectators—could see the end of all this coyness and blushing as well as if we were in church at the wedding.

From four to five o'clock on a summer's day is a sort of second noon for heat; and now that we were up on this breezy height, it seemed so disagreeable to think of going once more into the close woods down below, and to brave the parched and dusty road, that we gladly and lazily resigned ourselves to stay a little later, and to make our jolly three o'clock tea serve for dinner.

So I strolled into the busy yard once more, and by watching my opportunity, I crossed between men, women, boys, sheep, and barking dogs, and got to an old man, sitting under the sycamore, who had been pointed out to me as the owner of the sheep and the farm. For a few minutes he went on, doggedly puffing away; but I knew that this reserve on his part arose from no want of friendliness, but from the shy reserve which is the characteristic of most Westmoreland and Cumberland people. By-and-by he began to talk, and he gave me much information about his sheep. He took a 'walk'* from a landowner with so many sheep upon it; in his case one thousand and fifty, which was a large number, about six hundred being the average. Before taking the 'walk,' he and his landlord each appointed two 'knowledgeable people' to value the stock. The 'walk' was taken on lease of five or seven years, and extended ten miles over the Fells* in one direction—he could not exactly say how far in another, but more; yes! certainly more. At the expiration of the lease, the stock are again numbered, and valued in the same way. If the sheep are poorer, and gone off, the tenant has to pay for their depreciation in money; if they have improved in quality, the landlord pays him; but one way or another the same number must be restored, while the increase of each year, and the annual fleeces form the tenant's profit. Of course they were all of the black-faced or mountain breed, fit for scrambling and endurance, and capable of being nourished by the sweet but scanty grass that grew on the Fells. To take charge of his flock he employed three shepherds, one of whom was my friend Tom. They had other work down on the farm, for the farm was 'down' compared with the airy heights to which these sheep will scramble. The shepherd's year begins before the twentieth of March, by which time the ewes must be all safely down in the home pastures, at hand in case they or their lambs require extra care at yeaning* time. About the sixteenth of June the sheep-washing begins. Formerly, said my old man, men stood bare-legged in a running stream, dammed up so as to make a pool, which was more cleansing than any still water, with its continual foam, and fret, and struggle to overcome the obstacle that impeded its progress: and these men caught the sheep, which were hurled to them by the people on the banks, and rubbed them and soused them well; but now (alas! for these degenerate days) folk were content to throw them in head downwards, and thought that they were washed enough with swimming to the bank. However, this proceeding was managed in a fortnight after the shearing or clipping came on; and people were bidden to it from twenty miles off or better; but not as they had been fifty years ago. Still, if a family possessed a skilful shearer in the person of a son, or if the good wife could fold fleeces well and deftly, they were sure of a gay week in clipping time, passing from farm to farm in merry succession, giving their aid, feasting on the fat of the land ('sweet butter' amongst other things, and much good may it do them!) until they in their turn called upon their neighbours for help. In short, good old-fashioned sheep-shearings are carried on much in the same sort of way as an American Bee.*

As soon as the clipping is over, the sheep are turned out upon the Fells, where their greatest enemy is the fly. The ravens do harm to the young lambs in May and June, and the shepherds scale the steep grey rocks to take a raven's nest with infinite zest and delight; but no shepherd can save his sheep from the terrible fly—the common flesh fly—which burrows in the poor animal, and lays its obscene eggs, and the maggots eat it up alive. To obviate this as much as ever they can, the shepherds go up on the Fells about twice a week in summer time, and, sending out their faithful dogs, collect the sheep into great circles, the dogs running on the outside and keeping them in. The quick-eyed shepherd stands in the midst, and, if a sheep make an effort to scratch herself, the dog is summoned, and the infected sheep brought up to be examined, the piece cut out, and salved. But, notwithstanding this, in some summers scores of sheep are killed in this way: thundery and close weather is peculiarly productive of this plague. The next operation which the shepherd has to attend to is about the middle or end of October, when the sheep are brought down to be salved, and an extra man is usually hired on the farm for this week. But it is no feasting or merry-making time like a clipping. Sober business reigns. The men sit astride on their benches and besmear the poor helpless beast with a mixture of tar and bad butter, or coarse grease, which is supposed to promote the growth and fineness of the wool, by preventing skin diseases of all kinds, such as would leave a patch bare. The mark of ownership is renewed with additional tar and raddle, and they are sent up once more to their breezy walk, where the winter winds begin to pipe and to blow, and to call away their brethren from the icy North. Once a week the shepherds go up and scour the Fells, looking over the sheep, and seeing how the herbage lasts. And this is the dangerous and wild time for the shepherds. The snows and the mists (more to be dreaded even than snow) may come on; and there is no lack of tales, about the Christmas hearth, of men who have gone up to the wild and desolate Fells and have never been seen more, but whose voices are yet heard calling on their dogs, or uttering fierce despairing cries for help; and so they will call till the end of time, till their whitened bones have risen again.

Towards the middle of January, great care is necessary, as by this time the sheep have grown weak and lean with lack of food, and the excess of cold. Yet as the mountain sheep will not eat turnips, but must be fed with hay, it is a piece of economy to delay beginning to feed them as long as possible; and to know the exact nick of time, requires as much skill as must have been possessed by Emma's father in Miss Austen's delightful novel, who required his gruel 'thin, but not too thin—thick, but not too thick.'* And so the Shepherd's Calendar* works round to yeaning time again! It must be a pleasant employment; reminding one of Wordsworth's lines—

> In that fair clime, the lonely herdsman stretched
> On the soft grass, through half the summer's day, &c.*

and of shepherd boys with their reedy pipes, taught by Pan,* and of the Chaldean shepherds studying the stars;* of Poussin's picture of the Good Shepherd,* of the 'Shepherds keeping watch by night!'* and I don't know how many other things, not forgetting some of Cooper's delightful pieces.*

While I was thus rambling on in thought, my host was telling me of the prices of wool that year, for we had grown quite confidential by this time. Wool was sold by the stone; he expected to get ten or twelve shillings a stone; it took three or four fleeces to make a stone: before the Australian wool* came in, he had got twenty shillings, ay and more; but now—and again we sighed over the degeneracy of the times, till he took up his pipe (not Pandean*) for consolation, and I bethought me of the long walk home, and the tired little ones, who must not be worried. So, with much regret, we took our leave; the fiddler had just arrived as we were wishing goodbye; the shadow of the house had overspread the yard; the boys were more in number than the sheep that remained to be shorn; the busy women were dishing up great smoking rounds of beef; and in addition to all the provision I had seen in the boilers, large-mouthed ovens were disgorging berry pies without end, and rice-puddings stuck full of almonds and raisins.

As we descended the hill, we passed a little rustic bridge with a great alder bush near it. Underneath sat Isabel, as rosy red as ever, but dimpling up with smiles, while Tom lay at her feet, and looked up into her eyes; his faithful sheep-dog sat by him, but flapped his tail vainly in hope of obtaining some notice. His master was too much absorbed for that. Poor Fly! Every dog has his day, and yours was not this tenth of July.

THE GREY WOMAN

PORTION I

THERE is a mill* by the Neckar-side,* to which many people resort for coffee, according to the fashion which is almost national in Germany. There is nothing particularly attractive in the situation of this mill; it is on the Mannheim (the flat and unromantic) side of Heidelberg. The river turns the mill-wheel with a plenteous gushing sound; the out-buildings and the dwelling-house of the miller form a well-kept dusty quadrangle. Again, further from the river, there is a garden full of willows, and arbours, and flower-beds not well kept, but very profuse in flowers and luxuriant creepers, knotting and looping the arbours together. In each of these arbours is a stationary table of white painted wood, and light moveable chairs of the same colour and material.

I went to drink coffee there with some friends in 184 –.* The stately old miller came out to greet us, as some of the party were known to him of old. He was of a grand build of a man, and his loud musical voice, with its tone friendly and familiar, his rolling laugh of welcome, went well with the keen bright eye, the fine cloth of his coat, and the general look of substance about the place. Poultry of all kinds abounded in the mill-yard, where there were ample means of livelihood for them strewed on the ground; but not content with this, the miller took out handfuls of corn from the sacks, and threw liberally to the cocks and hens that ran almost under his feet in their eagerness. And all the time he was doing this, as it were habitually, he was talking to us, and ever and anon calling to his daughter and the serving-maids, to bid them hasten the coffee we had ordered. He followed us to an arbour, and saw us served to his satisfaction with the best of everything we could ask for; and then left us to go round to the different arbours and see that each party was properly attended to; and, as he went, this great, prosperous, happy-looking man whistled softly one of the most plaintive airs I ever heard.

'His family have held this mill ever since the old Palatinate days;* or rather, I should say, have possessed the ground ever since then, for two successive mills of theirs have been burnt down by the French. If you want to see Scherer in a passion, just talk to him of the possibility of a French invasion.'

But at this moment, still whistling that mournful air, we saw the miller going down the steps that led from the somewhat raised garden into the mill-yard; and so I seemed to have lost my chance of putting him in a passion.

We had nearly finished our coffee, and our *Kuchen*,* and our cinnamon cake, when heavy splashes fell on our thick leafy covering; quicker and quicker they came, coming through the tender leaves as if they were tearing them asunder; all the people in the garden were hurrying under shelter, or seeking for their carriages standing outside. Up the steps the miller came hastening, with a crimson umbrella, fit to cover everyone left in the garden, and followed by his daughter, and one or two maidens, each bearing an umbrella.

'Come into the house—come in, I say. It is a summer-storm, and will flood the place for an hour or two, till the river carries it away. Here, here.'

And we followed him back into his own house. We went into the kitchen first. Such an array of bright copper and tin vessels I never saw; and all the wooden things were as thoroughly scoured. The red tile floor was spotless when we went in, but in two minutes it was all over slop and dirt with the tread of many feet; for the kitchen was filled, and still the worthy miller kept bringing in more people under his great crimson umbrella. He even called the dogs in, and made them lie down under the tables.

His daughter said something to him in German, and he shook his head merrily at her. Everybody laughed.

'What did she say?' I asked.

'She told him to bring the ducks in next; but indeed if more people come we shall be suffocated. What with the thundery weather, and the stove, and all these steaming clothes, I really think we must ask leave to pass on. Perhaps we might go in and see Frau Scherer.'

My friend asked the daughter of the house for permission to go into an inner chamber and see her mother. It was granted, and we went into a sort of saloon, overlooking the Neckar; very small, very bright, and very close. The floor was slippery with polish; long narrow pieces of looking-glass against the walls reflected the perpetual motion of the river opposite; a white porcelain stove, with some old-fashioned ornaments of brass about it; a sofa, covered with Utrecht velvet,* a table before it, and a piece of worsted-worked carpet* under it; a vase of artificial flowers; and, lastly, an alcove with a bed in it, on which lay the paralysed wife of the good miller, knitting busily, formed the furniture. I spoke as if this was all that was to be seen in the room; but, sitting quietly, while my friend kept up a brisk conversation in a language which I but half understood, my eye was caught by a picture in a dark corner of the room, and I got up to examine it more nearly.

It was that of a young girl of extreme beauty; evidently of middle rank. There was a sensitive refinement in her face, as if she almost shrank from the gaze which, of necessity, the painter must have fixed upon her. It was not over-well painted, but I felt that it must have been a good likeness, from this strong impress of peculiar character which I have tried to describe. From the dress, I should guess it to have been painted in the latter half of the last century. And I afterwards heard that I was right.

There was a little pause in the conversation.

'Will you ask Frau Scherer who this is?'

My friend repeated my question, and received a long reply in German. Then she turned round and translated it to me.

'It is the likeness of a great-aunt of her husband's.' (My friend was standing by me, and looking at the picture with sympathetic curiosity.) 'See! here is the name on the open page of this Bible, "Anna Scherer, 1778." Frau Scherer says there is a tradition in the family that this pretty girl, with her complexion of lilies and roses, lost her colour so entirely through fright, that she was known by the name of the Grey Woman. She speaks as if this Anna Scherer lived in some state of life-long terror. But she does not know details; refers me to her husband for them. She thinks he has some papers which were written by the original of that picture for her daughter, who died in this very house not long after our friend there was married. We can ask Herr Scherer for the whole story if you like.'

'Oh yes, pray do!' said I. And, as our host came in at this moment to ask how we were faring, and to tell us that he had sent to Heidelberg for carriages to convey us home, seeing no chance of the heavy rain abating, my friend, after thanking him, passed on to my request.

'Ah!' said he, his face changing, 'the aunt Anna had a sad history. It was all owing to one of those hellish Frenchmen; and her daughter suffered for it—the cousin Ursula, as we all called her when I was a child. To be sure, the good cousin Ursula was his child as well. The sins of the fathers are visited on their children.* The lady would like to know all about it, would she? Well, there are papers—a kind of apology the aunt Anna wrote for putting an end to her daughter's engagement—or rather facts which she revealed, that prevented cousin Ursula from marrying the man she loved; and so she would never have any other good fellow, else I have heard say my father would have been thankful to have made her his wife.' All this time he was rummaging in the drawer of an old-fashioned bureau, and now he turned round, with a bundle of yellow MSS* in his hand, which he gave to my friend, saying, 'Take it home, take it home, and if you care to make out our crabbed German writing, you may keep it as long as you like, and read it at your leisure. Only I must have it back again when you have done with it, that's all.'

And so we became possessed of the manuscript of the following letter, which it was our employment, during many a long evening that ensuing winter, to translate, and in some parts to abbreviate. The letter began with some reference to the pain which she had already inflicted upon her daughter by some unexplained opposition to a project of marriage; but I doubt if, without the clue with which the good miller had furnished us, we could have made out even this much from the passionate, broken sentences that made us fancy that some scene between the mother and daughter—and possibly a third person—had occurred just before the mother had begun to write.

'Thou dost not love thy child, mother! Thou dost not care if her heart is broken!' Ah, God! and these words of my heart-beloved Ursula ring in my ears as if the sound of them would fill them when I lie a-dying. And her poor tear-stained face comes between me and everything else. Child! hearts do not break: life is very tough as well as very terrible. But I will not decide for thee. I will tell thee all; and thou shalt bear the burden of choice. I may be wrong; I have little wit left, and never had much, I think; but an instinct serves me in place of judgment, and that instinct tells me that thou and thy Henri must never be married. Yet I may be in error. I would fain make my child happy. Lay this paper before the good priest Schriesheim, if, after reading it, thou hast doubts which make thee uncertain. Only I will tell thee all now, on condition that no spoken word ever passes between us on the subject. It would kill me to be questioned. I should have to see all present again.

My father held, as thou knowest, the mill on the Neckar, where thy new-found uncle, Scherer, now lives. Thou rememberest the surprise with which we were received there last vintage twelvemonth. How thy uncle disbelieved me when I said that I was his sister Anna, whom he had long believed to be dead, and how I had to lead thee underneath the picture, painted of me long ago, and point out, feature by feature, the likeness between it and thee; and how, as I spoke, I recalled first to my own mind, and then by speech to his, the details of the time when it was painted; the merry words that passed between us then, a happy boy and girl; the position of the articles of furniture in the room; our father's habits; the cherry-tree, now cut down, that shaded the window of my bedroom, through which my brother was wont to squeeze himself, in order to spring on to the topmost bough that would bear his weight; and thence would pass me back his cap laden with fruit to where I sat on the window-sill, too sick with fright for him to care much for eating the cherries.

And at length Fritz gave way, and believed me to be his sister Anna, even as though I were risen from the dead. And thou rememberest how he fetched in his wife, and told her that I was not dead, but was come back to the old home once more, changed as I was. And she would scarce believe him, and scanned me with a cold, distrustful eye, till at length—for I knew her of old as Babette Müller—I said that I was well-to-do, and needed not to seek out friends for what they had to give. And then she asked—not me, but her husband—why I had kept silent so long, leading all—father, brother, everyone that loved me in my own dear home—to esteem me dead. And then thine uncle (thou rememberest?) said he cared not to know more than I cared to tell; that I was his Anna, found again, to be a blessing to him in his old age, as I had been in his boyhood. I thanked him in my heart for his trust; for were the need for telling all less than it seems to me now I could not speak of my past life. But she, who was my sister-in-law still, held back her welcome, and, for want of that, I did not go to live in Heidelberg as I had planned beforehand, in order to be near my brother Fritz, but contented myself with his promise to be a father to my Ursula when I should die and leave this weary world.

That Babette Müller was, as I may say, the cause of all my life's suffering. She was a baker's daughter in Heidelberg—a great beauty, as people said, and, indeed, as I could see for myself. I, too—thou sawest my picture—was reckoned a beauty, and I believe I was so. Babette Müller looked upon me as a rival. She liked to be admired, and had no one much to love her. I had several people to love me—thy grandfather Fritz, the old servant Kätchen, Karl, the head apprentice at the mill—and I feared admiration and notice, and the being stared at as the *Schöne Müllerin*,* whenever I went to make my purchases in Heidelberg.

Those were happy, peaceful days. I had Kätchen to help me in the housework, and whatever we did pleased my brave old father, who was always gentle and indulgent towards us women, though he was stern enough with the apprentices in the mill. Karl, the oldest of these, was his favourite; and I can see now that my father wished him to marry me, and that Karl himself was desirous to do so. But Karl was rough-spoken, and passionate—not with me, but with the others—and I shrank from him in a way which, I fear, gave him pain. And then came thy uncle Fritz's marriage; and Babette was brought to the mill to be its mistress. Not that I cared much for giving up my post, for, in spite of my father's great kindness, I always feared that I did not manage well for so large a family (with the men, and a girl under Kätchen, we sat down eleven each night to supper). But when Babette began to find fault with Kätchen, I was unhappy at the blame that fell on faithful servants; and by-and-by I began to see that Babette was egging on Karl to make more open love to me, and, as she once said, to get done with it, and take me off to a home of my own. My father was growing old, and did not perceive all my daily discomfort. The more Karl advanced, the more I disliked him. He was good in the main, but I had no notion of being married, and could not bear anyone who talked to me about it.

Things were in this way when I had an invitation to go to Karlsruhe to visit a schoolfellow, of whom I had been very fond. Babette was all for my going; I don't think I wanted to leave home, and yet I had been very fond of Sophie Rupprecht. But I was always shy among strangers. Somehow the affair was settled for me, but not until both Fritz and my father had made inquiries as to the character and position of the Rupprechts. They learned that the father had held some kind of inferior position about the Grand Duke's court,* and was now dead, leaving a widow, a noble lady, and two daughters, the elder of whom was Sophie, my friend. Madame Rupprecht was not rich, but more than respectable—genteel. When this was ascertained, my father made no opposition to my going; Babette forwarded it by all the means in her power, and even my dear Fritz had his word to say in its favour. Only Kätchen was against it—Kätchen and Karl. The opposition of Karl did more to send me to Karlsruhe than anything. For I could have objected to go; but when he took upon himself to ask what was the good of going a-gadding, visiting strangers of whom no one knew anything, I yielded to circumstances—to the pulling of Sophie and the pushing of Babette. I was silently vexed, I remember, at Babette's inspection of my clothes; at the way in which she settled that this gown was too old-fashioned, or that too common, to go with me on my visit to a noble lady; and at the way in which she took upon herself to spend the money my father had given me to buy what was requisite for the occasion. And yet I blamed myself, for everyone else thought her so kind for doing all this; and she herself meant kindly, too.

At last I quitted the mill by the Neckar-side. It was a long day's journey, and Fritz went with me to Karlsruhe. The Rupprechts lived on the third floor of a house a little behind one of the principal streets, in a cramped-up court, to which we gained admittance through a doorway in the street. I remember how pinched their rooms looked after the large space we had at the mill, and yet they had an air of grandeur about them which was new to me, and which gave me pleasure, faded as some of it was. Madame Rupprecht was too formal a lady for me; I was never at my ease with her; but Sophie was all that I had recollected her at school: kind, affectionate, and only rather too ready with her expressions of admiration and regard. The little sister kept out of our way; and that was all we needed, in the first enthusiastic renewal of our early friendship. The one great object of Madame Rupprecht's life was to retain her position in society; and as her means were much diminished since her husband's death, there was not much comfort, though there was a great deal of show, in their way of living; just the opposite of what it was at my father's house. I believe that my coming was not too much desired by Madame Rupprecht, as I brought with me another mouth to be fed; but Sophie had spent a year or more in entreating for permission to invite me, and her mother, having once consented, was too well bred not to give me a stately welcome.

The life in Karlsruhe was very different from what it was at home. The hours were later, the coffee was weaker in the morning, the pottage was weaker, the boiled beef less relieved by other diet, the dresses finer, the evening engagements constant. I did not find these visits pleasant. We might not knit, which would have relieved the tedium a little; but we sat in a circle, talking together, only interrupted occasionally by a gentleman, who, breaking out of the knot of men who stood near the door, talking eagerly together, stole across the room on tiptoe, his hat under his arm, and, bringing his feet together in the position we called the first at the dancing-school, made a low bow to the lady he was going to address. The first time I saw these manners I could not help smiling; but Madame Rupprecht saw me, and spoke to me next morning rather severely, telling me that, of course, in my country breeding I could have seen nothing of court manners, or French fashions, but that that was no reason for my laughing at them. Of course I tried never to smile again in company. This visit to Karlsruhe took place in '89, just when everyone was full of the events taking place at Paris;* and yet at Karlsruhe French fashions were more talked of than French politics. Madame Rupprecht, especially, thought a great deal of all French people. And this again was quite different to us at home. Fritz could hardly bear the name of a Frenchman; and it had nearly been an obstacle to my visit to Sophie that her mother preferred being called Madame to her proper title of Frau.

One night I was sitting next to Sophie, and longing for the time when we might have supper and go home, so as to be able to speak together, a thing forbidden by Madame Rupprecht's rules of etiquette, which strictly prohibited any but the most necessary conversation passing between members of the same family when in society. I was sitting, I say, scarcely keeping back my inclination to yawn, when two gentlemen came in, one of whom was evidently a stranger to the whole party, from the formal manner in which the host led him up, and presented him to the hostess. I thought I had never seen anyone so handsome or so elegant. His hair was powdered, of course, but one could see from his complexion that it was fair in its natural state. His features were as delicate as a girl's, and set off by two little *mouches*,* as we called patches in those days, one at the left corner of his mouth, the other prolonging, as it were, the right eye. His dress was blue and silver. I was so lost in admiration of this beautiful young man, that I was as much surprised as if the angel Gabriel had spoken to me, when the lady of the house brought him forward to present him to me. She called him Monsieur de la Tourelle, and he began to speak to me in French; but though I understood him perfectly, I dared not trust myself to reply to him in that language. Then he tried German, speaking it with a kind of soft lisp that I thought charming. But, before the end of the evening, I became a little tired of the affected softness and effeminacy of his manners, and the exaggerated compliments he paid me, which had the effect of making all the company turn round and look at me. Madame Rupprecht was, however, pleased with the precise thing that displeased me. She liked either Sophie or me to create a sensation; of course she would have preferred that it should have been her daughter, but her daughter's friend was next best. As we went away, I heard Madame Rupprecht and Monsieur de la Tourelle reciprocating civil speeches with might and main, from which I found out that the French gentleman was coming to call on us the next day. I do not know whether I was more glad or frightened, for I had been kept upon stilts of good manners all the evening. But still I was flattered when Madame Rupprecht spoke as if she had invited him, because he had shown pleasure in my society, and even more gratified by Sophie's ungrudging delight at the evident interest I had excited in so fine and agreeable a gentleman. Yet, with all this, they had hard work to keep me from running out of the salon the next day, when we heard his voice inquiring at the gate on the stairs for Madame Rupprecht. They had made me put on my Sunday gown, and they themselves were dressed as for a reception.

When he was gone away, Madame Rupprecht congratulated me on the conquest I had made; for, indeed, he had scarcely spoken to anyone else, beyond what mere civility required, and had almost invited himself to come in the evening to bring some new song, which was all the fashion in Paris, he said. Madame Rupprecht had been out all morning, as she told me, to glean information about Monsieur de la Tourelle. He was a *propriétaire*,* had a small château on the Vosges mountains;* he owned land there, but had a large income from some sources quite independent of this property. Altogether, he was a good match, as she emphatically observed. She never seemed to think that I could refuse him after this account of his wealth, nor do I believe she would have allowed Sophie a choice, even had he been as old and ugly as he was young and handsome. I do not quite know—so many events have come to pass since then, and blurred the clearness of my recollections—if I loved him or not. He was very much devoted to me; he almost frightened me by the excess of his demonstrations of love. And he was very charming to everybody around me, who all spoke of him as the most fascinating of men, and of me as the most fortunate of girls. And yet I never felt quite at my ease with him. I was always relieved when his visits were over, although I missed his presence when he did not come. He prolonged his visit to the friend with whom he was staying at Karlsruhe, on purpose to woo me. He loaded me with presents, which I was unwilling to take, only Madame Rupprecht seemed to consider me an affected prude if I refused them. Many of these presents consisted of articles of valuable old jewellery, evidently belonging to his family; by accepting these I doubled the ties which were formed around me by circumstances even more than by my own consent. In those days we did not write letters to absent friends as frequently as is done now, and I had been unwilling to name him in the few letters that I wrote home. At length, however, I learned from Madame Rupprecht that she had written to my father to announce the splendid conquest I had made, and to request his presence at my betrothal. I started with astonishment. I had not realized that affairs had gone so far as this. But when she asked me, in a stern, offended manner, what I had meant by my conduct if I did not intend to marry Monsieur de la Tourelle—I had received his visits, his presents, all his various advances without showing any unwillingness or repugnance—(and it was all true; I had shown no repugnance, though I did not wish to be married to him,—at least, not so soon)—what could I do but hang my head, and silently consent to the rapid enunciation of the only course which now remained for me if I would not be esteemed a heartless coquette all the rest of my days?

There was some difficulty, which I afterwards learnt that my sister-in-law had obviated, about my betrothal taking place from home. My father, and Fritz especially, were for having me return to the mill, and there be betrothed, and from thence be married. But the Rupprechts and Monsieur de la Tourelle were equally urgent on the other side; and Babette was unwilling to have the trouble of the commotion at the mill; and also, I think, a little disliked the idea of the contrast of my grander marriage with her own.*

So my father and Fritz came over to the betrothal. They were to stay at an inn in Karlsruhe for a fortnight, at the end of which time the marriage was to take place. Monsieur de la Tourelle told me he had business at home, which would oblige him to be absent during the interval between the two events; and I was very glad of it, for I did not think that he valued my father and my brother as I could have wished him to do. He was very polite to them; put on all the soft, grand manner, which he had rather dropped with me; and complimented us all round, beginning with my father and Madame Rupprecht, and ending with little Alwina. But he a little scoffed at the old-fashioned church ceremonies which my father insisted on; and I fancy Fritz must have taken some of his compliments as satire, for I saw certain signs of manner by which I knew that my future husband, for all his civil words, had irritated and annoyed my brother. But all the money arrangements were liberal in the extreme, and more than satisfied, almost surprised, my father. Even Fritz lifted up his eyebrows and whistled. I alone did not care about anything. I was bewitched,—in a dream,—a kind of despair. I had got into a net through my own timidity and weakness, and I did not see how to get out of it. I clung to my own home-people that fortnight as I had never done before. Their voices, their ways were all so pleasant and familiar to me, after the constraint in which I had been living. I might speak and do as I liked without being corrected by Madame Rupprecht, or reproved in a delicate, complimentary way by Monsieur de la Tourelle. One day I said to my father that I did not want to be married, that I would rather go back to the dear old mill; but he seemed to feel this speech of mine as a dereliction of duty as great as if I had committed perjury; as if, after the ceremony of betrothal, no one had any right over me but my future husband. And yet he asked me some solemn questions; but my answers were not such as to do me any good.

'Dost thou know any fault or crime in this man that should prevent God's blessing from resting on thy marriage with him? Dost thou feel aversion or repugnance to him in any way?'

And to all this what could I say? I could only stammer out that I did not think I loved him enough; and my poor old father saw in this reluctance only the fancy of a silly girl who did not know her own mind, but who had now gone too far to recede.

So we were married, in the Court chapel, a privilege which Madame Rupprecht had used no end of efforts to obtain for us, and which she must have thought was to secure us all possible happiness, both at the time and in recollection afterwards.

We were married; and after two days spent in festivity at Karlsruhe, among all our new fashionable friends there, I bade goodbye for ever to my dear old father. I had begged my husband to take me by way of Heidelberg to his old castle in the Vosges; but I found an amount of determination, under that effeminate appearance and manner, for which I was not prepared, and he refused my first request so decidedly that I dared not urge it. 'Henceforth, Anna,' said he, 'you will move in a different sphere of life; and though it is possible that you may have the power of showing favour to your relations from time to time, yet much or familiar intercourse will be undesirable, and is what I cannot allow.' I felt almost afraid, after this formal speech, of asking my father and Fritz to come and see me; but, when the agony of bidding them farewell overcame all my prudence, I did beg them to pay me a visit ere long. But they shook their heads, and spoke of business at home, of different kinds of life, of my being a Frenchwoman now. Only my father broke out at last with a blessing, and said, 'If my child is unhappy—which God forbid—let her remember that her father's house is ever open to her.' I was on the point of crying out, 'Oh! take me back then now, my father! oh, my father!' when I felt, rather than saw, my husband present near me. He looked on with a slightly contemptuous air; and, taking my hand in his, he led me weeping away, saying that short farewells were always the best when they were inevitable.

It took us two days to reach his château in the Vosges, for the roads were bad and the way difficult to ascertain. Nothing could be more devoted than he was all the time of the journey. It seemed as if he were trying in every way to make up for the separation which every hour made me feel the more complete between my present and my former life. I seemed as if I were only now wakening up to a full sense of what marriage was, and I dare say I was not a cheerful companion on the tedious journey. At length, jealousy of my regret for my father and brother got the better of M. de la Tourelle, and he became so much displeased with me that I thought my heart would break with the sense of desolation. So it was in no cheerful frame of mind that we approached Les Rochers,* and I thought that perhaps it was because I was so unhappy that the place looked so dreary. On one side, the château looked like a raw new building, hastily run up for some immediate purpose, without any growth of trees or underwood near it, only the remains of the stone used for building, not yet cleared away from the immediate neighbourhood, although weeds and lichens had been suffered to grow near and over the heaps of rubbish; on the other, were the great rocks from which the place took its name, and rising close against them, as if almost a natural formation, was the old castle, whose building dated many centuries back.

It was not large nor grand, but it was strong and picturesque, and I used to wish that we lived in it rather than in the smart, half-furnished apartment in the new edifice, which had been hastily got ready for my reception. Incongruous as the two parts were, they were joined into a whole by means of intricate passages and unexpected doors, the exact positions of which I never fully understood. M. de la Tourelle led me to a suite of rooms set apart for me, and formally installed me in them, as in a domain of which I was sovereign. He apologized for the hasty preparation which was all he had been able to make for me, but promised, before I asked, or even thought of complaining, that they should be made as luxurious as heart could wish before many weeks had elapsed. But when, in the gloom of an autumnal evening, I caught my own face and figure reflected in all the mirrors, which showed only a mysterious background in the dim light of the many candles which failed to illuminate the great proportions of the half-furnished salon, I clung to M. de la Tourelle, and begged to be taken to the rooms he had occupied before his marriage, he seemed angry with me, although he affected to laugh, and so decidedly put aside the notion of my having any other rooms but these, that I trembled in silence at the fantastic figures and shapes which my imagination called up as peopling the background of those gloomy mirrors. There was my boudoir, a little less dreary—my bedroom, with its grand and tarnished furniture, which I commonly made into my sitting-room, locking up the various doors which led into the boudoir, the salon, the passages—all but one, through which M. de la Tourelle always entered from his own apartments in the older part of the castle. But this preference of mine for occupying my bedroom annoyed M. de la Tourelle,

I am sure, though he did not care to express his displeasure. He would always allure me back into the salon, which I disliked more and more from its complete separation from the rest of the building by the long passage into which all the doors of my apartment opened. This passage was closed by heavy doors and *portières*,* through which I could not hear a sound from the other parts of the house, and, of course, the servants could not hear any movement or cry of mine unless expressly summoned. To a girl brought up as I had been in a household where every individual lived all day in the sight of every other member of the family, never wanted either cheerful words or the sense of silent companionship, this grand isolation of mine was very formidable; and the more so, because M. de la Tourelle, as landed proprietor, sportsman, and what not, was generally out of doors the greater part of every day, and sometimes for two or three days at a time. I had no pride to keep me from associating with the domestics; it would have been natural to me in many ways to have sought them out for a word of sympathy in those dreary days when I was left so entirely to myself, had they been like our kindly German servants. But I disliked them, one and all; I could not tell why. Some were civil, but there was a familiarity in their civility which repelled me; others were rude, and treated me more as if I were an intruder than their master's chosen wife; and yet of the two sets I liked these last the best.

The principal male servant belonged to this latter class. I was very much afraid of him, he had such an air of suspicious surliness about him in all he did for me; and yet M. de la Tourelle spoke of him as most valuable and faithful. Indeed, it sometimes struck me that Lefebvre ruled his master in some things; and this I could not make out. For, while M. de la Tourelle behaved towards me as if I were some precious toy or idol, to be cherished, and fostered, and petted, and indulged, I soon found out how little I, or, apparently, anyone else, could bend the terrible will of the man who had on first acquaintance appeared to me too effeminate and languid to exert his will in the slightest particular. I had learnt to know his face better now; and to see that some vehement depth of feeling, the cause of which I could not fathom, made his grey eye glitter with pale light, and his lips contract, and his delicate cheek whiten on certain occasions. But all had been so open and above board at home, that I had no experience to help me to unravel any mysteries among those who lived under the same roof. I understood that I had made what Madame Rupprecht and her set would have called a great marriage, because I lived in a château with many servants, bound ostensibly to obey me as a mistress. I understood that M. de la Tourelle was fond enough of me in his way—proud of my beauty, I dare say (for he often enough spoke about it to me)—but he was also jealous, and suspicious, and uninfluenced by my wishes, unless they tallied with his own. I felt at this time as if I could have been fond of him too, if he would have let me; but I was timid from my childhood, and before long my dread of his displeasure (coming down like thunder into the midst of his love, for such slight causes as a hesitation in reply, a wrong word, or a sigh for my father), conquered my humorous* inclination to love one who was so handsome, so accomplished, so indulgent and devoted. But if I could not please him when indeed I loved him, you may imagine how often I did wrong when I was so much afraid of him as to quietly avoid his company for fear of his outbursts of passion. One thing I remember noticing, that the more M. de la Tourelle was displeased with me, the more Lefebvre seemed to chuckle; and when I was restored to favour, sometimes on as sudden an impulse as that which occasioned my disgrace, Lefebvre would look askance at me with his cold, malicious eyes, and once or twice at such times he spoke most disrespectfully to M. de la Tourelle.

I have almost forgotten to say that, in the early days of my life at Les Rochers, M. de la Tourelle, in contemptuous indulgent pity at my weakness in disliking the dreary grandeur of the salon, wrote up to the milliner in Paris from whom my *corbeille de mariage** had come, to desire her to look out for me a maid of middle age, experienced in the toilette, and with so much refinement that she might on occasion serve as companion to me.*

PORTION II

A Norman woman, Amante by name, was sent to Les Rochers by the Paris milliner, to become my maid. She was tall and handsome, though upwards of forty, and somewhat gaunt. But, on first seeing her, I liked her; she was neither rude nor familiar in her manners, and had a pleasant look of straightforwardness about her that I had missed in all the inhabitants of the château, and had foolishly set down in my own mind as a national want. Amante was directed by M. de la Tourelle to sit in my boudoir, and to be always within call. He also gave her many instructions as to her duties in matters which, perhaps, strictly belonged to my department of management. But I was young and inexperienced, and thankful to be spared any responsibility.

I daresay it was true what M. de la Tourelle said—before many weeks had elapsed—that, for a great lady, a lady of a castle, I became sadly too familiar with my Norman waiting-maid. But you know that by birth we were not very far apart in rank: Amante was the daughter of a Norman farmer, I of a German miller; and besides that, my life was so lonely! It almost seemed as if I could not please my husband. He had written for someone capable of being my companion at times, and now he was jealous of my free regard for her—angry because I could sometimes laugh at her original tunes and amusing proverbs, while when with him I was too much frightened to smile.

From time to time families from a distance of some leagues drove through the bad roads in their heavy carriages to pay us a visit, and there was an occasional talk of our going to Paris when public affairs should be a little more settled. These little events and plans were the only variations in my life for the first twelve months, if I except the alternations in M. de la Tourelle's temper, his unreasonable anger, and his passionate fondness.

Perhaps one of the reasons that made me take pleasure and comfort in Amante's society was, that whereas I was afraid of everybody (I do not think I was half as much afraid of things as of persons), Amante feared no one. She would quietly beard

Lefebvre, and he respected her all the more for it; she had a knack of putting questions to M. de la Tourelle, which respectfully informed him that she had detected the weak point, but forbore to press him too closely upon it out of deference to his position as her master. And with all her shrewdness to others, she had quite tender ways with me; all the more so at this time because she knew, what I had not yet ventured to tell M. de la Tourelle, that by-and-by I might become a mother—that wonderful object of mysterious interest to single women, who no longer hope to enjoy such blessedness themselves.

It was once more autumn; late in October. But I was reconciled to my habitation; the walls of the new part of the building no longer looked bare and desolate; the debris had been so far cleared away by M. de la Tourelle's desire as to make me a little flower-garden, in which I tried to cultivate those plants that I remembered as growing at home. Amante and I had moved the furniture in the rooms, and adjusted it to our liking; my husband had ordered many an article from time to time that he thought would give me pleasure, and I was becoming tame to my apparent imprisonment in a certain part of the great building, the whole of which I had never yet explored. It was October, as I say, once more. The days were lovely, though short in duration, and M. de la Tourelle had occasion, so he said, to go to that distant estate the superintendence of which so frequently took him away from home. He took Lefebvre with him, and possibly some more of the lacqueys; he often did. And my spirits rose a little at the thought of his absence; and then the new sensation that he was the father of my unborn babe came over me, and I tried to invest him with this fresh character. I tried to believe that it was his passionate love for me that made him so jealous and tyrannical, imposing, as he did, restrictions on my very intercourse with my dear father, from whom I was so entirely separated, as far as personal intercourse was concerned.

I had, it is true, let myself go into a sorrowful review of all the troubles which lay hidden beneath the seeming luxury of my life. I knew that no one cared for me except my husband and Amante; for it was clear enough to see that I, as his wife, and also as a *parvenue*,* was not popular among the few neighbours who surrounded us; and as for the servants, the women were all hard and impudent-looking, treating me with a semblance of respect that had more of mockery than reality in it; while the men had a lurking kind of fierceness about them, sometimes displayed even to M. de la Tourelle, who on his part, it must be confessed, was often severe even to cruelty in his management of them. My husband loved me, I said to myself, but I said it almost in the form of a question. His love was shown fitfully, and more in ways calculated to please himself than to please me. I felt that for no wish of mine would he deviate one tittle from any predetermined course of action. I had learnt the inflexibility of those thin, delicate lips; I knew how anger would turn his fair complexion to deadly white, and bring the cruel light into his pale blue eyes. The love I bore to anyone seemed to be a reason for his hating them, and so I went on pitying myself one long dreary afternoon during that absence of his of which I have spoken, only sometimes remembering to check myself in my murmurings by thinking of the new unseen link between us, and then crying afresh to think how wicked I was. Oh, how well I remember that long October evening! Amante came in from time to time, talking away to cheer me—talking about dress and Paris, and I hardly know what, but from time to time looking at me keenly with her friendly dark eyes, and with serious interest, too, though all her words were about frivolity. At length she heaped the fire with wood, drew the heavy silken curtains close; for I had been anxious hitherto to keep them open, so that I might see the pale moon mounting the skies, as I used to see her—the same moon—rise from behind the Kaiser Stuhl at Heidelberg;* but the sight made me cry, so Amante shut it out. She dictated to me as a nurse does to a child.

'Now, madame must have the little kitten to keep her company,' she said, 'while I go and ask Marthon for a cup of coffee.' I remember that speech, and the way it roused me, for I did not like Amante to think I wanted amusing by a kitten. It might be my petulance, but this speech—such as she might have made to a child—annoyed me, and I said that I had reason for my lowness of spirits—meaning that they were not of so imaginary a nature that I could be diverted from them by the gambols of a kitten. So, though I did not choose to tell her all, I told her a part; and as I spoke, I began to suspect that the good creature knew much of what I withheld, and that the little speech about the kitten was more thoughtfully kind than it had seemed at first. I said that it was so long since I had heard from my father; that he was an old man, and so many things might happen—I might never see him again—and I so seldom heard from him or my brother. It was a more complete and total separation than I had ever anticipated when I married, and something of my home and of my life previous to my marriage I told the good Amante; for I had not been brought up as a great lady, and the sympathy of any human being was precious to me.

Amante listened with interest, and in return told me some of the events and sorrows of her own life. Then, remembering her purpose, she set out in search of the coffee, which ought to have been brought to me an hour before; but, in my husband's absence, my wishes were but seldom attended to, and I never dared to give orders.

Presently she returned, bringing the coffee and a great large cake.

'See!' said she, setting it down. 'Look at my plunder. Madame must eat. Those who eat always laugh. And, besides, I have a little news that will please madame.' Then she told me that, lying on a table in the great kitchen, was a bundle of letters, come by the courier from Strasburg that very afternoon: then, fresh from her conversation with me, she had hastily untied the string that bound them, but had only just traced out one that she thought was from Germany, when a servant-man came in, and, with the start he gave her, she dropped the letters, which he picked up, swearing at her for having untied and disarranged them. She told him that she believed there was a letter there for her mistress; but he only swore the more, saying, that if there was it was no business of hers, or of his either, for that he had the strictest orders always to take all letters that arrived during his master's absence into the private sitting-room of the latter—a room into which I had never entered, although it opened out of my husband's dressing-room.

I asked Amante if she had not conquered and brought me this letter. No, indeed, she replied, it was almost as much as her life was worth to live among such a set of servants: it was only a month ago that Jacques had stabbed Valentin for some jesting talk. Had I never missed Valentin—that handsome young lad who carried up the wood into my salon? Poor fellow! he lies dead and cold now, and they said in the village he had put an end to himself, but those of the household knew better. Oh! I need not be afraid; Jacques was gone, no one knew where; but with such people it was not safe to upbraid or insist. Monsieur would be at home the next day, and it would not be long to wait.

But I felt as if I could not exist till the next day, without the letter. It might be to say that my father was ill, dying—he might cry for his daughter from his death-bed! In short, there was no end to the thoughts and fancies that haunted me. It was of no use for Amante to say that, after all, she might be mistaken—that she did not read writing well—that she had but a glimpse of the address; I let my coffee cool, my food all became distasteful, and I wrung my hands with impatience to get at the letter, and have some news of my dear ones at home. All the time, Amante kept her imperturbable good temper, first reasoning, then scolding. At last she said, as if wearied out, that if I would consent to make a good supper, she would see what could be done as to our going to monsieur's room in search of the letter, after the servants were all gone to bed. We agreed to go together when all was still, and look over the letters; there could be no harm in that; and yet, somehow, we were such cowards we dared not do it openly and in the face of the household.

Presently my supper came up—partridges, bread, fruits, and cream. How well I remember that supper! We put the untouched cake away in a sort of buffet, and poured the cold coffee out of the window, in order that the servants might not take offence at the apparent fancifulness of sending down for food I could not eat. I was so anxious for all to be in bed, that I told the footman who served that he need not wait to take away the plates and dishes, but might go to bed. Long after I thought the house was quiet, Amante, in her caution, made me wait. It was past eleven before we set out, with cat-like steps and veiled light, along the passages, to go to my husband's room and steal my own letter, if it was indeed there; a fact about which Amante had become very uncertain in the progress of our discussion.

To make you understand my story, I must now try to explain to you the plan of the château. It had been at one time a fortified place of some strength, perched on the summit of a rock, which projected from the side of the mountain. But additions had been made to the old building (which must have borne a strong resemblance to the castles overhanging the Rhine), and these new buildings were placed so as to command a magnificent view, being on the steepest side of the rock, from which the mountain fell away, as it were, leaving the great plain of France in full survey. The ground-plan was something of the shape of three sides of an oblong; my apartments in the modern edifice occupied the narrow end, and had this grand prospect. The front of the castle was old, and ran parallel to the road far below. In this were contained the offices and public rooms of various descriptions, into which I never penetrated. The back wing (considering the new building, in which my apartments were, as the centre) consisted of many rooms, of a dark and gloomy character, as the mountainside shut out much of the sun, and heavy pine woods came down within a few yards of the windows. Yet on this side—on a projecting plateau of the rock—my husband had formed the flower-garden of which I have spoken; for he was a great cultivator of flowers in his leisure moments.

Now my bedroom was the corner room of the new buildings on the part next to the mountain. Hence I could have let myself down into the flower-garden by my hands on the window-sill on one side, without danger of hurting myself; while the windows at right angles with these looked sheer down a descent of a hundred feet at least. Going still farther along this wing, you came to the old building; in fact, these two fragments of the ancient castle had formerly been attached by some such connecting apartments as my husband had rebuilt. These rooms belonged to M. de la Tourelle. His bedroom opened into mine, his dressing-room lay beyond; and that was pretty nearly all I knew, for the servants, as well as he himself, had a knack of turning me back, under some pretence, if ever they found me walking about alone, as I was inclined to do, when first I came, from a sort of curiosity to see the whole of the place of which I found myself mistress. M. de la Tourelle never encouraged me to go out alone, either in a carriage or for a walk, saying always that the roads were unsafe in those disturbed times; indeed, I have sometimes fancied since that the flower-garden, to which the only access from the castle was through his rooms, was designed in order to give me exercise and employment under his own eye.

But to return to that night. I knew, as I have said, that M. de la Tourelle's private room opened out of his dressing-room, and this out of his bedroom, which again opened into mine, the corner-room. But there were other doors into all these rooms, and these doors led into a long gallery, lighted by windows, looking into the inner court. I do not remember our consulting much about it; we went through my room into my husband's apartment, through the dressing-room, but the door of communication into his study was locked, so there was nothing for it but to turn back and go by the gallery to the other door. I recollect noticing one or two things in these rooms, then seen by me for the first time. I remember the sweet perfume that hung in the air, the scent bottles of silver that decked his toilet-table, and the whole apparatus for bathing and dressing, more luxurious even than those which he had provided for me. But the room itself was less splendid in its proportions than mine. In truth, the new buildings ended at the entrance to my husband's dressing-room. There were deep window recesses in walls eight or nine feet thick, and even the partitions between the chambers were three feet deep; but over all these doors or windows there fell thick, heavy draperies, so that I should think no one could have heard in one room what passed in another. We went back into my room, and out into the gallery. We had to shade our candle, from a fear that possessed us, I don't know why, lest some of the servants in the opposite wing might trace our progress towards the part of the castle unused by anyone except my husband. Somehow, I had always the feeling that all the domestics, except Amante, were spies upon me, and that I was trammelled in a web of observation and unspoken limitation extending over all my actions.

There was a light in the upper room; we paused, and Amante

would have again retreated, but I was chafing under the delays. What was the harm of my seeking my father's unopened letter to me in my husband's study? I, generally the coward, now blamed Amante for her unusual timidity. But the truth was, she had far more reason for suspicion as to the proceedings of that terrible household than I had ever known of. I urged her on, I pressed on myself; we came to the door, locked, but with the key in it; we turned it, we entered; the letters lay on the table, their white oblongs catching the light in an instant, and revealing themselves to my eager eyes, hungering after the words of love from my peaceful, distant home. But just as I pressed forward to examine the letters, the candle which Amante held, caught in some draught, went out, and we were in darkness. Amante proposed that we should carry the letters back to my salon, collecting them as well as we could in the dark, and returning all but the expected one for me; but I begged her to return to my room, where I kept tinder and flint, and to strike a fresh light; and so she went, and I remained alone in the room, of which I could only just distinguish the size, and the principal articles of furniture: a large table, with a deep, overhanging cloth, in the middle, escritoires and other heavy articles against the walls; all this I could see as I stood there, my hand on the table close by the letters, my face towards the window, which, both from the darkness of the wood growing high up the mountainside and the faint light of the declining moon, seemed only like an oblong of paler purpler black than the shadowy room. How much I remembered from my one instantaneous glance before the candle went out, how much I saw as my eyes became accustomed to the darkness, I do not know, but even now, in my dreams, comes up that room of horror, distinct in its profound shadow. Amante could hardly have been gone a minute before I felt an additional gloom before the window, and heard soft movements outside—soft, but resolute, and continued until the end was accomplished, and the window raised.

In mortal terror of people forcing an entrance at such an hour, and in such a manner as to leave no doubt of their purpose, I would have turned to fly when first I heard the noise, only that I feared by any quick motion to catch their attention, as I also ran the danger of doing by opening the door, which was all but closed, and to whose handlings I was unaccustomed. Again, quick as lightning, I bethought me of the hiding-place between the locked door to my husband's dressing-room and the *portière* which covered it; but I gave that up, I felt as if I could not reach it without screaming or fainting. So I sank down softly, and crept under the table, hidden, as I hoped, by the great, deep table-cover, with its heavy fringe. I had not recovered my swooning senses fully, and was trying to reassure myself as to my being in a place of comparative safety, for, above all things, I dreaded the betrayal of fainting, and struggled hard for such courage as I might attain by deadening myself to the danger I was in by inflicting intense pain on myself. You have often asked me the reason of that mark on my hand; it was where, in my agony, I bit out a piece of flesh with my relentless teeth, thankful for the pain, which helped to numb my terror. I say, I was but just concealed when I heard the window lifted, and one after another stepped over the sill, and stood by me so close that I could have touched their feet. Then they laughed and whispered; my brain swam so that I could not tell the meaning of their words, but I heard my husband's laughter among the rest—low, hissing, scornful—as he kicked something heavy that they had dragged in over the floor, and which lay near me; so near, that my husband's kick, in touching it, touched me too. I don't know why—I can't tell how—but some feeling, and not curiosity, prompted me to put out my hand, ever so softly, ever so little, and feel in the darkness for what lay spurned beside me. I stole my groping palm upon the clenched and chilly hand of a corpse!

Strange to say, this roused me to instant vividness of thought. Till this moment I had almost forgotten Amante; now I planned with feverish rapidity how I could give her a warning not to return; or rather, I should say, I tried to plan, for all my projects were utterly futile, as I might have seen from the first. I could only hope she would hear the voices of those who were now busy in trying to kindle a light, swearing awful oaths at the mislaid articles which would have enabled them to strike fire. I heard her step outside coming nearer and nearer; I saw from my hiding-place the line of light beneath the door more and more distinctly; close to it her footstep paused; the men inside—at the time I thought they had been only two, but I found out afterwards there were three—paused in their endeavours, and were quite still, as breathless as myself, I suppose. Then she slowly pushed the door open with gentle motion, to save her flickering candle from being again extinguished. For a moment all was still. Then I heard my husband say, as he advanced towards her (he wore riding-boots, the shape of which I knew well, as I could see them in the light),—

'Amante, may I ask what brings you here into my private room?'

He stood between her and the dead body of a man, from which ghastly heap I shrank away as it almost touched me, so close were we all together. I could not tell whether she saw it or not; I could give her no warning, nor make any dumb utterance of signs to bid her what to say—if, indeed, I knew myself what would be best for her to say.

Her voice was quite changed when she spoke; quite hoarse, and very low; yet it was steady enough as she said, what was the truth, that she had come to look for a letter which she believed had arrived for me from Germany. Good, brave Amante! Not a word about me. M. de la Tourelle answered with a grim blasphemy and a fearful threat. He would have no one prying into his premises; madame should have her letters, if there were any, when he chose to give them to her, if, indeed, he thought it well to give them to her at all. As for Amante, this was her first warning, but it was also her last; and, taking the candle out of her hand, he turned her out of the room, his companions discreetly making a screen, so as to throw the corpse into deep shadow. I heard the key turn in the door after her—if I had ever had any thought of escape it was gone now. I only hoped that whatever was to befall me might soon be over, for the tension of nerve was growing more than I could bear. The instant she could be supposed to be out of hearing, two voices began speaking in the most angry terms to my husband, upbraiding him for not having detained her, gagged her—nay, one was for killing her, saying he had seen her eye fall on the face of the dead man, whom he now kicked in his passion. Though the form of their speech was as if they were speaking to equals, yet in their tone there was something of fear. I am sure my husband was their superior, or captain, or somewhat. He replied to them almost as if he were scoffing at them, saying it was such an expenditure of labour having to do with fools; that, ten to one, the woman was only telling the simple truth, and that she was frightened enough by discovering her master in his room to be thankful to escape and return to her mistress, to whom he could easily explain on the morrow how he happened to return in the dead of night. But his companions fell to cursing me, and saying that since M. de la Tourelle had been married he was fit for nothing but to dress himself fine and scent himself with perfume; that, as for me, they could have got him twenty girls prettier, and with far more spirit in them. He quietly answered that I suited him, and that was enough. All this time they were doing something—I could not see what—to the corpse; sometimes they were too busy rifling the dead body, I believe, to talk; again they let it fall with a heavy, resistless thud, and took to quarrelling. They taunted my husband with angry vehemence, enraged at his scoffing and scornful replies, his mocking laughter. Yes, holding up his poor dead victim, the better to strip him of whatever he wore that was valuable, I heard my husband laugh just as he had done when exchanging repartees in the little salon of the Rupprechts at Karlsruhe. I hated and dreaded him from that moment. At length, as if to make an end of the subject, he said, with cool determination in his voice,—

'Now, my good friends, what is the use of all this talking, when you know in your hearts that, if I suspected my wife of knowing more than I chose of my affairs, she would not outlive the day? Remember Victorine. Because she merely joked about my affairs in an imprudent manner, and rejected my advice to keep a prudent tongue—to see what she liked, but ask nothing and say nothing—she has gone a long journey—longer than to Paris.'

'But this one is different to her; we knew all that Madame Victorine knew, she was such a chatterbox; but this one may find out a vast deal, and never breathe a word about it, she is so sly. Some fine day we may have the country raised, and the gendarmes down upon us from Strasburg, and all owing to your pretty doll, with her cunning ways of coming over you.'

I think this roused M. de la Tourelle a little from his contemptuous indifference, for he ground an oath through his teeth, and said, 'Feel! this dagger is sharp, Henri. If my wife breathes a word, and I am such a fool as not to have stopped her mouth effectually before she can bring down gendarmes upon us, just let that good steel find its way to my heart. Let her guess but one tittle, let her have but one slight suspicion that I am not a *grand propriétaire*, much less imagine that I am a chief of Chauffeurs,* and she follows Victorine on the long journey beyond Paris that very day.'

'She'll outwit you yet; or I never judged women well. Those still silent ones are the devil. She'll be off during some of your absences, having picked out some secret that will break us all on the wheel.'

'Bah!' said his voice; and then in a minute he added, 'Let her go if she will. But, where she goes, I will follow; so don't cry before you're hurt.'

By this time, they had nearly stripped the body; and the conversation turned on what they should do with it. I learnt that the dead man was the Sieur de Poissy, a neighbouring gentleman, whom I had often heard of as hunting with my husband. I had never seen him, but they spoke as if he had come upon them while they were robbing some Cologne merchant, torturing him after the cruel practice of the Chauffeurs, by roasting the feet of their victims in order to compel them to reveal any hidden circumstances connected with their wealth, of which the Chauffeurs afterwards made use; and this Sieur de Poissy coming down upon them, and recognizing M. de la Tourelle, they had killed him, and brought him thither after nightfall. I heard him whom I called my husband laugh his little light laugh as he spoke of the way in which the dead body had been strapped before one of the riders, in such a way that it appeared to any passer-by as if, in truth, the murderer were tenderly supporting some sick person. He repeated some mocking reply of double meaning, which he himself had given to someone who made inquiry. He enjoyed the play upon words, softly applauding his own wit. And all the time the poor helpless outstretched arms of the dead lay close to his dainty boot! Then another stooped (my heart stopped beating), and picked up a letter lying on the ground—a letter that had dropped out of M. de Poissy's pocket—a letter from his wife, full of tender words of endearment and pretty babblings of love. This was read aloud, with coarse ribald comments on every sentence, each trying to outdo the previous speaker. When they came to some pretty words about a sweet Maurice, their little child away with its mother on some visit, they laughed at M. de la Tourelle, and told him that he would be hearing such woman's drivelling some day. Up to that moment, I think, I had only feared him, but his unnatural, half-ferocious reply made me hate even more than I dreaded him. But now they grew weary of their savage merriment; the jewels and watch had been apprised, the money and papers examined; and apparently there was some necessity for the body being interred quietly and before daybreak. They had not dared to leave him where he was slain for fear lest people should come and recognize him, and raise the hue and cry upon them. For they all along spoke as if it was their constant endeavour to keep the immediate neighbourhood of Les Rochers in the most orderly and tranquil condition, so as never to give cause for visits from the gendarmes. They disputed a little as to whether they should make their way into the castle larder through the gallery, and satisfy their hunger before the hasty interment, or afterwards. I listened with eager feverish interest as soon as this meaning of their speeches reached my hot and troubled brain, for at the time the words they uttered seemed only to stamp themselves with terrible force on my memory, so that I could hardly keep from repeating them aloud like a dull, miserable, unconscious echo; but my brain was numb to the sense of what they said, unless I myself were named, and then, I suppose, some instinct of self-preservation stirred within me, and quickened my sense. And how I strained my ears, and nerved my hands and limbs, beginning to twitch with convulsive movements, which I feared might betray me! I gathered every word they spoke, not knowing which proposal to wish for, but feeling that whatever was finally decided upon, my only chance of escape was drawing near. I once feared lest my husband should go to his bedroom before I had had that one chance, in which case he would most likely have perceived my absence. He said that his hands were soiled (I shuddered, for it might be with life-blood), and he would go and cleanse them; but some bitter jest turned his purpose, and he left the room with the other two—left it by the gallery door. Left me alone in the dark with the stiffening corpse!

Now, now was my time, if ever; and yet I could not move. It was not my cramped and stiffened joints that crippled me, it was the sensation of that dead man's close presence. I almost fancied—I almost fancy still—I heard the arm nearest to me move; lift itself up, as if once more imploring, and fall in dead despair. At that fancy—if fancy it were—I screamed aloud in mad terror, and the sound of my own strange voice broke the spell. I drew myself to the side of the table farthest from the corpse, with as much slow caution as if I really could have feared the clutch of that poor dead arm, powerless for evermore. I softly raised myself up, and stood sick and trembling, holding by the table, too dizzy to know what to do next. I nearly fainted, when a low voice spoke—when Amante, from the outside of the door, whispered, 'Madame!' The faithful creature had been on the watch, had heard my scream, and having seen the three ruffians troop along the gallery down the stairs, and across the court to the offices in the other wing of the castle, she had stolen to the door of the room in which I was. The sound of her voice gave me strength; I walked straight towards it, as one benighted on a dreary moor, suddenly perceiving the small steady light which tells of human dwellings, takes heart, and steers straight onward. Where I was, where that voice was, I knew not; but go to it I must, or die. The door once opened—I know not by which of us—I fell upon her neck, grasping her tight, till my hands ached with the tension of their hold. Yet she never uttered a word. Only she took me up in her vigorous arms, and bore me to my room, and laid me on my bed. I do not know more; as soon as I was placed there I lost sense; I came to myself with a horrible dread lest my husband was by me, with a belief that he was in the room, in hiding, waiting to hear my first words, watching for the least sign of the terrible knowledge I possessed to murder me. I dared not breathe quicker, I measured and timed each heavy inspiration; I did not speak, nor move, nor even open my eyes, for long after I was in my full, my miserable senses. I heard someone treading softly about the room, as if with a purpose, not as if for curiosity, or merely to beguile the time; someone passed in and out of the salon; and I still lay quiet, feeling as if death were inevitable, but wishing that the agony of death were past. Again faintness stole over me; but just as I was sinking into the horrible feeling of nothingness, I heard Amante's voice close to me, saying—

'Drink this, madame, and let us be gone. All is ready.'

I let her put her arm under my head and raise me, and pour something down my throat. All the time she kept talking in a quiet, measured voice, unlike her own, so dry and authoritative; she told me that a suit of her clothes lay ready for me, that she herself was as much disguised as the circumstances permitted her to be, that what provisions I had left from my supper were stowed away in her pockets, and so she went on, dwelling on little details of the most commonplace description, but never alluding for an instant to the fearful cause why flight was necessary. I made no inquiry as to how she knew, or what she knew. I never asked her either then or afterwards, I could not bear it—we kept our dreadful secret close. But I suppose she must have been in the dressing-room adjoining, and heard all.

In fact, I dared not speak even to her, as if there were anything beyond the most common event in life in our preparing thus to leave the house of blood by stealth in the dead of night. She gave me directions—short condensed directions, without reasons—just as you do to a child; and like a child I obeyed her. She went often to the door and listened; and often, too, she went to the window, and looked anxiously out. For me, I saw nothing but her, and I dared not let my eyes wander from her for a minute; and I heard nothing in the deep midnight silence but her soft movements, and the heavy beating of my own heart. At last she took my hand, and led me in the dark through the salon, once more into the terrible gallery, where across the black darkness the windows admitted pale sheeted ghosts of light upon the floor. Clinging to her I went; unquestioning—for she was human sympathy to me after the isolation of my unspeakable terror. On we went, turning to the left instead of to the right, past my suite of sitting-rooms where the gilding was red with blood, into that unknown wing of the castle that fronted the main road lying parallel far below. She guided me along the basement passages to which we had now descended, until we came to a little open door, through which the air blew chill and cold, bringing for the first time a sensation of life to me. The door led into a kind of cellar, through which we groped our way to an opening like a window, but which, instead of being glazed, was only fenced with iron bars, two of which were loose, as Amante evidently knew, for she took them out with the ease of one who had performed the action often before, and then helped me to follow her out into the free, open air.

We stole round the end of the building, and on turning the corner—she first—I felt her hold on me tighten for an instant, and the next step I, too, heard distant voices, and the blows of a spade upon the heavy soil, for the night was very warm and still.

We had not spoken a word; we did not speak now. Touch was safer and as expressive. She turned down towards the high road; I followed. I did not know the path; we stumbled again and again, and I was much bruised; so doubtless was she; but bodily pain did me good. At last, we were on the plainer path of the high road.

I had such faith in her that I did not venture to speak, even when she paused, as wondering to which hand she should turn. But now, for the first time, she spoke:—

'Which way did you come when he brought you here first?'

I pointed, I could not speak.

We turned in the opposite direction; still going along the high road. In about an hour, we struck up to the mountainside, scrambling far up before we even dared to rest; far up and away again before day had fully dawned. Then we looked about for some place of rest and concealment: and now we dared to speak in whispers. Amante told me that she had locked the door of communication between his bedroom and mine, and, as in a dream, I was aware that she had also locked and brought away the key of the door between the latter and the salon.

'He will have been too busy this night to think much about you—he will suppose you are asleep—I shall be the first to be missed; but they will only just now be discovering our loss.'

I remember those last words of hers made me pray to go on;

I felt as if we were losing precious time in thinking either of rest or concealment; but she hardly replied to me, so busy was she in seeking out some hiding-place. At length, giving it up in despair, we proceeded onwards a little way; the mountainside sloped downwards rapidly, and in the full morning light we saw ourselves in a narrow valley, made by a stream which forced its way along it. About a mile lower down there rose the pale blue smoke of a village, a mill-wheel was lashing up the water close at hand, though out of sight. Keeping under the cover of every sheltering tree or bush, we worked our way down past the mill, down to a one-arched bridge, which doubtless formed part of the road between the village and the mill.

'This will do,' said she; and we crept under the space, and climbing a little way up the rough stonework, we seated ourselves on a projecting ledge, and crouched in the deep damp shadow. Amante sat a little above me, and made me lay my head on her lap. Then she fed me, and took some food herself; and opening out her great dark cloak, she covered up every light-coloured speck about us; and thus we sat, shivering and shuddering, yet feeling a kind of rest through it all, simply from the fact that motion was no longer imperative, and that during the daylight our only chance of safety was to be still. But the damp shadow in which we were sitting was blighting, from the circumstance of the sunlight never penetrating there; and I dreaded lest, before night and the time for exertion again came on, I should feel illness creeping all over me. To add to our discomfort, it had rained the whole day long, and the stream, fed by a thousand little mountain brooklets, began to swell into a torrent, rushing over the stones with a perpetual and dizzying noise.

Every now and then I was wakened from the painful doze into which I continually fell, by a sound of horses' feet over our head: sometimes lumbering heavily as if dragging a burden, sometimes rattling and galloping, and with the sharper cry of men's voices coming cutting through the roar of the waters. At length, day fell. We had to drop into the stream, which came above our knees as we waded to the bank. There we stood, stiff and shivering. Even Amante's courage seemed to fail.

'We must pass this night in shelter, somehow,' said she. For indeed the rain was coming down pitilessly. I said nothing. I thought that surely the end must be death in some shape; and I only hoped that to death might not be added the terror of the cruelty of men. In a minute or so she had resolved on her course of action. We went up the stream to the mill. The familiar sounds, the scent of the wheat, the flour whitening the walls—all reminded me of home, and it seemed to me as if I must struggle out of this nightmare and waken, and find myself once more a happy girl by the Neckar-side. They were long in unbarring the door at which Amante had knocked: at length, an old feeble voice inquired who was there, and what was sought? Amante answered shelter from the storm for two women; but the old woman replied, with suspicious hesitation, that she was sure it was a man who was asking for shelter, and that she could not let us in. But at length she satisfied herself, and unbarred the heavy door, and admitted us. She was not an unkindly woman; but her thoughts all travelled in one circle, and that was, that her master, the miller, had told her on no account to let any man into the place during his absence, and that she did not know if he would not think two women as bad; and yet that as we were not men, no one could say she had disobeyed him, for it was a shame to let a dog be out such a night as this. Amante, with ready wit, told her to let no one know that we had taken shelter there that night, and that then her master could not blame her; and while she was thus enjoining secrecy as the wisest course, with a view to far other people than the miller, she was hastily helping me to take off my wet clothes, and spreading them, as well as the brown mantle that had covered us both, before the great stove which warmed the room with the effectual heat that the old woman's failing vitality required. All this time the poor creature was discussing with herself as to whether she had disobeyed orders, in a kind of garrulous way that made me fear much for her capability of retaining anything secret if she was questioned. By-and-by, she wandered away to an unnecessary revelation of her master's whereabouts: gone to help in the search for his landlord, the Sieur de Poissy, who lived at the château just above, and who had not returned from his chase the day before; so the *intendant** imagined he might have met with some accident, and had summoned the neighbours to beat the forest and the hillside. She told us much besides, giving us to understand that she would fain meet with a place as housekeeper where there were more servants and less to do, as her life here was very lonely and dull, especially since her master's son had gone away—gone to the wars. She then took her supper, which was evidently apportioned out to her with a sparing hand, as, even if the idea had come into her head, she had not enough to offer us any. Fortunately, warmth was all that we required, and that, thanks to Amante's cares, was returning to our chilled bodies. After supper, the old woman grew drowsy; but she seemed uncomfortable at the idea of going to sleep and leaving us still in the house. Indeed, she gave us pretty broad hints as to the propriety of our going once more out into the bleak and stormy night; but we begged to be allowed to stay under shelter of some kind; and, at last, a bright idea came over her, and she bade us mount by a ladder to a kind of loft, which went half over the lofty mill-kitchen in which we were sitting. We obeyed her—what else could we do?—and found ourselves in a spacious floor, without any safeguard or wall, boarding, or railing, to keep us from falling over into the kitchen in case we went too near the edge. It was, in fact, the store-room or garret for the household. There was bedding piled up, boxes and chests, mill sacks, the winter store of apples and nuts, bundles of old clothes, broken furniture, and many other things. No sooner were we up there, than the old woman dragged the ladder, by which we had ascended, away with a chuckle, as if she was now secure that we could do no mischief, and sat herself down again once more, to doze and await her master's return. We pulled out some bedding, and gladly laid ourselves down in our dried clothes and in some warmth, hoping to have the sleep we so much needed to refresh us and prepare us for the next day. But I could not sleep, and I was aware, from her breathing, that Amante was equally wakeful. We could both see through the crevices between the boards that formed the flooring into the kitchen below, very partially lighted by the common lamp that hung against the wall near the stove on the opposite side to that on which we were.

PORTION III

FAR on in the night there were voices outside reached us in our hiding-place; an angry knocking at the door, and we saw through the chinks the old woman rouse herself up to go and open it for her master, who came in, evidently half drunk. To my sick horror, he was followed by Lefebvre, apparently as sober and wily as ever. They were talking together as they came in, disputing about something; but the miller stopped the conversation to swear at the old woman for having fallen asleep, and, with tipsy anger, and even with blows, drove the poor old creature out of the kitchen to bed. Then he and Lefebvre went on talking—about the Sieur de Poissy's disappearance. It seemed that Lefebvre had been out all day, along with other of my husband's men, ostensibly assisting in the search; in all probability trying to blind the Sieur de Poissy's followers by putting them on a wrong scent, and also, I fancied, from one or two of Lefebvre's sly questions, combining the hidden purpose of discovering us.

Although the miller was tenant and vassal to the Sieur de Poissy, he seemed to me to be much more in league with the people of M. de la Tourelle. He was evidently aware, in part, of the life which Lefebvre and the others led; although, again, I do not suppose he knew or imagined one-half of their crimes; and also, I think, he was seriously interested in discovering the fate of his master, little suspecting Lefebvre of murder or violence. He kept talking himself, and letting out all sorts of thoughts and opinions; watched by the keen eyes of Lefebvre gleaming out below his shaggy eyebrows. It was evidently not the cue of the latter to let out that his master's wife had escaped from that vile and terrible den; but though he never breathed a word relating to us, not the less was I certain he was thirsting for our blood, and lying in wait for us at every turn of events. Presently he got up and took his leave; and the miller bolted him out, and stumbled off to bed. Then we fell asleep, and slept sound and long.

The next morning, when I awoke, I saw Amante, half raised, resting on one hand, and eagerly gazing, with straining eyes, into the kitchen below. I looked too, and both heard and saw the miller and two of his men eagerly and loudly talking about the old woman, who had not appeared as usual to make the fire in the stove, and prepare her master's breakfast, and who now, late on in the morning, had been found dead in her bed; whether from the effect of her master's blows the night before, or from natural causes, who can tell? The miller's conscience upbraided him a little, I should say, for he was eagerly declaring his value for his housekeeper, and repeating how often she had spoken of the happy life she led with him. The men might have their doubts, but they did not wish to offend the miller, and all agreed that the necessary steps should be taken for a speedy funeral. And so they went out, leaving us in our loft, but so much alone, that, for the first time almost, we ventured to speak freely, though still in a hushed voice, pausing to listen continually. Amante took a more cheerful view of the whole occurrence than I did. She said that, had the old woman lived, we should have had to depart that morning, and that this quiet departure would have been the best thing we could have had to hope for, as, in all probability, the housekeeper would have told her master of us and of our resting-place, and this fact would, sooner or later, have been brought to the knowledge of those from whom we most desired to keep it concealed; but that now we had time to rest, and a shelter to rest in, during the first hot pursuit, which we knew to a fatal certainty was being carried on. The remnants of our food, and the stored-up fruit, would supply us with provision; the only thing to be feared was, that something might be required from the loft, and the miller or someone else mount up in search of it. But even then, with a little arrangement of boxes and chests, one part might be so kept in shadow that we might yet escape observation. All this comforted me a little; but, I asked, how were we ever to escape? The ladder was taken away, which was our only means of descent. But Amante replied that she could make a sufficient ladder of the rope lying coiled among other things, to drop us down the ten feet or so—with the advantage of its being portable, so that we might carry it away, and thus avoid all betrayal of the fact that anyone had ever been hidden in the loft.

During the two days that intervened before we did escape, Amante made good use of her time. She looked into every box and chest during the man's absence at his mill; and finding in one box an old suit of man's clothes, which had probably belonged to the miller's absent son, she put them on to see if they would fit her; and, when she found that they did, she cut her own hair to the shortness of a man's, made me clip her black eyebrows as close as though they had been shaved, and by cutting up old corks into pieces such as would go into her cheeks, she altered both the shape of her face and her voice to a degree which I should not have believed possible.

All this time I lay like one stunned; my body resting, and renewing its strength, but I myself in an almost idiotic state—else surely I could not have taken the stupid interest which I remember I did in all Amante's energetic preparations for disguise. I absolutely recollect once the feeling of a smile coming over my stiff face as some new exercise of her cleverness proved a success.

But towards the second day, she required me, too, to exert myself; and then all my heavy despair returned. I let her dye my fair hair and complexion with the decaying shells of the stored-up walnuts, I let her blacken my teeth, and even voluntarily broke a front tooth the better to effect my disguise. But through it all I had no hope of evading my terrible husband. The third night the funeral was over, the drinking ended, the guests gone; the miller put to bed by his men, being too drunk to help himself. They stopped a little while in the kitchen, talking and laughing about the new housekeeper likely to come; and they, too, went off, shutting, but not locking the door. Everything favoured us. Amante had tried her ladder on one of the two previous nights, and could, by a dexterous throw from beneath, unfasten it from the hook to which it was fixed, when it had served its office; she made up a bundle of worthless old clothes in order that we might the better preserve our characters of a travelling pedlar and his wife; she stuffed a hump on her back, she thickened my figure, she left her own clothes deep down beneath a heap of others in the chest from which she had taken the man's dress which she wore; and with a few francs in her pocket—the sole money we had either of us had about us when we escaped—we let ourselves down the ladder, unhooked it, and passed into the cold darkness of night again.

We had discussed the route which it would be well for us to take while we lay *perdues** in our loft. Amante had told me then that her reason for inquiring, when we first left Les Rochers, by which way I had first been brought to it, was to avoid the pursuit which she was sure would first be made in the direction of Germany; but that now she thought we might return to that district of country where my German fashion of speaking French would excite least observation. I thought that Amante herself had something peculiar in her accent, which I had heard M. de la Tourelle sneer at as Norman patois; but I said not a word beyond agreeing to her proposal that we should bend our steps towards Germany. Once there, we should, I thought, be safe. Alas! I forgot the unruly time that was overspreading all Europe, overturning all law, and all the protection which law gives.

How we wandered—not daring to ask our way—how we lived, how we struggled through many a danger and still more terrors of danger, I shall not tell you now. I will only relate two of our adventures before we reached Frankfurt. The first, although fatal to an innocent lady, was yet, I believe, the cause of my safety; the second I shall tell you, that you may understand why I did not return to my former home, as I had hoped to do when we lay in the miller's loft, and I first became capable of groping after an idea of what my future life might be. I cannot tell you how much in these doubtings and wanderings I became attached to Amante. I have sometimes feared since, lest I cared for her only because she was so necessary to my own safety; but, no! it was not so; or not so only, or principally. She said once that she was flying for her own life as well as for mine; but we dared not speak much on our danger, or on the horrors that had gone before. We planned a little what was to be our future course; but even for that we did not look forward long; how could we, when every day we scarcely knew if we should see the sun go down? For Amante knew or conjectured far more than I did of the atrocity of the gang to which M. de la Tourelle belonged; and every now and then, just as we seemed to be sinking into the calm of security, we fell upon traces of a pursuit after us in all directions. Once I remember—we must have been nearly three weeks wearily walking through unfrequented ways, day after day, not daring to make inquiry as to our whereabouts, nor yet to seem purposeless in our wanderings—we came to a kind of lonely roadside farrier's and blacksmith's. I was so tired, that Amante declared that, come what might, we would stay there all night; and accordingly she entered the house, and boldly announced herself as a travelling tailor, ready to do any odd jobs of work that might be required, for a night's lodging and food for herself and wife. She had adopted this plan once or twice before, and with good success; for her father had been a tailor in Rouen, and as a girl she had often helped him with his work, and knew the tailors' slang and habits, down to the particular whistle and cry which in France tells so much to those of a trade. At this blacksmith's, as at most other solitary houses far away from a town, there was not only a store of men's clothes laid by as wanting mending when the housewife could afford time, but there was a natural craving after news from a distance, such news as a wandering tailor is bound to furnish. The early November afternoon was closing into evening, as we sat down, she cross-legged on the great table in the blacksmith's kitchen, drawn close to the window, I close behind her, sewing at another part of the same garment, and from time to time well scolded by my seeming husband. All at once she turned round to speak to me. It was only one word, 'Courage!' I had seen nothing; I sat out of the light; but I turned sick for an instant, and then I braced myself up into a strange strength of endurance to go through I knew not what.

The blacksmith's forge was in a shed beside the house, and fronting the road. I heard the hammers stop plying their continual rhythmical beat. She had seen why they ceased. A rider had come up to the forge and dismounted, leading his horse in to be reshod. The broad red light of the forge-fire had revealed the face of the rider to Amante, and she apprehended the consequence that really ensued.

The rider, after some words with the blacksmith, was ushered in by him into the house-place* where we sat.

'Here, good wife, a cup of wine and some *galette** for this gentleman.'

'Anything, anything, madame, that I can eat and drink in my hand while my horse is being shod. I am in haste, and must get on to Forbach tonight.'

The blacksmith's wife lighted her lamp; Amante had asked her for it five minutes before. How thankful we were that she had not more speedily complied with our request! As it was, we sat in dusk shadow, pretending to stitch away, but scarcely able to see. The lamp was placed on the stove, near which my husband, for it was he, stood and warmed himself. By-and-by he turned round, and looked all over the room, taking us in with about the same degree of interest as the inanimate furniture. Amante, cross-legged, fronting him, stooped over her work, whistling softly all the while. He turned again to the stove, impatiently rubbing his hands. He had finished his wine and *galette*, and wanted to be off.

'I am in haste, my good woman. Ask thy husband to get on more quickly. I will pay him double if he makes haste.'

The woman went out to do his bidding; and he once more turned round to face us. Amante went on to the second part of the tune. He took it up, whistled a second for an instant or so, and then the blacksmith's wife re-entering, he moved towards her, as if to receive her answer the more speedily.

'One moment, monsieur—only one moment. There was a nail out of the off-foreshoe which my husband is replacing; it would delay monsieur again if that shoe also came off.'

'Madame is right,' said he, 'but my haste is urgent. If madame knew my reasons, she would pardon my impatience. Once a happy husband, now a deserted and betrayed man, I pursue a wife on whom I lavished all my love, but who has abused my confidence, and fled from my house, doubtless to some paramour; carrying off with her all the jewels and money on which she could lay her hands. It is possible madame may have heard or seen something of her; she was accompanied in her flight by a base, profligate woman from Paris, whom I, unhappy man, had myself engaged for my wife's waiting-maid, little dreaming what corruption I was bringing into my house!'

'Is it possible?' said the good woman, throwing up her hands.

Amante went on whistling a little lower, out of respect to the conversation.

'However, I am tracing the wicked fugitives; I am on their track' (and the handsome, effeminate face looked as ferocious as any demon's). 'They will not escape me; but every minute is a minute of misery to me, till I meet my wife. Madame has sympathy, has she not?'

He drew his face into a hard, unnatural smile, and then both went out to the forge, as if once more to hasten the blacksmith over his work.

Amante stopped her whistling for one instant.

'Go on as you are, without change of an eyelid even; in a few minutes he will be gone, and it will be over!'

It was a necessary caution, for I was on the point of giving way, and throwing myself weakly upon her neck. We went on; she whistling and stitching, I making semblance to sew. And it was well we did so; for almost directly he came back for his whip, which he had laid down and forgotten; and again I felt one of those sharp, quick-scanning glances, sent all round the room, and taking in all.

Then we heard him ride away; and then, it had been long too dark to see well, I dropped my work, and gave way to my trembling and shuddering. The blacksmith's wife returned. She was a good creature. Amante told her I was cold and weary, and she insisted on my stopping my work, and going to sit near the stove; hastening, at the same time, her preparations for supper, which, in honour of us, and of monsieur's liberal payment, was to be a little less frugal than ordinary. It was well for me that she made me taste a little of the cider-soup she was preparing, or I could not have held up, in spite of Amante's warning look, and the remembrance of her frequent exhortations to act resolutely up to the characters we had assumed, whatever befell. To cover my agitation, Amante stopped her whistling, and began to talk; and, by the time the blacksmith came in, she and the good woman of the house were in full flow. He began at once upon the handsome gentleman, who had paid him so well; all his sympathy was with him, and both he and his wife only wished he might overtake his wicked wife, and punish her as she deserved. And then the conversation took a turn, not uncommon to those whose lives are quiet and monotonous; everyone seemed to vie with each other in telling about some horror; and the savage and mysterious band of robbers called the Chauffeurs, who infested all the roads leading to the Rhine, with Schinderhannes* at their head, furnished many a tale which made the very marrow of my bones run cold, and quenched even Amante's power of talking. Her eyes grew large and wild, her cheeks blanched, and for once she sought by her looks help from me. The new call upon me roused me. I rose and said, with their permission my husband and I would seek our bed, for that we had travelled far and were early risers. I added that we would get up betimes, and finish our piece of work. The blacksmith said we should be early birds if we rose before him; and the good wife seconded my proposal with kindly bustle. One other such story as those they had been relating, and I do believe Amante would have fainted.

As it was, a night's rest set her up; we arose and finished our work betimes, and shared the plentiful breakfast of the family. Then we had to set forth again; only knowing that to Forbach we must not go, yet believing, as was indeed the case, that Forbach lay between us and that Germany to which we were directing our course. Two days more we wandered on, making a round, I suspect, and returning upon the road to Forbach, a league or two nearer to that town than the blacksmith's house. But as we never made inquiries I hardly knew where we were, when we came one night to a small town, with a good large rambling inn in the very centre of the principal street. We had begun to feel as if there were more safety in towns than in the loneliness of the country. As we had parted with a ring of mine not many days before to a travelling jeweller, who was too glad to purchase it far below its real value to make many inquiries as to how it came into the possession of a poor working tailor, such as Amante seemed to be, we resolved to stay at this inn all night, and gather such particulars and information as we could by which to direct our onward course.

We took our supper in the darkest corner of the *salle-à-manger,** having previously bargained for a small bedroom across the court, and over the stables. We needed food sorely; but we hurried on our meal from dread of anyone entering that public room who might recognize us. Just in the middle of our meal, the public *diligence** drove lumbering up under the *porte-co-*

chère,* and disgorged its passengers. Most of them turned into the room where we sat, cowering and fearful, for the door was opposite to the porter's lodge, and both opened on to the wide-covered entrance from the street. Among the passengers came in a young, fair-haired lady, attended by an elderly French maid. The poor young creature tossed her head, and shrank away from the common room, full of evil smells and promiscuous company, and demanded, in German French, to be taken to some private apartment. We heard that she and her maid had come in the *coupé*,* and, probably from pride, poor young lady! she had avoided all association with her fellow-passengers, thereby exciting their dislike and ridicule. All these little pieces of hearsay had a significance to us afterwards, though, at the time, the only remark made that bore upon the future was Amante's whisper to me that the young lady's hair was exactly the colour of mine, which she had cut off and burnt in the stove in the miller's kitchen in one of her descents from our hiding-place in the loft.

As soon as we could, we struck round in the shadow, leaving the boisterous and merry fellow-passengers to their supper. We crossed the court, borrowed a lantern from the ostler, and scrambled up the rude steps to our chamber above the stable. There was no door into it; the entrance was the hole into which the ladder fitted. The window looked into the court. We were tired and soon fell asleep. I was wakened by a noise in the stable below. One instant of listening, and I wakened Amante, placing my hand on her mouth, to prevent any exclamation in her half-roused state. We heard my husband speaking about his horse to the ostler. It was his voice. I am sure of it. Amante said so too. We durst not move to rise and satisfy ourselves. For five minutes or so he went on giving directions. Then he left the stable, and, softly stealing to our window, we saw him cross the court and re-enter the inn. We consulted as to what we should do. We feared to excite remark or suspicion by descending and leaving our chamber, or else immediate escape was our strongest idea. Then the ostler left the stable, locking the door on the outside.

'We must try and drop through the window—if, indeed, it is well to go at all,' said Amante.

With reflection came wisdom. We should excite suspicion by leaving without paying our bill. We were on foot, and might easily be pursued. So we sat on our bed's edge, talking and shivering, while from across the court the laughter rang merrily, and the company slowly dispersed one by one, their lights flitting past the windows as they went upstairs and settled each one to his rest.

We crept into our bed, holding each other tight, and listening to every sound, as if we thought we were tracked, and might meet our death at any moment. In the dead of night, just at the profound stillness preceding the turn into another day, we heard a soft, cautious step crossing the yard. The key into the stable was turned—someone came into the stable—we felt rather than heard him there. A horse started a little, and made a restless movement with his feet, then whinnied recognition. He who had entered made two or three low sounds to the animal, and then led him into the court. Amante sprang to the window with the noiseless activity of a cat. She looked out, but dared not speak a word. We heard the great door into the street open—a pause for mounting, and the horse's footsteps were lost in distance.

Then Amante came back to me. 'It was he! he is gone!' said she, and once more we lay down, trembling and shaking.

This time we fell sound asleep. We slept long and late. We were wakened by many hurrying feet, and many confused voices; all the world seemed awake and astir. We rose and dressed ourselves, and coming down we looked around among the crowd collected in the courtyard, in order to assure ourselves *he* was not there before we left the shelter of the stable.

The instant we were seen, two or three people rushed to us. 'Have you heard?—Do you know?—That poor young lady—oh, come and see!' and so we wêre hurried, almost in spite of ourselves, across the court, and up the great open stairs of the main building of the inn, into a bedchamber, where lay the beautiful young German lady, so full of graceful pride the night before, now white and still in death. By her stood the French maid, crying and gesticulating.

'Oh, madame! if you had but suffered me to stay with you! Oh! the baron, what will he say?' and so she went on. Her state had but just been discovered; it had been supposed that she was fatigued, and was sleeping late, until a few minutes before. The surgeon of the town had been sent for, and the landlord of the inn was trying vainly to enforce order until he came, and, from time to time, drinking little cups of brandy, and offering them to the guests, who were all assembled there, pretty much as the servants were doing in the courtyard.

At last the surgeon came. All fell back, and hung on the words that were to fall from his lips.

'See!' said the landlord. 'This lady came last night by the *diligence* with her maid. Doubtless, a great lady, for she must have a private sitting-room ——'

'She was Madame the Baroness de Roeder,' said the French maid.

—— 'And was difficult to please in the matter of supper, and a sleeping-room. She went to bed well, though fatigued. Her maid left her ——'

'I begged to be allowed to sleep in her room, as we were in a strange inn, of the character of which we knew nothing; but she would not let me, my mistress was such a great lady.'

—— 'And slept with my servants,' continued the landlord. 'This morning we thought madame was still slumbering; but when eight, nine, ten, and near eleven o'clock came, I bade her maid use my pass-key, and enter her room ——'

'The door was not locked, only closed. And here she was found—dead is she not, monsieur?—with her face down on her pillow, and her beautiful hair all scattered wild; she never would let me tie it up, saying it made her head ache. Such hair!' said the waiting-maid, lifting up a long golden tress, and letting it fall again.

I remembered Amante's words the night before, and crept close up to her.

Meanwhile, the doctor was examining the body underneath the bed-clothes, which the landlord, until now, had not allowed to be disarranged. The surgeon drew out his hand, all bathed and stained with blood; and holding up a short, sharp knife, with a piece of paper fastened round it.

'Here has been foul play,' he said. 'The deceased lady has been murdered. This dagger was aimed straight at her heart.' Then, putting on his spectacles, he read the writing on the bloody paper, dimmed and horribly obscured as it was:—

NUMÉRO UN.
Ainsi les Chauffeurs se vengent.*

'Let us go!' said I to Amante. 'Oh, let us leave this horrible place!'

'Wait a little,' said she. 'Only a few minutes more. It will be better.'

Immediately the voices of all proclaimed their suspicions of the cavalier who had arrived last the night before. He had, they said, made so many inquiries about the young lady, whose supercilious conduct all in the *salle-à-manger* had been discussing on his entrance. They were talking about her as we left the room; he must have come in directly afterwards, and not until he had learnt all about her, had he spoken of the business which necessitated his departure at dawn of day, and made his arrangements with both landlord and ostler for the possession of the keys of the stable and *porte-cochère*. In short, there was no doubt as to the murderer, even before the arrival of the legal functionary who had been sent for by the surgeon; but the word on the paper chilled everyone with terror. Les Chauffeurs, who were they? No one knew, some of the gang might even then be in the room overhearing, and noting down fresh objects for vengeance. In Germany, I had heard little of this terrible gang, and I had paid no greater heed to the stories related once or twice about them in Karlsruhe than one does to tales about ogres. But here in their very haunts, I learnt the full amount of the terror they inspired. No one would be legally responsible for any evidence criminating the murderer. The public prosecutor shrank from the duties of his office. What do I say? Neither Amante nor I, knowing far more of the actual guilt of the man who had killed that poor sleeping young lady, durst breathe a word. We appeared to be wholly ignorant of everything: we, who might have told so much. But how could we? We were broken down with terrific anxiety and fatigue, with the knowledge that we, above all, were doomed victims; and that the blood, heavily dripping from the bed-clothes on to the floor, was dripping thus out of the poor dead body, because, when living, she had been mistaken for me.

At length Amante went up to the landlord, and asked permission to leave his inn, doing all openly and humbly, so as to excite neither ill-will nor suspicion. Indeed, suspicion was otherwise directed, and he willingly gave us leave to depart. A few days afterwards we were across the Rhine, in Germany, making our way towards Frankfurt, but still keeping our disguises, and Amante still working at her trade.

On the way, we met a young man, a wandering journeyman from Heidelberg. I knew him, although I did not choose that he should know me. I asked him, as carelessly as I could, how the old miller was now? He told me he was dead. This realization of the worst apprehensions caused by his long silence shocked me inexpressibly. It seemed as though every prop gave way from under me. I had been talking to Amante only that very day of the safety and comfort of the home that awaited her in my father's house; of the gratitude which the old man would feel towards her; and how there, in that peaceful dwelling, far away from the terrible land of France, she should find ease and security for all the rest of her life. All this I thought I had to promise, and even yet more had I looked for, for myself. I looked to the unburdening of my heart and conscience by telling all I knew to my best and wisest friend. I looked to his love as a sure guidance as well as a comforting stay, and, behold, he was gone away from me for ever!

I had left the room hastily on hearing of this sad news from the Heidelberger. Presently, Amante followed:

'Poor madame,' said she, consoling me to the best of her ability. And then she told me by degrees what more she had learned respecting my home, about which she knew almost as much as I did, from my frequent talks on the subject both at Les Rochers and on the dreary, doleful road we had come along. She had continued the conversation after I left, by asking about my brother and his wife. Of course, they lived on at the mill, but the man said (with what truth I know not, but I believed it firmly at the time) that Babette had completely got the upper hand of my brother, who only saw through her eyes and heard with her ears. That there had been much Heidelberg gossip of late days about her sudden intimacy with a grand French gentleman who had appeared at the mill—a relation, by marriage—married, in fact, to the miller's sister, who, by all accounts, had behaved abominably and ungratefully. But that was no reason for Babette's extreme and sudden intimacy with him, going about everywhere with the French gentleman; and since he left (as the Heidelberger said he knew for a fact) corresponding with him constantly. Yet her husband saw no harm in it all, seemingly; though, to be sure, he was so out of spirits, what with his father's death and the news of his sister's infamy, that he hardly knew how to hold up his head.

'Now,' said Amante, 'all this proves that M. de la Tourelle has suspected that you would go back to the nest in which you were reared, and that he has been there, and found that you have not yet returned; but probably he still imagines that you will do so, and has accordingly engaged your sister-in-law as a kind of informant. Madame has said that her sister-in-law bore her no extreme good-will; and the defamatory story he has got the start of us in spreading, will not tend to increase the favour in which your sister-in-law holds you. No doubt the assassin was retracing his steps when we met him near Forbach, and having heard of the poor German lady, with her French maid, and her pretty blonde complexion, he followed her. If madame will still be guided by me—and, my child, I beg of you still to trust me,' said Amante, breaking out of her respectful formality into the way of talking more natural to those who had shared and escaped from common dangers—more natural, too, where the speaker was conscious of a power of protection which the other did not possess—'we will go on to Frankfurt, and lose ourselves, for a time, at least, in the numbers of people who throng a great town; and you have told me that Frankfurt is a great town. We will still be husband and wife; we will take a small lodging, and you shall housekeep and live indoors. I, as the rougher and the more alert, will continue my father's trade, and seek work at the tailors' shops.'

I could think of no better plan, so we followed this out. In a back street at Frankfurt we found two furnished rooms to let on a sixth story. The one we entered had no light from day; a dingy lamp swung perpetually from the ceiling, and from that, or from the open door leading into the bedroom beyond, came our only light. The bedroom was more cheerful, but very small. Such as it was, it almost exceeded our possible means. The money from the sale of my ring was almost exhausted, and Amante was a stranger in the place, speaking only French, moreover, and the good Germans were hating the French people right heartily. However, we succeeded better than our hopes, and even laid by a little against the time of my confinement. I never stirred abroad, and saw no one, and Amante's want of knowledge of German kept her in a state of comparative isolation.

At length my child was born—my poor worse than fatherless child. It was a girl, as I had prayed for. I had feared lest a boy might have something of the tiger nature of its father, but a girl seemed all my own. And yet not all my own, for the faithful Amante's delight and glory in the babe almost exceeded mine; in outward show it certainly did.

We had not been able to afford any attendance beyond what a neighbouring *sage-femme** could give, and she came frequently, bringing in with her a little store of gossip, and wonderful tales culled out of her own experience, every time. One day she began to tell me about a great lady in whose service her daughter had lived as scullion, or some such thing. Such a beautiful lady! with such a handsome husband. But grief comes to the palace as well as to the garret, and why or wherefore no one knew, but somehow the Baron de Roeder must have incurred the vengeance of the terrible Chauffeurs; for not many months ago, as madame was going to see her relations in Alsace, she was stabbed dead as she lay in bed at some hotel on the road. Had I not seen it in the *Gazette?* Had I not heard? Why, she had been told that as far off as Lyons there were placards offering a heavy reward on the part of the Baron de Roeder for information respecting the murderer of his wife. But no one could help him, for all who could bear evidence were in such terror of the Chauffeurs; there were hundreds of them, she had been told, rich and poor, great gentlemen and peasants, all leagued together by most frightful oaths to hunt to the death anyone who bore witness against them; so that even they who survived the tortures to which the Chauffeurs subjected many of the people whom they plundered, dared not to recognize them again, would not dare, even did they see them at the bar of a court of justice; for, if one were condemned, were there not hundreds sworn to avenge his death?

I told all this to Amante, and we began to fear that if M. de la Tourelle, or Lefebvre, or any of the gang at Les Rochers, had seen these placards, they would know that the poor lady stabbed by the former was the Baroness de Roeder, and that they would set forth again in search of me.

This fresh apprehension told on my health and impeded my recovery. We had so little money we could not call in a physician, at least, not one in established practice. But Amante found out a young doctor for whom, indeed, she had sometimes worked; and offering to pay him in kind, she brought him to see me, her sick wife. He was very gentle and thoughtful, though, like ourselves, very poor. But he gave much time and consideration to the case, saying once to Amante that he saw my constitution had experienced some severe shock from which it was probable that my nerves would never entirely recover. By-and-by I shall name this doctor, and then you will know, better than I can describe, his character.

I grew strong in time—stronger, at least. I was able to work a little at home, and to sun myself and my baby at the garret-window in the roof. It was all the air I dared to take. I constantly wore the disguise I had first set out with; as constantly had I renewed the disfiguring dye which changed my hair and complexion. But the perpetual state of terror in which I had been during the whole months succeeding my escape from Les Rochers made me loathe the idea of ever again walking in the open daylight, exposed to the sight and recognition of every passer-by. In vain Amante reasoned—in vain the doctor urged. Docile in every other thing, in this I was obstinate. I would not stir out. One day Amante returned from her work, full of news—some of it good, some such as to cause us apprehension. The good news was this: the master for whom she worked as journeyman was going to send her with some others to a great house at the other side of Frankfurt, where there were to be private theatricals, and where many new dresses and much alteration of old ones would be required. The tailors employed were all to stay at this house until the day of representation was over, as it was at some distance from the town, and no one could tell when their work would be ended. But the pay was to be proportionately good.

The other thing she had to say was this: she had that day met the travelling jeweller to whom she and I had sold my ring. It was rather a peculiar one, given to me by my husband; we had felt at the time that it might be the means of tracing us, but we were penniless and starving, and what else could we do? She had seen that this Frenchman had recognized her at the same instant that she did him, and she thought at the same time that there was a gleam of more than common intelligence on his face as he did so. This idea had been confirmed by his following her for some way on the other side of the street; but she had evaded him with her better knowledge of the town, and the increasing darkness of the night. Still it was well that she was going to such a distance from our dwelling on the next day; and she had brought me in a stock of provisions, begging me to keep within doors, with a strange kind of fearful oblivion of the fact that I had never set foot beyond the threshold of the house since I had first entered it—scarce ever ventured down the stairs. But, although my poor, my dear, very faithful Amante was like one possessed that last night, she spoke continually of the dead, which is a bad sign for the living. She kissed you—yes! it was you, my daughter, my darling, whom I bore beneath my bosom away from the fearful castle of your father—I call him so for the first time, I must call him so once again before I have done—Amante kissed you, sweet baby, blessed little comforter, as if she never could leave off. And then she went away, alive.

Two days, three days passed away. That third evening I was sitting within my bolted doors—you asleep on your pillow by my side—when a step came up the stair, and I knew it must be for me; for ours were the topmost rooms. Someone knocked; I held my very breath. But someone spoke, and I knew it was the good Doctor Voss. Then I crept to the door, and answered.

'Are you alone?' asked I.

'Yes,' said he, in a still lower voice. 'Let me in.' I let him in, and he was as alert as I in bolting and barring the door. Then he came and whispered to me his doleful tale. He had come from the hospital in the opposite quarter of the town, the hospital which he visited; he should have been with me sooner, but he had feared lest he should be watched. He had come from Amante's death-bed. Her fears of the jeweller were too well founded. She had left the house where she was employed that morning, to transact some errand connected with her work in the town; she must have been followed, and dogged on her way back through solitary wood-paths, for some of the wood-rangers belonging to the great house had found her lying there, stabbed to death, but not dead; with the poniard again plunged through the fatal writing, once more; but this time with the word 'un' underlined, so as to show that the assassin was aware of his previous mistake.

Numéro *Un*.
Ainsi les Chauffeurs se vengent.

They had carried her to the house, and given her restoratives till she had recovered the feeble use of her speech. But, oh, faithful, dear friend and sister! even then she remembered me, and refused to tell (what no one else among her fellow workmen knew), where she lived or with whom. Life was ebbing away fast, and they had no resource but to carry her to the nearest hospital, where, of course, the fact of her sex was made known. Fortunately both for her and for me, the doctor in attendance was the very Doctor Voss whom we already knew. To him, while awaiting her confessor, she told enough to enable him to understand the position in which I was left; before the priest had heard half her tale Amante was dead.

Doctor Voss told me he had made all sorts of detours, and waited thus, late at night, for fear of being watched and followed. But I do not think he was. At any rate, as I afterwards learnt from him, the Baron Roeder, on hearing of the similitude of this murder with that of his wife in every particular, made such a search after the assassins, that, although they were not discovered, they were compelled to take to flight for the time.

I can hardly tell you now by what arguments Dr Voss, at first merely my benefactor, sparing me a portion of his small modicum, at length persuaded me to become his wife. His wife he called it, I called it; for we went through the religious ceremony too much slighted at the time, and as we were both Lutherans,* and M. de la Tourelle had pretended to be of the reformed religion, a divorce from the latter would have been easily procurable by German law both ecclesiastical and legal, could we have summoned so fearful a man into any court.

The good doctor took me and my child by stealth to his modest dwelling; and there I lived in the same deep retirement, never seeing the full light of day, although when the dye had once passed away from my face my husband did not wish me to renew it. There was no need; my yellow hair was grey, my complexion was ashen-coloured, no creature could have recognized the fresh-coloured, bright-haired young woman of eighteen months before. The few people whom I saw knew me only as Madame Voss; a widow much older than himself, whom Dr Voss had secretly married. They called me the Grey Woman.

He made me give you his surname. Till now you have known no other father—while he lived you needed no father's love. Once only, only once more, did the old terror come upon me. For some reason which I forget, I broke through my usual custom, and went to the window of my room for some purpose, either to shut or to open it. Looking out into the street for an instant, I was fascinated by the sight of M. de la Tourelle, gay, young, elegant as ever, walking along on the opposite side of the street. The noise I had made with the window caused him to look up; he saw me, an old grey woman, and he did not recognize me! Yet it was not three years since we had parted, and his eyes were keen and dreadful like those of the lynx.

I told M. Voss, on his return home, and he tried to cheer me, but the shock of seeing M. de la Tourelle had been too terrible for me. I was ill for long months afterwards.

Once again I saw him. Dead. He and Lefebvre were at last caught; hunted down by the Baron de Roeder in some of their crimes. Dr Voss had heard of their arrest; their condemnation, their death; but he never said a word to me, until one day he bade me show him that I loved him by my obedience and my trust. He took me a long carriage journey, where to I know not, for we never spoke of that day again; I was led through a prison, into a closed courtyard, where, decently draped in the last robes of death, concealing the marks of decapitation, lay M. de la Tourelle, and two or three others, whom I had known at Les Rochers.

After that conviction Dr Voss tried to persuade me to return to a more natural mode of life, and to go out more. But although I sometimes complied with his wish, yet the old terror was ever strong upon me, and he, seeing what an effort it was, gave up urging me at last.

You know all the rest. How we both mourned bitterly the loss of that dear husband and father—for such I will call him ever—and as such you must consider him, my child, after this one revelation is over.

Why has it been made, you ask. For this reason, my child. The lover, whom you have only known as M. Lebrun, a French artist, told me but yesterday his real name, dropped because the bloodthirsty republicans* might consider it as too aristocratic. It is Maurice de Poissy.

EXPLANATORY NOTES

A Dark Night's Work

1 *about forty years ago*: although published in 1863, 'A Dark Night's Work' was, according to a letter from Elizabeth Gaskell to George Smith (*Letters*, 697), begun in about 1858. The story's opening sentence therefore suggests that the early events of the tale take place sometime between 1815 and 1820.

conveyancing attorney: the term attorney was commonly used synonymously for solicitor for much of the nineteenth century. The lower social standing of the solicitor, compared to the Oxford or Cambridge-educated barrister, is important for the history of the Wilkins family.

the meet . . . the brush: the gathering of men, horses, and hounds for the purpose of fox-hunting, traditional recreation of the landed gentry. When the fox is caught, its tail or brush is cut off and awarded to the rider who has led the chase.

2 *Christ Church*: one of the oldest and most prestigious colleges of Oxford University.

3 *sixteen quarterings*: when two families entitled to bear coats of arms were allied by a marriage, the couple could quarter the arms. A single shield was divided into four equal areas and heraldic devices from the two families' arms were combined in a new arrangement. A large number of quarterings indicated the noblest ancestry.

minuets . . . country dances . . . quadrilles . . . waltzing: the fortunes of the Hamley assemblies reflect changing fashions in dancing. The slow, stately minuet was at the height of its popularity during the period 1650 to 1750. The more lively, traditional country dances persisted into the nineteenth century. The quadrille, a dance for four couples which became popular early in the century, was complicated and formal, while the newly fashionable waltz created a scandal because it required partners to dance in an embrace.

allied sovereigns: the alliance between Britain, Prussia, Russia and Austria, formed against Napoleon, was made official by the Treaty of Chaumont in March 1814, and the visit to Britain by the Emperor of Russia and the King of Prussia in June of the same year.

'muckle-mou'ed': (dialect) large-mouthed.

5 *they did covet the horses and hounds he possessed*: echoes the tenth commandment: 'Thou shalt not covet thy neighbour's house, thou shalt not covet thy neighbour's wife, nor his manservant, nor his maidservant, nor his ox, nor his ass, nor any thing that is thy neighbour's' (Exodus 20: 17).

11 *the famous Adam and Eve in the weather-glass*: a barometer with two figures, one representing fine weather and the other representing rain, mounted so that as one appears the other disappears. In a letter of 1850 to Eliza Fox (*Letters*, 130), Gaskell describes herself and her husband as being 'like Adam and Eve in the weather glass' due to their custom of taking separate holidays.

12 *recherché*: (French) choice, select.

the woolsack: an allusion to the office of Lord Chancellor, Speaker of the House of Lords and the highest judicial position to which a barrister could aspire. The Lord Chancellor's seat in the House is made of a large square bag of wool.

14 *riding a-tilt*: literally referring to combat with lances on horseback (Shakespeare, *1 Henry VI*, III. ii. 50–1: 'break a lance, And run a tilt at death'); figuratively, showing that, despite his youth, Ralph Corbet is confident enough to meet his opponents head-on in argument.

16 *dipped*: in debt, mortgaged.

Herald's College: a royal corporation with the authority to grant coats of arms. In the nineteenth century many of the middle class who had made their fortunes from industry, commerce, or the professions paid for a genealogical search in the hope of discovering an ancestral right to bear arms.

17 *brougham . . . dog-cart . . . gig*: the elder Mr Wilkins uses a light, open, two-wheeled vehicle while his son first drives a larger, heavier cart, and then a more expensive, fashionable closed carriage.

21 *potters*: (dialect) confuses, troubles, or perplexes. Gaskell's use of dialect owes much to her husband's knowledge of etymology. William Gaskell's *Two Lectures on the Lancashire Dialect* were appended to the fifth (1854) edition of *Mary Barton*. In the same year, Gaskell sent a copy of the lectures to Walter Savage Landor, and confessed 'I sometimes "potter" and "mither" people' by using dialect words and expressions (*Letters*, 292).

fid-fad: a reduction of 'fiddle-faddle', denoting triviality or fussiness.

23 *Horace*: Latin poet (65–8 BC) whose *Satires*, *Odes*, *Epistles*, and

critical works, particularly the *Ars Poetica*, exerted a profound influence on English literary life from the seventeenth to the nineteenth century. His works were studied so widely in schools and at the universities that it is unlikely that there was any great demand for Mr Ness's new edition.

27 *Boeotian*: the inhabitants of Boeotia, a region of ancient Greece, were proverbially equated with dullness and stupidity.

Plantagenets: the dynasty which ruled England from 1154 to 1485. Founded by the union between Geoffrey, Count of Anjou, and the empress Matilda, daughter of the English king Henry I; their descendants divided into the houses of Lancaster and York, and the power struggle between them led to the Wars of the Roses.

28 *'thought of eating and drinking'*: a paraphrase of Matthew 24: 38—'For as in the days that were before the flood they were eating and drinking'—or Isaiah 22: 13—'let us eat and drink; for tomorrow we shall die.'

30 *Middle Temple*: one of London's four Inns of Court, or ancient colleges of law, at which a university graduate undertakes study of the law as the pupil of an established barrister.

'come out': the ritual by which young women made a formal entry into society, being presented under chaperonage at an important occasion such as a ball. Gaskell mocks the pretensions so often attached to the ceremony in her account, in *Wives and Daughters*, of Molly Gibson and Cynthia Kirkpatrick 'coming out' (ch. 21).

31 *he was thankful he was not as other men*: Luke 18: 11—the parable of the Pharisee and the Publican.

32 *he would and he would not*: Shakespeare, *Measure for Measure*, II. ii. 33: 'At war 'twixt will and will not.'

34 *wisdom of Solomon*: Jewish king of the Old Testament famed for his wisdom (1 Kings 3: 16–28, and 4: 29–34).

a peer of James the First's creation: James I of England and James VI of Scotland (1566–1625), only son of Mary Queen of Scots, was the first Stuart king of England.

portions: used here in the sense of dowry or marriage settlement.

post-obits: Reginald, Ralph's elder brother and the Corbet heir, has been able to borrow money on the strength of his future inheritance. Although accepted practice, it indicated a lack of feeling as the guarantee for the loan was one's father's death. Earlier in the story (p. 13) Mr Corbet had complained, apparently in a reference to his eldest son and heir, of 'Edward's extravagance'. Thus Ralph's mention of Reginald's post-obits would seem to be an instance of Gaskell's well-known carelessness with proper names.

34 *Flanders mare*: (colloquial) a plain or ugly woman; derived from King Henry VIII's opinion of his fourth wife, Anne of Cleves, as reported in Smollett's *Complete History of England* (3rd edn., 1759, vi. 68).

a silver penny to cross herself with: (proverbial) having no money; the English penny used to be made of silver, with a cross on the reverse.

35 *éclat*: (French) social distinction or brilliance.

42 *Ophelia*: in Shakespeare's *Hamlet*, daughter of Polonius and lover of Hamlet. Aspects of Ophelia's history, particularly the death of her father and her rejection by her lover, prefigure events in Ellinor's life.

43 *drab breeches and gaiters*: a description of the cloth of Mr Wilkins's garments rather than their colour. Drab is a kind of hempen, linen, or woollen cloth which accords well with the old gentleman's unaffected style of dress.

the old heathen saying, 'Let no man be envied till his death.': Gaskell may be referring to the saying, attributed to Solon, Athenian legislator and poet, 'Call no man happy till he dies, he is at best but fortunate' (Herodotus, *Histories*, i. 32). A slightly different version is found in the Apocrypha, Ecclesiasticus 11: 28—'Judge none blessed before his death.'

44 *a thorn in her father's side*: 2 Corinthians 12: 7—'there was given to me a thorn in the flesh, the messenger of Satan.'

45 *Lord Chancellor's wife—wigs and woolsacks*: see note to p. 12.

47 *living*: appointment to a parish.

Ruskin's works: John Ruskin (1819–1900), art critic, architect, and first Slade professor of art at Oxford, was one of the Victorian age's most influential men of letters. Elizabeth Gaskell and Charlotte Brontë discussed Ruskin's works when they first met in 1850 (*Letters*, 124). It is likely that the conversation between Ellinor and Mr Livingstone concerns the first volume of *Modern Painters* (1843), the work which first brought Ruskin significant public attention.

48 *Dante*: Dante Alighieri (1265–1321), medieval Italian poet and philosopher.

51 *brandy and hartshorn*: administered as stimulants. The horn or antler of the hart (male deer or stag) was the source of ammonia used in sal-volatile (smelling-salts).

51 *Rechabite*: originally 'one of a Jewish family descended from Jonadab, son of Rechab, which refused to drink wine or live in houses' (*OED*). More generally used to describe one who avoids or abstains from alcohol. The biblical account of the obedience of the Rechabites (Jeremiah 35) has ironic implications for Ellinor's own history. She becomes a 'tent-dweller' in the sense that she loses her permanent home on the death of her father; like the Rechabites, she obeys her father (in the matter of concealing Dunster's murder), but her obedience brings her not blessings but sorrow.

60 *P. P. C.-ing*: (French) 'pour prendre congé'; to take one's leave: often written on calling cards.

62 *rending their garments and crying aloud*: Jeremiah 36: 24, Leviticus 10: 6, 2 Chronicles 34: 27.

64 *burnt and scared with affliction*: the Knutsford edition of 'A Dark Night's Work' (*The Works of Mrs. Gaskell*, ed. A. W. Ward, 1906, vii. 474) corrects what may be a compositor's misreading of this phrase from the original manuscript to 'burnt and seared with affliction'.

67 *'standing afar-off'*: Luke 18: 13—the parable of the Pharisee and the Publican.

68 *Bath-chair*: a large chair on wheels, precursor of the modern wheelchair, for the use of invalids.

69 *foumart*: polecat; figuratively, a term of contempt.

74 *Autolycus's song*: Shakespeare's *Winter's Tale* IV. iii. 121–4:

> Jog on, jog on, the footpath way,
> And merrily hant the stile-a:
> A merry heart goes all the day,
> Your sad tires in a mile-a.

75 *malice prepense*: legal term for premeditated malice, a wrong or injury purposely done.

76 *collegiate*: originally endowed as a cathedral but with no bishop appointed.

'hardening her heart': Exodus 8: 15 and 14: 8.

81 *fly*: light, one-horse carriage with a collapsible roof; usually a hired vehicle, especially at railway stations.

action brought against him for breach of promise: a lawsuit could be brought against a man who reneged on a promise of marriage. A young man's career could be severely damaged if he were named in a breach of promise suit; however, the process often resulted in worse damage to the woman's reputation.

83 *the feast of wit or reason*: Alexander Pope, *Imitations of Horace*, Satire I, Book II, 'To Mr. Fortescue', l. 128: 'The feast of reason and the flow of soul.'

ménages: (French) households, domestic arrangements.

94 *Orestes and the Furies*: upon his victorious return from the Trojan War Agamemnon was murdered by his wife Clytemnestra and revenged by his son Orestes. Orestes murdered Clytemnestra and her lover Aegisthus but was pursued by the Furies (Eumenides), goddesses of vengeance who punished wrongdoers, particularly those who had committed crimes against ties of kinship. This story of retribution for past crimes, which has such significance for the guilty Mr Wilkins, is told in *The Oresteia*, a dramatic trilogy by the Greek poet Aeschylus.

95 *bear the sins of thy father*: Exodus 34: 7.

98 *the morning mail*: the coach (Hamley does not yet have the railway) used to convey letters and parcels as well as passengers; hence, the system of sending material by post.

102 *I am but forty*: Gaskell has made an error of chronology here for Miss Monro is described as 'a plain, intelligent, quiet woman of forty' p. 11 when she enters Mr Wilkins's service and approximately ten years have passed since then.

106 *canons*: cathedral clergy (as distinct from parish clergy such as Mr Ness).

precentor: a minor canon who leads the singing of the choir or congregation, and may chant the responses during the service.

chapter: the body of canons, headed by the dean, attached to the cathedral.

108 *a second spring*: Thomas Gray, 'Ode on a Distant Prospect of Eton College', ll. 15–16, 20. The lines are misquoted in both the original serial publication, in which l. 16 is given as 'A momentary youth bestow'; and in the 1863 volume publication, which reads, 'A momentary bless bestow'. The correct version, given in the Knutsford edition of Gaskell's works (vii. 524), is 'A momentary bliss bestow'. The misquotation may be unconscious on Gaskell's part or a deliberate comment on Miss Monro's rather haphazard education of Ellinor.

110 *frank*: convey free of charge.

111 *Queen's Counsel*: the highest rank a barrister may attain, distinguished by a silk gown worn in court and the initials QC added after the name, restricting him to plead in higher courts, and a prerequisite for promotion to be a judge

113 *by this time East Chester had got a railway*: construction of new railway lines in Britain reached a peak in the 1840s; the Great Western Railway's line from London to Bristol, on which Ellinor travels when she returns from Rome, was completed in 1841.

empressement: (French) effusive cordiality.

114 *the 'Wedding March'*: the 'Wedding March' from Felix Mendelssohn's *Midsummer Night's Dream* (1842) was performed at the marriage of the Princess Royal in 1858, after which it became the fashionable accompaniment for weddings. This date accords with the time at which 'A Dark Night's Work' was written rather than with the chronology of the story.

116 *in the year 1829*: this date does not fit the chronology of the story so far. When Ellinor is ill she is approximately nineteen; if the date of her illness is 1829, then the story begins before 1810, earlier than the date suggested by the 'forty years ago' of the opening paragraph, and the reference to the visit of the allied sovereigns in 1814. Moreover, a few days before she falls ill, Ellinor and Mr Livingstone discuss Ruskin's works, but even the earliest of Ruskin's works were not published until the mid-1830s.

rara avis: (Latin) literally, rare bird; a remarkable person.

'sacerdotal face': I have been unable to find any other use of this phrase.

122 *blood will out*: proverbial; also Chaucer, *The Prioress's Tale*, 'Mordre wol out, certeyn, it wol nat faille' (Fragment VII, l. 576: Group B2, l. 1766); and Shakespeare, *Macbeth*, 'It will have blood, they say: blood will have blood' (III. iv. 123).

122 *the Athenaeum*: this influential literary and philosophical magazine was published weekly in London from 1828 to 1921. The Gaskells were subscribers from 1849 to 1858 and Elizabeth Gaskell wrote that it 'seems to fill an absolute want in literature, and to be universally read in all circles' (*Letters*, 810).

Virgil: Publius Vergilius Maro (70–19 BC), Roman poet known particularly for his use of the pastoral and the epic (the *Aeneid*) modes. His influence on English literature can be traced from the Middle Ages and his works were widely studied in schools and universities in the nineteenth century.

123 *Nova Zembla*: Novaya Zemlya; an archipelago lying north of Russia (USSR) in the Arctic Ocean.

128 *Murray*: an extremely popular series of travellers' guidebooks, several written by John Murray III (1808–92) and published by the firm established by his grandfather John Murray I (1745–93). Gaskell owned a copy of Murray's *Handbook for Travellers in Central Italy* (5th edn., London, 1861); this volume, with enclosed handwritten notes, some in the author's own hand, is in the Gaskell collection of the Manchester Central Library.

129 *the Carnival*: festivities celebrated in many Roman Catholic countries prior to the austerity of Lent. Traditionally, the Carnival runs for three days in the week before Lent, ending on Shrove Tuesday. Elizabeth Gaskell was in Rome on Shrove Tuesday, 24 February 1857 and, like Ellinor Wilkins, viewed the scene from a balcony on the Via del Corso.

fourth piano, No. 36, Babuino: fourth floor, 36 Via del Babuino, a street running off the Piazza di Spagna, which formed the centre of a colony of English and American writers and artists in nineteenth-century Rome. During her visit to Rome in 1857, Gaskell stayed in lodgings not far from the Spanish Steps as the guest of William Wetmore Story, the American sculptor and writer.

facchino: (Italian) porter.

Pinelli: Bartolommeo Pinelli (1781–1835) was known primarily for his chalk drawings, water-colours, and etchings of scenes illustrating Italian life and costume, and views of Rome and Tivoli. Some of his plates were brought to England and printed there shortly before his death as *Views in Rome* (London, 1834).

Condotti . . . Corso: the Via del Babuino and the Via Condotti meet in the Piazza di Spagna, the Via Condotti running between the Piazza and the principal street of Rome, the Via del Corso.

130 *domino*: (Spanish) a cloak, with a mask for the upper part of the face, worn at masquerades and festivals.

confetti: (Italian) can refer to bon-bons or to little bits of coloured paper or plaster made in imitation of these.

moccoletti: (Italian) thin wax candles.

contadini: (Italian) country people.

senators who received Brennus and his Gauls: Brennus was the chief of a band of Gauls thought to have captured Rome about AD 390. He was paid a ransom by the city and withdrew his forces.

130 *a familiar face*: the first meeting between Elizabeth Gaskell and Charles Eliot Norton, student of art history and later professor at Harvard, took place in a similar fashion to Ellinor's recognition of Canon Livingstone. Gaskell was standing on the balcony on the Corso hired by the Storys to view the Carnival when Norton was recognized in the crowd below and asked to join the group (see Winifred Gérin, *Elizabeth Gaskell* (Oxford, 1980), ch. 16).

131 *the Angleterre*: Murray's *Handbook for Travellers in Central Italy* (1861) recommends the 'Hôtel d'Angleterre, in the Via Condotti, excellent in every respect both for families and bachelors' (p. 421)

132 *griping*: (archaic) grasping or seizing.

135 *Civita*: Civitavecchia, the principal port for Rome, situated on the west coast of Italy, approximately 40 miles from the capital.

136 *Dr Livingstone*: Gaskell can be quite careless with titles and names. For example, up to this point the canon has been given the title 'Mr', but from here on he is called 'Dr Livingstone'.

141 *stound*: violent impact, or the noise thereof.

the engine is broken . . . return to Civita: the breakdown of the ship between Civitavecchia and Marseilles may be based on Gaskell's own experience on her outward journey to Rome in 1857. The Gaskell party had been at sea for 30 hours when engine failure forced them to return to Marseilles.

142 *diligence*: (French) public stage-coach used in Europe.

sala: (Italian) waiting-room or hall.

144 *Galignani*: *Galignani's Messenger*, an English newspaper, published twice-daily in France from 1814, and widely circulated among English residents and travellers in Europe.

no electric telegraph in those days: although several telegraph companies in England adopted Cooke and Wheatstone's single-needle instrument for public use as early as 1846, it was not until 1859 that a district telegraph system with branch offices was established in London.

146 *white soup*: Mrs Beeton's recipe for white soup, given in her *Book of Household Management* (1861), contains sweet almonds, veal or poultry, bread, lemon-peel, mace, cream, and the yolks of hard-boiled eggs.

147 *white-wine whey*: a medicinal drink made by boiling milk with wine or sherry until the milk curdles. The whey, the watery product of coagulation, is strained off and sweetened.

148 *moreen*: thick wool, or wool and cotton, material, which may be plain or watermarked.

se'ennight: (archaic) seven nights, i.e. a week.

149 *the lion of the place*: the sight most worth seeing. The phrase derives from the custom of showing visitors the lions formerly kept at the menagerie in the Tower of London.

151 *the Hullah system*: John Pyke Hullah (1812–84), conductor, composer, and teacher, but principally known for his work in musical education. He studied Continental systems of teaching music to large groups and started his own classes in Manchester in 1842. In the original serial publication Mrs Johnson and Ellinor discuss the tonic sol-fa system, the main alternative to the Hullah system for musical notation and training, and the method which ultimately gained far wider acceptance.

152 *I'd as lief*: or 'I'd liefer' (archaic), 'I would rather', 'I would as willingly'.

153 *Botany Bay*: site on the east coast of Australia at which Captain James Cook landed in 1770. Although the British colony and penal settlement was subsequently established at Port Jackson, 'Botany Bay' remained in common parlance as the term for transportation to New South Wales.

154 *main and sorry*: (dialect) 'main' or 'main and' before an adjective means 'very' or 'greatly'.

163 *wisest, best*: Milton, *Paradise Lost*, Book VIII, l. 550: 'wisest, virtuousest, discreetest, best'.

164 *home*: the Knutsford edition of 'A Dark Night's Work' (p. 588) suggests the more likely reading of 'Rome' here

Libbie Marsh's Three Eras

168 *house-place*: the name given, in many parts of England, to the common living-room and kitchen in a farmhouse or cottage.

169 *'the blue sky, that bends over all'*: Coleridge, 'Christabel', I. 331.

170 *'till her name was up'*: 'His name is up; he may lie abed till noon', i.e. once you have a reputation, for example as an early riser or, in Mrs Hall's case, as a termagant, nothing you can do will change it (*Oxford Dictionary of English Proverbs*, 189).

172 *St Valentine's day*: the custom of giving presents or cards to a sweetheart on 14 February is related not to the saints which bear

this name but from the association of that date with the beginning of the mating season for birds. Therefore it is appropriate that Libbie gives Frankie Hall a canary as a valentine.

172 *the widow's mite*: Mark 12: 42.

173 *nesh*: (dialect) soft, weakly, tender.

174 *the grapes that were beyond her reach*: an allusion to Aesop's fable of the fox who, unable to get the grapes beyond his reach, pronounced them sour. It is illustrative of Libbie's character that she does not give in to 'sour grapes' but is happy with what is within her means.

175 *Whitsuntide*: Whit Sunday, the seventh Sunday after Easter, and the week following; a traditional holiday in Britain.

176 *Dunham*: Dunham Massey Hall, set in ancient woods south-west of Manchester, was the seat of the Earls of Stamford and Warrington. I am indebted to Mrs Joan Leach, secretary of the Gaskell Society, for the following information regarding Dunham Massey: 'In Mrs Gaskell's day the family lived mainly at their other house in Staffordshire, which is possibly why they allowed free access to Manchester workers travelling via the Bridgewater canal which skirted the park.' Gaskell's original rough sketch for *Mary Barton* included a visit to Dunham during Whitsun week, but the episode was not included in the finished novel.

Alderley: Alderley Edge, a sandstone escarpment about 12 miles south of Manchester. Railway construction in the 1830s and 1840s opened up this scenic spot to Manchester residents, much to the annoyance of the Stanley family, who considered themselves the owners of Alderley. Representatives of the railways proposed a roster system for access to the area—private days for the Stanley family, open days for the working classes, and restricted days for the 'Cottontots', as the Stanleys disparagingly called the Manchester gentry. See *The Ladies of Alderley*, ed. Nancy Mitford (London, 1967), 60–4.

dove . . . olive branch: both ancient symbols of peace; in the Old Testament, the receeding of the flood, symbolizing the decline of God's anger against man, is shown to Noah by the return to the ark of a dove with an olive leaf in her beak (Genesis 8: 11)

178 *'slay'*: the context suggests a meaning of treating, paying on behalf of another; however, I have been unable to find any other example of such a usage.

Macadamized: a relatively cheap and rapid method of road construction invented by John Loudon McAdam (1756–1836), which greatly facilitated transport in the early nineteenth century.

179 *gimp*: a decorative trimming made of twisted silk, worsted, or cotton with a cord or wire running through it.

'sweet hour of prime': William Wordsworth, *The Excursion*, VI. 823: 'In the prime hour of sweetest scents and airs'.

180 *old men and maidens, young men and children*: in Psalms 148: 12 all creation, including 'young men, and maidens; old men, and children', is exhorted to praise God.

'the Duke': Francis Egerton, 3rd Duke of Bridgewater (1736–1803), founder of the canal system in Britain. He commissioned James Brindley to build a canal to transport coal from his mines at Worsley to Manchester, a distance of 10 miles. The Bridgewater Canal, completed in 1761, was extended in 1776 from Manchester to Liverpool, an extra 30 miles. The subsequent growth of Manchester's canal network culminated in the opening of the Manchester Ship Canal in 1894, which linked the city to the Irish Sea. However, from the 1840s the canals faced competition from the developing railways.

'verdurous walls': John Keats, 'Ode to a Nightingale', l. 40: 'Through verdurous glooms and winding mossy ways'.

182 *'under the greenwood tree'*: song from Shakespeare's *As You Like It*, II, v, 1–8.

Puck or Robin Goodfellow: originally an evil or malicious demon; from the sixteenth century, the name of a mischievous goblin or sprite, also called Hobgoblin. The name is used in the latter sense in Shakespeare's *Midsummer Night's Dream*, II. i. 32–42.

top-strings: spinning-tops, conical, circular, or oval, usually made of wood, were spun by means of a string, a whip, or a twist of the hand

183 *Welly*: (dialect) nearly, almost; a contraction of well-nigh.

oud smoke-jack: 'old smoke-jack'; term of endearment for Manchester. The city, like a smoke-jack which is fixed in a chimney to turn a spit, cannot operate without smoke.

184 *'Dot'*: a diminutive person or thing

heaven, 'which is our home': William Wordsworth, 'Ode: Intimations of Immortality', l. 65: 'God, who is our home'.

'Here we suffer grief and pain': hymn for children (*The Union Hymn Book*, no. 287) composed by Thomas Bilby (1794–1872), an active supporter of infant schools.

185 *Michaelmas*: (29 September) the feast of St Michael and All Angels, traditionally celebrated by eating goose.

187 *the fourteenth chapter of St John's Gospel*: in which Jesus promises that the Holy Spirit will comfort the disciples.

'Father's house': 'In my Father's house are many mansions . . . I go to prepare a place for you' (John 14: 2).

188 *'flesh is grass,' Bible says*: Isaiah 40: 6 and 1 Peter 1: 24.

189 *Jemmie*: *Howitt's Journal*, 1 (1847), 346 has 'Jeannie', but the name is corrected in the 1855 Chapman and Hall edition to 'Jemmie' in order to tally with Libbie's mention of a 'little brother long since dead' (p. 168).

Six Weeks at Heppenheim

195 *Lincoln's Inn*: one of London's four Inns of Court, the others being Gray's Inn, Inner Temple, and Middle Temple (see note to p. 30).

Heppenheim, on the Berg-Strasse: situated about 12 miles west of the Rhine, Heppenheim lies on the Bergstrasse (literally 'mountain street'), an ancient migration route which runs parallel to the Rhine between Darmstadt in the north and Heidelberg in the south.

196 vis inertiae: (Latin) inertia.

201 *a chasse*: (French) an exclusive right to hunt game in a particular tract of country.

Odenwald: elevated wooded region, studded with castles and ruins, situated east of the Rhine. As hunting ground of the Nibelungen, the Odenwald forms the setting for the thirteenth-century German epic poem the *Nibelungenlied*.

the chevreuil: (French) roe-deer, the culinary term for which is venison.

202 *the Halbmond*: the 'Half-Moon'. The 12th edn. of Murray's *Handbook for Travellers on the Continent* (London, 1858) recommends the 'Halber Mond' in Heppenheim as 'good', with 'capital trout, and wine of the country' (p. 530).

'Thekla, Thekla, liebe Thekla': 'Thekla, Thekla, dear Thekla'.

redded up: arranged, put in order.

204 *perdu*: or perdue (French), hidden.

205 *honi soit qui mal y pense*: 'evil be to him who evil thinks' (literally, 'shame to him who thinks evil of it'); motto of the Order of the Garter, highest British civil and military honour, founded by Edward III probably in 1348

206 *tisane*: (French) an infusion (of herbs, tea, etc.), slightly medicinal.

209 *the church at Heppenheim . . . built by the great Kaiser Karl*: Murray's *Handbook for Travellers on the Continent* (1858) notes that the church at Heppenheim was founded by Charlemagne (p. 530).

Castle of Starkenburg . . . Abbots of Lorsch: the ruined castle of Starkenburg was built in 1064 by abbots from the even older monastery at nearby Lorsch as a defence against the powerful German emperors.

Melibocus: a high granite hill (1,696 ft.), about 6 miles north of Heppenheim, which forms the highest point of the Odenwald.

211 *Grand Duke*: before unification in 1871, Germany consisted of hundreds of fragmented, independent states. From 1803 Heppenheim was part of the state of Hesse-Darmstadt. In 1806, Louis X (1753–1830) of Hesse-Darmstadt took the title of Grand Duke Louis I on Hesse-Darmstadt's entry into the French-controlled Confederation of the Rhine. Louis III (1807–77) was Grand Duke from 1848.

212 *Bacchus:* (Dionysus), classical god of wine, and, more generally, fruitfulness.

Aufwiedersehen: the German form of farewell, literally translated as 'to-meet-again'.

213 *the Adler*: the Eagle, a rival hotel.

216 *place*: the Knutsford edition of 'Six Weeks at Heppenheim' (*The Works of Mrs. Gaskell*, ed. A. W. Ward, 1906, VII. 386) substitutes the more likely word 'plan' here.

217 *doing evil that possible good might come*: Romans 3: 8.

219 *All Saints' Day*: or All Hallows' Day (1 November), a festival of the Christian church held to honour the saints and martyrs.

222 *to each country its own laws*: Geoffrey Chaucer, *Troilus and Criseyde*, II. vi. 42: 'Forthi men seyn, ecch contree hath his lawes.'

her hand was against everyone's: Genesis 16: 12—'his hand will be against every man, and every man's hand against him.'

'Methinks the lady doth profess too much': a misquotation (the error may be Gaskell's or the narrator's) of *Hamlet*, III. ii. 234: 'The lady doth protest too much, methinks.'

227 *German harvest-hymn*: 'Wir pflügen'—music by Johann Abraham Peter Schultz (1747–1800); words by Matthias Claudius (1740–1815); English translation by Jane Montgomery Campbell (1817–78):

We plough the fields, and scatter
The good seed on the land,
But it is fed and watered
By God's almighty hand;
He sends the snow in winter,
The warmth to swell the grain,
The breezes and the sunshine,
And soft refreshing rain.
All good gifts around us
Are sent from heaven above,
Then thank the Lord, O thank the Lord,
For all His love.

228 *Dicker-milch*: (German) curd, or solidified sour milk.

cates: choice foods, delicacies.

chemisette: (French) bodice or blouse.

230 *Mrs Inchbald's pretty description of Dorriforth's anxiety in feeding Miss Milner*: in Elizabeth Inchbald's prose romance *A Simple Story* (1791), the beautiful flirt, Miss Milner, is in despair as she loves her guardian Dorriforth, a Catholic priest. She is unable to eat through unhappiness and Dorriforth tempts her with morsels he has selected from her plate.

232 *All Souls*: (2 November) a holy day of the Roman Catholic Church devoted to prayers for the souls of the faithful departed. Abolished in the Church of England at the Reformation, All Souls' Day continued to be observed among many European Protestants. This paragraph suggests that All Saints' Day follows All Souls' Day; however, All Saints' Day falls on 1 November, the day before All Souls'.

immortelles: everlasting flowers which keep their colour after drying.

Cumberland Sheep-Shearers

233 *Three or four years ago*: Elizabeth Gaskell holidayed often in the Lake District and knew the area well. It is not possible to identify a specific incident on which 'Cumberland Sheep-Shearers' is

based. However, Gaskell's description of a party consisting of 'two grown up persons and four children, the youngest almost a baby' suggests that she may have drawn on memories of the holiday she took with her husband and four daughters at Skelwith in July 1849, merely changing the location to 'the neighbourhood of Keswick'. In 1849 Marianne Gaskell, the eldest child, was 15 and Julia, the youngest, was 3.

233 *Keswick*: principal town of the Lake District, which became an important tourist centre in the nineteenth century, especially after the arrival of the railway in 1865.

Statesman: used in the Cumberland and Westmoreland dialect to denote a small landowner, who cultivates his own land. The term implies the social position of a respectable countryman, but not a gentleman. In his *Guide Through the District of the Lakes* (5th edn., 1835) Wordsworth mentions the 'estatesmen' whose lands are being bought up by wealthy tourists.

234 *a green gloom in a green shade*: Andrew Marvell (1621–78), 'The Garden', l. 48—'a green thought in a green shade'.

the 'fat and scant of breath' quotation: *Hamlet*, v. ii. 297.

235 *the Scotch name of a 'town'*: in Scottish dialect, the house or group of buildings belonging to a single farm. For many centuries Cumbria was a battleground in the Border disputes between England and Scotland. It was occupied and raided many times by the Scots and many Scottish words were incorporated into the dialect of the region.

Derwent Water: one of the principal lakes from which the district takes its name; assuming the party walked south from Keswick, they would have had Derwent Water in view on their right for much of the journey.

Cat Bell: or Cat Bells, an area of fells or high ground lying west of Derwent Water.

236 *equinox*: the time of the year in which days and nights are of equal length. Gaskell appears to be using the term incorrectly to refer to the hottest part of the day.

house-place: see note to p. 168.

chimney corners: seat or nook on either side of an open fireplace; the warmest spot in any house and thus the most sought-after seat in winter.

Rydal Mount: Rydal Mount was William Wordsworth's home at

Ambleside in the Lake District. He moved there with his family in 1813, having previously lived at Allan Bank and Dove Cottage, Grasmere, both also in the Lakes area. The early creative period in which Wordsworth produced his best poetry was over by 1813 and the years spent at Rydal Mount saw his adoption of a conservative, public role. He died there in 1850.

236 *'Do at Rome as the Romans do'*: proverbial contraction of a statement attributed to St Ambrose (*c.*340–97), Bishop of Milan; follow the customs and habits of those around you.

water-gruel: liquid food, often for invalids, made by boiling oatmeal or other starch in water. Mrs Beeton (*The Book of Household Management*, 1861) recommends 1 tablespoon of Robinson's patent groats to 1 pint of boiling water.

237 *Coleridge—*

> *This sycamore (oft musical with bees—*
> *Such tents the Patriarchs loved) &c., &c.:*

the opening lines of 'Inscription for a Fountain on a Heath' by Samuel Taylor Coleridge (1772–1834).

*yellow asphode*l: related to the daffodil and common on British moors; also, in poetry, an immortal flower, said to cover the meadows of Elysium in Greek mythology.

linsey: usually linsey-woolsey; coarse dress material of wool loosely woven on a linen or cotton warp.

238 *Olympics*: famous athletic games of ancient Greece. The modern revival of the Olympic games dates only from 1896, so Gaskell's reference is specifically classical.

score: a group of twenty, presumably from the practice, in counting livestock, of numbering from one to twenty, and making a score or notch on a stick before continuing counting.

when Greek meets Greek: from the commonly misquoted 'When Greeks joined Greeks, then was the tug of war' in Nathaniel Lee's play *The Rival Queens* (1677). The line refers to the determined resistance of the Greek cities in war against the Macedonian kings Philip and Alexander the Great. The proverb implies that the struggle between two forces of equal courage and strength, armies or expert shearers, will be great.

Langdale Head: head of the Langdale valley near Skelwith, where Gaskell stayed on two visits to the Lake District; it is approximately 11 miles south of Keswick.

239 *shandries*: in north-west dialect, a light cart on springs. The *OED* cites Gaskell's use of the term in 'The Sexton's Hero' (*Howitt's Journal*, 1847).

raddle, or ruddle: a red ochre used for colouring, especially for marking sheep.

240 *'Old men and maidens . . .' of the Psalmist*: see note to p. 180.

'Saint's Tragedy': a drama in blank verse by Charles Kingsley, published in 1848. It presents the life of St Elizabeth of Hungary, including a scene in which Elizabeth's husband departs for the Crusades, bidden farewell by the whole population of the town.

241 *Fiery Cross*: a wooden cross carried from settlement to settlement in the Scottish Highlands in order to summon a clan before its chieftain. Another example of the Scottish influence in the Cumbrian district.

green and black tea: Mrs Beeton recommends that 'For mixed tea, the usual proportion is four spoonfuls of black to one of green.' Rather than 'masking', that is, infusing, the green and black leaves together, the usual method of blending tea, Gaskell's Cumberland housewife prefers to mix green and black tea after it has brewed. Miss Matty, in Gaskell's *Cranford* (1851–3), was convinced that green tea was 'slow poison, sure to destroy the nerves, and produce all manner of evil' (ch. 15). In her biography, *Elizabeth Gaskell: Her Life and Work* (London, 1952), Annette Hopkins tells of 'the green tea episode' which took place during Charlotte Brontë's visit to the Gaskells' home in Manchester in 1851: 'Charlotte's insistence that she could not sleep if there were the least fragment of green leaf in her tea, and her hapless hostess's resourcefulness. Elizabeth had only a blend of black and green tea at hand and could procure nothing else at that hour of the night. So she served without comment her guest, who announced the next morning that she had slept "splendidly" ' (p. 352).

oat-cake or 'clap-bread': oatmeal mixture, beaten or rolled thin, and baked hard.

242 *Camacho's wedding*: Camacho, a rich farmer in Cervantes' famous tale *Don Quixote* (1605, 1615), prepares a magnificent wedding feast for his bride Quiteria.

Watendlath: a small farming hamlet in a secluded valley approximately 5 miles south of Keswick. Its location suggests that the farm in this story is situated in high country somewhere between Watendlath to the south and the southern tip of Derwent Water to the north.

243 *Eleusinian circle*: refers to mysteries or religious ceremonies held in Eleusis in ancient Greece. The mysteries honoured Demeter, the goddess of Earth and Fertility, and her daughter Persephone, carried off to the underworld by Hades but allowed to return to earth for half of each year. Persephone's story explains the cycle of the seasons which controls the sheep-farmer's yearly work while Gaskell links the circle of women in the farmhouse with the female fertility embodied by Demeter.

244 *'walk'*: a tract of land used for grazing sheep, also known as a sheep-walk.

Fells: north-country term for high ground, lacking dense vegetation but sustaining the grazing of animals.

yeaning: (archaic, dialect) the process of giving birth, particularly in sheep.

245 *American Bee*: a social gathering for the purpose of work. The bee is a well-known symbol of industry.

246 *Emma's father . . . 'not too thick'*: Mr Woodhouse, father of Jane Austen's heroine Emma in the novel of the same name (1816), is a querulous invalid. In *Household Words* (22 January 1853, 451), the reference is to 'Eunice's father', probably a compositor's misreading of Gaskell's manuscript rather than an authorial error. The name has been silently corrected in this text.

the Shepherd's Calendar: an allusion either to Spenser's *Shepheardes Calendar* (1579) or, more probably, to John Clare (1793–1864), whose verse, including *The Shepherd's Calendar* (1827), evokes rural landscapes with great power.

Wordsworth's lines—

> *In that fair clime, the lonely herdsman stretched*
> *On the soft grass, through half the summer's day, &c.*:

The Excursion, IV. 851–2.

Pan: Pan, in Greek mythology, is the god of pastures, forests, flocks, and herds. The Pan-pipes are an ancient wind instrument from which a scale of notes is produced by blowing across the open ends of graduated pipes.

Chaldean shepherds . . . stars: the Chaldeans were of an ancient civilization known for occult learning and astrology. In Wordsworth's *Excursion*, 'Chaldean Shepherds . . . | Looked on the polar star, as on a guide' (IV. 694–7).

246 *Poussin's . . . Good Shepherd*: Nicholas Poussin (1594–1665), one of the leading French painters of the late Renaissance. There does not appear to be a painting by Poussin called 'The Good Shepherd'. However, Gaskell may have in mind one of Poussin's many biblical (or possibly classical) figures in a painting of a different name.

'Shepherds keeping watch by night!': refers to the Nahum Tate hymn 'While Shepherds Watched Their Flocks by Night', which paraphrases Luke 2: 8–15.

Cooper's delightful pieces: although the context suggests that Gaskell is adding another artist to the list which includes Poussin, the nature of 'Cooper's delightful pieces' is not clear. The reference is probably to Thomas Sidney Cooper (1803–1902) who exhibited his paintings continuously at the Royal Academy from 1833 to 1902, and also at the British Institution between 1833 and 1863. His favourite and constant subject was sheep and cattle in landscapes.

Australian wool: the exports to Britain from the wool industry developing in the colonies in the first half of the nineteenth century increased more than sixfold in the period 1831 to 1840, and were regarded as a serious threat by domestic wool growers.

Pandean: pertaining to Pan.

The Grey Woman

249 *There is a mill*: the manuscript version of 'The Grey Woman' (John Rylands University Library, Manchester) begins, 'The story I am going to relate is true as to its main facts, and as to the consequence of those facts, from which this tale takes its title.' This sentence is omitted in the serial and first volume publication of the story.

Neckar-side: the Neckar River, in Germany, flows through Heidelberg and joins the Rhine at Mannheim.

I went to drink coffee . . . in 184–: Gaskell visited Heidelberg in 1841, as part of a tour of the Continent with her husband; and she returned there in autumn 1858 and summer 1860 with three of her daughters.

250 *the old Palatinate days*: the Palatinate territory extended east and west of the Rhine and the court of the Electors Palatine was situated at Heidelberg. The history of the Palatinate is marked by repeated French invasions. Murray's *Handbook for Travellers on the*

Continent (1858) comments that it was at the seige of Heidelberg in 1693 that the French displayed 'the most merciless tyranny, and . . . excesses worthy of fiends rather than men . . . which will ever render the name of Frenchman odious in the Palatinate' (p. 532). During the wars with Napoleon, the land west of the Rhine was ceded to France and the remainder of the territory was divided between other German principalities.

250 *Kuchen*: (German) cake, flan or pastry.

251 *Utrecht velvet*: strong, thick fabric used in upholstery originating from the Dutch city of Utrecht.

worsted-worked carpet: a loosely woven canvas completely covered with embroidery in highly twisted, heavy, coloured woollen yarn.

252 *The sins of the fathers are visited on their children*: Exodus 34: 7—'visiting the iniquity of the fathers upon the children, and upon the children's children, unto the third and to the fourth generation.'

MSS: manuscripts.

254 *Schöne Müllerin*: (German) 'the Fair Maid of the Mill'.

255 *the Grand Duke's court*: Karlsruhe, approximately 28 miles south of Heidelberg, was founded in 1715 as the capital of the Grand Duchy of Baden, another of the independent German states. The Grand Duke or Margrave Karl Friedrich ruled Baden from 1746 to 1811.

257 *events taking place at Paris*: the French Revolution which began in 1789 and was symbolized in the popular consciousness by the storming of the Bastille prison in Paris on 14 July of that year.

mouches: (French) patches; artificial beauty-spots made of black silk or court-plaster (silk coated with isinglass), used to hide blemishes or enhance the complexion.

258 *propriétaire*: (French) landowner.

Vosges mountains: range of mountains lying west of the Rhine in France.

259 *with her own*: in the manuscript version of the story there is an additional sentence at the end of this paragraph which reads, 'Alas, if all were but known and foreseen.'

261 *Les Rochers*: (French) The Rocks; literally, high, pointed rocks or crags.

263 *portières*: (French) fabric panels or curtains hung over doorways to exclude draughts or for decoration.

264 *humorous*: used here not to suggest amusement, but with regard to the temperament or disposition. Derived from medieval physiology, which held that the individual's state of mind was determined by the relative proportions of the four principal fluids (cardinal humours) in the body—phlegm, blood, choler, and black choler or bile.

corbeille de mariage: (French) wedding presents offered by the bridegroom to his bride.

companion to me: the manuscript version of 'The Grey Woman' contains no chapter breaks. At this point in the manuscript there is an additional sentence which reads, 'This was rather a risk it is true; but it answered well, as I have good reason to say.'

266 *parvenue*: (French) upstart; person of humble birth who has obtained wealth or higher social position but not the manners appropriate to such a position.

267 *the Kaiser Stuhl at Heidelberg*: literally, the 'Emperor's Seat'; also known as the Königstuhl, this mountain towers over the city of Heidelberg.

276 *Chauffeurs*: (French) literally, stokers, firemen, for example, for a blacksmith's furnace; here, the name given to a band of robbers who torture their victims by fire.

282 *intendant*: (French) steward, bailiff, or manager.

287 *perdues*: see note to p. 204.

288 *house-place*: see note to p. 168.

galette: (French) round, flat, thin cake.

291 *Schinderhannes*: Johannes Bückler (1778–1803), a notorious robber captain who operated in the region of the Rhine, taking advantage of the general unrest during the Revolutionary period and the Napoleonic wars.

salle-à-manger: (French) dining-room.

diligence: see note to p. 142.

292 *porte-cochère*: (French) carriage entrance or gateway into a courtyard.

coupé: (French) separate, private compartment situated at the front or back of a continental *diligence*.

295 *Numéro Un. Ainsi les Chauffeurs se vengent.*: 'Number One. Thus the Chauffeurs are avenged.'

298 *sage-femme*: (French) midwife.

302 *Lutherans*: in his introduction to vol. VII of the Knutsford edition of *The Works of Mrs. Gaskell* (London, 1906), in which 'The Grey Woman' is reprinted, A. W. Ward comments that

> The complications which mark the religious history of the Palatinate have . . . involved the narrator of poor Anna's history in one or two inconsistencies. She bids her daughter lay her story 'before the good priest Schriesheim'; but it is elsewhere stated that she was of the Lutheran, and her husband of the 'Reformed' persuasion. . . . The grounds on which Anna justified to herself her second marriage, while her villainous first husband was still alive, must be described as hazy (p. xxviii).

303 *bloodthirsty republicans*: after the removal of King Louis XVI from the throne in September 1792, France became a Republic. The Law of Suspected Persons, passed by the governing body, the Convention, in September 1793, allowed the imprisonment and execution of many noblemen and others suspected of Royalist sympathies. It is an indication of the excesses of the Reign of Terror that Maurice de Poissy could have been arrested on no other evidence than an aristocratic name.